Flight Into Fear

Holmes shouted, "Watson! Watson! Hang on, man! Lupin, quick, help me bash through!"

The two men hurled themselves at the bookcase, clawing volumes from the shelves. "Assistance, if you please, Monsieur et Madame Hammelin," said Lupin, without interrupting his task.

The large woman thrust both men aside and after a few harsh slams, her girth cracked the wood enough that Holmes was able to reach through the broken, splintered boards and slide the cross bar until, with a pop, the bookcase swung into the room. Lupin slipped through first, then Holmes dashed up the stone stairs, three at a time, his walking stick held before him. At the top of the stairs, he flung back a smaller wooden door in time to see Arsene Lupin leap off the parapet.

The Frenchman snagged a rope swinging from a most incredible airship. It had just cast off from its mooring atop the very tower on which they stood.

From the pages of history and literature, the most colorful personalities of all time match wits with the incomparable **Sherlock Holmes** *and his trusted assistant, Dr. John H. Watson! Journey with the Great Detective through diabolical and devious crime as he teams up with Harry Houdini, Calamity Jane, Arsene Lupin, Professor Challenger, the Great and Powerful Oz and many more from the files of* ***The Crossovers Casebook!***

DEDIDCATION

This volume is respectfully dedicated to
Howard Hopkins (1961-2012), our friend
and collaborator, whose contributions to
Moonstone Books and new pulp fiction were
considerable.

*"Some days it is more difficult being a writer than others. Some days the words won't
come, or the ones that do just suck. Or maybe
sales take a dump or somebody leaves you a
bad review. Maybe the sound of your author
'voice' sounds like nails on a chalkboard. But
we need those days...because it is in times
like that you either 'hold 'em or fold 'em.' It's
when you grow, and know that, 'Yeah, this is
my passion, what I was meant to be.'"*

Howard Hopkins
January 11, 2012

SHERLOCK HOLMES
THE CROSSOVER CASEBOOK

edited by
Howard Hopkins

Howard Hopkins
Editor

David Smith
Editorial Assist

Timothy Lantz
Cover Artwork

Sidney Paget
Title Page Artwork

Logo and Cover Design by Erik Enervold/Simian Brothers Creative

Interior Book Design by Rich Harvey/Bold Venture Press

Sherlock Holmes: The Crossover Casebook
ISBN: 10: 1-933076-99-2
ISBN: 13: 978-1-933076-99-7

PUBLISHER'S NOTE:

Published by
Moonstone Entertainment, Inc.
582 Torrence Ave.,
Calumet City, IL 60409
www.moonstonebooks.com

CONTENTS

A Study in Awareness

by
Howard Hopkins

"**B**ut I'm really not a Sherlock Holmes fan…"

That's what I recall saying to writer/Holmesian Martin Powell when, many moons ago, he queried me about writing a new Sherlock Holmes tale for the volume you now hold in your hands. It took a bit of convincing. "Have you read one of the original stories?" I believe he asked. Well, I had to admit, not really. My familiarity with the character was confined mostly to bits and pieces of old movies, the guy with the deerstalker cap and curved pipe, and his semi-bumbling sidekick, Watson. I wasn't sure I wanted to add to that perception, but said yes anyway, thinking it might be a challenge to bring something new to that portrayal, and because Martin told me this was to be a volume of "team-ups", pairing the Great Detective with some of fiction and history's most interesting figures to help solve the mystery.

He then gave me a list of stories to read for research, and though I was somewhat less than enthusiastic about poring through old text for a character I was not particularly fond of, I dug in.

And got quite a shock.

They were nothing like the snatches of movies I had seen. Watson was neither bumbling nor an incompetent stooge clinging to Holmes' coattails. He was eminently efficient and the narrator of the stories. Holmes was still a genius, but more of a cluttered one, not the quite the dapper, deerstalker cap wearing gentleman portrayed by Basil Rathbone. He was physically

fit and an accomplished boxer, among other things. No effete dandy here.

But beyond that, the stories were brilliant mysteries and studies in the relationship between a somewhat aloof detective and his right-hand man. Watson, in his reports of Holmes' exploits, had what Holmes perceived to be an embellished perspective; and Watson, in his assessment of his long-time friend, was often bluntly realistic and his outlook towards the detective's superior attitude usually one of annoyance and a bit of one-upsmanship. Yet they understood each other, as old friends do, and were inseparable.

The more tales I read, the more I was drawn into Holmes' Victorian world of detection and intrigue. The more I was dazzled.

This was also about the time the big-budget Sherlock Holmes movie starring Robert Downey, Jr. and Jude Law hit the theaters, something I probably would have skipped had it not been for my growing affection for the Great Detective. The movie sealed the deal. I was hooked. Sherlock Holmes was so much more real than I had given him credit for being, and Sir Arthur Conan Doyle, an author I had avoided reading to that point, a master craftsman who breathed life into one of the greatest literary creations of all time.

With that epiphany, I set to work on my own story, now a bit apprehensive about the grand responsibility I had to the character and mythos. Not long after writing the tale, probably the most difficult story I have ever written,

I signed on as editor for this anthology.

No, "I'm not really a Sherlock Holmes fan…" I am now a devoted and enthusiastic reader and follower of the Great Detective.

In closing I would like to thank Martin Powell and Joe Gentile not only for their Holmes expertise and faith in allowing me to helm the good ship S.S. Watson, but for giving me a deep appreciation of the character and his world. Any errors in this book are mine and I hope they will not detract from the enjoyment of the excellent authors involved with the project, and the grand mystery and adventure that is Sherlock Holmes.

Now, read on, the game's afoot!

Sherlock Holmes *in* the Lost World

by

Martin Powell

Author's Note

John H. Watson, M.D. wishes to state that both the restriction for restraint and the libel action have been withdrawn unconditionally by Professor George Edward Challenger, who, being content that no criticism or observation in this narrative is meant in an offensive spirit, has guaranteed that he will place no obstruction to its publication.

Prologue

THE *cave man's stomach felt as empty as his head.*

Days and nights of starvation, by no means an uncommon happenstance upon the Plateau, had dimmed his distinctive wisdom and he'd reluctantly ventured down from the relative shelter of the vine-tangled trees in search of sustenance.

He crawled through the open grass on his hairy belly like a filth-encrusted beetle, short spear gripped in a black-bristled paw, with a razor-edge blade made of bone clenched in his broad square teeth. The deer was grazing only a few short yards away.

The cave man scarcely breathed, hungrily eyeing his quarry with mouth-watering expectations. He was down-wind of the slight breeze as planned—he'd not yet lost total reason—and rapid glances over both wide bushy shoulders did not yet reveal a rival predator stalking the same prey. From a kneeling position he raised his spear. Perhaps, this was his lucky day.

The deer's head sprang up in instant vigilance. The deadly double pair of antlers, and the Y-shaped horn upon its snout at once would have made the otherwise graceful creature utterly unearthly to the typical modern Londoner. Large liquid eyes darted for the coming danger. Before the batting of another long lash the fleet-footed deer sprang away in a series of lofty leaps were almost miraculous in their prowess.

The cave man hadn't time for disappointment. At first he sensed the commotion rather than heard it, rather like the thudding of an inaudible drum-beat. Alarm flashed in his deep-set, sweat-reddened eyes as he suddenly felt the rumbling earth beneath him.

Stampede!

A bank of swirling grasses, twelve feet high, parted and exploded outward with an eruption of the thundering brontotherium and her galloping calf. The frenzied terror of the massive beasts prompted the cave man to race for the salvation of the high branches at least a hundred yards distant. Still, he had to try. The brontotheres feared few enemies.

The pack of creodonts swarmed after the massive grass-eaters in all their yellow-eyed, jagged jawed horror. The grisly devils virtually slithered rather than ran, their low, long, ductile feline forms fluidly racing and flowing in the heat of the hunt. Bone-crushing wolfish snouts dripped and snarled with the stuff of nightmares.

The clodding of the cave man's overly-wide, loutish feet betrayed him. A lone, lean creodont broke from the panting pack and instantaneously sized him up as easier game. No chance of out-running the racing red-tongued demon. The cave man whirled, a bull-like bellow blasting from his thirsty lips as he hurled the stubby stone-tipped spear with all his shrinking, starving strength—transfixing the fiend from sternum to coccyx.

The dead beast's berserker brethren rampaged on through the grassy plain, unaware of the spore of the cave man. After a bit, fearsome screams in the distant thicket gave evidence that the hunters would long be occupied with their ponderous feast.

He swatted away skulking black buzzards and little flying lizards, hastily slinging the weighty carcass over his apish shoulder. No time to waste. More formidable scavengers were certain to follow.

The cave man had lived past another noon.

Act One
"Nothing less could lure you from those infernal bees."

As I alighted from the motorcar at the very doorstep of the Diogenes Club, I reflected upon the realization that, despite all the many years of our peculiar association, I didn't know Mycroft Holmes very well.

An urgent telegram demanding my presence in London upon that date at noon sharp vexed my good nature, but also piqued my curiosity. Such an august individual, who was once described by his own brother as the "British Government, Personified", could not easily be denied. Not even by an old retired army surgeon.

I was duly shown to the Strangers Room, the only place within the eccentric building that allowed normal conversation, and immediately recognized the imposing figure of Mycroft Holmes, much greyer and less corpulent than I remembered from our last encounter. A small perfectly elegant lady, dark-haired and eyed, was seated mournfully by a window. She was very handsome, if worry-worn, her fine features denoting a more exotic heritage than the usual, attractive English woman. I would certainly have remembered if I'd met her before. Standing stalwartly beside Mycroft Holmes, much to no small amazement upon my part, was the solemn iron-mustached Prime Minister himself.

"Dr. Watson, good of you to come." Mycroft Holmes offered his great flipper of a hand. "You know the Prime Minister."

The Prime Minster hardly nodded, remaining as motionless as his official portrait. Although the lady was not introduced, she favoured me with a sad yet attractive smile.

Mycroft Holmes consulted his watch, snapping it shut again with a distinctive air of conviction.

"I perceive a multitude of queries forming behind your brows, Doctor. Pray remain silent one minute longer and all shall be revealed."

He spanned the space of the room in three prodigious strides, swinging open the door, revealing—to my great surprise—his celebrated brother, and my old friend, Mr. Sherlock Holmes, upon the threshold.

"Welcome, Sherlock. I apologize for the deception, but I surmised nothing less could lure you from those infernal bees." Mycroft Holmes tilted his massive head in my direction.

I hadn't seen Sherlock Holmes in nearly a year. He was leaner, and as a result seemed taller, than ever. At Holmes' first sight of me, the steely fierceness burning in his gray eyes immediately dimmed. I thought for a moment to detect something akin to sentiment settling in his hawkish features, but with a blink he was the aloof Holmes of old once more.

Without so much as a glance toward the Prime Minister, Holmes pressed my hand.

"My dear, Watson, it's quite gratifying to discover the full extent of my brother's rather imaginative exaggeration." He faintly smiled, presenting a crumpled telegram which I read with astonishment.

DR. WATSON DECEASED. COME AT ONCE. MYCROFT.

I didn't know what to remark, so I remained quiet within the uncomfortable silence of the room.

"Well, Doctor," said Sherlock Holmes, "since I somewhat inexplicably find myself suddenly in London, I suggest that we take advantage of the new Greek and Etruscan vase exhibit at the British Museum. What do you say?"

My old friend hooked my elbow with his wiry forearm.

"Mr. Holmes, I protest your cavalier manner, sir." The Prime Minister came suddenly to livid life. "I ordered your brother to arrange your presence before us. He has done so, as was his duty. Your country has need of you, sir."

Holmes continued to spirit me hastily from the room.

"My country," replied Sherlock Holmes, "appears to suffer from a chronic form of reprehensible and conscienceless embellishment. Good day to you. Come along, Watson."

"The Prime Minister does not exaggerate, Mr. Holmes," the lady abruptly spoke out. "I am Mrs. George Edward Challenger. I understand you've met my husband."

Holmes halted, sighed slightly, and turned to face her.

"Once, more than a decade ago." A smile hinted at the notorious name. "I can certainly personally testify to the professor's scientific proficiency… as well as his rather brutal bare-knuckled straight left."

Mrs. Challenger beamed, brightening her dark beauty.

"However brief your meeting may have been, George always spoke of you with great respect, Mr. Holmes. A rare and difficult thing for a man like my husband, as I trust you can appreciate."

Holmes narrowed his eyes, regarding the lady for an instant, then stabbed rapid glances at his brother and, lastly, the Prime Minister. A shadow of apprehension veiled his pale gaunt features. Shoulders settling back he assumed his old unique comportment of authority.

"Allow me a moment to propose my suspicions as to my role in this dubious matter," he stated bluntly. "I take it that I have been engaged to locate and reveal the exact whereabouts of the infamous Professor George Edward Challenger, who—according to the London *Times*—has been missing and is presumed dead these last twenty-seven months. I further infer that Mrs. Challenger believes that her husband is very much alive."

The Prime Minister's moustache visibly twitched in surprise.

"How in Hades did you guess that, sir?"

Holmes grimaced impatiently.

"I never guess," he snapped.

Mycroft Holmes stamped a flustered boot heel.

"Now see here, Sherlock—these theatric antics of yours are heinously out of place." The elder brother's neck bloomed a deep crimson. "I assure you that this is a desperately secret matter of the very deepest concern for all of England. Why, the very lives of hundreds of thousands are at stake—"

The Prime Minister touched Mycroft Holmes upon the sleeve.

"Your brother never spoke more truly, sir," his voice more grave by several degrees than mere moments before. "I demand to know exactly how you came by this information. Mr. Phelps has been missing for two days and if there has been some clandestine breach in our security I must know about it immediately."

Sherlock Holmes turned his back upon the bristling mustache and resigned himself to an armchair. His hooded eyes nearly disguised his growing interest in the matter, though his mouth remained fixed and determined. Automatically, he lighted a cigarette and blew the blue smoke toward the lofty ceiling.

"You may call off our watchdogs, Mr. Prime Minister; the secrets of the Crown are quite safe for now." Holmes exhaled with an exaggerated weariness. "You should be aware of my methods."

The Prime Minister puffed his annoyance.

"You mean to say, sir, that this is more of your deductive reasoning nonsense." His face was starting to purple.

Holmes allowed himself a slight smile.

"Is it nonsense to deduce, after being rather intimately aware of the workings of this government, that the presence of the presumed widow of a private scientific adventurer would suggest such an obvious inference? Why else would the lady be present within this selective company, were that not the case? As to Mrs. Challenger herself being convinced of her husband's survival, well, that is also simplicity itself. The lady would be wearing black, certainly not the stylish dove-grey dress we all perceive, if she were, in fact, in genuine mourning."

I noticed an immediate glint of affirmation in the lady's dark, lustrous eyes and a considerable weight of the earlier anxiety had perceptibly eased from her proud yet delicate shoulders.

The Prime Minister regained his stalwart composure.

"I see," he nodded. "Now that you've explained yourself, it's really not so very clever at all. Well, sir, now that we understand each other—"

"There is one small detail I need to possess before we proceed," my friend interrupted. "Why is the Crown so interested in locating the Professor?"

The mustache fluttered angrily again.

"That is privileged information, sir." The Prime Minister glowered.

Holmes fully opened his eyes and tossed his half-spent cigarette into the fireplace. Abruptly, he rose to his feet and donned his top hat.

"Quite so. Good day, madam. Come, Watson, a gallery of Greek and Etruscan marvels await us."

The Prime Minister's violet complexion deepened.

"Very well," he spoke directly to Mycroft Holmes. "Show him the damned thing!"

The elder Holmes revealed a steel infantry helmet from a wooden case, handing it to my friend with the reverence of a Holy Relic. It was no different than any other soldier's helmet I'd seen, though I did notice immediately that it had been violently pierced by a rifle bullet.

"The Germans have advanced the effectiveness of their artillery, sir," the Prime Minister spat with no little amount of disgust.

Sherlock Holmes was upon the brink of an inquiry when his brother explained the meaning of the grisly artifact.

"Sherlock," he began, "Mrs. Challenger recently discovered a hidden notebook belonging to her husband wherein he had enthusiastically experimented with a formula, of his own invention, for a new lightweight steel alloy dozens of times stronger than what is currently possible."

I broke my long silence.

"I don't understand," I said, frankly. "It was my impression that Professor Challenger's expertise was, uh, rather is, zoology. How could a zoologist conceive of such a sophisticated formula?"

"My George has a restless mind, Dr. Watson. He rarely sleeps and constantly studies. I dare say, one day, he may well know just about everything." Mrs. Challenger smiled proudly, making her look younger and even more charming by some dozen years.

Sherlock Holmes rubbed his squared, prominent chin.

"The lady hardly exaggerates, my dear fellow." His long white finger morbidly traced around the helmet's bullet hole. "I've read Challenger's monographs on the practical applications of chemistry and physics with keen interest. Regardless of how he is ridiculed by his colleagues, they can't hold a candle to him. George Edward Challenger may well be the greatest scientific mind in all of Europe, if not the world."

The Prime Minister reinstated himself into the proceedings.

"A rather clumsy and discourteous scientific mind, I'll wager," he growled, peering at Mycroft Holmes.

"Yes, gentlemen," he explained to us, "it appears that Professor Challenger's actual formula resided purely within his own head."

"My George memorized everything." The lady sparkled. "He claimed it considerably reduced the clutter of his filing cabinets."

Sherlock Holmes moved to the window, putting a match to another cigarette.

"Allow me to refresh my own memory..." His eyes took on a momentary pensive aspect. "After Challenger returned from South America, he proposed to prove his claims of having discovered a hellish plateau, a lost world—if you will—still populated by the surviving denizens from the ancient Age of the Dinosaurs. As I recall, Challenger delivered such authentication by exhibiting, in person, a pterodactyl which he had captured and brought back alive to London."

Mrs. Challenger moved to my friend, her dark doe-like eyes suddenly tragic.

"That's exactly as it happened, Mr. Holmes." Her fine porcelain features flushed with feminine ferocity. "But the creature escaped and the assembly of scientists almost immediately pronounced it a hoax. Two of my husband's most trusted colleagues, dear old Summerlee and young Mr. Malone of the Daily Gazette—both of them sworn eye-witnesses—were ridiculed into professional and public exile. My husband was furious. Even with such a temper like his, I don't think I ever saw him so close to cold-blooded murder as he was toward the entire academic community in those weeks that followed. In the end, George vowed that he'd go back to that primordial purgatory and, once and for all time, return with positive proof of its reality for the entire world to witness."

The heavy silence in the room was remindful of a wake. The dear lady fought back tears, more of outrage than of sorrow. Sherlock Holmes extinguished his cigarette and smiled at her kindly, if sadly.

"Madam, what you ask is impossible." He spoke to her as if they were alone together in the room. "Surely you must see that I am at my own limits, considering my age, and for me to even begin such a journey would be madness. It is my opinion that your brave, brilliant husband met an honourable end to his noble life somewhere upon that mysterious plateau. There are no existing maps or charts of this lost world. No way to even find it, let alone search for clues, now some two years old, of his possible whereabouts. I very much regret that services such as mine are useless to you in this endeavor."

Mrs. Challenger sank back against a chair as if all strength had left her. I felt powerfully sympathetic toward her plight, but Holmes, of course, was quite correct in his assertion. Without a map, without a guide, it would be like seeking a single lost speck of sand from among all the beaches of the world.

"Now see here, sir." The Prime Minister blocked the door. "We do not request, but rather, command this duty of you, Mr. Sherlock Holmes. It is by royal decree that you undertake this mission, regardless of your personal feelings in the matter. Whatever the chances, or the odds, England must have that formula or our boys fighting for our liberty in the trenches will be slaughtered like sitting fowl. Even if there's only the merest possibility of Challenger's miraculous survival, surely the World's Greatest Detective can discover this lone indispensable needle in a haystack for the sake of his nation?"

I didn't like the hot rapacious gleam in Holmes' eyes as he stalked so closely to the Prime Minister that his aquiline nose nearly brushed the suddenly fluttering mustache. A quiet knock at the door stayed his reply, for the moment.

Mycroft Holmes opened the door, receiving a calling card from the butler. His watery gray eyes were astonished as he read the name aloud.

"Apparently, Professor Challenger is…here."

The room was silent as a confessional until broken by the clack of a lady's boots.

Into the chamber stepped a tall, golden-haired young woman of twenty-eight or thirty. Her striking features were, somehow, familiar and yet the intense gray-green eyes almost buried her beauty behind a gaze of such piercing intelligence that I have never before witnessed upon one so young and so fair. She was, at once, Athena and Artemis, molded into the same divine being.

"Indeed, gentlemen." Her voice was low though not unmusical, supremely confident in her rapid inflection. "Professor Jessica Cuvier Challenger—doctor of medicine, zoology, and anthropology."

Mrs. Challenger was clearly aghast.

"Jess…you promised—" she startled and stammered, but the vicarious Amazon waved her aside.

"Not the first time I've broken such a ridiculous oath, Mother, dear." Professor Challenger held a telegram in her graceful hand. "As is my habit, I've managed to discover the very thing that all of you are so desperately searching for. I am, in truth, my father's daughter!"

She turned her cool scientist's eyes upon each of us and finally relinquished the telegram to Sherlock Holmes. After scanning it, Holmes handed it to me with a smile of satisfaction. It was sent from Central America. I'm reprinting the message below exactly as written:

DELIGHTED TO GUIDE MR. SHERLOCK HOLMES
TO LOST WORLD. WILL LAY ODDS THAT OLD SON
OF A BITCH CHALLENGER IS STILL ALIVE.
     LORD JOHN ROXTON

Interlude

The cave man had slept for two full days. His belly again gnawed at him to be filled, but it was the desiccation of his painfully parched throat which provoked the descent from his protective little grotto fortress in the limestone cliff. He had chosen this refuge principally because of the small stream of fresh water which perennially poured near its hidden entrance, but an aberrant ten day drought had caused the flow to vanish.

There was no avoiding it. Gathering up his club and spear, slipping his treasured doeskin medicine bag around his burly neck, a chill raised the hackles along the caveman's spine. His aching, adventure-etched body was already going through the motions before his clouded mind caught up with it. He must return to that monstrous river or die.

The long, snakishly winding, narrow river was an awful place, indeed. It was there that many of the terrible, most massive creatures of the Plateau came to sate their unfathomable thirst. Canopied in black-green shadows from towering vine-webbed branches, even at high noon, the river banks were a twilight world of creeping, crawling, living delirium and unseen impending death.

The cave man waited impatiently behind a concealing boulder, his swollen tongue raking across cracked lips. He knew what he was doing, the strategy worked flawlessly a thousand times past. The safest place among giants was to form an alliance with them.

The massive jagged-spined stegosaur wouldn't do. The hulking reptile was docile enough, except when roused, but the two tons worth of meandering, slashing, spike-tipped tail itself made the beast a companion of unpredictable peril. The cave man warily kept his eye on the fin-backed flesh-eating dimetrodons, but the entire pride was too immersed in glutting themselves with the muddy water to notice him.

He'd nearly resolved to select the company of two enormous exotically crested duck-billed hadrosaurs, but then a great baritone bellow trumpeted the arrival of a lone hundred-year-old deinotherium. Even better, the cave man recognized the elephantine goliath from long-healed foreleg scars caused from the claws of great saber-toothed cats, the splintered skulls of which were embedded forever in the pads of a ponderous front paw, resulting in a familiarly distinctive limp.

Gathering up a bouquet of succulent orchids, the cave man showed himself plainly to the colossal matriarch. Her melon-size left eye regarded the snack tentatively for just a moment, then the long muscular proboscis snatched the juicy blossoms high above to her pink hook-tusked mouth. The cave man had chosen his allies carefully, knowing from endless hours of observation that the deinotherium were predominantly gentle, intelligent and entirely fearless, even in the face of the Plateau's most fearsome flesh-eaters.

Confidently, the caveman followed alongside his lumbering guardian behemoth—safe in the shadow of her protective company—and drank his fill beside her from the edge of the beetle-infested, worm-writhing green-brown river. A swelling wave suddenly engorged the odious surface and for a scant second the cave man found his entire head submerged beneath the water. Coughing up the sulfur-flavored refreshment, he bitterly observed his leather medicine bag floating rapidly away from him. No chance of rescuing the precious little pouch, already it glided among sharp-beaked snapping turtles twice his own weight. The cave man's sole luxury, absolutely irreplaceable, was bade a tender farewell through his tear-filled eyes.

Abruptly, the source of the rising river became alarmingly clear as a wading herd of leviathan long-necked sauropods emerged from the bend of the river, the thunder lizards enormously dwarfing every other colossus among them. These majestic treetop browsers, the cave man knew, where the real lords of the Plateau, especially when they gathered in such abundant numbers. The danger of a panicked stampede of the lesser giants around him was a very real possibility.

With a rapid, final, and regretful glance, the cave man scurried away to his lonely lair.

ACT TWO:
"Two of them in the world is rather over-doing it."

"There, lady and gentlemen, is our Plateau!" Lord John Roxton pointed with a weathered bronze forefinger.

Our ominous destination jutted up through the eerie morning mist like a dark green jungle-haunted obelisk. Already the dizzying height within the balloon's carriage had threatened to rob me of my meager breakfast as the humid tropical atmosphere rocked and swayed like an angry sea. It was, however, an excellent and even awe-inspiring view of our perilous objective. Lord Roxton remarked, jabbing an elbow playfully into my ribs, that he felt like a boy living out a Jules Verne adventure. Sherlock Holmes had said nothing at all since we'd cast off and he clung white-knuckled to the carriage handrails.

The last two months had been a flurry of planning, packing, and speeding away at a dizzying pace by motor, rail, sail, and steam. Twice

Sherlock Holmes cautioned me that we were being followed, but would say no more about it afterward, even with me pressing him firmly.

Holmes had spent a goodly portion of our journey in silent study of Professor Challenger's recovered notebook. The missing scientist's distinctive barbed-wire scrawl contained enough chemical details on the mysterious super-steel formula to convince my friend of its possibility. Even so, he'd laboriously bemoaned leaving his little Sussex bee-farm and direly confided to me that all we were likely to find was Challenger's bones upon that Plateau, perhaps to eventually jumble with our own. A sobering prediction, indeed, especially as the terrible formation loomed up before us and was, at last, an incredible reality.

"Is that the region you and my father ascended?" The young professor indicated a treacherous slope seemingly somewhat more passable than the others in our sight.

Lord Roxton laughed cheerily.

"No, Miss, we can't see it from this angle. It's climbable, obviously, but more than a mite dangerous. I like this balloon idea of yours much better—saves on lots of sweat, blistered fingers, and potential broken-necks!"

She glowered at him, lifting up her pretty chin.

"Refer to me as 'Professor', if you please, Roxton," her tone was as cold as it was arrogant. "I'm not some mere Kensington school mistress out on holiday."

Holmes took a sharp long breath and let it out slowly.

"Oh, beggin' your pardon, Mi—uh, Professor Challenger," Lord Roxton grinned, winking at me, then spoke low into my ear. "Two of them in the world is rather over-doing it—what?"

I must say, however frequently disagreeable she could be, Professor Jessica Cuvier Challenger conducted the piloting of our little airship with the valiant hand of a seasoned expert. In truth, during the past several weeks I'd come to the pleasurable realization that the young lady was most remarkable in nearly every aspect.

Her knowledge of medicine was far in advance to my own, having studied in both Vienna and America in the highest of her class. She flattered me personally, as well, with a profound familiarity of my written accounts of the cases of Sherlock Holmes—correcting some of my careless chronological blunders from her own prodigious memory—and finally interrogated me most brazenly upon the exact anatomical location of my

Afghan War wound.

Indeed, despite her arrogant, quick-tempered, and almost artificial personae, both the lady's keenly disciplined brain, utter fearlessness, and her unrivaled physical beauty had charmed me completely.

Suddenly I noticed and followed Holmes' gaze at a small flock of birds pursuing us at a distance.

"An impulsive beak or talon might well rend a gape in this contraption," my friend mused matter-of-factly. "I take it, Professor, that you've a perceived notion preventing such a catastrophe?"

She lifted her excellent field-glasses, nodding calmly.

"The silk is chemically reinforced, Mr. Holmes. I doubt less than a rifle bullet could pierce it. Also, I noticed you warily detecting the electrical charge in the air. You needed be concerned, there's no chance of fire as these pressure tanks contain helium, not hydrogen."

Holmes rolled his gray eyes at me. The altitude was making him a bit green.

"You seem to have thought of everything," he said curtly.

The Professor lowered the glasses, her breath slightly quickened.

"Everything, perhaps, but the simple fact that my father may have been absolutely correct in all his outrageous contentions. Roxton—have you a rifle handy? Those are most certainly not birds."

They were hideous creatures, such as the tortured nightmares of a madman might concoct. Indeed, the flying monstrosities were not birds nor like any other animal I've ever seen, rather they resembled flapping bat-like crocodilians with wing-spans at least twice as great as that of an albatross. The enraged ear-splitting shrieks made it plain that our balloon was encroaching upon their aerial territory.

I'm delighted to confirm that Lord Roxton's marksmanship was every bit as legendary as reports of his world-wide adventures have claimed. Each time he shouldered his rifle, another winged demon squawked and spiraled away to vanish into the thick mists below. After the momentary danger died away, a different surge of excitement impressed us, even Holmes. Professor George Edward Challenger, and Lord John Roxton, had not exaggerated in the least. Such a "Lost World" as both men had long proclaimed, and established science had denounced, did, indeed, truly exist!

"Isn't it marvelous, Holmes!" I could hardly contain my exhilaration.

The passionless machine-like concentration had returned to his pale, gaunt face.

"I would suggest that those high limestone cliffs may be rather more imperative to the core of our quest, old fellow. I distinctly observed at least one cave located near the top that might have served as an excellent long-term refuge."

Professor Challenger focused her field-glasses once again, then lowered them with a quick nod and a beaming smile.

"Excellent, Mr. Holmes!" she agreed, looking quite lovely. "You are truly the first of detectives. Forgive me, in my excitement, I didn't notice those formations. Pterodactyls have been my favorites since I was a girl and seeing them alive is quite a thrill. Brace yourselves, gentlemen—we're going to land!"

Our landing was, if anything, even more dreadful than our daredevil launch. I've never had such a helpless sensation of vertigo. Densely dark jungle cloaked most of the Plateau's terrible denizens from our eyes, and perhaps that was for the best, but the hissing howls, blood-freezing screams, and thunderous footfalls could not be shut out.

At one point of our descent the balloon carriage, which contained us and all our provisions, slightly scraped the slime-skimmed surface of a prehistoric lake filled with such brethren of Hell as only Dante might have imagined. At first what I took to be gigantic swimming crocodiles were, in reality, undulating thirty foot long marine monitor lizards. One of the beasts was lethally ensnared in the strangling tentacles of a massive snail-shelled octopus, the likes of which—according to the Professor—hadn't been seen upon this earth for over sixty-five million years. Swooping kite-tailed pterodactyls soared upwards again with fanged beaks full of lobe-finned silver-scaled fish, while magnificent long-necked reptiles with the acrobatic streamlined bodies of sea lions gracefully rolled and sailed through the emerald algae rich waves.

We touched the earth, finally, near the base of Holmes' limestone cliff, as there was no safe landing area upon its peak. Professor Challenger rapidly set about the task of deflating our balloon and sealing it, along with the cleverly designed collapsible carriage, inside a crate which she buried under a mammoth fern fully one-hundred feet tall. At her own orders, Lord Roxton, Holmes and I stood guard with our rifles. She didn't need to tell us. We were taking no chances.

The Professor and Lord Roxton then commenced hurling grappling hooks attached to stout lengths of rope at the narrow cave entrance. I was amazed how swiftly and expertly that was accomplished. The cave above and beyond beckoned to be investigated.

"My father may be up there. Blood and brains before brawn, Roxton," Professor Challenger insisted after it was suggested there may be an element of danger within the cave itself.

She clambered up the cliff, in her high laced boots and riding britches, as effortlessly as a spider monkey. Before Lord Roxton could follow, Holmes surprised me by grasping the other rope.

"I'm afraid your old shoulder wound will be a nuisance here, Watson," he said ruefully. "However, I will trouble you for your service revolver. Take care of him, Lord Roxton. I'm lost without my Boswell."

With my pistol tucked into his belt, Holmes bounded up the line as fluidly deft as any man in his early sixties could ever hope to be. It was difficult to believe, at times like these, that he was only two years younger than me. When the scent of the chase was upon him, my friend could evoke an almost Herculean prowess as I'd witnessed, and chronicled, many times in our long association.

Lord Roxton let out a low whistle as he watched Holmes climb up and disappear into the cave. He grinned at me and revealed a silver hipflask.

"Is he a bloodhound or a squirrel—what? Care for a nip of whisky while we're waitin', Doctor?"

I confess to taking a few sips.

"After narrowly escaping from this Plateau seven years ago, I don't suppose that you'd ever imagined being back here again," I said to my famous companion, the steadying warmth of the whisky making me more social.

"Wouldn't miss it for the world." He sounded as if he meant it between swallows from the flask. "Besides this time there's more at stake than just the old bastard's bloomin' reputation, eh? What do you think of our young Miss?"

He offered me the flask again, but I thought the better of it.

"A most capable lady, surely," I replied.

"She's that, and more," Lord Roxton's leathery face lapsed into a moment of solemnity. "Reminds me a bit of my son, Richard. Fearless. Head strong. Maybe even a little crazy. He's fighting against Germany even as we speak. Youngest major in the American infantry, so they tell me. Guess I'm here as much for his sake as anything. Say, Doctor, does Mr. Holmes really think we'll find old Challenger alive, and deliver him and his formula back to Mother England?"

World-famous adventurer and explorer, proud father, patriot—there was a depth and temperament to Lord Roxton that, even with just those few words, established not merely his profound decency but also elevated his character to the almost mythic level that one hoped to expect of him. I found myself very glad to be in his acquaintance.

"Well, I dare say we wouldn't be here now, if he believed such a thing was impossible," I answered, in all honestly.

A wiggle of the ropes caught our attention.

"Hope you're right, Doctor," his easy grin returned. "They're comin' back down—and I've never seen such a pair of long faces."

We scouted the base of the cliff for more caves, finally finding one more assessable for our camp. Lord Roxton knew that night dropped swiftly, like a great black curtain over the Plateau, and we had a bright fire blazing at the cave entrance well before the first visible stars. Neither Holmes nor Professor Challenger had yet spoken of their morning adventure within the cave. Going along with her suggestion that we eat off the land, to lighten our packs, we were all dining on roasted Archaeopteryx, a bizarre toothed bird from the Jurassic Period, and some unknown, though very succulent fruits, when Holmes revealed his discoveries.

"This lady's father had, indeed, been a resident within the cave," my friend stated in his cool, unemotional manner. "There was evidence of scratches upon the cave floor, unmistakable nail-marks from the soles of worn-out British-made boots in his unusual size. Although we found no journals or scientific equipment, there were two rifles and a revolver in the cave, all without ammunition and badly rusted. Most telling, perhaps, were these…"

Holmes displayed a half dozen cigar stubs.

"The ends are cut, not bitten," the lady explained, "and Mr. Holmes has identified the tobacco which I easily confirmed as my father's special blend."

Lord Roxton kicked a stone into the fire and walked away, murmuring a quiet curse. I felt my own shoulders suddenly sag.

"So," I ventured hesitatingly. "Challenger was in the cave…but the condition of his weapons suggest that—"

"Without a good rifle, no one could survive twenty four hours in this infernal bloody jungle," Lord Roxton said, bitterly.

I wasn't ready to give up.

"Why, the Professor may have another rifle with him!"

Holmes shook his head.

"Challenger hasn't occupied that cave for better than a year, Watson," he said, grimly filling his pipe. "The condition of the firearms, and especially the cigar stubs, make that plain. There also were signs that a more savage entity has since claimed the refuge. I must concur with Lord Roxton's opinion, tragic though it is. Professor George Edward Challenger, and his team of five companions, perished somewhere here upon the Plateau many months ago."

The lady herself remained even more aloof than my friend.

"Mr. Holmes and I are quite in agreement on this," she added, frankly. "There is no hope. We leave tomorrow. Tonight, I'll take the first watch— no arguments, Roxton. Get some rest, gentlemen."

Though exhausted, I little more than dozed for a few hours. The ache in my heart—and the incessant chattering drone of Plateau insects the size of alley cats—disrupted any chance for real slumber. While Holmes napped restlessly, I rose a bit after midnight, finding Lord Roxton dourly at watch. I observed that the Professor was not in her sleeping bag.

"Think she needed some privacy." He winked without the usual humor. "Headed off toward those reeds. Give her a few minutes."

I did as he suggested, but grew anxious as time wore on. Finally I found her sitting on a fallen log. Tears glistened on her exquisite cheeks in the blue moonlight. Silently, I sat down next to her and patted her soft cool hand.

"We never got on together, you know," she almost whispered. "He was never supportive of my education. Never believed women could be as clever as men. Father and I always argued, even when I was a little girl. From the pronouncements of Darwin, to my refusal to eat Mother's awful omelets, we fought about everything. He was always gone—distant—even when he was home. Brilliant as he was, he never really knew me. Now he never will."

She dabbed at her eyes with a dirty sleeve and somehow the effect was quite elegant. Gazing at her, torn and bruised from the adventures of yesterday, quietly weeping in utter heartbreak, I knew I was looking at the most beautiful woman I'd ever seen.

She regained her dignity with a purposeful shrug, her unpinned golden hair draping her shoulders.

"What would Father say if he saw me now, eh, Dr. Watson?" She managed a lovely, if sardonic, smile.

I smiled back, more gently.

"I've no doubt that he'd be very proud of that same little girl, who wouldn't eat her mother's omelets."

Jessica's lips dropped suddenly, but her sad eyes gleamed with tenderness as she leaned forward and kissed my rough old cheek.

Suddenly, it seemed the sky was falling.

From out of the dense jungle canopy, shaggy black hulks fell all around, surrounding us. An iron-gripped hairy paw snatched my revolver from my hand the very moment I stood, taking some of my skin away with it. The two of us were hopelessly, horribly outnumbered by a savage tribe of what I can only describe as subhuman ape-men.

Jessica managed one frantic shot with her rifle before the weapon was wrenched away, nearly tearing her arms from their sockets. Two of the devils leaped upon my back, crashing me to the fetid filth and decay on the jungle floor. I kicked and struck back like a madman, with no effect upon the beast-men at all.

Through the dim shadows I watched in horror as one of the larger brutes snared Jessica with a single long hooked arm, bounding back toward the trees. Fighting furiously, I was a mere child against monsters. I could do nothing, but die.

Abruptly, the ogre carrying Jessica shrieked then flopped dead to the ground, limp as a puppet. The remaining horde paused, sniffing the air. Suddenly another one dropped dead. And another. There was no sound of a firearm, no indication at all of what was causing the mute, invisible slaughter happening inexplicably before our eyes.

The surviving ape-men fled back into the trees, screaming in terror as two more of their number were struck dead as they ran. The entire horrific incident had lasted probably less than a minute, yet we saw the lanterns of

Holmes and Lord Roxton already rushing to our defense.

After rapidly establishing our safety, Lord Roxton spied the branches with his rifle ready, while Holmes bent to examine one of the fallen fiends.

"Watson…" He indicated the hideous creature in the lantern glow. "You've just witnessed the most mysterious assassination in history."

"I don't understand," I admitted.

"Observe for yourself." He smiled grimly as Jessica drew nearer, also fascinated. "We heard only one rifle report—presumably from one of you—and yet each of these creatures has been expertly shot through the skull, without noise or sufficient light in which to properly aim a weapon. Quite a puzzle. How do you explain it, my dear fellow?"

The magnitude of the weird circumstance suddenly dawned upon me in full. Immediately, one of Holmes' favourite axioms immediately sprang to mind:

When you have eliminated the impossible, whatever remains—however improbable—must be the truth.

We weren't the only human hunters upon the Plateau.

Interlude Two

The cave man spied on the predators from the high jungle branches, watching them with a cold fascination. Caught too far away from his cave while in pursuit of food, he resigned himself to spending the terrible black night in the comparative security of the trees. He'd been munching on tree lizards when he first heard the uproar of the ape-men, rival hunter-scavengers, always dangerous in numbers. The cave man furtively moved to investigate among the gloom of the branches with the practiced ease of a gibbon.

He'd arrived in time to witness their unearthly deaths, almost the entire clan, slaughtered as if by a phantom killer. The ape-men had simply dropped dead. Most of them didn't even have time to scream. Their intended prey, a burly old man and a tall, radiant-haired young woman, seemed as perplexed as the cave man himself. Then, from among the shielding high branches, he caught sight of the executioners as they skulked away into the shadows among the giant ferns.

Interestingly, the killers were only men.

Something more than instinct assured the cave man that these three new invaders would murder him, too, if given the chance. There was a feral, cruel press to their features. Even in the darkness their evil nature was obvious. He didn't take more than an instant to decide to alter the odds of survival in his favor.

The cave man's spear and stone-headed club expertly found their targets, and two of the villains fell dead almost without a sound. Their older leader, more experienced and mercurial, escaped wraithlike into the jungle.

A rare glint of humour brightened his deep-set hostile eyes and the cave man allowed himself a rare chuckle of amusement.

He was looking forward to tomorrow.

ACT THREE:
"Doctor Watson—I presume?"

The hot, humid dawn couldn't come soon enough. Hardly surprising that none of us slept.

Lord Roxton held his rifle ready in a steely vigil toward the trees, while Jessica and Holmes performed a grotesque firelight autopsy on one of the dead subhumans. As for me, I stood guard against whatever other horrors lurked among the mazes of the jungle, puzzling fruitlessly over the inexplicable events of the night, and taking some small comfort in the weight of the high-powered rifle in my arms.

The first morning light had barely touched the damp mossy earth of the Plateau when I discovered Sherlock Holmes upon his hands and knees in the slime, intensely studying a boulder-heaped area about sixty yards from the massacre of the ape-men. He was there such a significant length of time, searching and researching, that Jessica and Lord Roxton anxiously sought us out.

"There were three of them, Watson." He refrained from glancing up, still scrutinizing with his lens. "All Londoners, I'll wager, from the make of these square-toed boots. Two of them are young and very athletic, skilled mountaineers, no doubt. The other is quite a bit older and, although quite dependant on them, appears to be the leader. We really must remain at our most vigilant now."

Lord Roxton bent to one knee, nodding appreciatively.

"I'll be damned." He smiled, suddenly more himself again.

Jessica also inspected the tracks. She admirably hid her aching heart.

"I'd hoped for a moment…but, no. None of these footprints are nearly large enough to belong to my father. Even so, this is an extraordinary circumstance, Mr. Holmes!"

Sherlock Holmes sprang to his feet. The keen fire of the chase burned again in his eyes, much like the old days. I could tell he was well satisfied with himself. For me, the mystery had merely grown murkier.

"Holmes," I was struggling to make sense of it, "do these mysterious saviours of ours have anything to do with your comment that we'd been followed since leaving London?"

We accompanied Holmes as he dashed back over the spongy terrain, to the ape-men killing ground. He minutely examined several of the great tree trunks surrounding us, then took his pocket-knife and dug meticulously into the scaly bark.

"I'd have thought that would be obvious, old fellow," he stated frankly. "And I'd hardly describe them as saviours. We're being kept alive for a practical purpose."

"You sound as if you already know these men." Lord Roxton couldn't quite hide his hint of skepticism.

Holmes withdrew the blade with a snap, letting a shapeless dull gray lump, about the size of a grape, drop into his hand.

"I suspect Watson does, too." He offered me the artifact.

I scraped its surface with my thumbnail, leaving a mark. It was made of lead.

"A soft-nosed rifle bullet," I mused aloud, when an incredible idea struck me. "My God—Holmes! But it can't be. He's dead."

"Are you so sure? I highly doubt it. This entire mystery is falling into place."

Without another word Holmes returned to the footprints, with the rest of us, again, breathlessly on his heels. He was utterly inexhaustible, racing and weaving among the thick undergrowth, on the scent of the almost invisible trail of our trio of stalkers. Less than five minutes later, we were investigating two more murders.

Holmes examined the corpses hastily, and with difficulty, as they were being devoured before our eyes by a fearlessly scampering flock of crow-sized winged reptiles.

"It's the young pair...dead about four hours," Holmes specifically pointed out their square-toed boots, which were barely intact. "However, they weren't killed by these little fiends. It appears that a stone-tipped spear and a heavy club were used against them, quite efficiently, too."

Lord Roxton eyed the upper tree boughs.

"Looks like we'd best find the other one quickly."

Sherlock Holmes indicted the single pair of continuing tracks, leading deeper into the swamp.

"Unless I am entirely mistaken..." He motioned for us to follow. "I highly suspect that it is *he* who will find us."

The swamp was crawling with an unimaginable multitude of vermin and parasites. Anemic-hued needle-toothed lampreys plagued us, biting through our clothing. Dragonflies as huge as hawks swooped over our heads, the droning of their wings almost deafening. Extremely bizarre coin-sized arthropods—Jessica identified them as trilobites—attached to us like armored leeches, oozing even into our boots.

The sticky mist surrounded us, swirling in dense steaming ribbons. Every step we took was a calculated risk. None of us, not even Sherlock Holmes, could see more than twenty feet away in any direction. Abruptly, and with no small alarm, we discovered our path blocked by two huge saurians, each easily heavy as elephants, and at least thirty feet long. Their ponderous faces, vaguely horse-like despite the thick scaly hide, seemed unimpressed by our diminutive comparison.

"It's only a couple Iguanodons." Jessica's educated tone was in contrast to her expression of wonder. "They're herbivorous and harmless, unless we get stepped on."

Almost as if on cue, the hulking dinosaurs became visibly agitated and galloped away, narrowly missing us. A series of tremors, each growing stronger, vibrated through the soles of our boots when a tremendous splashing followed, as if a barrage of boulders were being plummeted deep into the swamp. The creature that began to emerge from the mist was so immense, so utterly colossal, that it seemed to create its own eclipse.

The long serpentine neck arched slightly downward, its lizard-like head bowing toward us suspiciously. Even standing there in its regal presence, it was difficult to comprehend how something so enormous could actually be alive.

"A Diplodocus!" Jessica breathed. "I saw some egg casings along the edge of the swamp. She thinks we're invading her nesting ground. We've got to get away from here quickly—without panicking her."

Without a warning, the hundred foot long behemoth began a rhinoceros-like charge at us, a living avalanche of muscle, scale, and bone. There was nowhere for us to run.

Then, quite rapidly, before our astonished eyes, the monster began to explode into pieces. Yet, perhaps, that is the wrong word, for we heard no actual explosion at all—though the effect was as if the beast was caught in a bombardment of canon-fire. The ground rumbled as the ravaged remains of the mangled giant crashed wetly to the earth.

We gazed at each other, silent in the moment of our reprieve. Each of us, so I believe, knew the real storm was about to strike.

"Drop all your weapons to the ground," an English voice growled from behind us. "You're not going anywhere."

I could barely see his outline now, a tall stoop-shouldered figure standing in the curtain of mist. An extraordinary-looking firearm was pointed in our direction. We complied, relinquishing our rifles.

Even unarmed, Sherlock Holmes moved assertively toward the intruder.

"On the contrary, Colonel Moran," Holmes said coldly, "it would appear that it is you who aren't going anywhere. Not without us, that is. And you damn well know it."

Colonel Sebastian Moran glared at Holmes with pure hot murder in his eyes.

"Aware of the fate of my companions, are you, Holmes?" he snarled beneath a heavy iron-gray mustache.

"I know much more than that," Holmes stepped closer to the barrel of Moran's amazing weapon. "How tragic for your scheme, that Challenger's secret formula has died with him. No doubt, had you tortured the data from him, you would have possessed a king's ransom. More than enough to rebuild the late and unlamented Professor Moriarty's decayed criminal empire."

Colonel Moran grimaced, showing his stained tusk-like teeth.

"That's quite close enough, Holmes." He raised the remarkable rifle against his ursine shoulder. "You're correct, of course. The existence of such a formula made this damnable gamble a risk well worth taking. Not that there haven't been other rewards for a man such as myself. Never in all the world, since the beginning of time, has there been such a hunt for big game—the biggest game—as I have relished in this Primordial Hell. I've proven myself as the chief predator, almost a god. Ironic, isn't it, Holmes, that I was protecting all of you from harm, just so the World's Greatest Detective could guide me to Challenger and all his secrets!"

The grizzled old murderer was nearly raving. There was a mad yellowish cast to his eyes that bespoke, perhaps, of malaria, syphilis, or both. Moran was no longer the roguishly distinguished tiger-hunter Holmes and I once battled, but he was every bit as dangerous as he was more than twenty years before.

"Your cleverness has faded, Moran." Holmes thinly smiled. "You need us to help you escape from this Plateau. You cannot possibly leave the way you came, aided by your mountaineering henchmen. Even demented as you are, it should come as no great surprise that we utterly refuse to grant you passage."

Moran pressed a lever with his thumb and the fantastic rifle softly hummed like an electrical dynamo.

"You're wrong, Holmes." Moran sneered as he pointed the weapon directly at me. "Quite an improvement upon my old silent air-gun model, eh? You observed what it did to that forty-ton monstrosity. There won't be enough left of Dr. Watson to fill a jelly jar—unless you do as I demand."

Both Lord Roxton and Jessica made angry motions toward Moran.

"Pull that trigger and this Plateau will be your goddamned grave," Lord Roxton swore to the madman.

Jessica gazed at me with tear-brimmed eyes. The pain on her bruised, scratched face intensified her beauty.

"I'd say this is good a time as any, if you please," Holmes said, with a studied ease, directing his voice toward the branches above us.

No sooner had the first furrows of confusion appeared on Moran's murderous face than he was struck almost instantly to the earth, impaled with a Stone Age spear.

We stood aghast as the troglodyte dropped down from the trees, into our midst. He was covered with filth, crusted blood, and animal skins only slightly shaggier than his own brutish nearly naked hide, and a rich blue-black beard reaching nearly to his waist. Although his height was scarcely a few inches over five feet, the bull-like shoulders and broad apish chest gave the impression of a powerful hammered-down Hercules. In nearly every respect, except one, he was the very image of a Neanderthal Man museum exhibit brought to life. The only major disparity was the unusually high-domed intelligent forehead.

The cave man paid us no heed, leaping toward Moran and snatching up the weird rifle.

"Under normal circumstances, I'd sooner deface the Mona Lisa than destroy such an ingenious instrument," he, astonishingly, said to Holmes and then smashed the weapon against a boulder into a thousand pieces.

Moran uttered a wet rattling groan, coughing up blood. In my physician's instinct I immediately bent to his side, but there was nothing I could do. The spear had pierced his left lung, narrowly missing the heart by less than an inch. He would be dead in minutes.

Holmes and our shaggy champion studied each other for a moment in silence. Jessica was pale as a ghost, and even Lord Roxton's bronze complexion had become ashen. Then, the savage's piercing blue-gray eyes fell briefly upon each of us.

"Sherlock Holmes…but why…?" he mused aloud to himself, then slapped an enormous hand against his naked thigh. "Of course! This is about my *steel*, isn't it? I doubt they sent you here out of concern for my health. The war-mongering bastards."

He nodded at Lord Roxton.

"Obviously you still know your way around, Roxton. Full marks, you damned old campaigner. Delighted to see you."

Next, his eyes narrowed at Jessica, who'd started to tremble slightly.

"No keeping you away, was there?" he said almost reproachfully, then slightly smiled. "You get it naturally, I suppose. Remind me to describe the peculiar sub-species of living pseudosuchian that I discovered, as yet unknown even in the fossil record. I think you'll be very interested."

Finally, he bowed to me, formally as any English gentleman might.

"Ah, yes…" His smile brightened. "Dr. Watson, I presume?"

Only Holmes was left not stunned, and still capable of speech.

"Forgive me, dear fellow, I'd forgotten that the two of you never met," he said as if in the normalcy of a London street. "Allow me to present Professor George Edward Challenger."

He stood before my eyes, yet I could hardly believe it. Challenger, the man we'd come to find had not only survived—but had even thrived in that terrible place.

Challenger's surprisingly amiable smile abruptly vanished. I was startled and disturbed to see him literally sniff the humid breeze.

"Starved as I am for human conversation," he spoke with some haste, "I'm not the only hungry biological entity upon this Plateau. The blood-scent of the slain sauropod, and this wicked son of a bitch, is luring—"

Before he could say another word, a horrendous creature, more terrible than the most nightmarish dragon of myth, leapt suddenly from the jungle, pouncing upon the saurian carcass with a meteoric impact. I would dream in cold sweat of this forty-foot long scaly demon in the years that have followed this adventure. It was an Allosaurus, the Challengers later explained, although both scientists conceded the animal was considerably larger than its fossilized kin. Perhaps best described as a composite of bipedal crocodile and a wingless bird of prey, the fiend's grinding, snapping jaws towered twenty feet from the ground, or possibly more. In hideous rips and gulps it swallowed whole masses of meat and bone half as large as a London cab.

As can well be appreciated and understood, all of us ran for our lives—not daring even the quickest backward glance. We couldn't help but hear Moran, still barely alive, wailing one last shrill and piteous scream of terror.

A hellish death, even for such an evil man.

As for we who survived, our only thoughts were of our balloon and the safety of the skies above. I'm certain that even Holmes relished the notion.

Epilogue

Two months later, the secret formula for Professor George Edward Challenger's super-steel had reached the battlefields and the tide of the Great War turned to Britain's advantage. It was amusing to Challenger and to Sherlock Holmes that they both had the distinction of refusing knighthoods as a result.

Holmes and I had received a special invitation to Challenger's long-planned, and highly anticipated, lecture at the prestigious Zoological Institute—the very place a few years before that had deemed his experiences within the Lost World a fraud. Unfortunately, the weight limitations of the balloon, and our frenzied speed of departure from the Plateau did not allow for the collection of species to submit as evidence. However, Challenger and his daughter had written prodigiously since their return to civilization and were prepared to publish their proclamations following the lecture.

Both seemed unaffected by the probable fact that, once again, the scientific community would ridicule their discoveries.

We found them waiting for us just outside the Hall. Challenger struck quite a different figure in his immaculate white tie and tails, with his great black beard re-sculpted to spade-shaped perfection. Jessica Cuvier Challenger was radiant, reveling in the company of her father, and bravely ready to face the stormy trial of mockery that, doubtlessly, awaited them.

"Listen," Challenger scoffed, beard bristling. "You can already hear the bloody vultures deviously calculating to pick us apart. No matter to them that all of my courageous exploration team—and their own hand-picked associates—perished by beast and disease in the very place whose existence they all continue to deny."

His daughter affectionately touched his muscle-thick shoulder.

"No matter, sir," she laughed. "Last time even a live pterodactyl didn't convince them. After it escaped though the window, flying out to sea, all were convinced they'd witnessed nothing more than an elaborate conjurer's trick. We know what we saw, and studied. No one can ever take that away. And, believe us or burn us, they damn well will hear us out."

Challenger laughed uproariously, embracing Jessica and lifting her high above his head, as if she was a toddler.

"Ah, one thing before you start," Holmes remarked, "Dr. Watson and I have a small presentation. For the both of you."

This was news to me. I was as curious as were the Challengers as Holmes revealed a cigar box from his inner coat pocket.

"Ah—!" Challenger's eyes gleamed and, again, he laughed uproariously. "My only weakness! I've become even more addicted to the damned things since returning to London. I'd saved a single cigar while on the Plateau, wearing it in a pouch around my neck, resisting the temptation to put a match to it for over a year. It was a very sad day when I lost it in the river."

Jessica laughed heartily, as well.

"A presentation for both of us? You're suggesting, perhaps, that I take up the odious habit, Mr. Holmes?" She genuinely sparkled, ever so lovely in the glow of the street lamps.

Holmes nodded to her with hooded eyes.

"Open and see," he calmly directed.

She laughed again and opened the box, then became solemnly silent. Challenger also looked at the inner contents, glanced up at Holmes, back to his daughter, then down again into the box. He was, finally, at a lost for words.

"Lord Roxton delivered it to me. It had managed to conceal itself in his boot," Sherlock Holmes explained. "Fascinating little creature— and extremely tenacious, I might add. As you'll observe, somewhat miraculously, it has remained very much alive."

Jessica reached inside and extended her palm as the trilobite energetically scuttled across the fabric of her glove.

The
SCION *of* FEAR

by
Christopher Sequeira

For Jacqueline Amy Sequeira – The Greatest Treasure of All; Inspiration.

BY the year 1897, I had been back in residence at Baker Street for some time. Life had taken on a strange, invigorating quality, for although I deeply mourned the loss of my wife, Mary, the return of my friend Sherlock Holmes and my moving back into the old digs we shared had produced in me an effect like the re-winding of an emotional spring. I often carried the verve and confidence of the man I'd been in the eighties, ready for adventure, unswayed by fear. Looking back, I am sure that part of me also dreamed of a day when Mary might come back from the beyond, as miraculously as Holmes had. I imagined she'd appear in the doorway as a client in need of support as when first I'd met her. A fantasy, but one can see how it might appeal to a widower in his forties.

1897 was at the same time notable for some of Holmes' most challenging and dangerous cases, although these were sometimes hampered by the fact he had become such a notable public figure. For this reason I have refrained from publishing many of that year's exercises. The consultation he did for the United States of America in the Greenbrier Ghost case has been withheld; as has our return encounter with the King of Bohemia after the disastrous April Ordinance. Holmes himself placed an embargo on details of the shocking and deadly plot foiled during Queen Victoria's Diamond Jubilee ceremonies; and I will not reveal the labyrinthine scheme that had to be deciphered by Holmes and the Secret Society of Scribes—an affair wherein Holmes' old sparring partner Arthur Conan Doyle and his associates Bram Stoker, Mark Twain and the newly-released from prison

Oscar Wilde had been threatened by a maniacal adversary with the ability to read minds. The case I now recount, also, for reasons that shall become clear, must stay unpublished for some time until after my death.

I had just begun to think the year's frantic pace was abating one day late in the year, when, after a week of relative peace marred only by Holmes' disputes with a new sales clerk at Bradley's tobacconist, there came a tread on the stairs after lunch. Holmes looked up from his music sheets and queried me.

"I fancy those footfalls are unlike most, Watson; can you hazard any guess as to the features of our impending visitors?"

"You are right," I declared. "That clumping sound—someone is dragging a heavy object—no, *two* people are dragging it?"

Holmes laughed and reached for his black frockcoat from a chair-back.

"Ah, your ears are keen, old fellow! But you misinterpret a detail and it leads you astray."

Holmes then crossed to the door and flung it wide before Inspector Athelney Jones could rap.

"Mr. Holmes, I should have warned you of my coming, but sensitivity needs to be used here. I am going to cause you some surprise, at least I hope I might." Before my friend could object Jones entered, but he ushered another gentlemen in ahead of him. I stood up from my chair in sheer amazement, for the other man was known to both Holmes and me.

It was a man Holmes and I had last seen ten years earlier, Jonathan Small. Small was a remarkable figure. At about sixty-five he was lathe-thin, his face well-lined and his body a little bent, but still wiry and hard-looking. He sported a wooden leg as he had of old; it was the legacy of a horrifying encounter with a crocodile whilst swimming in the Ganges—this it had been which had made the heavy noise on the stairs. He was dressed cleanly and plainly.

It was such a surprise to see him that I almost reached out to touch this ghost—this man who had been arrested following his spectacular pursuit along the Thames by Holmes and me in the same case which introduced me to my late wife. That case had involved an Indian treasure chest, murder and oaths of fealty. Small had been the surviving criminal; sentenced to life, lucky to avoid the rope.

Jones spoke without any ado.

"Mr. Holmes, I arranged Mr. Small's release on a temporary basis, with the possibility of his sentence being reduced if he assisted us, but your involvement will also be needed."

Holmes clapped his hands with glee and rang the bell for Mrs. Hudson. The three of us looked quizzically at Small.

"My word, Jonathan Small!" said Holmes. "Sir, this is singular—I shall have Mrs. Hudson fetch tea for you!"

"Thank you, sir," Small said, amiably enough, displaying his unfettered wrists. "As you see, the Inspector doesn't need the darbies on me, and neither shall you."

Athelney Jones cocked an eyebrow. "Most courteous of you, Mr. Holmes, but what makes you think we have time for—"

Holmes waved the two men to chairs—a move which made me feel most uncomfortable.

"Jones, relax yourself, and, Watson, cease looking as if you think Small might take the silverware. If the good inspector has arranged for Mr. Small's release then clearly it is a police matter most serious, requiring Small's unique knowledge or attributes. However, if it were one of impending death, Mr. Jones would not have brought the man here but summonsed us by messenger to meet the two of them at a scene of criminal evidence."

Small laughed wildly. The brash, self-righteous cast of the man came back to the forefront of my memory—and did not reduce my apprehensions—although I tried to conceal this.

"That tea'd be right nice, Mr. Holmes!" said Small. "My current home in Dartmoor Prison ill affords the niceties. I must thank *you*, though. In Stir the fact I know you—and gave you a little run for yer money ten-year ago—has granted me some status amongst the lads."

Holmes smiled expansively. "No, I thank you, Mr. Small. Your case remains unique in my annals. Now sit, Jones, and explain this visit."

Holmes arranged seating near the fire for us all, and took a spot nearest Small. As we spoke, Holmes nodded towards him at times like an old school-chum. Rarely has my friend's contrary social manner infuriated me more. Sensing my discomfort, he tried to calm me.

"Watson, surely you must realize that Mr. Small's liberation from Dartmoor depends on his following Jones' instructions to the letter; if he attempts escape he will spend his every remaining day in prison. He does not want that, so you may relax."

Holmes then leaned back in his chair and closed his eyes.

"Now, to the affair of the garment district attacks."

Small and Jones were open-mouthed.

Holmes did not move. "Come, come, gentlemen, the facts, as today's newspaper makes plain. Firstly, two persons in the city of London have reported being attacked by a strange assailant in the past week, and in each case the description of the culprit is reported as 'not for release at this time'. But I notice three common factors in the abbreviated—one might be unkind and say 'censored'—accounts. Firstly, the victims were assaulted, physically struck in some fashion; secondly, the crime appears motiveless—these are not written of as 'robberies', 'arguments' or the like; and, thirdly, the victims provided the police with 'accurate description which should make capture inevitable,' yet the said description is not included in the report. Suggestive, sirs, that the press is assisting you."

Athelney Jones spoke. "Yes, Mr. Holmes, we have asked the papers to support our efforts, because I was worried we might have a serious threat on our hands."

Holmes opened his eyes and leaned forward.

"Indeed. And with Mr. Small's presence I complete an hypothesis as he has capabilities few or no other men in England possess – he speaks the language of one of the Andaman Island ethnic tribes, a native group most hostile to Europeans, I believe, and Small also knows the details of the deadly poison that tribe uses in its spears and darts."

Small nodded. "Aye, sir, Mr. Jones came to Dartmoor last night and asked if I would help him. He said the victims had been attacked by a man from the same tribe as my late friend, the Andaman Tonga."

"My word, that fearsome creature! I'll never forget the hideous look on the dead face of Sholto's corpse after that poison had done its work!"

Small nodded. "I could not believe another such as Tonga prowled our shores—they despise foreigners—but I said I shall come and assist, and to be honest, if some time comes off my sentence that be a thought that fair motivates me, I must also say."

Jones chimed in. "Two assaults, Mr. Holmes, let me detail them. One a clerk, name of Garrick, doing inventory late at night in a warehouse six days ago. Innocuous fellow. I think he surprised someone in the warehouse who should not have been there. Garrick described a figure covered almost completely in Hindu-style robes—a very small man, dark of skin, might have been hiding in a bay in the warehouse. The fellow sprung on Garrick and hit him with a wooden plank, but what was worse—and near turned my blood cold with evil memories, Mr. Holmes—was when Garrick hit the ground, the attacker pulled out a wooden tube, a blowpipe apparently, and was about to use it on the victim. But a shout or cry in the night outside, probably drunken passers-by according to the account, stopped him cold and he turned and fled. However, he dropped the pipe when he escaped. See—I have it here."

Holmes examined the proffered tube, even using his lens, turning it carefully.

"Small, my less practiced eye certainly would say the wood is not local, and the cutting and finishing done simply and without modern blade or tool, what about you?"

"I agree, and would stake my cursed life this is Andaman. Just as one of Tonga's, it is."

Jones continued. "I was of a similar mind, a pipe like the one from the one case that's haunted my nightmares since the Sholto death, what Watson called the 'Case of Four' or whatnot. I thought of Small at once, but I'll confess, I tried to put it down to coincidence at first—some other perpetrator, I thought."

Holmes was intrigued. "Jones, you did not seek out Small—or myself for that matter? Why?"

"Well, Garrick, who came to see me at the Yard, seemed too excitable, to be honest. I was fearful he had read the old case by Dr. Watson and worked himself into a lather, and that the pipe was coincidence. A mislaid curio in a warehouse seemed more likely."

Holmes chuckled as he lit a fresh cigarette. "But your hard-headed police instincts succumbed when a second report was received days later?"

Small laughed again and I was sure Holmes winked encouragingly at the man!

"Yes, the second report changed my mind, two days ago. For a woman was shot at with a dart! An Indian family, Mukhergee, with a small tailoring business in the city, were the victims. She was working, sewing late into the night and the husband thought he heard a noise—and voices. He heard a scream, then he raced downstairs to investigate and saw the figure, identical to Garrick's depiction, running out the back door into a laneway into the night. The wife described a strange native man who had appeared and begun yammering at her in a strange tongue; she understood none of it, although she speaks five Indian dialects. The figure was not angry at first, but seemed to be trying to seek her aid. But with the failure to make himself understood he grew angry and moved to slap her! She blocked his blow and he was enraged. He pulled a blowpipe—she describes it as a mate to the one we have—and actually launched a dart at her! She had thrown up an empty sewing basket in defense and this saved her, for the dart stuck in it."

"Miraculous!" declared Small.

"The husband had come down, and here we have corroboration, he saw the man, who was seething with rage. The native actually plucked the dart from the basket, whisked it into a pouch on a necklace and ran out the back door and into the night. Mukhergee admits he did not immediately go in pursuit; his wife was screaming and refused to let him follow at first. By the time he did, there was nothing."

"Needless to say, gentlemen, when the family reported the matter to me, I contacted Dartmoor immediately and got dispensation to see Mr. Small."

I was sure I could see Jones' line of reasoning. "You had to try and prepare in case it was another Tonga, another Andamaner? You might need a man who could speak his language if pursued or captured, or a man who could confirm the poison dart was the same type?"

Jones confirmed this. "I was sure the past was re-living itself, sirs, so I sought an expert. And now, seeing you, Mr. Holmes, I am consulting the only other living expert."

Holmes frowned. "Yes, yes. But to business, leaving the reunion aside. The killer retrieved the dart and took it with him. Odd."

"As far as I can tell, yes, sir," said Athelney Jones "Must have assumed the dart might incriminate him, give him away."

"No, no, Inspector, too dependent on an appreciation of our legal system and criminology methods. I favor instead…" Holmes' voice trailed off as a thought suddenly interrupted his words. He stood, silently, scratched his head and then stretched, almost absent-mindedly, which gave the appearance he was uninterested, but which I knew full well only signified he was throwing off the boredom of contemporary existence to embrace this case. Surely enough, after extending his arms to the utmost he brought his hands together with a little clap.

"That he was ensuring he has a plentiful supply of darts to complete a task he has before him! Ha!"

Jones and Small looked confused but Holmes left them little time to ponder.

"To it, then, sirs!" Holmes said. "The picture painted is that of a frightened native of other climes to deal with. A dangerous prey, too, armed as he is. We need to find him or what he has come here for. Is there any antidote to that poison, Small?"

The old convict spoke grimly. "Mr. Holmes, that stuff was diabolical; it killed pretty quick. Tonga brewed it from plants on his island and I was kept well away when he did. The mere smell as he smoked and blended them together boded danger. If a man survived a dart, by strength of constitution, he'd be given naught but goat's milk for days until his fever broke, but there was few that did live."

"Well, then we'd best get a move on, and run this culprit down," said Holmes, shuffling on his overcoat and cap.

Jones, Small and myself stood, mystified. We were in ignorance as to where Holmes was suggesting we go.

"Chase the culprit?" I asked. "By talking to the family, or the warehouse, is it?"

"No, no," said my friend. "Let us talk to the person responsible for bringing the killer to our fair city, and the London Harbormaster should make that possible."

Holmes, as usual, had his methods, and they opened doors that were at times closed to others. A four-wheeler was obtained and it took us to Whitehall, where we held a brief meeting with Holmes' brother.

Mycroft Holmes, as my readers may recall, held a crucial role that spanned the boundaries of several government portfolios. He was a valued clearing-house of information and his assessments upon inter-departmental matters were highly valuable to the civil service. His ability to analyze large quantities of numerical data and statistics was extraordinary, and his memory was rumored to be almost photographic. Suffice to say, if information were required, he often had it or had the means to procure it.

The portly Mycroft—as massive as his younger brother was lean—heard out Holmes' account of the matter. At one stage they retired in private—and then had a letter prepared for us that would immediately provide entrée to the London Harbormaster's Office. As we ended our short discussion Mycroft made a point of shaking my hand warmly. "You continue to chronicle Sherlock's efforts with élan, Doctor, and I am well aware you have kept him from some of his more reckless pursuits since his return to us. The dismantling of the Moriarty organization that almost took Sherlock's life—it is appreciated, sir."

"The least I can do, Mr. Holmes," I said. "He is my friend."

Mycroft looked me in the eye. "And no easy friendship that, I am sure, knowing my younger brother's habits! Dr. Watson, it is no small thing that you assist on this case and go over the old matters of the Agra treasure. I know it must bring back certain memories for you—and sad ones, too, may your dear wife rest in peace."

The huge man turned to Holmes, then. "Sherlock, all the records and paraphernalia associated with the Agra case were lodged with Indian diplomatic services via my office once the police had finished with them. Let me know if there's anything you fellows desire in this investigation. It shall be put at your disposal."

Holmes clasped his brother's shoulder. "Thank you, Mycroft, I think your letter shall be all we need."

Our trip to the Harbormaster's office was protracted but unremarkable. Holmes and Athelney Jones required a list of all vessels that had entered the port of London from Indian waters over a week ago, and their next destination, and purpose of voyage. He and Athelney Jones were engaged with clerks for the better part of two hours, and argued and fussed over a number of registers.

Holmes finally seemed satisfied and with a map of the docks also in his pocket we left just as the day was ending. Holmes explained his plans.

"There are five ships that have come from the waters anywhere near the Andaman Islands that had textiles or clothing as their cargo."

"Why is the cargo of import, Holmes?" said I. "Surely any vessel from the home of the Andamans is worthy of examination?"

Holmes expounded: "Vessels from Indian waters number fifteen. But forget not that India is a primary producer of some of the highest quality cloths and weaves, and consequently exports some to London. I surmise that if a man comes to this city wielding a deadly poison known to originate on an India-region island, and that that man is then later seen in a textiles warehouse, and then later still reported running from a London tailor, that the miscreant is in all likelihood connected to the textile industry."

"Connected? A savage?" Jones said. "But how—why?"

Holmes shrugged. "Possibly in the most tangential of ways, possibly only in the events that led to the arrival in London. And be wary of the word 'savage', Jones. It oft denotes lack of guile and resourcefulness, and since our quarry has defied capture for a week I'd suggest he lacks neither. Perhaps our man's passage or stowaway status was arranged on a textile vessel by a passenger or principal in that voyage, and then once berthed in London the foreigner has followed a connection to a textile customer—to their receiving customer's warehouse, perhaps."

"Could they have been stowed away with bolts of cloth and suchlike and taken to the warehouse, from whence they emerged from hiding?" I said, excitedly, understanding my friend's reasoning.

Holmes agreed. "It is possible. And thence a pre-arranged plan was that a customer of that warehouse, the tailor, or one of his suppliers was to take care of this new arrival. Would you not think this likely, Small?"

Small shook his head. "Sirs, I can make no sense of this! The Andaman Islanders—Tonga's friendship with me was a rare thing. His trust in me came about through an injury that forced him into my care. His folk—they do not trust white men so readily—Lord, they kill them most times rather than look at us! Are ye sure 'tis right? Maybe it's another white man is helping this fellow?"

Holmes actually snorted derisively, a distinct change from his earlier mien. "Preposterous. Your own life experiences could not be replicated without stretching credibility. No, I suggest our man is a lone stowaway. Let us have no more debate on the matter without further contrary data; an Andaman Islander is loose in the city. The thread that connects this is that of the sub-continent's well-known textile industry, and we must see if it is unbroken or binding. Come. There are five worthy vessels to investigate."

In relating the cases my friend has investigated, I have, of course, employed artistic license whilst trying to hew to the facts. At times Holmes' inquiries take months and I must contract the events or skip over unfruitful leads in preparing a narrative version for the public.

The inquiries on the five freight ships out of India that Holmes led formed a perfect example of this situation, Holmes was able, using his reputation, his insightful understanding of authority figures and sheer guile to get us on to the bridge of all five vessels and allow us to speak to all the captains or senior officers-on-deck.

To no avail. Three hours later we had not one shred of a clue and no reason to think any man had lied to us. I ventured to ask if the right vessel had sailed away already. Holmes laughed, although Small looked blackly angry. "Watson," said Holmes, "you have not lost that imaginative streak." And infuriatingly he would say no more.

Holmes called Jones over for a quiet conference and I was left watching Small. He stared at me unflinchingly.

"He's a clever man, your Mr. Holmes. Not many get the best of him."

"None do," I said, regretting it the minute I spoke it, realizing how childishly I was trying to show Small I would brook no familiarity from such as he.

"None, then, all right, none, then," he said. "Doctor. Years ago when we first met I saw you as a man of strength and character—surely there's no threat you see in me?"

"Mr. Small, you caused my late wife no small amount of grief, even if you thought you were avenging yourself on those that had wronged you. I cannot forgive you that."

He looked at me, puzzled, then blinked and nodded.

"Ah, the treasure. You would have been a rich man if not for me tossing the jewels out of the iron box and into the river Thames."

I bristled. I wrestled with myself and tried not to speak, but I failed.

"You will recall, Small, that after you secretly dumped the treasure in the Thames, you re-locked the box that contained it. It was then taken by myself, and I took it to the woman who was to become my wife. It was opened and found to be empty! And my heart leapt to find it empty, for if my beloved Mary had been the recipient of a magnificent fortune, I would never have proposed to her. No gentlemen would."

Small looked surprised. A look of consideration flitted across his face, then he fixed upon me.

"Forgive me, Doctor. The treasure went to the riverbed; it lies there with the body of little Tonga, because it is *cursed*. It killed him, it cursed me, ruined my life and that of the three others who swore the blood-oath of the Sign of the Four. I'm sorry about your wife, Doctor, but she and you were better off without the damned things."

"I don't believe in curses, Mr. Small. I believe in the actions of men, their actions for good or ill."

He stared at me. "What a man believes often comes from what life has given him, or taken. Since I lost me leg and life turned sour I've known that; since the treasure I've wished it were otherwise, but it's not, sir. It all depends on the life ye've had. Mine's been harder than some, and easier than others, but I was once promised riches and glory, and to have spent decades in stone prisons instead, well, please indulge me if I call that a curse."

I was moved to rebuke the man but Holmes interrupted, and called us back.

"Watson, Mr. Small. Your attention, please—I fear we must abandon—"

"Inspector, Inspector!" a young voice cried out. A lad of perhaps fourteen years was cantering down the docks towards us, waving a paper. The boy was some sort of messenger employed by the Yard. Jones studied the offering intently, then passed it to Holmes.

"A note," explained Jones to Small and myself. "Garrick has seen the man again, in the premises next the textile warehouse, an empty engineering parts place, but he refuses to go in. Gentlemen, this is presumably an opportunity we should not pass up."

Holmes was in agreement. "Despite the danger, I would ask you come with us, Small. Your presence may redeem the day."

"Aye, sir, I'll go."

The building where the fugitive had been seen caused me serious concerns when I sighted it. Massive, and filled with broken metal industrial wheels, and boiler parts, it was a dangerous place to hunt a man. And I immediately wondered if we were not exposing ourselves to risk of a serious accident or even a fatal attack in this place of haphazardly stacked iron and steel mechanisms.

Night had thrown its concealing cloak over the domain. The bull's-eye lanterns we had secured before assailing the place gave me little comfort; shadows danced everywhere we swung them.

Ultimately Holmes and Jones pursued one artificial corridor of floor-space between mountains of twisted and rusting metal, whilst Small and I traversed ahead in another corridor, his wooden leg tapping behind me.

Ten minutes of such wandering saw no result and the four of us met up at an intersection between alleyways. I opened my mouth to complain and Holmes silenced me with a raised finger. He pointed to a new alleyway, and he and Jones disappeared down it.

I stood in silence with Small, realizing his wooden leg would not allow any stealthy advancement. Then I saw it, a figure in white clothing, a somewhat smaller than average form, emerging from a bulk of rusted gears and heading towards Holmes. I turned to Small, to tug his sleeve and make him aware of what I'd seen—only to see him begin to charge up and ahead, like a madman, his hands outstretched, screaming with rage!

I nearly fell over as he bowled past me, but the carefully wrapped figure in white was more effected. It stopped in its tracks and looked back and looked forward, then back—it seemed completely hesitant. And then Small was upon it—he jumped for the person.

Small was a snarling wild man, trying to hold the white-garbed one. It was a bizarre tableaux. The two figures were hidden in shadows as they rolled and pushed back and forth across two aisles and three piles of old iron parts. I could scarcely make out what was going on

I was wondering what had become of Holmes when a terrible ripping noise sounded, like the tearing of wood. There was a scream, then a splash of water. "It's all right," I heard Small yell, "It's all right!"

We must have made a strange sight, Holmes, Jones and I, shuffling towards Small's voice and bringing light with us.

A huge section of floorboards had rotted and fallen away. The heavy machinery had bowed the timbers here some time previously. The sewer below the building now seemed to have swallowed up the Andamaner.

Small clutched a turban-like swath of linen and a wicked knife that dripped crimson, but he had not a cut nor mark upon his own body. He was beaming like a proud schoolboy.

"I'm sorry, sirs, but I had no choice. He was going to do for me."

I checked Small for wounds or fatigue; he seemed well enough. Jones shook his head, angrily.

"I put your life at risk, Small, a man your age, against some sort of human animal—Lord, I am sorry, man!"

"Don't be," said Holmes quietly.

Even I was taken aback at my friend's rudeness on this occasion. "Holmes, that is really unfunny."

Holmes stretched his arms, and cracked his knuckles. "Watson, I'm not attempting a joke. Small was not at risk, because this entire case has been a fabrication from the start."

Jones started; I thought he looked angrier than Small.

"No—Mr. Holmes, no, please!"

Holmes' voice was calm, yet steely. "I'm sorry, but my own charade at Mycroft's, at the harbor, on those vessels, probably did not adequately prepare one for this. But the facts are indisputably the facts. Firstly, why was it you had no independent evidence of this mad Andaman Islander? Why was there a blowpipe, not a difficult thing to make, but no actual poison dart—which would have been extremely hard to produce? And the crowning fact: these people sought out you, Jones, the one man in Scotland Yard who would react to these tales of a deadly cannibal tribesman by securing the release of Mr. Small."

Small looked nothing other than crushed in spirit, now. Holmes spoke to him, a hint of sympathy in his voice. "Small, you gave a good game. But played it a tiny piece too far. It was that ridiculous story about the native retrieving his dart—that struck me as being inconsistent with leaving a pipe behind, but of course your story had to fall out that way. I tested the truth of things by pretending to be convinced the pipe was made of foreign wood—it was not. Being raised by country folk I'm afraid I know a briar root when I see it, but Small in his eagerness took my bait. Now it remains to know—"

A scream echoed through that dank place and it came from behind us. A figure in white burst out from behind some old fittings and ran towards us, a pistol extended in its hand!

I fumbled for my service revolver, but Jones, with speed I'll remember to my dying day, drew his own pistol. They both fired. The man in white missed, his bullet ricocheting. I felt a flash of something—perhaps some metallic fragment—crease my temple. Jones did not miss, however, and the white figure spasmed as he was hit. But as he fell, his gun discharged almost point-blank into Small's chest.

Small's mouth frothed and twisted; his face was sheened in sweat. Blood erupted from his upper body as he hit the timbers. Holmes got to him before I did, and Jones went to the other man, removing a scarf of white.

"Lord! Called himself Mukhergee, he did. He was the tailor."

Holmes was leaning down to Small's lips, which were croaking. Small tried to clutch at him, then flailed at his own bloody upper body, his face twisted in pain. He was clutching his ribcage. He gasped "chest", "side"; then his eyes froze.

I started to walk, felt something throbbing at my temple, and I fell.

The blow that had glanced across my head had done some damage, it seemed, for I began to feel a boiling heat, as if I were in a furnace. Sounds began to recede; my vision blurred. Holmes loomed before me.

I fell into blackness.

When I regained consciousness some time later, I was at Baker Street and in my own bed, the framed bedside picture of my late beloved Mary on my night-table, as usual decked with the small chaplet of six pearls—the pearls that had propelled her into the matter of the Sign of the Four, that event which had brought us together and which only death had put asunder.

I staggered up and gradually gained my senses. I threw on a dressing gown.

Right outside my door I almost stepped on a Stradivarius violin. Holmes lay slumped on the floor on a massive pile of cushions outside my room, sound asleep. Nearby was a foul ashtray over-flowing with cigarette butts. He still held a cold pipe in his fingers. My old friend had kept vigil at my door.

We took luncheon with Athelney Jones once I was recovered, who was as relieved that he had narrowly avoided the embarrassment of his career as he was that I was unharmed.

"I don't know how I could have been so stupid. It maddens me, sirs, I can tell you!"

Holmes was calm and reassuring.

"Friend Jones, the Sholto case left a rather nasty scar on your memory. You were reacting to that, and Small played upon your gullibility due to that cause."

"But I was so thick, so daft!"

"No, sir. He was so clever, and so elegantly clever because his plan was so simple. He made you think of the proposition yourself. But our late convict colleague had many a year to scheme and plot, so one must acknowledge he had time aplenty to consider how to play this best, and he had nothing in the world to lose—he was never expected to be released."

"I suspected that the young Indian that aided him was involved with the nefarious Four, perhaps a son of one of the other three sentenced to life in an Indian prison; a scion of the fear pact that led to so much misery in India those many years gone. At some juncture he tracked Small to England and made contact, visited him in jail—perhaps originally to chastise Small for his failure to hold onto the treasure. Small then recognized a kindred spirit, a man with courage, desperation and a complete lack of principles. Small also had a charisma. He was party to murder but could tell his tale and evoke sympathy. I would submit it is a skill many murderers have put to great use in their trade, particularly in the courtroom. In any event the idea was conceived: create a scenario where it appeared a dangerous fugitive was at large and only Jonathan Small—old, harmless Small—could stave off disaster, avoid a terrible fatality of an innocent person."

"Would such a person go to all that trouble?" I asked. "Why? And why become so murderous once exposed?"

"I shall be honest and confess that I must use conjecture, but that I think greed may be the drawcard," said my friend, his gray eyes staring into space, searching realms beyond this world. "Yes, Small threw the treasure into the Thames all those years ago – but what if he told Mukhergee that he had hidden it somewhere, given it to an accomplice, or buried it? The story might then have power, and make a man take a wild chance. But we shan't be able to ask them. Perhaps if the other accomplices knew much, and they turn up?"

"So, regardless," said Holmes, "those accomplices were gathered, told what was needed, and stories of 'Garrick' and 'Mukhergee' were crafted, and just enough evidence manufactured to hook you, Jones. Yet there was no poison, for they had none that matched the obscure Andaman mixture and would not have been foolish enough to provide some other that would fail a chemist's toxicity tests. The climax was supposed to have been Small's great heroic moment with the vanishing—never to be recovered—'Andamaner'. The case would close and Small would be free for being such significant help to the Crown. It is in one sense, the most perfect prison escape plan I've ever come across—a completely legal exit from captivity."

"I was not sure where it would lead so I was happy to play along. The exercise with freighter captains was all nonsense, although it was not inconsistent with what I would have done if I thought a wild aborigine had recently arrived in port! I had made my mind up whilst I was with Mycroft to see this matter through, for I took advantage of the fact he has authority to use a telephone in his office and so I sent a question to Dartmoor Prison when we were at the Whitehall office."

Jones was intrigued. "You telephoned them, about Small?"

Holmes stabbed decisively in the air with his fork. "To find out if he'd had any visitors, of course—and the answer was, yes, in the last four months a man of Indian appearance made regular trips, said he was a nephew's friend. Again, the man going as Mukhergee, unless I miss my guess. If his so-called wife can be found she will give him quite another name, I think."

Jones sighed. "Doctor, I'm sorry you went through all this."

I laughed. "Jones, Holmes is right—I always said the Sign of the Four case transformed my life, this just proved the effect was longer lasting than I thought."

It was almost eleven that night when I arrived at the Diogenes Club, but as I expected a doorman escorted me into its confines with neither fuss nor delay. I sat in the dark-paneled Strangers Room, and barely had had time to start a pipe when Mycroft Holmes entered, accompanied by a footman wheeling a wooden trolley upon which rested a large object covered by a brown cloth. Once the trolley was delivered to a spot in the room before me, the footman bowed and wordlessly withdrew, closing the door behind him. As if from habit, Mycroft sighed and spoke for the first time.

"Doctor, there are few men worthy of me breaking my ritual dinner at Marcini's but you are one. You will deduce I not only received your note but have acted upon it. Behold." And he removed the brown cloth.

Upon the trolley sat an object that I knew only too well, the iron box that Sherlock Holmes and I had pursued Jonathan Small for ten years earlier—the box that Small had explained he emptied of its precious gemstones straight into the Thames rather than give any up to the police.

"Thank you, sir. Now please let me put to use the knowledge I have."

I leaned over the chest and studied it, lifted its lid and examined its vacant interior. I pressed its sturdy walls and ran my fingers over its beautiful if rather crudely embossed surface. Then finally finding what I sought, I pushed the small metal handle on one of its sides whilst pressing a corner stud.

An almost inaudible metallic click sounded, and then from one of the solid metal sides—two-thirds of an inch thick—slid upwards, via some concealed spring, a metal drawer from the side of the chest! This drawer had a flat lid to it, which I lifted. Revealed within, nestling in three, snug velvet-lined compartments, were three enormous yellow stones—yellow diamonds! There was a fourth space—for an identical stone, it appeared— but this was empty.

Mycroft raised an eyebrow. He removed one stone and studied it.

"I was once required to write a paper for the diplomatic corps on certain errant valuables that had created some problems for the crown by being smuggled out of India. I was given a schooling on gems as a result."

"If these stones are what I believe they are, their value eclipses the rest of the recorded Agra treasure, which supposedly went to the bottom of the Thames."

"I would have suspected so," I said. "And Jonathan Small's dying words— 'chest', 'side'—make me certain he knew, too."

"The fact that you requested this meeting without the presence of brother Sherlock informs me that you have something of import to conceal from him. My conclusion is that you did not just now find out that this treasure was concealed here—did you, Doctor?"

I hesitated, then answered, as I knew I must.

"No, sir, I did not. I have known it lay here these ten years."

Mycroft studied me, and in those gray eyes I felt the scrutiny that his brother had turned on many a weaker mind. "You are saying that you have known or suspected this hidden treasure lay secreted here these past ten years and you have kept this fact from my brother – never told him?"

"Yes," I said firmly. "Sir, I give you my word, perhaps ironically. I ask that you trust me when I say there is no man I value more highly than your brother. But during the case I came to call the Sign of the Four, ten years ago, I was faced with an impossible position. I could reveal I had found the treasure and see it fall into the hands of a young woman, Mary Morstan; or keep my secret, and propose to her and make her my wife."

Mycroft Holmes heaved a sigh. "Forgive my question, sir, for romance is not the strong suit of Holmes men. You could not have asked her regardless? She loved you, did she not?"

I smiled, and felt my eyes brimming. "She did. But a man of honor, a man almost completely insolvent as I was then, could not put a woman in that position. She would always wonder whether I loved her or her fortune. She had been so cruelly manipulated by her family until then—I could not—would not do so."

Mycroft stared at me. He was silent for a little time; he was wrestling with divulging something.

"Doctor, these diamonds are of some consequence. They are a part of a series of four 'moonstones' that adorned temple-idols at four compass points in the Indian sub-continent. They have bizarre and bloody lineages. The fourth one was recovered some years ago after much drama. The rightful owners have only ceased chasing these three because they were thought lost by the Rajah who stole them all those years ago and subsumed them into his treasure vaults until the Sepoy mutiny frightened him into fleeing. There exist secret diplomatic arrangements that if they are recovered, they are to be returned, whereupon British relations with locals in some very contentious matters can be smoothed over. Simply put, sir, the British Interest in India will greatly appreciate the return of these and remunerate the finder well."

"Mr. Holmes, I have no need of money, thanks to my returns from writing—which stem from your marvelous brother's confidence in me - and I have no fear of life without it in any case."

Mycroft scratched his chins. He looked at me sharply. I was baffled for a moment at his next question.

"Doctor, forgive me. You and your late wife had no children?"

"Her illness and early passing prevented that, sir."

"And I recall Sherlock or you saying she aided charitable agencies from time to time?"

"Yes. Not short of compassion for the less fortunate, was Mary."

Mycroft Holmes was amused with himself. "Well, Doctor, the Diogenes Club has a number of charities it discreetly funds; orphanages, destitute mothers, other causes that perhaps your wife would have looked kindly upon. We see to their needs without fanfare or recognition. Keeps our motives pure, you might say. If the remuneration for the treasure were put to such a use, my brother need never find out...?"

"Thank you, sir," I stammered. "I would be, be most honored."

"Excellent, Doctor! I shall generate the appropriate commitments."

He shook my hand at the door, warmly, a thing he had never done before.

"It is possible Sherlock did at least entertain the solution to the treasure's location, but that he discarded that notion or decided not to further act on the supposition. Because he had a pressing reason not to."

"Sir?"

"Doctor, do not repeat this. Sherlock considers you the highest caliber friend a fellow could have. Therefore if a solution to a case produced a result that might harm you, I doubt he would pursue such a solution if no other innocent life or limb were in jeopardy."

I nodded.

"Well, he always has a fine sense of justice, your brother does."

Mycroft Holmes grinned. "Another Holmesian trait. Good night, sir."

The
PETRIFYING WELL

by
Martin Gately

IT had been nearly two years since I had cause to record the details of one of my cases myself—that being the singular adventure of the Lion's Mane, in July, 1907—and as I stated then, I seldom saw my dear Watson during my "retirement" except for the occasional weekend visit. I was therefore delighted when he suggested that we should undertake a walking holiday in Derbyshire, using as our base the popular inland resort of Matlock Bath—where the well-to-do and genteel go to imbibe the refreshing and, some claim, healing waters.

It seemed we had hardly unpacked our bags when we became embroiled in a series of crimes noteworthy only for their brutality. I refer to the matter of Foxwell, the "Lumsdale Horse Slasher," whose depravities, capture and trial were reported in sufficient detail in *The Times* to satisfy even the most bloodthirsty student of malfeasance. I shall not seek to repeat that sordid narrative here. However, it was during the cornering of Foxwell in an isolated barn on the Derbyshire moors that Dr. Watson suffered incapacitating injuries: a deep gash across the scalp, lacerations to his forearm, a knife wound to the thigh and a mild concussion. I berated myself for my failure to protect him and thereby swore to bring him back to full health; although by temperament and ability I am something of a poor nursemaid. In any event, it was necessary to extend our stay beyond the originally planned two weeks to allow time for Watson's recuperation. So it was, one cool June morning in our suite at the "County and Station" Hotel that our breakfast was interrupted by a knock at the door. I admitted to the room a slim fair-haired young man of about twenty-one years of age. His face was noble, his eyes bright and intense, but he carried with him a great sadness, as if all the troubles of the world were upon him.

"Mr. Holmes, it is fortunate indeed that you have not yet returned to London. A dreadful thing has occurred that is both ghastly and inexplicable, and it has robbed my closest friend of his brother."

"Pray sit down, sir. First tell me your name and every detail of these inexplicable events, for it is only when every fact is in its correct position that the algebra of truth can be calculated and proper answers revealed."

"My name is Ned Lawrence and I am a history student at Oxford University. I have a particular interest in medieval architecture and have been studying local churches prior to my main summer holiday cycling in France and the Near East, where I shall survey crusader castles. I have been staying with the Hassett family—who are well known local landowners. I am particular friends with the Sir Ambrose Hassett's eldest son, Ian, who is a mining engineer."

I assisted Watson from the breakfast table to a comfortable position on the sofa and bade Lawrence continue.

"Now I must tell you of the events of yesterday morning. The whole family breakfasted early and heartily on porridge and fruit: taciturn Sir Ambrose at the head of table, larger than life Ian Hassett and his quieter brother, James. I had obtained permission to ascend the St. John's church tower with a borrowed double-length ladder to examine its unusual gargoyles. James had no plans other than to walk his terrier, Bob, in the fields and Ian had business in Chesterfield. And so, not long after, I was perched precariously on the external ledge of the St. John's bell tower, making a sketch. This vantage point, perhaps seventy feet above the ground, afforded me an excellent view of the Hassett's stable-yard. I saw James Hassett exit the main house into the stable-yard with the dog. Looking up, he spotted me and gave a cheery wave of the hand. As he did so the terrier fell still at his feet. When he crouched to examine the little fellow, he too keeled over and lay prone on the cobblestones. He clawed at his throat momentarily and then was still. I edged around the bell tower ledge back towards my ladder so that I could climb down and assist, but when I reached the far side of the tower my ladder had vanished. By this point I was frantic and I considered attempting to descend directly down the stone work—I have done some little climbing here on the cliffs at Matlock Bath with minimal equipment—but there were no handholds and it seemed I would merely die a futile death in the attempt. I was at a complete loss when I saw in the lane Ian Hassett about to embark on his journey to Chesterfield in a pony and trap. I shouted to him at the top of my voice, gesticulating wildly. He rode into the yard and tried to rouse his brother, but he was already dead."

"The facts as you relay them suggest to me that you witnessed a murder," I said. "A most extraordinary murder. I can tell that you have discounted the commonplace since you regard the event as inexplicable. A Scotland Yard official would assume poisoning, but you have not mentioned poisoning. Why?"

"The family and I ate the same breakfast and drank the same Darjeeling—none of the rest of us suffered any ill-effects at all. Then there is the matter of the terrier. It died the instant before its master and yet they had consumed nothing in common. I am not given to fancies, but it is almost as if the grim reaper waited for them in the stable-yard. There must be an answer, Mr. Holmes, and I mean to find it."

"Your case presents many interesting aspects, Mr. Lawrence. Would that I were free to commence an investigation, but as you can see my friend and colleague, Dr. Watson, is totally reliant on my ministrations at present."

"Good grief, Holmes! The care provided by the humblest scullery maid in this hotel could hardly be less than a ten-fold improvement on the clumsy assistance you've rendered. Go with young Mr. Lawrence here and engage your God-given faculties for their proper use. Get to the bottom of this business, I implore you."

Later that same morning, I stood before the heavy oak door of Sir Ambrose Hassett's study in his palatial property.

"I should probably warn you that Sir Ambrose is rather eccentric and subscribes to some peculiar beliefs," said Lawrence.

He knocked and we both entered. Sir Ambrose sat at the far end of his study at a leather-topped desk. His plum-colored smoking jacket was hung on the back of his throne-like chair, his shirt sleeves were rolled up—showing that his forearms were a mass of scar tissue and partially covered with soiled wound dressings. As we approached, he placed a bloodstained scalpel into a pewter tankard which sat on his desktop, where several other surgical blades also resided.

"Ah, Ned, you are a welcome distraction from my grief," said the old man. "When a father has to make the arrangements for his son's funeral it is enough to deplete both mental and physical energy."

"Sir Ambrose, this is Sherlock Holmes, the famous consulting detective. He was on holiday here and I have presumed to ask him to investigate your son's death."

"Sir Ambrose," I began, "I was greatly saddened to hear of the death of your son. Have you also suffered some other misfortune? These injuries to your arms…" I mentioned them explicitly because I could not account for them. I once saw a man dig birdshot from his flesh after a hunting accident, but the desktop was bereft of the lead pellets that would mark a shotgun wound as the likely explanation.

"Mr. Holmes, the misfortune I suffer is a malady that plagues my family. It is as uncommon as it is repulsive. The Hassett's are susceptible to infestation by blood lice. These parasitic insects burrow into our skin and sup on our blood. I would not in any way be surprised to find that James' death was caused by these creatures. They may have passed through his veins directly into his heart and caused some form of coronary arrest."

He led us to an octagonal rosewood table near the fireplace upon which sat a large brass microscope.

"Look for yourselves. On the slide are some blood lice I removed from my flesh earlier."

I looked through the eyepiece and adjusted the focus. Under high magnification the lice looked like titanic monsters. They seemed to writhe and fight over the remaining blood droplets on the glass slide. I moved away and young Lawrence took his turn at the microscope. He blanched slightly and almost immediately started involuntarily scratching at the skin of his own forearms through his shirt. Thereafter, we left, having obtained permission from Sir Ambrose to question his family and servants as we saw fit; although plainly he thought the solution lay with the strange parasitic lice.

"Mr. Holmes, I have never heard blood lice mentioned until I came to this place. Do you really think they could be responsible for James Hassett's death?"

"I sincerely doubt it, Ned, since there are no such things as blood lice. The creatures we saw under the microscope are called 'springtails'— harmless enough little arthropods. They devour leaf litter and can be found in practically any woodland setting. Though sure enough, they look like they were created by the devil himself, if you are unfamiliar with them. I hesitated to press Sir Ambrose for answers because he is subject to delusions rather than eccentricity. The question is: how has he come to believe so wholeheartedly in their existence? Is the belief a product of his own imaginings or has their reality been suggested to him by someone else?"

"To what end?"

"Once again, murder, of course. If he digs around with filthy scalpels every day I'm surprised he hasn't already fallen victim to septicemia. Suggestion is a weapon every bit as powerful as a gun. For instance, you are a highly intelligent young man and yet one look through that microscope and you were scratching your forearms because you feared that you too had been infected with blood lice during your stay here."

We walked together for nearly an hour in the bright summer sun along bracken-lined lanes to reach Cromford Lake, where Ned Lawrence said we would find Ian Hassett. As we talked I became more and more impressed with him—he had the mind of a scientist, the heart of soldier and the soul of a poet.

"I seldom dream when sleeping," he told me. "Yet all my waking hours are filled with daydreams of what I might do when I am older. There is a siren song calling me to a destiny in the Eastern deserts. I'm sure I will find a greater purpose there than studying crusader architecture."

"Such men as you are dangerous," I smiled. "Those who dream with their eyes open may act out their dreams, making them possible and real."

When we reached the lake, Hassett was there with three other men standing on a large pontoon which floated about twenty yards out from the shore. Two of the men were dressed in full diving gear; their burnished copper helmets gleamed dazzlingly. Also on the pontoon was a great brass and steel engine from which emanated a pneumatic drumming sound. This was the compressor which supplied the divers with air.

Upon seeing us, Ian Hassett climbed into a small rowing boat that had been moored on the far side of the pontoon and rowed across to greet us. He had the look of a man from another age—a swashbuckler. He might have been a privateer rowing to a desert isle to deposit his booty.

"I'm pleased to meet you, Mr. Holmes," he said, once on dry land. "You will no doubt think me harsh, but I have little time for grief at the moment. I am by profession a mining engineer, a specialist in the design of electric compressors and pumps used in coal mining. At the moment I am adapting these mechanisms to provide compressed air for the divers of the Maracot Expedition to the deep Atlantic. They leave in less than a week and if a compressor were to fail with a diver perhaps several hundred feet beneath his diving bell it would mean certain death. I am therefore working night and day to perfect these systems."

"Then I shall keep my questions to a minimum. You were the first on the scene after your brother's death. What do you believe was the cause of his demise?"

"Some obstruction of his windpipe or lungs...I noticed that his lips were turning blue from lack of air, likewise his face was starting to blacken."

"And his dog died at almost exactly the same moment...how do you account for that?"

"Dogs are such loyal creatures. The sight of his master so distressed possibly caused a fatal seizure in the animal."

"No doubt."

"From what I saw, I believe the terrier died first," interjected Lawrence.

"I have just a few other questions but I will not keep you from your work for long."

Around noon, I stood with Ned Lawrence in the cobbled stable-yard where James Hassett had died. The yard, surrounded on three sides by brick stable buildings, was roughly oblong in shape and at its center, where the terrain dipped slightly, was a metal drainage grate. I looked up at the bell tower in the adjacent church grounds.

"Where was your ladder found, Ned?"

"Scant yards away in the orchard—perhaps some local lad took it for a prank."

"The person who took the ladder saved your life, or at least intended to prevent you from becoming a victim. The yard rebounds with echoes of how the crime was committed. This place was both the scene of the crime and part of the murder weapon."

I walked along the perimeter of the yard until I came to a drainage ditch about four and a half feet deep. In the side of the ditch was the outflow pipe which drained excess rainwater from the yard.

"I'm going to jump into this ditch to look for clues. Do not follow me. If I feel unwell I will lift up my arms and you must pull me out as quickly as you can. Do not on any account enter the ditch yourself, whatever happens."

He nodded that he understood and I landed down in the ditch without ill-effect. Looking at the pipe itself I surmised that someone had deliberately filled it with a plug of mud and dirt and then sometime later poked out the blockage. I looked into the pipe.

"What can you see?" asked Lawrence.

"Rats. Dead rats."

Watson was asleep when we returned to the suite at the County and Station Hotel. I poured tea for Ned and myself and considered the events of the day.

"Mr. Holmes, I believe that you had solved this mystery very early in our first meeting before you ever even left this room for the Hassett estate. When I read your exploits in *Strand Magazine* I had thought your reticence to be some form of literary device employed by Dr. Watson to promulgate suspense, but experiencing it firsthand is most infuriating. This is a serious matter; a man has died. What is the solution?"

"Ned, you have a first class mind; the product of a first class education. It is not, if you will forgive my immodesty, so very different from my mind. My friend Watson sees everything and deduces nothing, while you are afraid to apply your deductive powers in case you do not like what they discover. Like a locomotive whose driver is desperate to avoid pulling into the station…you are thinking with the brakes pushed down hard."

"That's simply not true. I have no idea what happened here."

"And I have ideas but no proof. The workings of my brain are not admissible in a court of law. I need physical evidence—more than just a handful of dried mud. But what proof can there be of a murder weapon that is both invisible and intangible? Go and get some rest and I will see you in the morning."

I had no intention of resting. At around midnight I placed Watson's service revolver in the pocket of my coat, slipped out of the hotel and headed for Hassett Manor myself. I effected entry through unlocked French doors on the terrace and made my way into the library. Quietly, I lit a lamp and then made an examination of the encyclopedia and medical reference books that I found on the shelves. Where my eye detected interference to the bindings of the books, without exception, I found new pages had been inserted, expertly, and that these pages contained spurious information about the parasitical infestation of humans by creatures called "blood lice." The silence in the library was broken by a muffled sound from the adjoining room—Sir Ambrose Hassett's study. Even more stealthily I went to investigate. I opened the door to the study to find Sir Ambrose collapsed at his desk. I strode swiftly towards him with the aim of feeling for a pulse. After a couple of steps I stopped. There was no breathable air in the room. Instead, a vile miasma hung before me. It was odorless, yet pernicious, and I could feel the life giving oxygen being forced from my tissues. My head swam. I turned back to the door only to hear it slam and lock. My legs buckled beneath me and I found myself lying on my back. Now I could both smell and taste dampness and something like coal dust. Over to my right I could hear hissing, as if from a large angry snake. I reached into my coat for Watson's revolver. I did not have the strength to tug it from my pocket so I shot through the lining in the general direction of the window. My first shot hit the woodwork, but the following four blasted out the window panes and a stiff breeze served to refill the room with a restorative atmosphere.

Having heard the shots, Ned Lawrence raced from his bedroom and battered down the door. I was already on my feet investigating the source of the hissing sound. I reached up into the chimney cavity and removed a black metal cylinder with a wheel valve. I turned the wheel until no more gas issued out. And then quickly looked up the chimney; it had been blocked. Then, for the first time I noticed what was stencil painted on the side of the cylinder—a single word: "BLACKDAMP." I handed the cylinder to Ned.

"The proof of a weapon both invisible and intangible. Where is Ian Hassett?" I asked.

I sent Ned Lawrence to fetch the local police and then dispatched them to look for Ian Hassett, who had disappeared from the house with the pony and trap. I sat with Ned in the library and lit my pipe. There was much explaining to be done.

"I suppose it was Ian Hassett who told you of the unusual gargoyles on the bell tower. If they had not been there he would've had to concoct a different reason to preclude the possibility of your entering the stable-yard, for certainly, it was he who stranded you up in the bell tower. We both know that Ian Hassett was a mining engineer with access to compressors. I can tell you there are many deadly gases found in coal mines – one is known to miners as 'blackdamp'; it is a mixture of nitrogen, argon and water vapor. It displaces oxygen from the air and out of the very cells of the human body. It takes no more than a few breaths to bring unconsciousness and death. It is a simple matter for a mining engineer to capture such a gas with a compressor and place it in a pressurized cylinder like the one we found. Such a cylinder or perhaps many cylinders were concealed within the stable-yard drains with their valves open. The drain outflow was blocked with mud so the blackdamp seeped upwards and filled the yard. Its highest density was low to the ground, so the little terrier succumbed straightaway. As soon as James Hassett put his head near the ground to examine the dog he was doomed.

"But why? Why would Ian kill his own brother, his own father?"

"In such cases, the motive is virtually always financial. I searched his room when you went for the police and found evidence of extreme and growing gambling debts. Some time ago, Ian Hassett had the subtle idea to cause his father to infect himself with septicemia through making him believe that creatures were burrowing under his skin and that they could be dug out with a scalpel blade. Young Hassett even went to the trouble of having fictional pages on blood lice inserted into genuine medical books to show his father. In the miscreant's dresser are wound dressings peppered with springtail eggs. Springtails have no desire to live in human skin but if it is the only environment they have ever known they might well burrow into it just as they would the forest floor. This ingenious plan was frustrated by Sir Ambrose's fastidiousness—he kept the wounds and the blades sufficiently clean to avoid blood poisoning. With his debts increasing and his father steadfastly refusing to die, more desperate measures were called for. Around this time Ian Hassett must have wondered why he should share the inheritance with a brother and began to plot his sibling's demise, too."

"I cannot conceive of the fact that any friend of mine could be a murderer. How could my judgment be so faulty?"

"Do not rebuke yourself. Once it has taken root, evil grows quickly in a man's heart and is impossible to eradicate completely."

"You must be mistaken, Mr. Holmes. If Ian were responsible for the blackdamp in the yard then why did he enter it so soon after his brother's death, when it was still potentially fatal to do so?"

"Ah, note that he rode in on his pony and trap thereby disrupting and dissipating the cloud of blackdamp. On this point we will have to question him, but I suspect that open cylinders of oxygen or air were concealed in the trap—they would've minimized the danger."

Word came to us not long before dawn that Ian Hassett's pony and trap had been found near to the entrance to the Great Rutland Cavern, one of Matlock Bath's main tourist attractions. Lawrence and I joined the police in a thorough search of the underground tunnels. I had almost concluded that Hassett had left the trap outside as a ruse when we came upon his clothes next to a flooded section of tunnel. An examination of the footprints led me to believe that Hassett had entered the tunnel wearing diving gear—one of the suits from the Maracot expedition to the deep Atlantic. It was puzzling as to how he could do this without one of the large compressor engines we had previously seen on the pontoon at Cromford Lake feeding him air. When we located the Maracot Co. divers at their lodgings they explained that Hassett had also been experimenting with something called an "escape set," a light-weight diving suit with a handheld submersible compressor about the size of a suitcase. Lawrence was determined to pursue Hassett along the flooded tunnels, so we arranged for a large compressor and a diving suit to be transported from the Hassett estate to the Great Rutland Cavern. After ten minutes tuition from one of the Maracot men Lawrence entered the water.

Lawrence edged his way along the tunnel by the light of a slow-burning, submersible magnesium torch. He knew that he only had about ten minutes of light before the torch burnt out and he would be plunged into stygian darkness. It was cold and uncomfortable in the suit and the air from the compressor smelt and tasted foul. At first he thought his eyes were playing tricks or that he saw a reflection of his own light. Then it became obvious that someone was approaching him. The light ahead was a piercing blue-white flame surrounded by a halo of incandescent bubbles. It was an oxyacetylene blowlamp wielded by Ian Hassett. Hassett was not so encumbered as Lawrence, since he wore only the lighter "escape set" and was able to swim freely in the tunnel with the miniature compressor strapped to his back. It took only an instant for the blowlamp to slice through Lawrence's rubber air-hose. He realized immediately what had happened and thrust the magnesium torch towards Hassett's face, driving him away. Lawrence found the severed end of his air-hose and knotted it as best he could; that would stop the icy water from flowing into his suit, but he would be lucky to make it back to the dry caverns before the air in his helmet ran out. He abandoned the pursuit and started to head back.

It was a frozen and forlorn Lawrence who emerged from the water. As he was helped from the suit there was much discussion as to what could be done now. The police favored starving out the murderer; I was not in favor of this. I could easily imagine the wily and dangerous Hassett surprising a fatigued guard and getting clean away. One of the cavern tour guides explained to us that the flooded tunnel led into the ancient workings of a Roman lead mine. The uncharted Roman mine tunnels were regarded as too dangerous to enter and many of them were partially collapsed. Vertical ventilation shafts had been cut by the Roman miners down from the surface to the workings, and when I heard this I became concerned that Hassett could use them to make good his escape. We were reassured by the guide that ascent of the shafts would be difficult for a team of men with specialist equipment.

So it was that the shivering Ned and I crouched on the floor of the cavern, examining the police inspector's large-scale ordnance survey map of Matlock Bath by lamplight. I traced with my finger the zigzag pattern of the ventilation holes which pock-marked the countryside. They led away in the direction of the Arkwright gravel quarry. I examined the area of the quarry with my magnifying glass. Near the entrance to the quarry the tiny words "Sulis Cave" were inscribed in italics.

"What is the origin of the word 'Sulis'?" I asked.

"Sulis Minerva was a Romano-British goddess," explained Ned. "She would've been the main religion around the time the old lead mine was being worked."

"And what if this Roman cave is another exit from the Roman mine? We have assumed that Hassett is cornered here and taking refuge. What if he is, in fact, still making his escape? Borrow a bicycle from one of the policemen and cycle as quickly as you can to the cave mouth. Here, take Watson's service revolver."

Ned Lawrence rode hell for leather along the darkening lanes on a police bicycle, his mind theorizing on how long it might take Hassett to pick his way through the miles of hazardous tunnels to Sulis Cave. He'd bragged to Ned months ago that he knew every inch of the Matlock Bath countryside—every bird's nest, every rabbit hole. Had he perhaps explored beneath the surface, too? The diving suit had not been taken to Rutland Cavern on a whim. Ned turned a corner and saw that an old gray-snouted badger was sauntering across the lane. He skidded to avoid the creature and lost control of the bicycle. A split second later he had fallen and was sliding along the rough gravel surface of the lane with the skin being avulsed from his right arm and shoulder. He picked himself up—he now looked like a bloodied scarecrow—and remounted the bicycle. His speed was more cautious now; it had to be since the cycle's lamp had broken in the accident and the velvet gloom of twilight had descended.

Finally, he arrived at the quarry. The figure walking nonchalantly away from the Sulis Cave could only be Hassett. The "escape set" diving attire was unmistakable. The air was split by the crack of gunfire as Lawrence loosed two shots from the service revolver in Hassett's direction. The killer turned and ran back to the safety of the cave mouth, with Lawrence in close pursuit. Lawrence entered the cave and took cover behind a pile of rocks. He then reached into his pocket to retrieve a spare magnesium torch. He quickly lit it with a match and threw it into the depths of the cave. Suddenly the dark cavern was illuminated as if by the noon-day sun. Rocks not far away from Lawrence's head seemed to explode. Hassett had a gun too and he was an expert shot. Lawrence returned fire. A large black object arced towards him out of the distance and landed just a few feet from where he was concealed. It was one of Hassett's pressurized cylinders. Lawrence held his breath, expecting a noxious gas to spew forth. He looked at the cylinder again. It was not marked with the word "BLACKDAMP." Instead, it bore the legend "FIREDAMP." He guessed that in the descriptive slang of miners that could mean an inflammable or perhaps explosive gas. Hassett's bullets struck close to the cylinder. He was trying to make it explode by shooting it! Lawrence made a flying leap from behind the rocks out of the cave mouth. As he did so the firedamp cylinder detonated with a roaring blast that brought down the rock ceiling and sealed Sulis Cave.

"What is firedamp?" asked Ned when he found me outside the Great Rutland Cavern.

"I'll explain later. You need a doctor and I happen to know a very good one."

The following day I suggested to the police that the submerged tunnel be dynamited, thus marooning Ian Hassett permanently underground. I was surprised by the enthusiasm with which the suggestion was met and within two hours men from the Arkwright Quarry had done the job. I wrote half a dozen identical notes to Hassett and dropped them down the ventilation shafts tied to packets of candles and matches. The note urged him to go to the vertical shaft nearest the Great Rutland Cavern at noon so that we could converse. As the sun reached its zenith I stood near the edge of the shaft and called down.

"Can you hear me, Hassett?"

"I hear," was his only answer.

"The Roman Mine is your prison, now. To all intents and purposes it is escape proof. I have arranged with a local woman for food and flasks of clean drinking water to be lowered on thin twine once every three days. Her efforts shall not be wasted since I am sure that your colossal arrogance will prevent thoughts of suicide. Goodbye. We shall not speak again."

The sole reply was a combined whimper and throaty curse that might have been, "Damn you, Holmes," or something similar.

There have been very few occasions when I wished that there were brakes which could be applied to my deductive talents or that my faculties could be turned off as if with an electrical switch—but this is one. What am I to conclude from the slowness with which Dr. Watson's service revolver was returned to me, the sight of Ned Lawrence surreptitiously borrowing a length of rope from the Hassett stables, and the two swift barks of gunfire which echoed over the cliffs from the direction of the ventilation shaft near the Great Rutland Cavern? Is it deduction or imagination that allows me to see in my mind's eye Ned Lawrence luring Hassett into the light with the promise of the rope and then shooting him dead as he tried to ascend it? In any event, it was a happier more carefree Lawrence that a largely recovered Watson and I ran into on the Matlock Bath high street as we passed a final half hour before returning to our respective homes.

"Mr. Holmes! Dr. Watson! I'm so glad I've found you before you caught your train!" he cried with boyish enthusiasm.

"Ned, what's wrong?"

"Nothing! Follow me to the Petrifying Well at once. I've cleared everything with the proprietor. I just hope that you agree."

Further to this mysterious exhortation we followed Ned to a shop by the riverside, which had been converted to be a tourist attraction called "The Petrifying Well". Inside, the calcium-laden local water dripped over a variety of items which stood on shelves in stone tubs. Any item placed on these shelves turned to stone by a process of calcification within a few weeks. I could see birds' nests, tree branches and loaves of bread all undergoing the metamorphosis. Without warning, Ned relieved me of my deerstalker and Dr. Watson of his bowler and placed them on one of the shelves.

"The British public will be paying a halfpenny to see your hats until doomsday," he announced cheerfully.

Watson and I roared with laughter, bade him farewell and then walked back towards the railway station. On the journey home I could not help but think that this country, indeed this empire, will be safe in the hands of young men such as Thomas Edward Lawrence, no matter what storm clouds might be gathering even now.

Sherlock Holmes, 30th June, 1909

Editor's note: When the villa on the Sussex Downs which once belonged to Sherlock Holmes was refurbished in 1948, the preceding manuscript was discovered in a rusted strongbox beneath the floor boards. We can surmise that Holmes never intended the narrative for publication—at least not in the lifetime of T E Lawrence (later, Lawrence of Arabia). The original manuscript is preserved in the Sherlock Holmes Museum on upper Baker Street, where it may be viewed by appointment under the supervision of the curator.

Addendum: Holmes neglects to explain in the narrative that "firedamp" is concentrated methane. Howard Hopkins, 2010

THE ADVENTURE OF THE

FALLEN STONE

(Being the First Part of the Account of
The Dynamics of a Meteor)

by
John H. Watson, M.D.
edited by
Win Scott Eckert

AS I review my notes of the cases brought to a satisfactory conclusion by my friend, Mr. Sherlock Holmes, in that dark period during which the bloom of England's youth was decimated in the mud-filled trenches of France, my attention is drawn in particular to a singular exploit involving the theft of the rare flower *lotus vitae*.

The events in question occurred at a time when Holmes should have been comfortably ensconced in his retirement and free to tend his bees. The truth of the matter is that his retirement was a bit of a fiction, as he was repeatedly called into service by His Majesty's government both in the years leading up to and during the Great War. Shortly after Holmes ran the German spy Von Bork to ground, in a case I have recorded as "His Last Bow" (a title which, I assure you, I have come to regret, due to Holmes' continued inability to stave off further calls upon his unique abilities and fully bask in his retirement), he reopened his rooms on Baker Street, and thereafter split his time between London and the South Downs for the duration of the War.

April of '17, however, found Holmes at his small farm upon the downs, a cottage some five miles from the town of Eastbourne in East Sussex. The nearest small village was Fulworth, which is in a cove on the beach. Holmes' cottage was situated somewhat inland—a necessity for maintenance of his apiary—but nonetheless had a long view of the Channel.

It was early in my wife's condition that she took herself away to stay with her cousin Sir George Curtis and his family, freeing me to pay a rare visit to my long-standing friend. I had not disclosed my wife's status to Holmes, but rather made an excuse for my arrival, indicating that Nylepthah had indeed called upon relatives of her late father, Sir Henry Curtis, but omitting any reference to the forthcoming child.

How I ever hoped to hide the news from Holmes, I cannot imagine. I should have known better.

Holmes, however, played along with this minor deception, and only when he had occasion to pay me a London visit some two years later (he had come bearing gifts, a large financial payment from the English Lord of the Apes, the result of our African adventure in 1916) did he reveal that he had known of my wife's state and the subsequent birth of my son all along. Holmes was being kind during my visit by not mentioning it, since I clearly suffered some embarrassment at the prospect of fatherhood at my rather advanced age, despite the happy circumstances.

I had been at Holmes' cottage two days when our restful reunion was broken by an unfortunate event. Breakfast and coffee had just been cleared and Holmes, after stuffing his black briar with a thick shag and filling the sitting room with the dense blue smoke, was digging into the morning *Times* and the *Eastbourne Chronicle*.

He grunted in dissatisfaction and tossed the local paper to me.

"Watson, I call your attention to the story in the right-hand column," he said, curling up in his arm-chair and steepling his long fingers in front of his hawk nose.

I scanned the newspaper and recited the particulars back to him. "A murder in an alley behind a public house in Fulworth. The crime appears to be random, perhaps a robbery. The victim is a former seaman, 'Black' Mike Croteau, who, upon his retirement from shipboard life, supported himself with occasional gardening work for several local residents. Croteau, a known carouser of somewhat fiery temper, was stabbed and bled to death."

I looked up. "It appears fairly straightforward to me, Holmes..." I began, but my friend had already jumped up, pulling his mouse-colored dressing gown about him as he darted to the next room. There, I heard him utilizing the recently-installed telephone, and after several minutes he reached the local constabulary.

"Sherlock Holmes...*Holmes*...You should have called me...A pub fight? Simple robbery-murder? Surely not...I assume you've trampled all over the evidence...Moved the body as well? Yes, of course you have... Send a motor car around and I'll come examine the body..." He hung up without saying good-bye, and re-entered the sitting room.

Shaking his lean form out of the dressing gown, he said caustically, "Watson, while our friends at Scotland Yard have made some little advancement in criminal science since we began our fruitful association, progress in towns and villages outside of London is sadly lagging."

I made some noise in agreement but couldn't help notice that his gray eyes sparkled, and he bounded across the room energetically like a hound on the scent. He took a helmet and beekeeping veil from a hook on the wall by the door and called on his way out, "I must tend to the bees. The car will be 'round in an hour, if you'd care to accompany me."

A short time later we were in an alley behind the Belching Bull. The sea air was fresh and a mild breeze drove a fog in off the Channel, providing some relief against the dank and squalid odor of day-old fish hanging over the cobblestoned passageway behind the public house.

Holmes inspected the crime scene in his usual animated fashion, mumbled in particular over some dirt and soil on the pavement at the mouth of the alley, and inquired of the constable escorting us as to the orientation of the corpse when it was discovered, learning that the feet were nearer the mouth of the passage, with the head closer to the back exit of the pub.

As usual, I saw without observing.

From there, we were transported to the morgue—a small holding room in the back of the local police-station—where Holmes inspected the body of Black Mike Croteau.

"Is there anything in particular that you note regarding the knife wounds, Doctor?"

As on so many other occasions, I attempted to apply Holmes' methods, and bent over to examine the corpse. "The cuts seem to be centered on the left side of the body. Despite being on the far side of middle-age, the victim is large and muscular, and I would not care to meet him in a dark alley at night. Therefore, it is probable he was attacked from behind, and stricken before he could defend himself. Croteau was known to have a hot temper; thus the attack was no doubt in response to some insult or confrontation which occurred in the tavern. That is the extent of my own observations, I'm afraid," I concluded.

"Capital, Watson, capital!" Holmes exclaimed. To the police escort, he instructed, "Contact me immediately if there are any further developments," and from there we returned to Holmes' cottage. He ignored, as was his habit, my inquiry as to what led him to conclude there was more to the murder than a simple robbery or pub fight.

The police motor car dispatched us to the gate, and making our way up the drive and around a bend, bringing Holmes' abode into plain view, I was surprised to see a young man in his late twenties reclining on a cast-iron bench situated near the front of the cottage, evidently waiting upon us. He was lean and sharp-featured, looking much like Holmes himself did at that age.

"Hullo, Dickson!" greeted Holmes. "This is no great surprise, but nonetheless your appearance here is most welcome." Turning to me, he continued, "Watson, meet young Harry Dickson, whom some have labeled 'the American Sherlock Holmes—'"

"Mr. Holmes, I assure you—!"

"Now, now, Dickson, I know it is not an appellation to which you subscribe or encourage. Nevertheless you have made some small name for yourself in the field of consulting detectives. Watson, Dickson here has apprenticed with both Barker—my Surrey rival, you'll recall—and Blake, another consulting detective who has also set up rooms on Baker Street." Turning back to Dickson, Holmes' countenance became more serious. "I presume you're here about the flower."

"Yes, Mr. Holmes. M. sent me."

Without another word, Holmes entered the cottage and began packing a small leather valise as I stood, frankly, somewhat astonished by the fast-moving events.

"Well, are you coming?" Holmes asked impatiently. "Come, time is short; we just have ten minutes to catch the last train."

"You knew all along," said Sherlock Holmes.

The man sitting across the desk from him—gray-haired, and as rotund as Holmes was lean—nodded in agreement, his gray eyes twinkling. "Of course."

We were deep in the secret chambers beneath the stucco-fronted façade of the Diogenes Club in St. James's, where the true, if tangled, business of the British government was directed and organized. I had been here—in the underground headquarters, that is—twice, since the start of the Great War. A large plate window which served as one wall of Mycroft's office overlooked a huge gallery filled with table maps of various parts of Western Europe, banks of telephones, and rows of operators stationed at wireless equipment.

This was, to my knowledge, Holmes' first meeting with his brother Mycroft—the man who occasionally *was* the British government—since the prior year when Holmes and I had taken an assignment for King and Country, at Mycroft's behest, to hunt down Von Bork in Cairo.

On the London train, it had been explained that Dickson had served as one of Mycroft's best Secret Service agents during the War. Now he and I sat to one side, observing the tense reunion and trying to follow their conversation.

"You knew all along," Holmes continued, "that while tracking down Von Bork we would very likely be blown far south of Cairo in the forthcoming 'storm of the century.'"

"I admit it fully, Sherlock," Mycroft said. "You could have studied the meteorological forecasts as well as anyone. What did it matter, since Von Bork would also very likely be caught in the same storm?"

"You calculated that the storm would deposit us all in an area of Africa where we would very likely meet the fabled 'ape lord.' Furthermore, it is clear that you knew all along that this ape lord, although legitimately entitled to his dukedom, was in fact impersonating his dead cousin, William Clayton, the 7th Duke of Grey—"

"How so?" Mycroft interrupted.

"When you sent us on our ill-fated mission, you described our flier, Leftenant John Drummond, as the adopted son of the present ape lord. You took pains to remind me that I knew the Leftenant's great-uncle, the late 6th Duke. If you did not know of the ape man's impersonation, you should have referred to Leftenant Drummond as the grandson of the late 6th Duke."

Mycroft laughed heartily and slapped the desk in front of him. "I must say, Sherlock, that age has not dimmed your powers of observation in the least."

"Nor age your powers of guile," Holmes noted. "How did you come to know of the ape lord's impersonation?"

"William Clayton was not shipwrecked in Africa by happenstance," Mycroft replied. "He was an agent on a mission for the government, reporting directly to me. He must have encountered some misfortune and been killed; I never did get those details. When the man purporting to be William Clayton—who was really William's cousin, the ape lord, impersonating William—returned to England in 1910 and did not report in, I investigated and came to the conclusion that 'William' was in fact Clayton's second cousin. This man had survived a prior African shipwreck as an infant and was impersonating William to avoid the inevitable publicity which would be attendant on the discovery of a peer of the realm who had been suckled and raised by apes."

"The mission you sent Dr. Watson and me on last year served a dual purpose," Holmes said. "Certainly the stated purpose of tracking down the spy Von Bork and his bacillus was of import. But it is also clear you wanted us to run into the ape lord in Africa, and to discover his impersonation for ourselves. Why?"

"Why do you think," Mycroft challenged.

"Since our return from Africa, I've studied the fictional accounts published about the ape man, and done a bit of investigating about his exploits. He has a history of unlikely coincidences, of stumbling upon places and people who otherwise remain undiscovered and inaccessible."

"Yes," Mycroft prodded. "Our scientists call these phenomena 'human magnetic moments.'"

"The *lotus vitae*," Holmes said quietly. His gray eyes shone as they always did when that great brain crafted a solution out of varied and seemingly disconnected puzzle pieces.

"Your colleague, Doctor Shan Ming Fu, informed you of its existence almost ten years ago, and you've kept your eyes open for a sample of the flower ever since."

"Not my colleague," Holmes said. "An honorable adversary. In all events, you wished me to find it; you understood through some intelligence that it might be located in the depths of the Dark Continent, and you decided that if I were in the ape man's circle of 'human magnetic' influence, its discovery would be more likely. And so I did discover it, in the hidden valley of Zu-Vendis, although I asked Watson to eliminate that fact from his notes of the incident."

"And now the *lotus vitae* has been stolen from your garden," Mycroft replied. "Had you made any progress in getting your bees to collect its nectar?"

"Not as yet; this would have been the first season."

"A pity. It must be recovered. If your bees can be induced to sample its nectar, a particular honey may result."

"Indeed."

"The key ingredient in a singular brew…"

"Brew, what sort of brew?" I interjected. I had done my best to follow along in silence, but the brothers' cryptic tête-à-tête had finally tried my patience.

"Come now, old fellow," Holmes rejoined, "you know I've always had a taste for experimentation with the effects of certain substances upon human physiology."

"Yes, your own."

"My blushes, Watson, a hit, a distinct hit! But I was referring to my chemical researches, and, as I noted to you so many years ago, I have long been interested in solving the problems furnished by nature as opposed to those superficial ones caused by our artificial state of society."

"But this is alchemy, pure alchemy, Sherlock," Mycroft taunted. "You've never wasted time on anything that was not rational and scientific."

"Nonsense. There is a historical and scientific basis for such a formula—as you well know, or else you'd not have sent me off to Africa chasing after it in the first place."

"Touché," Mycroft said. "Now, to the business at hand. Do you know who took the flower?"

"Naturally."

"But how, Holmes?" I cried.

Dickson, sitting at my side, smiled in anticipation of the deductive display by his mentor.

"Croteau's feet were pointed toward the exit of the alleyway, with his head toward the back door of the pub, indicating that he was facing the passageway's exit when he was attacked. He fell backward. The murderer came into the alley and faced Croteau as the latter was departing. I'm afraid that dispenses with your theory that the victim was surprised from behind, Watson. However, as you noted, Croteau was a large man, if past his prime, and the only way to take him head-on would be if he were not expecting an assault and was unprepared to mount a defense. Therefore, Croteau knew his killer, and did not anticipate violence.

"As you noted, Doctor, the knife gashes were focused on the left side of Croteau's body. Since the killer faced him, this, in most circumstances, would indicate the murderer was right-handed. Not much help there. However, you failed to note the curious aspect that the wounds did not have a generally universal depth; some were quite deep, while others were rather shallow. This points to a lack of depth perception. The killer was one-eyed.

"Finally, you failed to recognize the significance of the bits of soil and dirt on the ground near where Croteau's feet rested—no, no, Doctor, don't blame yourself for missing it. The impact of Croteau's body hitting the ground shook the dirt from his boot soles. I knew the dirt would be there and was looking for it. The soil matches perfectly that from my own flower beds.

"Croteau took the flower," Holmes concluded, "met the killer in the alley behind the Belching Bull, and received payment in the currency of death."

"And the killer?" Mycroft asked.

"You know as well as I that it's Von Bork," Holmes replied with some asperity, and I recalled that the last time we had clashed with the German master spy, during our African adventure last year, Von Bork had had a glass eye in which he'd concealed the plans for a deadly bacillus.

"If you wouldn't continually turn him back over to his German masters," Holmes continued, "he'd have been hanged for espionage long ago and we'd be done with him."

"In point of fact," Mycroft said, "you're the one who turned him loose on the eve of the War, and sent him back to Germany."

"On your orders."

"There were reasons."

"Two years undercover as Altamont ruined," Holmes said, "on your orders to admit directly to Von Bork that much of the intelligence I'd gathered for him was planted, false, or exaggerated, and then to let him go free. This, followed by the so-called 'Hellbirds' incident, in which he escaped again, and your subsequent instructions to Watson to concoct and publish a fanciful and dramatic tale about him falling to his death from the Eiffel Tower.

"Finally, the bacillus escapade last year, and once again he's packed off to Germany rather than facing the penalty for his crimes. Germ warfare, Mycroft. The death toll could have been staggering. I cannot imagine any justification for such a move."

"Then don't imagine," Mycroft said. "Do what you do best. Reason it out. There is just one justification."

Holmes' gray eyes swirled. "There is someone behind Von Bork. Someone much bigger than he, whom you seek."

Mycroft nodded. "This could finally be it, Sherlock, a line on the real brain behind Von Bork's schemes, and many other plots only hinted at which haven't involved Von Bork."

"You knew Von Bork had re-entered England."

"From the moment he debarked at Southampton."

"Who is trailing him?"

"Sexton Blake."

"There are few better," Holmes admitted. "Why did Blake allow him to kill my gardener?"

"That was unexpected," Mycroft said. "Blake presumed Von Bork would render the man unconscious and take the flower."

"A fatal error. It could be anticipated that Von Bork would want to leave the man permanently incapable of identifying him."

Dickson spoke up for the first time. "It's not like Mr. Blake, I'll admit, Mr. Holmes, but nobody's perfect."

"Indeed, Dickson, indeed," Holmes said. "Very well, then, Blake is hot on Von Bork's trail, in hopes it will lead to the mastermind. Do we have a name?"

At a nod from Mycroft, Dickson continued. "He's been known by many names over the years, as far as we can tell: Wolf Larsen, Karl Woldheim, Carl Waldhaus. He's currently believed to be using the name Baron Ulf Von Waldman."

Mycroft took up the recitation. "Von Waldman is a scientist and inventor. Affects a monocle and is rarely seen without a large cigar in hand. Speaks perfect English, and probably several other languages as well. Charismatic and personally magnetic. Attractive to women—and vice versa; he is a great admirer of female beauty. Perhaps his Achilles' heel. A powerful man physically, mutton-chop whiskers, hazel eyes, hooked nose.

"He's high up in the German Command, and is believed to be the Commandant of a supposedly inescapable prison camp for incorrigible and inveterate prisoners of war, those who have already escaped from lesser camps and been recaptured. He's also reputed to conduct experiments on some of those prisoners—while they're still alive."

"And…" Dickson added, then paused.

"Well, Dickson, out with it!" Holmes said.

"Well, Mr. Holmes, there are rumors Baron Von Waldman is the son of someone with whom we're all familiar. Von Waldman supposedly denies the connection, but there are also indications he's the one who started the talk in the first place."

"This Baron seems like a wily character, and well-versed at keeping people off balance. Who is the purported father?"

"Professor James Moriarty," Dickson replied.

Holmes, Dickson, and I, accompanied by the enigmatically beautiful Isis Vanderhoek, descended from the horse-drawn landau and approached the finely-carved oak doors of Blakeney House, a large country manor in the Yorkshire Wolds.

We had left London the night before by late evening service from St. Pancras to Leeds, and thence had proceeded to the coastal town of Scarborough. A hired carriage brought us to our destination in the East Riding of Yorkshire, about ten or twelve miles south.

Our journey had been prompted by a brief but to-the-point wire from Blake to Mycroft:

> M—
> *Quarry headed for East Yorkshire. Will stay on trail and pinpoint more precise location.*
> —*Blake*

Mycroft had handed over the cable for Dickson to read and picked up a black telephone on the corner of his desk. "Send in Mrs. Vanderhoek."

He cradled the receiver and turned back to Dickson. "You and Isis will prepare to journey north by the first available train. Blake will undoubtedly wire more specifics, and our people here will forward the information along your route."

"Very good, sir, we'll check for messages at all stops."

"What about us?" Holmes asked.

"Sherlock, I couldn't possibly impose. Not after the lark I sent you and the good doctor upon last year—"

"Nonsense, Mycroft," my friend interrupted. "We insist on seeing it through. We may be old, but we're not done for yet."

I nodded in agreement.

Both Mycroft and Dickson gave slight smiles, as if this conclusion had been preordained, and Holmes' brother said, "Very well, if you both are adamant. Now then, we must craft our plan."

Mycroft looked up at us, his gray eyes sharp and bright; his soft and corpulent exterior did not belie the hard inner core of the man tasked with manipulating events and directing players on an international scale for the benefit of an Empire at war. "Von Waldman, as I recounted earlier, is a great admirer of women. This is our opening, our point of attack."

"M.," came a thrilling voice, French accented, from the shadowy corner of Mycroft's sanctum, "you flatter me."

The owner of the voice stepped forward, and my breath caught, for the vision of loveliness before me was as dark and enigmatic as that of my golden-tressed wife was open and bright. I daresay that despite his much-repeated admonition that the fair sex was my department, even Holmes was brought up short, if only momentarily, at the sight of this raven-haired beauty. For Dickson's part, his expression did nothing to conceal the fact that he was mesmerized.

"Mrs. Vanderhoek, here you are," Mycroft said. Turning back to us, he made introductions. "Isis has been with the Service for several months now," he concluded.

"Isis Vanderhoek," Holmes said. "Surely, though, that was a French accent?"

She gave Holmes a dazzling smile. "Yes, Mr. Holmes. My husband was Dutch. My late husband," she amended.

"My condolences," Holmes said. "I find you familiar," he continued, his gray eyes glittering.

"You may know of my father, Mr. Klaw. He used to run a curio shop, and had on occasion helped the police solve unusual and bizarre crimes."

"Ah, yes, the 'dreaming detective,'" Holmes replied contemptuously. He turned to Mycroft "Am I to understand that the branch of the Service now run through the Diogenes Club deigns to work with frauds and charlatans?"

Isis Vanderhoek's black eyes flashed, and Dickson opened his mouth to object, thinking better of it when Mycroft replied: "I fail to see how her father's methods pertain in any way to Mrs. Vanderhoek's skills as an agent in my department, Sherlock. In fact, the Club has more recently begun to focus on matters outré and unexplained, which still strike at the heart of the Empire. I believe our adversary, Baron Von Waldman, and the formula for the elixir he seeks, fall into these categories, do they not?"

Holmes paused at this, then smiled grimly. "Indeed they do. I take your point." Turning to Isis Vanderhoek, he bowed slightly and said, "Madame, you have my apologies. I look forward to any assistance which your talents can bring to bear on the matter at hand."

With Mrs. Vanderhoek—and her admirer Dickson—thus pacified, we concluded our planning, took supper at the Midland Grand Hotel, which fronted St. Pancras station, and thereafter departed, travelling in separate coaches to throw off potential observers.

The next morning found us approaching our final destination, which had been communicated to Dickson in Leeds via a coded cable from Blake:

> Have tracked Von Bork to the general vicinity. Meet at Blakeney House.
>
> —Blake

Our arrival was expected and the butler, one Deeds, had us quickly installed in lavishly appointed rooms. We gathered immediately before a blazing fire in the sitting room for a quick repast of cold beef, cheese, and bread, and Deeds delivered to Dickson another coded missive from Blake:

> Have wired Peter Blakeney in Richmond (we have common relatives back to mid-17th cent.) and he has placed Blakeney House and servants at our disposal (the country house is unoccupied, with Blakeney, Jr. off at war) as temporary base of operations. Am investigating an additional lead. Suggest you rest in advance of coming events.
>
> —Blake

We were preparing to take Blake's advice, for our journey had been a long one, when a loud banging drew us to the front door. Waving the butler away, Dickson drew his pistol. Before he reached the door, however, it flew open and banged against the interior wall, revealing the beet-red face of Holmes' long-standing adversary.

"Good Lord, Holmes," I cried, "it's Von Bork!"

The German master spy ploughed forward, spittle flying in rage from his open mouth, and Dickson made ready to fire. "Not another step!"

"Hold your fire, Dickson," came a voice behind Von Bork, and then the lean figure of Sexton Blake stepped from behind the villain. Blake also covered Von Bork with his revolver, and Dickson lowered his pistol in relief.

Von Bork turned an even deeper shade of red upon seeing Holmes and me, and began spewing obscenities.

Sherlock Holmes stepped forward and silenced him, laying him out with a quick jab to the mouth. He had been quite the pugilist in his college days and had not lost his touch.

Holmes smiled. "Satisfactory."

We quickly trussed up the unconscious Von Bork and locked him in the wine cellar. Holmes lifted the spy's eye patch, and inspected the empty orifice underneath. "No replacement glass eye," he murmured, letting the patch snap back down. He looked at me and said, "Just wanted to ensure he had nothing secreted there, as he did in our last encounter."

I nodded and, securing the cellar door, we all trudged up the narrow stairs to the main floor, when I noticed my friend trailed behind. "Holmes, is all well?" I called.

"Coming, Watson!" Holmes rounded a bend in the stair and caught up with me, a gleam in his eye.

We joined our comrades in the sitting room. Blake called for brandy, which Deeds promptly served. The butler stoked the waning fire back to life and left us.

Holmes settled deep in the cushions of an armchair and lit his briarwood pipe. Dickson sat on the settee near the fire with Mrs. Vanderhoek, and took a cigar I offered from my case. Blake declined my offer of a cigar, with a strange expression almost akin to regret, and also lit his pipe, clenching it between his strong jaws.

It was my first chance to observe the detective who had also set up a consulting practice on Baker Street, and I was favorably impressed. Long and slender, like Holmes, Blake was in his mid-forties, his temples shot with iron-gray.

"Too bad about Croteau, Blake," Holmes said.

"Yes, sorry about that, Holmes," Blake replied. "I bungled that one, I admit."

"Well, there's nothing for it now. Happens to the best of us, at any rate. You'll recall the tale of Openshaw? We discussed it several years back."

Blake looked non-committal and I interjected, "Ah, yes, Holmes, the case of the five—"

"In any event," Holmes went on smoothly, "the key questions now are why Von Bork is here, is Von Waldman with him, and what possible connection this place might have to the stolen *lotus vitae*. Blake, any ideas?"

"None, I'm afraid. I questioned Von Bork when I captured him, but he's a professional. We'll get nothing from him."

"Where did you pick him up?" Dickson asked.

"I traced him to a public house in Thwing "

"Thwing?" asked Mrs. Vanderhoek.

"A nearby village," Blake replied. "He came with little resistance once he saw he was cornered. There was no sign of the stolen flower, nor of Von Waldman—if indeed Von Waldman is even involved."

"Then we've hit a dead end," Dickson said.

"We could take Von Bork back to London for a proper interrogation," Blake proposed. "I imagine the Club can bring some persuasive methods to bear."

"What is it in particular about this area," Isis Vanderhoek pondered, "which is of interest to Von Bork and Von Waldman?"

"Very good, Mrs. Vanderhoek," Holmes said. "Dickson, what of it?"

Harry Dickson reached for his valise and retrieved several pamphlets which he had taken from the British Intelligence library archives before departing the Diogenes Club. "I studied these on the train, Mr. Holmes. There's not much to it; it's a quiet area. Let's see, East Riding of Yorkshire… We're in the Northern Wolds. Several towns nearby. Scarborough, which we came through. Bridlington, Driffield, Wold Newton, Rudston, and Thwing, which Mr. Blake mentioned. The area was ruled by the Parisii until the Romans invaded around 71 A.D. Several Neolithic henges in the Great Wold Valley. Rudston boasts the tallest standing stone in England, the Rudston Monolith. Many Bronze Age round barrow burial sites throughout the Wolds. Wold Newton, chiefly famous for a meteorite which struck in 1795. That's pretty much it, as far as distinctive features go."

"Not much of use there, Dickson," Blake said.

"I'm intrigued by this meteorite, Dickson," Holmes said. He leaned back and closed his eyes. "Pray, tell me more."

"Holmes, I really think we should consider getting Von Bork back to London," Blake said.

"In due time, Blake, in due time. Dickson, if you please."

Blake sucked on his pipe vigorously and leaned back, looking slightly impatient while Dickson rummaged through his papers and brought forth the pamphlet in question.

"Very well, Mr. Holmes, here we have it. The 'Wold Cottage' meteorite. On December 13, 1795, at approximately three o'clock p.m., the meteorite fell near the hamlet of Wold Newton, making, upon impact, a crater approximately three feet wide and one or two feet deep. It fell near the country house, the Wold Cottage, belonging to a gentleman farmer and magistrate, Major Edward Topham. Three people are recorded as being within several hundred feet when the impact came, during a raging thunderstorm, but no one was injured. Several years later Topham erected a monument on the exact spot where the meteorite fell, and inscribed it thusly:

Here
On this Spot, Decr 13th, 1795
fell from the Atmosphere
AN EXTRAORDINARY STONE
In Breadth 28 inches
In Length 30 inches
and
Whose Weight was 56 Pounds
THIS COLUMN
In Memory of it
was erected by
EDWARD TOPHAM
1799

"The Wold Cottage meteorite is generally credited as providing the first scientific proof that extraterrestrial matter exists. The stone itself is now held at the Natural History Museum in London, but not before various shards were cut off, which are likely in the hands of collectors around the world."

Dickson concluded his recitation and looked at Holmes, who didn't stir. Indeed, we might have thought Holmes had fallen asleep, but for the rapid inhalation and exhalation of dense pipe smoke, but I knew better from long experience. That great brain was processing facts, establishing connections, and making deductions.

This went on for thirty minutes or more, and as we all sat quietly, allowing Holmes to cogitate, I observed the others.

Isis Vanderhoek appeared to nap, her fluttering eyelids indicating a dream-state, and both Dickson and Blake watched her intently. Dickson was American by birth and perhaps such a liberty was excusable in his case, but Blake was British through and through, and I felt somewhat embarrassed at this performance.

I got up and paced a bit, eventually stopping at the French windows and staring intently at some point of interest in the garden outside.

Finally, Holmes' eyes snapped open and I saw that a great energy lay behind them. "We must visit this Wold Cottage and the monument where the meteorite hit," he said.

Mrs. Vanderhoek awoke with a start while Blake spoke up. "Really, Holmes, I cannot see the connection."

"Mrs. Vanderhoek asked what in this area might be of interest to Von Bork and Von Waldman. To put a finer point on her question, why did they bring the *lotus vitae* here? What did they plan to do with it? This meteorite fall is the only item of significance I can see right now, that may lead to an answer."

"They could just as easily have been heading for a port on the coast, to make good their escape back to Germany," Blake said.

"Presumably they could have done that without travelling from London across half of England," Holmes said. "Why here?"

"Holmes, I'm sorry," said Blake, "but I can see no logical reason for this line of investigation. I still say we take Von Bork to London and question him properly."

Holmes chuckled and said genially, "Humor me, if you will, Blake. A quick look around the Cottage and then we'll be off for London as you suggest."

"It can't hurt, Mr. Blake," Dickson said. "We may as well take a gander as long as we're here."

"I also feel that our path lies as Mr. Holmes indicates, Mr. Blake," Mrs. Vanderhoek added. She smiled winningly at him.

Sensing defeat, Blake gave a faint smile and acquiesced. "Very well, then, but let's make it fast."

"Capital!" Holmes exclaimed. He jumped up and was off like a shot, calling back over his shoulder: "I'll check that Von Bork is still secure, if you'll ring for Deeds, Blake, and have a carriage brought 'round."

The Wold Cottage was a Georgian country retreat, down a groomed driveway just off the Rainsburgh Lane which ran between the villages of Thwing and Wold Newton. The place was modest but pleasant, two stories with tall narrow windows dividing ivy-covered red brick. An ice house and cellars were situated to the right side of the house. Further to the side were the carriage house and stables, although these appeared empty at the moment.

Sherlock Holmes circumnavigated the house and outbuildings like a bloodhound, a scene to which I was long accustomed. Mrs. Vanderhoek stuck close to Blake, to his obvious pleasure and the dismay of young Dickson, who took solace in trailing along after Holmes. However, it was clear that the American detective was at as much of a disadvantage as I, not knowing what significance Holmes might have attached to the Cottage.

"The place looked untenanted, Holmes," Blake called, after about thirty minutes. "Think I'll have a look inside." He held out his arm and grinned at Mrs. Vanderhoek, who seemed all too ready to accompany Blake as he investigated the interior of the Cottage.

Holmes was back in a flash, and shook his head. "No, no, that won't do. We'll remain together. Come! Let's take a look at the monument."

He and Dickson and I set off, making our way across the back lawn and through some hedges, finding ourselves in the middle of a pasture populated by cattle. We could see Topham's stone pillar in the distance, perhaps a ten minute walk. I looked back a moment later, and to my consternation saw Blake and Isis Vanderhoek in a warm embrace. They saw me and waved, indicating they would follow shortly. I blushed and hurried poor Dickson along before he could see.

When Blake and Mrs. Vanderhoek arrived a few minutes later at the monument, a four-sided brick and stone column situated just off a narrow path in the middle of pastureland, Holmes had already concluded his brief investigation of the site. Dickson looked up at their arrival and the raven-haired beauty smiled and cocked her eyebrow at him, but he merely nodded stiffly and stood with Holmes.

"You're a bit behind, Blake," Holmes remarked, "although I suppose you can't be blamed, since you saw no value in our excursion. For my part, I commend to your attention the digging which has occurred around the pillar. Quite recent, if I'm not mistaken, as the edges of these holes are sharp. It rained yesterday, I understand, so the digging occurred after that."

"Holmes, I'll say it again," Blake rejoined, "I cannot imagine what you're getting at, why you dragged us out into the middle of a farm field, and what this could possibly have to do with your stolen flower. As for the flower itself, I am aware it may have unique biological-chemical properties, but what value this is to the Germans also escapes me. I'm afraid that, now that we've humored you, I must insist we return to London with our German captive and allow the proper authorities to interrogate him and get at the bottom of this." Mrs. Vanderhoek, by this point, stood hand in hand with Blake and nodded her agreement at his words, which concluded with, "We are at war, you know, and time is a-wasting."

"Oh, yes," Holmes murmured, "yes, indeed, we are at war. Very well, then, Blake, off we go. It shall be as you say."

With that, we marched at a fast pace back toward the Wold Cottage, and I tried to ignore the tension in the air which emanated from the disagreement amongst the two master detectives, and which also resulted from the indiscreet romance which caused our young friend Dickson such obvious pain.

As we walked past the Cottage, Holmes turned suddenly.

"I think we'll follow your earlier suggestion and have a look inside, Blake, after all. You have no objections, I trust?"

"Now see here, Holmes—"

Holmes produced his revolver and aimed it squarely at Blake. "Not another move, if you please," he said coolly.

"What is this!" Blake exclaimed, reaching inside his own jacket, but his arm was encumbered by the beautiful Isis, who took it by the wrist and wrenched it expertly behind his back.

Holmes handed his revolver to me. "Place the barrel to his temple, Watson, and on your life do not hesitate to pull the trigger if he so much as twitches!"

He also instructed Dickson to cover Blake with his own pistol, and to his credit that worthy did not hesitate.

Holmes reached inside Blake's jacket and retrieved his pistol, pocketing it. Before he could step away, though, Blake somehow tangled his feet in Isis Vanderhoek's and sent her tumbling to the ground. He sprang toward Holmes, an unearthly growl coming from his mouth, and I could not get a clear shot.

Holmes danced backward and proved his prowess from his boxing days, getting in two clean jabs and briefly stunning Blake.

Meanwhile Dickson, also lacking a clear shot, handed his pistol to me and dove into the fray. He ducked and whirled, putting Blake off balance before the latter could fully recover from Holmes' blows. Dickson pressed his opponent to the ground in an inescapable hold that demonstrated the value of Holmes' *Baritsu* training.

Isis Vanderhoek, having retrieved a sturdy rope from the yard during the scuffle, bound Blake securely while Dickson held him down. Dickson then helped her to her feet and delivered a courtly bow; she dusted herself off and grinned at him. "*Merci beaucoup.*"

Blake, face down on the ground, managed to turn his head and vent his rage. "Holmes! All of you! I demand to know the meaning of this!"

"The meaning, my dear Herr Von Waldman, should be quite clear," Sherlock Holmes said, and I marveled at this revelation. "Your ruse has failed. I suspected you from the moment you and Von Bork arrived at Blakeney House. Your disguise was impeccable—you are a true master—but you could not completely cover the reddish indentations around one eye. As far as I know, Sexton Blake's eyesight is perfect and he never wore a monocle. I also observed your displeasure at Blakeney House while Watson and Dickson shared cigars, but you could not partake, as Blake is a confirmed pipe smoker. I pretended to believe that Von Bork was your prisoner, and kept a close watch on him the whole time."

Holmes reached down and vigorously scrubbed at the disguising makeup, revealing the sharp features and hooked nose of Ulf Von Waldman. We had only seen photographs at the Diogenes Club, but it was undoubtedly the Baron.

Holmes continued. "You'll note that I beat you to the punch in volunteering to check on Von Bork immediately before our departure from Blakeney House, and you're no doubt disappointed to learn that in addition to confirming the strength of his bonds, I rendered him *hors de combat* with the careful application of a cloth soaked in chloroform. You'll have no relief from that direction, I'm afraid. The real Blake is imprisoned here in the cellars—"

"This way, Mr. Holmes," Isis Vanderhoek interjected. "I have dreamed it."

"No doubt," Holmes said dryly. "Whereas I deduced it from the set of footprints leading to the cellar door—much deeper, you'll note, due to Von Waldman carrying his burden, the unconscious Blake—and the lighter prints leading away. The prints are quite recent because, as I said, it rained yesterday. They are fresh and were made after the rain. Von Waldman should have done better at concealing his tracks, but he never expected us to come here in the first place."

Von Waldman gave a throaty growl at this comment, but we ignored him.

As we headed for the cellar doors, which were at the base of the right side of the Cottage and were accessible from the house's exterior, Mrs. Vanderhoek continued. "As we search for Mr. Blake, keep your eyes open for a bag or a box that doesn't fit, anything that could contain small stones or pieces of rock which would measure perhaps three to four inches in diameter."

Holmes turned to her, astonishment on his lean face. "How could you know that?"

"I told you Mr. Holmes. I dreamed it. When we rested at Blakeney House before proceeding here. I, too, knew that our false Blake was really Von Waldman. How do you think I was so well-prepared to interfere with him when you made your move? M. did indicate the Baron's Achilles' heel was a particular susceptibility to feminine charms."

"I cannot conceive of this so-called 'dream detecting,' but I do congratulate you on your deductive skills, which appear to rival my own," Holmes replied.

I could see that this remark put Dickson in a bit of an awkward position; his affection for Mrs. Vanderhoek demanded he come to her defense, but the high esteem in which he held his mentor prevented him from giving full voice to the remarks he wished to make.

"Tut, young Dickson," Holmes said before Dickson could speak, "I understand your position. You have always been much more an apologist for the supernatural and unexplained than I. I certainly do not believe in Mrs. Vanderhoek's 'powers,' but out of respect for the lady and for you, I'll say nothing more." Dickson appeared greatly relieved at this and Holmes continued. "Now, shall we proceed? I imagine Blake is not taking kindly to his extended confinement."

We entered the cellars, and quickly located the bound and gagged

Sexton Blake, along with a small metal box containing some grayish stones, as predicted by both Holmes and Isis Vanderhoek.

In the dark cellars, released from his bonds, Sexton Blake stretched his limbs and attempted to get the blood flowing. "You're a sight for sore eyes, that's for sure, Mr. Holmes—and all of you." He grinned. "Now, does anyone have a pipe and strong shag?"

With Blake thus accommodated, Holmes explained to him—and me, for I was apparently the only one of our little band still in complete darkness—how we had come to this point:

"You, Blake, left Blakeney House to follow up on a lead. No doubt this was a plant by Von Waldman and Von Bork."

"Indeed, Holmes. I had lost firm track of them after Scarborough, but apparently they had made me. A telegram arrived at Blakeney House indicating my quarry had been sighted. It smelled of a trap, of course, but I had no other leads and was obliged to investigate. I was coshed almost immediately after leaving the grounds of Blakeney House, and woke up here."

"Very good," said Holmes, "that fills in some blanks. To continue: the meteorite strike site was always Von Waldman's destination. They abducted Blake, came to the Cottage and incarcerated him, and thence made their way to the monument, where they hoped to find remnants of the meteorite itself. After quite a bit of digging, they did, apparently." Holmes gestured to the stones in the metal box. "They then implemented the plan to throw the rest of us off by handing over the 'imprisoned' Von Bork and proposing a return to London.

"Von Waldman wanted to get us away from Wold Newton as quickly as possible so that we would not stumble upon the truth. He came up with the plan to pass off Von Bork as his prisoner, and push for taking this valuable German spy back to London for interrogation as soon as possible. Von Waldman could always return at his leisure to the Cottage and retrieve the meteorite stones.

"But might Von Bork actually talk if it became clear that Von Waldman had abandoned him?" Dickson asked.

"Perhaps," said Holmes, "although it is likely Von Bork did not know the real value of the meteorite rocks, and thus could not disclose it under questioning. Still, he knew of Von Waldman's imposture of Blake, and it is possible that Von Waldman might even have planned an accidental demise for Von Bork before the latter could reveal anything."

"Holmes," I asked, "you mentioned the value of the meteorite stones. I cannot fathom what it is they want with these rocks?"

"While it is an error to unduly speculate in absence of all the facts," he replied, "I believe that we have enough before us to reasonably reconstruct their intent. The Germans must believe that exposing the stolen *locus vitae* plant to these remnants of the meteorite may have some beneficial effect."

"What sort of effect?" I cried incredulously.

"I suspect that Von Waldman wants to expose the plant, or perhaps seeds from the plant, to meteorite shards; the core meteorite itself might be preferable, but it is too heavily guarded at the Natural History Museum. Presumably their hypothesis is that the meteorite rocks may have some radiation inherent in them which could somehow stimulate and enhance the properties which the *lotus vitae* plant is rumored to have."

"You are speaking of life prolongation, Mr. Holmes, and yet you chastise me and Mrs. Vanderhock as believers in the outré and unexplained." Harry Dickson's gentle smile softened the cut of his words considerably.

"Yes, well," Holmes smiled in return, "it is only a theory, after all, and I am speaking of what the Germans believe, not what I necessarily believe."

"And yet you cultivate the *lotus vitae* plant, Mr. Holmes," said Isis Vanderhoek. She smiled brightly at him.

Holmes laughed genially. "Indeed, Mrs. Vanderhoek, indeed. You have found me out! But I'm afraid we spend far too much time here debating these matters, and not enough planning to transport our German spy friends to London and the gentle ministrations of Mycroft's interrogation division."

Alas, Holmes was correct, for when we emerged from the Wold Cottage cellars Von Waldman was gone, his ropes piled in a little heap, although we had only been absent for five minutes or less.

"Curse me for a fool, Watson," cried Holmes. "I should have known he was more wily than even I might anticipate."

"The plant!" I said. "Von Waldman has gotten away with the plant, Holmes."

"Very likely true, Doctor, as we have not seen any sign of it. Most likely he has concealed it somewhere along his escape route for easy recovery." Holmes looked as grim as I had ever seen him. "However," he continued, "I have seeds, and shall grow another plant. And now we have the meteorite stones…Perhaps I will entreat Mycroft to use his connections and grant us access to the whole meteorite at the Museum, and see if there is anything to the Germans' theories."

"And we finally have Von Bork," I added.

"Yes, Watson. His usefulness as Mycroft's bait to lure in the real German Intelligence mastermind is now at an end. I don't envy him his fate, as no doubt His Majesty's Secret Service will work him over quite thoroughly before he faces the firing squad, but there can be no argument that it is a fate well deserved."

"How do you think Von Waldman did it, Holmes?" Sexton Blake asked.

"How did he escape? The ropes were entirely secure. I confess I'm not quite sure, Blake. I mean to find out."

Holmes filled his pipe and resumed with an extraordinary statement. "I am guilty of underestimating Baron Ulf Von Waldman. He is certainly brilliant, a master of disguise, and he managed to penetrate British Intelligence to a certain extent, learning about the plant. He must also have reasons for thinking the Wold Cottage meteorite has certain properties, and those reasons still remain obscure to me. I also intend to lift the veil of that obscurity."

"Holmes," I asked, "do you think Von Waldman is really the son of Professor Moriarty?"

"I admit I am unsure what to think at this point, my dear Watson," he replied, and I could see my friend was quite humbled by the whole experience. He continued. "Mycroft's files on Von Waldman indicate the Baron was born in 1888, which seems to fit with the photographs and the man we saw revealed under the disguising makeup. And yet I was following the late Professor's career quite closely by that time, and there was no indication of a child born to him during that period."

"Was he someone else, then, Mr. Holmes?" Harry Dickson asked, and with his next question demonstrated the extraordinary imagination for which he was destined to become quite famous. "Someone much, much older? Someone who already had prior access to an elixir of life which has run out, and which he is trying to duplicate?"

For once, Holmes could not answer, and he puffed at his pipe broodingly.

And in that moment I knew our adventure was not over, for Holmes would not rest until Baron Ulf Von Waldman was brought to book.

The SECRET of GRANT'S TOMB

by
Joe Gentile

THE more Boothby North tried to appear relaxed, the more dread filled him. He leaned expectantly in the doorway of the dilapidated Black Horse Tavern. Smoke from his cigarette hung in front of him as the chilled thick twilight air pressed down upon him. Something had assuredly gone amiss.

He continued to peer through his tobacco exhalations into the empty London streets, but nothing stirred. His own intake smelled of dank Bourbon and worse, and he stifled a gag reflex. He was not much of a drinker or frequenter of this kind of establishment. His contact should have been here hours ago, but now the longer Boothby remained, the greater the risk to himself.

With his foot, he stubbed out his cigarette, deciding he had waited long enough. He pulled his tweed jacket closer about him and headed away from the tavern, his footsteps making soft splashes in the scattered puddles from the rain a few hours previous.

It started as a hushed echo. He wasn't even sure he had heard anything until it grew louder. Looking up the street that was filled with nothing but piles of refuse and a stray ex-Black Horse patron or two sleeping off their night of imbibing, he saw the man running towards him.

That little man was almost stumbling in his hurry. Boothby stood his ground, realizing that the odds of this being some kind of coincidence were high.

The furtive man reached him and collapsed in his arms. Boothby had not anticipated that, and fell with the weight of the man to the cobblestone pavement. The man had cuts and bruises aplenty, and his clothes were torn as if a desperate struggle had just taken place.

"Guv', you that reporter, right? North?" He asked the question with wide bloodshot eyes, and hung onto Boothby's collar, white-knuckled, as if his life depended upon it.

"Yes, now tell me what's going on, but we also need to get you to a hospital."

"There's no time. The treasure does exist! But if it stays an underground secret, there will be dead bodies piled up in the streets! It's up to you now."

At that moment, the sound of shoed-horses and the clattering of wooden wheels jolted the quiet fabric of the night. There were two black carriages headed towards them at an alarming speed.

"Good God!" breathed Boothby.

He was literally shaken back to reality by the injured man. "You gotta get out of here now!"

"I can't just leave you here."

"It's too late for me, and if you wait any longer, you won't have any choice in the matter!" He pushed him with all his might, but not before stuffing an envelope into Boothby's coat.

Boothby fell backwards awkwardly, but regained his balance quickly. He dove over a garbage bin as the first carriage raced past him, brushing against his jacket. He heard the small man scream as the horses trampled down on his limbs, snapping them like twigs. Boothby was a seasoned reporter, but had never been witness to such a gruesome death, and that made him pause.

The second carriage bore down on his new location. He scrambled to his feet, but he wasn't quick enough. The door to the unmarked black vehicle opened and struck him in the midsection like a kick from a mule. He went down, folded in half. Although he had no breath left, Boothby still managed to roll out of the way, avoiding the horses' thundering hooves.

Then, as if none of this ever happened, the carriages disappeared down the street past the horizon line, and all the racket was snuffed to a dead calm. Boothby North lay in the road, trying to catch his breath, and looked out through watering eyes at the again empty avenue. Oh, yes, there was a story here, indeed. He just needed to survive to be able to tell it.

As an army surgeon, I had performed many unpleasant but necessary amputations, but getting my friend Sherlock Holmes away from his bee farm in Sussex might have been the most challenging extraction I have ever enacted.

I hadn't seen him since the summer before, right after the *Lion's Mane* affair, but when I visited him, experience told me that he needed something to occupy that great racing engine of a mind of his. If he continued as he was, I feared his health would deteriorate. He most certainly did not appreciate my "meddling", and protested to no end as I refused to leave without him. But amidst his remonstrations, he also was well aware of how I get concerning his medical welfare…"dogged" he called it…so he relented.

Eventually, during the ride to London, he warmed to the idea of dining at Simpsons and perhaps calling upon Lestrade, to see what was new in the annals of London crime. Needless to say, this played right into my plan, so I did not complain. Now, I did not "plan" for an investigation to fall into our laps, but it did not surprise me when such a thing did occur…for those in need are drawn to Holmes like a moth to an open flame.

"Why, Mister Holmes, for what do I owe the honor for a visit from such an illustrious personage as yourself?"

"Ah, Inspector, it is oddly good to see you again as well."

"And a backwards compliment from you, what a new experience!"

Lestrade had a bright gleam in his eyes, and Holmes almost grinned, as they both paused to look at each other. My heart was filled with joy as I listened to their repartee that long ago had been honed to a fine craft. Their begrudging friendship was not as well known, but was usually bubbling just beneath the surface. They clapped each other on the shoulder and laughed. It was hard not to join in.

Lestrade's office at the Yard hadn't changed much over the years, except for perhaps the amount of stacks of paper strewn about on his desk, on top of file cabinets, and even on his lap. He was still a tireless crusader, and the years hadn't altered his appearance too noticeably, except perhaps for the fewer strands of hair on his head. He got up to shake our hands, and held onto the papers that were on his lap.

"So is this a social call, gentlemen? Not that I am averse to seeing you, but as you can see, the wheels of justice still move slowly."

"My doctor advocated a visit to our old stomping grounds for health reasons, of course."

"Of course. So am I supposed to nurse you back to health, for I fear my nurturing skills are sharply lacking." At this, Holmes frowned, but I found myself smiling.

"Inspector, what are you working on now?" I interjected, "Anything of particular interest?"

"What am I not working on would be the better question. I have a kidnapping, a murder, assorted rumors, and paperwork that never ends!"

"So crime has gotten dull, old boy?" Holmes smirked.

"Yes, without you, Mister Holmes, all there has been is just boring crime." Lestrade rolled his eyes.

"Oh, and here I thought it was dull because you had put to rest so many cases in my absence."

"Lestrade," I quickly said, "perhaps you could meet us at Simpsons for some dinner tonight if you are available?"

"Wouldn't miss it, gentlemen."

"Inspector Lestrade?" came an unsure voice from the doorway. The man appeared to have run here from some distance, as his flush face and shallow breath suggested. "I am sorry for the interruption, but I was told I could find you here." There was slight pause as we all were surprised at this.

"Lestrade, you might want to let this American reporter in," Holmes said.

"A reporter from Boston, sir, doesn't appear at my door every day, so please do come in." Lestrade motioned him in. Holmes raised his eyebrow at the inspector's observation.

"Yes, Mister Sherlock Holmes, from time to time I do manage to identify a person's accent without you."

"Indeed?" Holmes smiled.

"Sherlock Holmes? Why, this is unbelievable!" said the reporter. "The Professor would be so very interested in meeting you…he has read all of your monographs!" Holmes positively glowed at this.

The reporter was a young man, but with that look of having seen many things. My first impression was that he was quite intelligent and physically capable of handling himself. I liked him right away.

"Hutchinson Hatch, please calm yourself, and tell us what has happened to Professor Van Dusen."

Mister Hatch stood dumbfounded at being the target of my friend's deductions.

"My day would not have been complete without one of your parlor tricks, Mister Holmes, so thank you for that." Lestrade smirked.

Mister Hatch slowly sat down, looking at us one at a time.

"Mister Hatch, do not be alarmed, and I apologize if my small skills of observation set you ill at ease." Holmes said. "There really is nothing special about it. I had read of the professor's coming to London, for it a rare thing for him to venture out. And I know that he is usually accompanied by you, sir, an American reporter from Boston…"

"But how would you have known I was an American reporter at all?" a calmer Hatch asked.

"Oh, several minor indicators, such as the cut of your suit coat, the notebook in your pocket, your overall manner which frankly screams 'American', and even the word choice of your speech, which indicates an educated man of letters."

"Well, when you explain it like that, sir…" Hatch began.

"Yes, I don't know why I bother to explain it away." Holmes looked away.

"Mr. Hatch," Lestrade sharply said, "Would you mind telling me what has brought you into my office today?"

"Inspector, Professor Van Dusen is missing!"

We left Lestrade at the Yard, where he promised he would send out some inquiries concerning the professor, since news of a missing prominent tourist does raise eyebrows. But he did also say that he could only do so much since Van Dusen has only been missing a short time.

The three of us shared a cab, as Holmes decided he had to help the reporter find the Professor. I imagine the fact that the Professor read Holmes' monographs made it impossible for him to refuse.

Holmes sat with his fingertips pressed together and faced the reporter with interest.

"Mister Hatch, pray tell us what brought you and the Professor to our shores. Spare no detail, no matter how insignificant it may seem."

"It was my friend, Boothby. Boothby North. He was a fellow reporter, British, which I guess is obvious, my apologies. We began corresponding a couple of years ago.

"About two months ago, I received the first letter from him concerning a big story he was going to break. It was an unusually exciting tale about discovered sunken treasure. The next letter I got was more specific, and it went that way until the very last letter I received. In it, I could tell something had changed. His writing was oddly dark, and I sensed what I can only describe as fear.

"Then, just two weeks ago, word reached me that Boothby had been murdered. The official reports that I could find listed the crime as unsolved. I could not just sit and wonder, sir, so I came as soon as I could, hoping that I could be of some use to my friend. I enlisted the Professor's opinion, and he does not believe in coincidences, so we both came."

"What sunken treasure are we talking about?" I couldn't help myself, for my curiosity overtook me.

"If I remember all the facts, the treasure concerned the ship The GENERAL GRANT. It was a full-rigged ship of over eleven hundred tons, and in 1866 set out from London to Melbourne. Her manifest included many items, but of note was the large amount of gold bullion, as it was insured for 165,000 pounds. *En route*, in the pitch black of night, the ship struck something. Chaos ensued, which caused the ship to drift into a cave 250 yards deep, the roof of which forced the masts into the hull, and the ship went down. Only 14 of the 83 on board managed to survive (cargo stores lost), after spending 18 months marooned.

The intoxicating lure of the gold prompted two attempts to recover it, in 1869 and 1870, and were met with similar terrible results. And that brings us to the latest attempt, here in 1907, which ended in death yet again.

"You have a reporter's memory, Mister Hatch, well done. Tell us more about the content of these letters, if you will," Holmes said cooly.

"As I recall them, sir, Boothby mentioned that he had a source. Someone who knew where the treasure was. Someone who was going to give him the proof because he didn't want the person who was looking for it to have it. Sounded like the informant was holding something against that person. This man was run down by two carriages, which Boothby avoided. Before he died, he said that if the information didn't go public, there would likely be many more deaths."

"Boothby had just met this person before sending his last letter to me. He had the proof, but didn't tell me exactly what it was. We reporters don't tend to share such things, even among friends."

"And the crime scene where your friend was murdered?" Holmes asked.

"As you can imagine, Mister Holmes, by the time we arrived, it was weeks after the events, and—"

"Useless, as if a herd of buffalo trampled over the area?" Holmes interjected.

"Yes, sir."

"And his effects?"

"He was buried as he was, which means that whatever he had on him, he still does…in a way."

"A pity."

"All we know is that he was stabbed right outside his apartment, and his keys were still in his hand."

"Did the Professor find anything of use at the apartment?"

"I honestly don't know, Mister Holmes, although he did talk to some of the residents there and was out of my sight for a bit. After that, we went to our rooms to settle in. I soon went out to talk with Boothby's fellow reporters at the paper, but when I got back, the Professor was gone. He had left a small note saying he would be back within two hours, but did not return. The Professor usually has me running around gathering information for him, so the fact that he went himself…I am concerned."

Inside the drably appointed Great Northern Hotel at Paddington, Mister Hatch showed us to their lodgings.

Hatch was telling us how little time he was gone before returning to find the Professor missing, but Holmes' attention was elsewhere. I watched his eyes, trying in vain to see what he was seeing. All I could determine is that the room looked like two travelers had come in and unpacked their belongings. Everything else looked perfectly in place.

Mister Hatch stopped in mid sentence when he saw that my friend was not actually listening, but that he did have a bit of a glint in his eye. Something I had seen numerous times before.

"Mister Holmes?" he asked.

"Ah, forgive me, Mister Hatch, but Watson, what is the one item out of place here?"

For the life of me, I had no idea what Holmes was referring to, and the frustration of that has not lessened over all these years, as this conversation was not a first.

"Holmes, the room looks undisturbed. All of the usual items hotels leave for their visitors are still in place: the flower vase, the newspaper on the table, the fireplace, the furniture…"

"You have seen, Watson, but you have not observed."

My resigned expression gave Holmes the go ahead to continue.

"Mister Hatch, Watson…observe the newspaper."

Both of us went to the table and looked down at the folded newspaper, and both of us, almost simultaneously, looked back at Holmes with blank expressions.

"The paper has been folded over. Not an even crisp fold at a section of the paper, but an uncreased one in the middle of the paper."

"So, you are saying that the Professor looked at the paper before he disappeared?" I asked.

"Precisely, Watson, and it was the paper that caused him to leave. Mister Hatch, be so good as to read aloud the article that is face up on the open page, the one that was continued from the previous page."

Hatch responded, a little hesitantly at first: "…so when the jewels were discovered missing, her friends tried to console her. Well known international philanthropist and society member Bradlee Leighton even went as far as offering a reward for their return—

"Leighton!" Hatch exclaimed, his brow furrowed in anger.

"One in the same. Bradlee Cunnyngham Leighton. Well-heeled aristocrat, lover of all fine things, friend to all, but mostly a master—"

"Thief!" Hatch grumbled with a sneer.

Holmes smiled thinly. "This is not common knowledge, so I take it you have come across Mister Leighton before, then?"

"Oh, indeed we did. Leighton got away clean last time, but even though the Professor really didn't have full opportunity to capture him at his own game then—"

"It appears he wants to rectify that this time. So, gentlemen, if you will follow me," Holmes said, "we will catch up with the Professor, for there are only a few places where someone like Leighton would be staying. A talk of missing treasure and an infamous thief…as the Professor so wisely states, there is no such thing as coincidence.

Hutchinson Hatch and I followed Holmes, as he went about retracing the Professor's logical movements after reading that newspaper article.

The Professor posed a striking figure, as Hatch gave his description: tall, thin, stoop-shouldered, pale, squinting eyes with thick spectacles, and most striking of all, a tall broad brow topped with a heavy shock of bushy yellow hair. Needless to say, after talking with a few cabbies and constables, we found our quarry.

We entered a very finely appointed restaurant, where the metallic color of gold was strewn about too garishly for my taste. There was an upstairs that promised even more lavish lodgings. We found the Professor sitting alone at a table. To say that he stood out, would be belaboring the obvious.

Upon our arrival the Professor raised an eyebrow.

"Hatch? I see you brought along some friends. Mister Sherlock Holmes, I presume?" he said as he held out his hand.

Holmes shook the hand. "Professor, and this is my colleague, Doctor Watson."

"Of course it is. I take it we are all on the same tack here?" he asked as we all sat down.

"Professor, where have you been?" said an exasperated Hatch.

"After I read of Leighton's appearance, I thought I would ascertain his location, and make sure he was still there, which would then answer an important question I had.

"I had found him, and stood in the dark outside the establishment for more than an hour, and listened and observed. At that point where I had witnessed comings and goings of what I can only call the criminal class, and many of them had the look of longshoremen about them, I was almost run over by a lightless speeding black carriage! There were curtains over the windows and the driver wore a cloak and masked his features. The carriage itself had no distinctive marks, and it vanished nearly noiselessly as quickly as it came.

"This Leighton runs in powerful criminal circles," I said.

"Obviously, so needless to say, I removed myself to a second location and remained unseen for some time, as to not bring danger back with me to the hotel, unless it had already come.

"There is no doubt, Leighton is anxiously searching for information, but not finding it."

"Professor, I see that you are waiting to approach Leighton when he comes down from his rooms, and he does not know you are here?" Holmes asked.

"Very good, Mister Holmes, you observed my eyes darting to the stairway on more than one occasion, and no doubt noticed by slight nervous tick of my hand drumming on the table."

"As we wait for Mister Leighton, perhaps you can enlighten us on what you found at the murder scene?"

"Certainly. Little physical evidence remained of course, but many of the residents there heard the scuffle that night.

"The intruder had asked Mister Boothby for some information, but the reporter was not interested in giving it. There was a short struggle, which ended as we know. But, we do have a witness, so there is a description of the killer."

"Excellent," said Holmes, "we can give that description to Inspector Lestrade. He should be able to handle such a thing, I trust. Plus, if I am not mistaken, there is another Inspector at the Yard who has made Leighton his *raison d'etre*, who would be of some use…Inspector Conway, is it?"

"Yes, and I take it we agree that it was Leighton who sent this man to Boothby?" asked the Professor.

At that moment, a finely dressed gentleman approached our table, and there was no doubt that it was Mister Bradlee Leighton.

"What an incongruous assembly," he said, matter of factly. We all stood, not knowing what to expect.

Leighton had that slick handsome look of a villain from a melodrama, and just being near him made me ill at ease.

The Professor made the opening gambit: "We are here to determine the root of Boothby North's murder."

"Gentlemen, I assure you, I did not kill anyone. Really, it's just too messy of a business."

"We know you made inquiries about Boothby's information." Hatch added.

"You know very little, and making an inquiry is now a crime?"

"You seem to be man who leaves the so called 'messy business' to others, so you would have had someone else kill him." Hatch was more agitated, and I set myself for the pot to boil over.

"Absolutely not. The reporter's death was misfortunate, to be sure, but—"

"Misfortunate?" Hatch yelled and leaped across the table at Leighton with arms outstretched. The Professor's coffee cup fell over, the linen slid off the table, and chairs were overturned. Leighton stood his ground and merely smiled with tight lips, his thin mustache a straight line, as Holmes and I held Hatch back.

"Mister Hatch, is it? I know the death of your friend is upsetting, but I am not to blame. I am, however, gratified that you think me so clever and devious."

The situation cooled slightly as the Professor escorted Hatch outside. I felt a little unsure of what I should be doing, but I was keenly aware, as if at any moment, fire would erupt.

Holmes and Leighton stood a few feet apart from each other and just stared. Leighton was still cool and collected, but also with a look of defiance, which didn't help my nerves.

Holmes stared through Leighton, and even though I was not the recipient of such a stare, I felt it shiver through me regardless.

"Mister Leighton…" Holmes said as if with a bitter after taste in his mouth.

"Mister Holmes," was the calm response.

"Up until now, your activities were only of a slight interest to me. Most of your escapades barely registered my notice. You are clever, but just a common thief. There have been no deaths contributable to your name… until now. That will be your undoing."

"Mister Holmes, your reputation precedes you, but often it reads like exaggerated fantasy. An old detective does not instill fear in me, my good sir."

Holmes' eyes were on fire with that last comment, and he moved around the table to be closer to Leighton until their faces were mere inches away from each other.

"Your inflated ego spells your end. With Professor Van Dusen and myself on you, your time is over."

Leighton's eyes changed at this exchange. No longer was his look of confidence strong. It wavered as the color of his face went ashen for a moment, but then returned just as quickly.

They stood and looked at each other silently. Not a sound was heard.

Holmes stepped back, and gave a bow at the waist. "Good day, Mister Leighton." At that, the two of us went outside to meet up with the Professor and Hatch. We all walked for a bit in silence.

"You left him concerned, I take it?" the Professor asked.

"The trap is set."

"Trap? What trap?" I asked.

"Leighton would not have stopped looking for the treasure."

"Boothby was determined that the treasure was in fact recovered. He must have had proof," Hatch added.

"And if Boothby had given Leighton any information…" Holmes started.

"He would not have still been where we could find him," the Professor finished.

"Two plus two equals four," said Holmes.

"Not sometimes," said the Professor.

"But always," said Holmes, which caused a rare smile on the Professor's lips.

"But if Leighton has any clues about the treasure's location, his timetable should now be moved up."

"If he believes that his way of life might have dried up here…he will want to leave, and grab whatever valuables he can."

"Watson, you and Hatch here get a message to Lestrade by any means necessary. Tell him what Leighton is up to, and make sure they round up the hired killer, using the Professor's description. Also let him know that we are on the trail and will get further word to him, as to where Leighton may try to take his leave of the city."

After getting this information down, Hatch and I departed, leaving Holmes and the Professor on the hunt

From what he told me later, Holmes and the Professor waited out of sight. They walked with pedestrians, and moved with any passing vehicle, trying not to be too stationary. Both men did this on their own, one in front of the hotel, and one in the back, and they would switch positions every now and then as well. No conversation was deemed necessary between these two great deductive minds.

Word came in while Hatch and I were still at the Yard. Leighton was heading towards pier #31, which meant time was of the essence.

We arrived with both Lestrade and Conway, as well as a group of trusted constables. We still had to wait, for the dreary pier had a small boat docked, but no other traffic of any kind. We sat still in our cabs, almost out of sight from the pier, but then there was a change. There was a dull fog, which I had to keep blinking away to keep my eyes focused.

A tall man, in a long coat, approached the boat, which swayed softly in the almost still water. He was wearing a knit cap and had a scarf around his face and neck. From the cabin of the boat, a man exited. When that man met the man in the coat, I rose out of my seat and rushed towards the boat, followed by Hatch and the others.

The man in the coat had his hand out, as if to hand something to the man in the boat.

We all approached cautiously, hiding behind scaffolding and paint canisters that were left behind from the day's work.

"There are many addresses on this list," the man in the boat said. "That's not what I asked for."

"What did you ask for then?" asked the scarfed man.

"You bloody well know what I paid you for, you imbecile. Tell me which one it is now, or you don't get the rest of your money."

"Why would I give you something I could just as easily go get myself?"

"I am the one who uncovered the leads to track this damn treasure down! You would have nothing without me!" the man on the boat yelled.

"Which is exactly what you have now," he goaded.

"That treasure is mine!" he screamed.

Then, quicker than a snake, the scarfed man grabbed the man off the boat, and tossed him on the ground! Just as quickly, the coated man kneeled on the tossed man, expertly pinning him.

We leapt from our spot to see my old friend Sherlock Holmes as the man doing the pinning! And he was very pleased with himself, I do say. The man on the ground was Leighton, who was out of breath.

"Ah, well met, Watson, Lestrade, and I presume Inspector Conway?" Holmes said. "I assume you heard my scintillating conversation with

Mister Leighton here, yes? Now tell me we have this man's compatriot in custody?"

"Indeed we do, Mister Holmes," Lestrade said proudly, pushing back his shoulders. "And he will testify that it was Leighton who hired him."

"Excellent, Lestrade, excellent!"

"Just good old fashioned, police work, Mister Holmes."

"Oh, I think it's a little more than that, Inspector."

Lestrade smiled at the rare compliment, filing it away to savor at a later date.

"And now, Inspector?" Lestrade nodded to Conway.

"My pleasure, Inspector," was the gruff reply from the disheveled Conway.

Conway bent over Leighton, applying the handcuffs.

"It is my distinct pleasure to inform you, Mister Leighton, that you are under arrest for conspiracy to commit murder, sir."

Leighton looked up and grimaced at Conway, "This cannot be a victory for you, Inspector."

"Good enough for me. I don't care if I got you for not having a cab license, as long as you were doing time."

My friend walked to where Leighton was still lying prone, and crouched down close to him. Now his cloak was open and his scarf was off.

"Leighton(,) I thought I should point out that all of the addresses on that list were fake. There was only one person who knew where the treasure was, but you had him killed. I hope the thought of your failure will keep you warm through this coming long winter."

"Holmes," spit Leighton, "you self-righteous son of—"

Making a stop at Lestrade, my friend told him something too quietly for me to hear.

The four of us stood, watching Leighton get driven away to finally answer for at least one of his crimes.

"So, Holmes…" I started.

"The Professor and I followed Leighton to the pier, then hiding out of sight, waited for who we thought would be Leighton's contact to approach. We got to the contact, and basically I switched places with him. We dispatched him to the local constabulary."

"What about the treasure, I asked?"

Both Holmes and the Professor smiled.

"Professor, I assume you have the letter…?" Holmes said with a nod.

The Professor produced a letter out of his jacket pocket.

"The last letter from Boothby?" asked a shocked Mister Hatch.

"Indeed, Hatch, indeed. You had showed it to me, do you not remember? For in this, are all the clues we need to see about the treasure," the Professor said, slightly waving the letter.

"What kind of cipher?" asked Holmes.

"A very simple one, child's play, I assure you."

"He tells us where the treasure is in that letter? How could I have missed that?" Hatch said, upset with himself.

"You weren't looking for it," replied the Professor without a tone of emotion in his voice.

"Wait," I said. "you mean the treasure does exist?"

"Not quite, Doctor," answered the Professor, "all we know is where someone thought the treasure was. It is so well hidden, that even to go looking for it, may very well spell disaster."

"Then it might as well be still buried at sea," bemoaned Hatch.

"I told Lestrade that the secret of the lost treasure of The General Grant died with your friend, Mister Hatch; that he took it to the grave."

"This treasure has already cost too many lives. And the information is this letter would only keep the death toll counting, wouldn't you say, Professor?"

"Indeed," he said, handing Holmes the letter, "would you care to do the honors?"

My friend drew a match, lit the letter on fire, and set it on the ground. We all watched the paper with whatever kind of coded message it contained, slowly burn, shrivel, and turn to ash.

Not one of us spoke.

"Professor, it has been a distinct honor," Holmes said, extending his hand.

"Mister Holmes, the pleasure was all mine," came the surprising response from the Professor, as he struck me as a more distant type of fellow. After they were on their way, I turned to Holmes and grinned. "So, how's the 'old detective' feeling after that fight at the pier?"

He looked at me with what I can only describe as a smirk, which marked the second time such a rare expression crossed his face.

"How did it feel?" I asked.

"Invigorating, Watson, for I haven't had to expend that kind of energy in some time."

The
HAUNTED MANOR

by
Howard Hopkins

OFTEN it is with great admiration and respect that I look upon the accomplishments of my friend Sherlock Holmes and, much to his inevitable consternation, put pen to paper to relate the frequently extraordinary accounts of his exploits. At times, however, I find myself enveloped with an equal and proportionate quantity of irritation at his egotism and disputatious reprimands of my chronicling.

Today was such a day, though if the awaited visitor to this old room on Baker Street proved as satisfactory as I anticipated, I do believe my present mood would be immensely lightened.

Sherlock Holmes cast aside a copy of *The Times*, contributing to the already considerable clutter of the old room, extricated himself from his chair and went to the fireplace, at which he plucked, with tongs, a glowing cinder from the blaze. He touched it to his cherry-wood pipe, then returned the cinder and tongs to their proper place.

"I say, you have outdone yourself in your present embellishment of our last case, my dear Watson," said he, then puffed on his pipe and assumed that air of superiority I found particularly loathsome this dreary morning.

"How so?" said I, knowing his answer would only serve to augment the chill of the morning even the fire could not dispel.

Beyond the window a serpentine mist moved along the dun-colored houses, and inside the gas lighting cast a glow over white linen and china not yet cleared from the breakfast meal.

My friend turned to me, observably in no sweet temper, and I feared one of his lectures regarding my literary shortcomings was nigh.

"Is it not obvious, my good man," said he, "that the disposition of singular facts regarding the events of Mrs. Opiney's deceased husband by her own hand has, indeed, again, been supplanted by such copious exaggeration as to seem secondary and insignificant?"

"Ah, but the details of that case were novel and of far more interest than the simple logic of a woman, who, grown weary of her unvirtuous husband, subsequently sets to bring about his untimely disposal."

"Pshaw, my dear fellow," said he, plucking the pipe from his lips and employing a disapproving arch to his right eyebrow. "Facts must always supersede hyperbole. For as you are well aware my own little practice must dismiss the seemingly fantastic claims of the unobservant public in favor of genuine criminal originality, a commodity that is becoming exceedingly rare in our presently unrestrained and unimaginative society. But, that said, you are kind enough to interest yourself in these cases, so while eminently appreciative I would yet again perhaps caution literary restraint."

From beyond the window distant footsteps increased in volume, echoing in the gray swirls of fog. Little wishing to continue with my friend's opining of my literary persuasions, I smiled slightly, taking minor pleasure in my foreknowledge of our approaching visitor.

"Ah, as expected, a woman," said he, before I could sufficiently take pleasure in the moment. "Perhaps a trifle early…"

I wondered how he could have possibly deduced such a thing as appointment time from mere footsteps. Indeed, the woman was right on time, as per her note, which he could not possibly have seen.

My friend's face assembled into an expression of perplexity, however, as if he had begun to suspect his deduction had been errant in some aspect.

"Strange," said he. "I expected her at half past ten."

A tapping came from the door, whose opening immediately followed. Into the room stepped the woman—and I use the term in its broadest application—whom had informed me by telegram on the previous day of her impending visitation.

The woman was more than even I expected, with dark eyes and a visage that might only have been properly described as handsome. A curious and unwholesome odor preceded her and from the curious twitching of my friend's nostrils it did not go unnoticed.

"Miss Martha Jane Cannary, I presume," said he, in a tone that carried a degree of disapproval that brought fleeting satisfaction to my deflating mood. At least he had seen fit to forgo mention of her olfactory ambiance.

"That is a most peculiar scent, I might add," said he, and I realized with great consternation my conclusion had been premature.

"Why, skinned me a mule right 'fore I got on that big ol' boat to come to your little country—we kicked your britches right on outta ours, ya recollect. I reckon the odor's still about me."

My friend might have flinched but the expression passed too quickly for me to be certain.

"I believe that was a Cunard line ship, my good miss," said I.

She grinned with yellowed teeth. "Hell and Hootenanny, yeah, big ol' boat. Had me heavin' my giblets, what with all the rockin' and rollin' it did."

"Ah, perhaps that may be further attributed to the inexpensive liquor I detect radiating from your person?" said Holmes, always the diplomat.

"Cheap?" The woman's face assembled into an indignant arrangement. "Have you know that whiskey comes four bits a bottle. Say, you got yourself some of that English sherry I been hearin' tell of on the trip over?" She rubbed a soil-stained hand across her parchmentlike lips. "Mite dry, if I do say so myself."

It was eminently obvious from the whisk of her breath in my direction that was not the case.

"How do you know of Miss Cannary?" asked I of my friend. "And that she was expected this morning?"

"Hell, that's—you must be the Watson fella I writ to—" She proceeded to give me what I believe in America was referred to as the "once-over". It caused me a peculiar sensation of being undressed and the lascivious angle of her lips only furthered the impression. "Like I was sayin', that's *Mrs*. Married me James Butler Hickok, I did. That's Wild Bill, fastest gun the West ever did see, least up until the idjit got himself shot in the back of the head and left me with child."

"I recognized the manner in which Miss—*Mrs*. Cannary was dressed," said Holmes. "The buckskins. As well, I read of her arrival in England in connection with a possible future engagement of a Wild West production. I did not, however, expect her arrival here. In fact, I anticipated someone quite different."

"So ya heard of me?" said she, her masculine face nearly taking on a semblance of femininity.

"My good woman," said Holmes, "the accounts of your—how shall we phrase it?—*escapades* are extraordinarily more exaggerated than Watson's somewhat embroidered recountings of my own."

The woman nudged up her battered felt hat and scratched at her scalp. Her brows lifted appreciably. "Bit of a rude one, ain't he, Jeeves?" said she, eyeing me. "Lucky for him I'm a right polite guest." Her attention shifted back to my friend. "Hell's bells, no offense taken! But I reckon there ain't one damn bit of exaggeration involved in the adventures of Calamity Jane—that's what you kin call me, by the by, Calamity. All my friends do, on account of I'm a famous Indian scout—best damn one there is, doncha believe what that varmint, Cody, says—an' I saved an officer from calamity at the hands of war-pathin' redskins."

"Or perhaps because you cause it?" said he, and I suppressed a desire to wince.

"Hell, now, tall and wiry, you cain't be believin' everything you read."

My friend lifted an accusing eyebrow in my direction. This encounter was certainly not proceeding in the way I had imagined it would. Miss Calamity Jane instead of rousing my friend's irritation had, somehow, in the space of moments, supported his specious point regarding my writings.

Miss Calamity—I was well aware of the invalidity of her self-regaled marriage to the former James Butler Hickok, so refused the married appellation—hitched her thumbs in the pockets of her buckskin coat and proceeded to expel a shrill whistle.

"Well, Judas Priest, so these are the digs of the famous Sherlock Holmes—" She cast him a condescending eye. "Not as famous as me, of course, but you're right well-known in these parts, I hear tell. Always gotta get me a parley with the local celebrities, assumin' I don't take me a notion to marry 'em…" She gazed about the room, her focus lingering on the fireplace. "Hot as ol' Hell in here, ain't it? Feel like I should be in my naturalness."

"Perhaps you would be kind enough to tell us your business here, Mrs. Cannary," Holmes suggested, a bit piqued.

"Figgered I'd see me how one of you English detectives worked while I'm in town. Reckon you cain't be as good as the Pinkertons. Heard me some pretty wild tall tales of your cases on the trip over."

Holmes cast me another of those patronizing glances and I wondered just what had possessed me to accept this woman's calling.

"I'm a right fine detective myself," continued she, pride swelling her carriage.

"Do say?" said Holmes, the arch of his brow more skeptical.

"Hell and tarnation, I do say. Why, once I recollect I was scouting for Custer—Georgie, I calls him—and readin' Injun sign like it was writ in God's English on the leaves. Georgie says to me, Calamity, you're the best gawdamned—pardon my Apache—best gawdamned scout—"

"Mrs. Cannary," said Holmes, thankfully interrupting what promised to be a tedious and boastful account of her tracking prowess.

"Calamity," said she.

"Mrs. Cannary," said he. "You find yourself in providence. I should be hearing a case within the quarter, for a message was delivered to me late yesterday afternoon. In fact, before your most auspicious arrival, it was the sender whom I was expecting."

I acquired the distinct impression my friend had deduced my intention and was obliging this "woman" in a retaliatory effort that in all likelihood I had brought on myself.

"Well, hot damn!" said she, and not a moment later another young woman stepped through the door, explaining my friend's earlier puzzlement over Miss Calamity, for here was, indeed, the guest he had expected.

"Ah, Miss Bickford," said Holmes. "If I may, my colleague, Dr. Watson and Mrs. Cannary from America."

"Calamity Jane, Missy. The famous detective here cain't seem to git it right. Never had me that problem with the Pinkertons."

I do believe the American woman's exposition annoyed Holmes. With that, I found my spirits lifting.

"Miss Sarah Bickford," said Holmes, "a servant at Crownshield Manor."

Miss Bickford was attired in a full-length, long-sleeved maid's uniform, the frills of her cuffs noticeably bruised and sullied. Her satin apron and shoulder frills were impeccable, however. The apron was of white, and black ribbon detailed the shoulders and skirt's bottom tiers. Blonde hair framed her delicate face in tiny curls and soft terror resided in her robin's-egg eyes.

She curtsied and Miss Calamity made a discordant *pfft* of a sound, expressing her obvious scorn of such decorum. It was my opinion Miss

Calamity would not in the least be harmed by a lengthy sabbatical at a finishing school.

"Thank you for seeing me on such short notice, Mr. Holmes. If it were not of vital, perhaps even mortal, importance, Lady Crownshield would not have insisted upon such an abrupt time frame. But you see, as I indicated in my message, Master Crownshield is to meet his spectral death later today."

"All you folks talk so funny?" said Miss Calamity and my friend sighed. "What the tarnation you mean, 'spectral death'?"

"Ghosts, Mrs. Cannary," said Holmes.

"*Calamity*," said she in a tone of exasperation. "And there's no such varmints."

"Be that as it may," said Holmes, "the mystery Miss Bickford alluded to in her message is intriguing. Did Master Crownshield not recently become heir to Crownshield Manor and marry?"

"Indeed, he did, Mr. Holmes. Let me explain." Miss Bickford's gaze went to Miss Calamity with a display of questioning disdain.

"Well, by all means, Miss Little Uppity," said Miss Calamity with an exaggerated sweep of her arm.

"You see, Mr. Holmes," continued Miss Bickford, ever since Zephren Crownshield became master of the Manor and wed the former Miss Nellie Green, the house has been plagued by the ghost of its former Master, Lydell Crownshield, who passed some years ago."

Holmes nodded, his gaze intently focused on the young woman. "The Manor fell to Lady Crownshield upon his death?" said he.

"Yes, but she has become unfit," said Miss Bickford.

"Unfit?" said Holmes.

"Madness runs in the family, Mr. Holmes," said she. "It was Lady Crownshield who first observed her husband's ghost many months ago, but we all humored her, thinking it mere delusion."

"Ghost—*pfft!*" scoffed Miss Calamity.

"And this ghost," said Holmes, "has Master Crownshield seen him?"

"He denies that he has, but his actions over the past few weeks do not bear this out. I believe he refuses to accept that the madness may have been passed to him as well. He has become increasingly agitated and talks of the ghost in his sleep. He appears more and more unwell."

"Lady Crownshield insisted upon this meeting?" asked Holmes, his angular face thoughtful as he took a puff from his pipe.

Miss Bickford nodded. "After the letter."

"The letter?" Holmes' eyes brightened.

"This—" Miss Bickford reached into an apron pocket, then passed a folded note she extracted to Holmes, who accepted it with a slight bow. "It says Master Crownshield shall perish at tea this very afternoon at 12, in full view of witnesses."

"Is it signed 'the ghost'?" said Miss Calamity with undisguised ridicule.

"It is unsigned," said Holmes, deep lines creasing his brow. "And quite emphatic in its threat." He handed the note back to the young woman. "Should Master Crownshield meet with his doom by means mortal or otherworldly, who would Crownshield Manor and its holdings fall to?"

"Why, Nellie Crownshield," said Miss Bickford. "Indeed, the papers were drawn up soon after their nuptials."

"*Pfft*," said Miss Calamity again. "Case solved. There's your killer. That filly's got her greedy little eyes set on his gold saddlebags. Seen it a hunnert times."

"Oh, no," said Miss Bickford. "Nellie was a dear friend of mine for more than a year before she came to know Master Crownshield. I can wholeheartedly vouch for her integrity. In fact, she postponed the wedding many months after others criticized her station, for she worked as a servant prior to her betrothal."

"That's a good story," said Miss Calamity, her tone advising she did not for one moment believe an iota of it.

"I notice your cuffs, Miss Bickford," said Holmes. "They are certainly scuffed and soiled. Your hands exhibit reddish stains and scratches as well, and your fingernails evidence of soil."

"Don't need a detective to answer that," intruded Miss Calamity. "You got something going on with the old boy and he gits a mite rough, don't he? Maybe draws some blood."

The young woman's delicate face took on a bloom of rose, and she glanced at her fingers, as if distressed with herself for failing to clean them.

"I..." she started, face drawing tight. "Well, no, there has never been anything untoward between Master Crownshield and myself. Miss Nellie and I have been too close and I would not overstep the bounds of propriety, nor invade the sanctity of their union. But Master Crownshield, he...well, he forbade me to come here today and as of late his ill temper has become legendary at the Manor. I am afraid he pushed me rather ungently and I fell. He could not help himself, you see. It is this dreadful ghost business and I know he fears he is going insane. I had to promise not to come here this morning."

"But you did, indeed, come, Miss Bickford," said Holmes.

"I had to. If there is a chance this letter comes to pass…"

"Ghosts don't write letters," said Miss Calamity. "Even if such critters were real."

"Nevertheless," said Holmes, "my associates—" He glanced at Miss Calamity with an unreadable look he commonly reserved for me, forthright to dressing me down on some erroneous or misunderstood observation on my part. "—and I will call upon Crownshield Manor by half past eleven."

It was thus one hour hence I found myself in the corner of a first-class carriage *en route* to Crownshield Manor. My friend sat across, walking stick between his legs and his angular features framed beneath his ear-flapped traveling cap. Beside me and regrettably downwind, sat the buckskin-adorned Miss Calamity, a beaming smile upon her lips expressing her chronic delight with the comforts of the vehicle. Our dear woman had seen fit to let not one iota of silence remain undisturbed.

"Mind, gents?" said she, plunging a callused hand beneath her buckskin coat, bringing hither a resurgence in effluvium I could have done without. She liberated a tarnished flask, uncapped it, and as they say in America, "took a swig."

Miss Calamity wiped her mouth upon her forearm and returned the flask to the nether regions of her garments.

"My dear Mrs. Cannary…" said Holmes, a particularly pained expression on his face.

"I keep on tellin' ya, Holmes, it's *Calamity*." Her exasperation had acquired a stature rivaling that of her grand exposition regarding her scouting days, which she had chosen to regale us with the entire journey. "Hell an' tarnation, no wonder I had to solve your case for ya—ya cain't even recollect my name!" She turned to me and Holmes looked exceedingly dubious of his decision to allow her to accompany us on this expedition. "Jesus H., Jeeves, your accounts sure paint a rosy picture this fellow don't rightly deserve, don't they?"

"Madam," said he, "I merely wish to elucidate that with the palsy afflicting your digits I have heretofore observed, the considerably tawny nature of your epidermis, combined with evidence of parotid swelling and undeniable rhinophyma, your condition may well have become dangerously chronic."

Miss Calamity's brow became an expanse of confused lines. "What the hell'd he jest say?" asked she of me.

"I believe my friend is concerned with your health should you continue with your...habit."

Her brows relaxed. "Ah, I git it." She peered at Holmes, her demeanor now amiable. "Right kindly of you, but drinkin' keeps the consumption away, I've always said."

"You do not suffer from Tuberculosis, Madam," said he in all seriousness.

"Well, there ya go!" said she. "'Sides..." Her dark eyes lowered and a distinctly morose flavor betook her features. "You'd lost your ma to washtub pneumonia when you were a young'un you'da took to drinkin' too."

"I am certain," said I, before Holmes could add a match to her incendiary nature with one of his arrogant retorts.

Miss Calamity cast me an expression with which I found little comfort. "You're a right handsome fella there, Jeeves. You ever consider takin' yourself a Yank wife? War's been over a spell, ya know."

"I am certain I have not," said I.

Her hand moved to my knee and I am confident Holmes took far more delight in my dilemma than was appropriate.

"Usually have a fella pay for my favors, but might be willin' to spot ya some for free."

I am sure my groan was audible but a bit of fortune struck as Crownshield Manor came into view.

"Christ on a crutch!" said Miss Calamity, slapping her knee, which meant she thankfully removed her hand from mine. "Will ya git a load of them digs?"

"Them digs," as she expressed it, and in this case could be forgiven for such a display of exuberance, were, indeed, quite a sight. The building sprawled across the horizon in a stately display of architecture that included a moat with drawbridge, gatehouse watchtowers, stables and, according to legend, boasted the grandest conservatory filled with exotic plants and flowers country-wide.

"Reckon I can see as how that little filly Crownshield got hitched to might wanna see him go boots up. Might loosen Cody's saddle myself for a homestead like that."

"My dear woman," said Holmes as the carriage slowed. "It has far from been established by even circumstantial, let alone empirical, evidence that the newly matrimonied Mrs. Nellie Crownshield is guilty of anything more than a stroke of opportunity."

Miss Calamity, clearly a woman of fiery disposition beneath her continual chatter, was at present becoming increasingly disenchanted with my friend's constant contradictions of her exposition.

"You really ain't much of a detective, are ya?" said she.

"You have definitive evidence for Mrs. Crownshield's guilt?" said he.

"Gawdamn, who needs evidence? I have me a scout's intuition. Why, did I tell ya 'bout the time I saved Wyatt Earp's scrawny little ass jest a'cause I could *feel* them Injuns hidin' in the hills?"

"I believe the experiential substantiation of your admittedly colorful life's exaggerated accounts is as flimsy as your suppositions regarding this case."

"You're gettin' right on my last nerve, there, buckaroo." She cast him a most noxious gaze and I was eminently relieved when moments later we found ourselves in Crownshield Manor's grand hall before Miss Calamity decided skinning detectives held much more appeal than relieving mules of their hides.

"Hell's bells…" said she, her gaze sweeping the hall, as did mine. Only my friend appeared ill impressed by the chandeliers of crystal above and the magnificently bannistered center staircase that rose to a mezzanine hallway at its termination. Portraits of what I could only speculate were Crownshield ancestry adorned the walls and various rooms branched off to either side.

"That scent," said Holmes after the doorman had taken his departure.

"Almond, Mr. Detective," said Miss Calamity.

"Almond tea," said a soft voice and our attention traveled to the delicate form of Miss Bickford, who stepped from the drawing room to our right. "Lady Crownshield insists on almond tea. It is her favorite."

Miss Calamity's eyes narrowed as did those sharp orbs of my friend. "Almond tea, huh?" said she, but elaborated on her thoughts no further.

Miss Bickford motioned us to follow her into the drawing room. "Lady Crownshield would be most insulted if you did not partake."

"Long as I can put whiskey in it," said Miss Calamity. "Reckon this ghost of yourn ain't about to kill us all."

The pronouncement brought a peculiar look from Miss Bickford and a resulting one of mockery from Miss Calamity. It was clear there was little love lost between them.

Within the drawing room resided three others. An older woman, muttering to herself, round of stature and wrinkled of face, sat in a winged chair, teacup in her trembling, brown-spotted hands, while a young lady of extraordinary raven hair and exquisite mahogany eyes perched, small hands in her lap, upon the edge of the settee. Master Crownshield stood by the great windows, an expression of deep annoyance assembling on what I judged were once robust features. For Master Crownshield appeared anything but sturdy now, a man reflecting the strain of years yet unlived. It was apparent he was also quite agitated, perhaps even ill. Beads of perspiration stood out on his forehead and his pale flesh appeared mottled with patches of red.

"I forbade you to bring Holmes into it!" said Master Crownshield with entire bluntness and recrimination to Miss Bickford, who was now at the buffet pouring tea into fine China cups.

"Hush, Zephren!" said Lady Crownshield, somewhat more in possession of her faculties than I had believed. "I ordered the poor dear to bring him here. He is going to exorcise the ghost."

"In a manner of speaking," said Holmes.

Master Crownshield exhibited what might only have been described as a grunt, then took a hearty swallow of his tea. I am certain I am not the only one who noticed the manifest trembling of his hand as he lifted the cup to his lips.

Miss Bickford served Homes, Miss Calamity and myself, then went and sat herself beside the young woman on the settee. She tilted her head towards Mrs. Crownshield and placed a hand on the young woman's knee in comfort, but the present Mrs. Crownshield shied away, her carriage becoming rigid. She was struggling to maintain an air of composure, appear a woman of stately strength, but it was merely a façade. For what purpose, however, to display bearing or hide guilt, was as yet to be determined.

"Gawdamn!" said Miss Calamity. "This tastes like horse piss. Don't y'all have Arbuckle's in this country?"

Well, that went over with Lady Crownshield much like the passing of a kidney stone.

"And *wot* is *that?*" said the Lady with a dismissive brush of her head towards Miss Calamity. I did have to admit, however, the almond tea was not to my taste.

"Calamity Jane, straight from the U.S. of A., you ornery old cow," said Miss Calamity, and I was eminently relieved when my friend stepped in to prevent any further exchange of hostility.

"Master Crownshield," said Holmes, placing his tea on the table before the settee, after taking the merest of sips. "Your mother summoned us to the Manor with clear worry over your impending death. According to the note left by this apparition of the former Master of the house, your life was threatened to terminate in full view of witnesses on this very day, precisely in ten minutes, if I judge correctly."

"Hogwash, Mr. Holmes," said Master Crownshield. "There is no such thing as ghosts."

Holmes' sharp gaze studied the man's deathly countenance. "Ah, yet from your observed agitation I would surmise you have indeed glimpsed this specter?"

Master Crownshield shifted feet and his eyelids fluttered. Sweat freely streaked from his temples, which were touched with the merest hint of gray.

"I have seen…nothing," said he.

"Sir, if you intend to fabricate with any degree of efficacy," said Holmes, "perhaps a bit more attention to the modulation of your tone might be in order."

"What?" said Master Crownshield, a curious dilation coming to his eyes.

"You're lyin', bub," said Miss Calamity in a display of graciousness that rivaled the sometimes superior manner of my friend. "Even I got that."

I expected fully that Master Crownshield would take undue umbrage at the statement, but he merely raised a shaking teacup to his lips.

Holmes, who had retained his walking stick, swatted the cup from Master Crownshield's hand quite unceremoniously. It shattered upon the floor.

"How clumsy of me," said Holmes in all innocence.

"Why—" began Master Crownshield, then with great abruptness collapsed to the floor. My friend rushed to him, knelt beside the stricken man, who for a suspended moment clutched at his abdomen, then clearly expired.

A trembling scream came from Master Crownshield's new wife and she jumped to her feet. Miss Bickford rose as well, sought to comfort the distraught young woman by putting an arm about her slim shoulders, but Mrs. Crownshield pulled away, beyond consolation.

Lady Crownshield issued a cackling screech, altogether as unnerving a sound as I had ever heard, then promptly fainted.

"Hell and tarnation!" uttered Miss Calamity.

"I say," said I, "the ghost has made good on his claim." I knew better and without doubt that Holmes would presently enlighten me in his singular manner on that point. For once, I prayed that would be the case.

"Hardly a ghost, my dear fellow," said he, failing to disappoint.

"Bet your britches on that," said Miss Calamity. "Let me take this one, Mr. Detective. Reckon I have it all figgered out—an' you can stop your little act, Missy—" She gazed at Mrs. Crownshield. "We all know who stands to gain the most from your fella's death."

"Do enlighten us, Miss Cannary," said Holmes, rising to his feet.

"For the love of *Gawd*, Holmes, it's *Calamity*." She shook her head and frowned. "First lemme see that note this ghost supposedly writ."

Miss Bickford, with no great enthusiasm, I might add, stepped forward and, after extracting the missive from her apron, handed the paper to Miss Calamity. She then went to Lady Crownshield and made an effort to revive her by patting her brown-stained hands in rapid motion.

"Obliged," said Miss Calamity, but clearly was not. She perused the missive, nodding to herself, and I suspected she was enjoying the sound of her own ruminations.

"Well, Miss—" started Holmes, then hesitated as Miss Calamity cast him a disputatious glare. "—er, Calamity?" he completed.

Miss Calamity dropped the note on the table and gazed at the quivering bride of a few months. "Jest as I figgered. That ghost of yourn, reckon you said it was a man, the former owner of these digs?"

"That's right," said Miss Bickford, having gotten Lady Crownshield at least vaguely conscious. She moved over to Mrs. Crownshield, getting between her and Miss Calamity, as well as aside of Holmes.

"Well, I'm here to tell ya, that note was writ by a woman. Handwritin's too fancy to be a man."

"She's quite correct," said Holmes, nodding. "I noticed it myself upon first viewing. It is exceedingly certain the missive was penned by a woman's hand."

"Well, hell, you're actually good for somethin'," said Miss Calamity, more jest than derision in her tone. "If you'd be so kind…"

My friend issued a curt bow. "Pray continue, my good woman."

"Like I was sayin', the note was writ by a gal—that'd be you, Miss New Wife."

Mrs. Crownshield started. Lady Crownshield uttered a sigh and promptly fainted again.

"That is preposterous!" said Miss Bickford. "Nellie, Mrs. Crownshield, could never do such a thing. I suppose you will accuse her of his death next."

"Well, Missy, that's precisely what I aim to do. She killed him, plain as the nose on your face. She had everything to gain."

"And just how did she accomplish this feat?" asked Holmes, eyebrows assembling into a curiously amused arch.

"Poison!" proclaimed Miss Calamity. "Cyanide, in fact. Everybody knows Cyanide has a bitter almond stink to it."

"And the method of ingestion?" said I.

"Well, Hell's Bells, Jeeves, what does that there tea smell like?" She swung her gaze to my friend. "You knocked that cup outta his hand on purpose, didn't you, Holmes? You suspected he'd probably been drinking it in small doses over the last few weeks."

"Ah, madam," said he. "I must confess I did, indeed."

"Well, see, maybe you're a better detective than I gave you credit for. Case closed—hang the filly and be done with it."

I was forced to admit perhaps Miss Calamity had just, in her unique way, put my friend in his place. The new Mrs. Crownshield did, indeed, stand to profit the most from her husband's untimely death and perhaps her background was now as questionable as rumor had alleged it. Coupled with the feminine handwriting and cyanide delivery in almond tea used to cover the scent…

I noted a sudden hole in Miss Calamity's theory and from the satisfied expression upon my friend's sharp features I knew I was about to hear it stated directly and succinctly.

"Quite an admirable conclusion, my dear—Calamity," said he. "But quite erroneous."

"Huh?" said she.

"I did not kill my husband!" Miss Crownshield spoke up for the first time, her voice as shrill as the upper notes of a violin.

"Indeed, you did not," said Holmes. "And, indeed, Master Crownshield was poisoned."

"But we all drank the tea," said I, stating my perceived flaw in Miss Calamity's theory.

"Undeniably, my dear Watson," said Holmes. "But the solution to that is elementary. The poison was delivered in Master Crownshield's tea, and his tea only, but it was not cyanide. The indicators are quite different."

"If not cyanide, then what?" asked Miss Calamity.

"Note the symptoms: irritability, as stated by Miss Bickford, the red patches upon his flesh and obvious excessive perspiration. He clutched his abdomen before expiring and I noted an extreme dilation of his pupils an instant before I knocked the cup from his hand. His observance of the ghost, despite his denial, was brought on by suggestion and the hallucinatory nature of the toxin."

"Well, spit it out, Mr. Detective," said Miss Calamity. "I'm getting' downright antsy with all this talk"

"An irony, no doubt," said Holmes. "Convallaria majalis."

"Conva-what?" Miss Calamity's brows reached distinctly for her hairline beneath her battered hat, which she had seen fit not to remove.

"A plant that bears orange-red, fleshy berries," said Holmes. "All parts of it are poisonous, even the water. The poison is a glycoside called convallaxotoxin. More commonly it is referred to as Lily of the Valley."

"Where the hell would someone get that?" asked Miss Calamity.

"Crownshield Manor has the most renowned conservatory in England," said I.

"Ok, then how did it get in just his tea and not ours?" Miss Calamity motioned her head towards the body.

"I am sure Miss Bickford might explain that," said Holmes, gazing to the maid, who jolted, a look of guilt assembling on her delicate face.

"How might *I* explain it?' she asked, voice startled.

Holmes took her hands in his, sharp gaze observing their form. They were now clean. "Earlier, your hands were stained with red, but it was not blood from a fall or salacious activities, as my dear Calamity indicated at Baker Street, nor are the scratches the result of such, for they are on the back of your hands. The soil that was beneath your nails and on your ragged cuffs indicated more than a casual acquaintance with the

Crownshield conservatory, I do believe. I would postulate perhaps one of your duties involves tending to the various species of fauna and flora? Ah, yes, indeed it does, I am certain from the increase in perspiration on your palms."

Miss Bickford pulled her hands free. "I do not know what you are alluding to, sir," said she.

"I believe you do, Miss Bickford," said Holmes. "You alone had access to the individual teacups, did you not?"

"I…"

"Perhaps you would be so kind as to provide us with a sample of your handwriting, then?"

A tear rolled down Miss Bickford's face, as good as a confession.

"Hell, I don't git—" Miss Calamity hesitated. "Oh, I see it now. Little Miss Prissy Pants here's in love. I can see it on her face. She wanted Mr. Dead as a Doornail there all to her ownself and when she found she couldn't have him she figgered nobody else would, neither. Hell hath no fury, I'm bettin'. That about nail the coffin closed, Mr. Detective?" Miss Calamity appeared entirely proud of her deduction. I might have informed her from experience of the adage concerning pride and falls.

"Not entirely," said Holmes. "Miss Bickford is, indeed, in love, but not with Master Crownshield. One of an observant persuasion might have noted Miss Bickford's previous predilection with comforting Mrs. Crownshield through the difficulties, perhaps the tilt of her head towards the young woman and the blush on her face. I believe Mrs. Crownshield knew of her friend's—perhaps former friend's—affection and spurned it. She noticeably retracted from Miss Bickford's console." Mrs. Crownshield nodded, tears running down her face. She uttered a small sound and stepped back from the maid. "Need I continue, Miss Bickford?" Holmes added.

"No…" said Miss Bickford.

"Oh, my," said I.

"Oh, hell…" said Miss Calamity.

It was thus with merely a blink Miss Bickford drew a derringer from the folds of her apron and sought to bring it to bear on my friend.

My friend issued a causal snap of his walking stick, sending the derringer to the floor. At the same instant, Miss Calamity produced an overly large firearm from the depths of her buckskin coat in what I believe the Americans refer to as "the fast draw." To say I was amazed she had concealed it upon her person the entire time was perhaps an understatement.

"You're right fast there, Mr. Detective," said she, giving my friend an approving nod and a regrettable expression of awe at his deductive prowess I was all too familiar with.

"Likewise," said he, kicking the derringer away. Miss Bickford remained massaging her hand, but offered no further resistance or threat, while Mrs. Crownshield knelt and wept beside the body of her husband.

"Maybe you *do* deserve your reputation, after all," said Miss Calamity, moments later as we rode in the carriage back to Baker Street.

"Perhaps yours is not as…overstated as I originally believed," said Holmes, though I took the distinct impression he was being merely patronizing.

"You ever find yourself in need of a wife…" Miss Calamity chuckled and withdrew a worn, leather-covered notebook and stub of a pencil from beneath her buckskins.

"What is that for, Miss Calamity?" said I, as she opened the notebook and began writing.

"Hell and tarnation," said she. "Somebody's gotta write this down and I've heard you're prone to exaggeration."

I nodded, Holmes' casual smile of satisfaction no greater than my inward pleasure as I noted Miss Calamity's first line: "How I Saved Sherlock Holmes…"

THE ADVENTURE OF THE
SINISTER CHINAMAN

by
Barbara Hambly

As the reputation of Mr. Sherlock Holmes advanced, his freedom to choose his cases—adhered to even in early days when the pair of us were occasionally beholden to Mrs. Hudson's grace in the matter of rent—increased. Astute investments by Holmes' brother, Mycroft, eventually freed him from the need to accept cases that did not present features of interest to him which would broaden his own experience.

One exception which he made to this rule was in the spring of 1901, when he agreed to investigate the persecution of American railroad magnate Hollis Connington, a case which both bored and annoyed him and which he undertook—I believe—for the sole reason that it followed hard upon my own near-fatal bout of pleurisy. Dr. Stamford at Bart's was adamant in recommending a sea voyage for my cure, and Connington's mansion and headquarters lay in San Francisco.

When Holmes informed Connington by telegram that my assistance was a condition of his handling the case, Connington—a miser who had, by Holmes' later count, twenty-four active candidates for the role of chief suspect in the attempts upon his life—reluctantly agreed, but took a petty revenge. While Holmes was lodged in the Palace Hotel in the city itself, I was put up in a modest boarding establishment across the bay in Berkeley. This circumstance led us both into a case which, Holmes said, made the entire California excursion worthwhile, and introduced us to that extraordinary madman, the balloonist and prestidigitator, Oscar Zoroaster Diggs.

Mrs. Ellen Carey's boarding-house on Telegraph Avenue was patronized chiefly by members of the local theatrical profession: actors, vaudevillians, magicians, acrobats, chorus-girls, a keeper of trained dogs, and a Central European harpist who spoke no language intelligible to anyone in the city. Holmes naturally found this company far more congenial than anything on offer at the Palace Hotel, and formed the habit of arriving for dinner—having swiftly won the approval of Mrs. Carey— and remaining all evening to listen to the professional small-talk in the parlor. Diggs was frequently the center of this group, partly on account of his truly astonishing adeptness in the arts of illusion, and partly on account of the warm friendliness of his personality, which accepted all humanity as sisters and brothers encountered upon a wonderful journey. He was, as Hamlet says, "mad north north-west," seeming perfectly sane in all respects except for the delusion—apparently believed in firmly by himself—that he had spent the past forty years of his life stranded in Fairyland due to a ballooning accident. His adventures there formed a cycle of tales that made him a great favorite with Mrs. Carey's four children and the assorted juvenile vaudevillians of the household, and which, I must confess, hugely entertained me as well.

On a certain Friday evening, Diggs had undertaken to teach Holmes the Illusion of the Seven Knives, so Holmes was at first vexed upon his arrival to discover that the little wizard was not at the communal supper-table. But his annoyance was swiftly swept away when Enzo Moretti (of the Flying Moretti Brothers) explained, with great concern, that Diggs had gone down to the Geary Street Precinct House in the city, to see what could be done for the Celestial Sorcerer, Li. "And he's a braver man than I, Mr. Holmes," said Moretti, shaking his head. "They arrested Li last night after the show, but when men get drinking after work, and talking each other up in the saloons along Market Street, there's danger they'll mob the jail, and lynch Li out of hand."

I said, "What on earth for?" and Holmes asked, "Have they found some further proof?" I had spent the day walking among the astounding beauties of the near-by California forests with friends I had met on the voyage, while Holmes, in between tracking down the movements of a number of Mr. Connington's relations, had been drinking coffee, smoking, and reading newspapers. Of course, he had already heard the story which was related to me.

Julian Li was a young illusionist of Chinese extraction, though both his parents had been born in California to immigrants from the great Gold Rush of 1849. He was well-known in the vaudeville circuits of the Western states and promised to become one of the finest practitioners of his trade in the country. The finale of his act involved what our table-mates referred to as a "Magic box gag," meaning that a member of the audience was placed in a cabinet on one part of the stage, and "miraculously" transported to a corresponding box on the other side of the stage – both boxes being ostensibly suspended in mid-air. On the previous evening, the sixth of June, at the Californian Theater in San Francisco, the subject of this illusion had been a six-year-old girl from the near-by community of Sausolito, Emily Redwalls. She had entered the "magic cabinet" at one side of the stage, but after the obligatory flash of light and puff of smoke, when the second cabinet was opened, the child was nowhere to be seen.

Antonio Rosales, the stagehand who had helped Li, swore that he had placed the child in the second cabinet (which was a great deal closer to the backdrop than the illusory lighting had led the audience to believe). The child's parents were distraught, and rumor had flashed through the white community that Li had kidnapped the little girl for unspeakable purposes: "Though surely if one were to descend to the unspeakable," commented Holmes dryly, "even the most sinister criminal would hardly care to do so in front of four hundred people."

"Three-hundred and eighty-seven," corrected Mrs. Carey, who had a very good sense of any performance's daily "gate."

"Oz said this afternoon he'd go across and see what could be done about posting bail," said Mrs. Pellingham, a diminutive actress who specialized in ingénue roles despite the possession of daughters almost old enough to take on such roles themselves. "We all chipped in for bail, of course, but I told him he's wasting his time. A Chinese that's kidnapped a little white girl? He'll be lucky if the police don't kill him themselves. Oz allowed I had the right of it," she added sadly, "but he said, he couldn't not go."

Holmes glanced across at me, and within minutes, he and I were in a cab, hastening to catch the last ferry of the evening. The dense fog that characterizes the city was rising from the bay by the time we arrived at the Geary Street Station, and found, to our alarm, a considerable crowd of rough-clothed workingmen, as Enzo Moretti had predicted, gathered on the station-house steps in furious altercation with the station chief and O.Z. Diggs himself. Since a number of these men were armed—some with the tools of various trades, such as hammers and crowbars, but several, in proper American fashion, with pistols and rifles—I was just as happy to see they were already beginning to disperse as Holmes and I approached. I heard one of the men on the steps snarl, "He's a goddamn *Chinaman*, for Chrissakes! How do I know why he'd do it?"

And another added as he passed me, "They don't think like we do," and tapped the side of his head. "Inscrutable. It's like they ain't even human—"

"And what do you call human?" I began angrily, but Holmes took me by the elbow and propelled me up the steps.

"Fifty years ago I heard the police in New York say that about the Irish," sighed Diggs, and the station-chief—just closing the door behind us as we entered the gaslight of the watchroom—bridled.

"That ain't the same thing," he objected. "You have only to look at him—"

"Do I, sir?" retorted the little wizard. "In my carpet-bag I have two bottles and a jar whose contents will transform you, sir, into a Mexican or a Comanche or a Chinaman yourself...Good Heavens, Holmes, am I glad to see you! And Dr. Watson! Captain O'Day, allow me to present Mr. Sherlock Holmes, of London, and Dr. Watson—gentlemen who have been retained to investigate the circumstances of Miss Redwalls' disappearance and to act in Mr. Li's defense."

Since neither of us had spoken one word to Diggs, my surprise at this prescience must have shown on my face. As Holmes was shaking Captain O'Day's hand, Diggs sidled up to me and murmured, "To the Great Oz the minds of lesser men are an open book—particularly men with whose decency and goodness of heart he is familiar. Why else would you have rushed from dinner to take the last ferry over here? Thank you."

Meanwhile Captain O'Day, a pink-faced Hibernian to the toes of his boots, was saying doubtfully, "And who'll it be that's retaining you, Mr. Holmes? There's not a lawyer in the city'll touch the case."

"A situation which may alter tomorrow," replied Holmes smoothly. "By which time, valuable evidence at the scene of the disappearance may be ineradicably lost. Suffice it to say that I am being retained—" He produced a letter of introduction from his pocket and displayed the signature of Hollis Connington, then slipped it away again as the Captain's eyes widened. "—by one who wishes, for the time being, to remain completely anonymous."

"Of course, Mr. Holmes. Any way that I may be of assistance to you—"

"First, I think," said Holmes, "we need to visit the Californian Theater."

"Of course. Will you wish to see Li before you go down?"

"When we return. Will Mr. Rosales be at the theater?"

"He should be by now, Mr. Holmes. The theater being closed today, he and Diaz, the day man, have been there merely as watchmen, but they may be clearing the place up for tomorrow's performance."

O'Day escorted us to the theater himself—so far did awe of Hollis Connington's name run in California, though as far as I knew the man himself was responsible for the deaths of hundreds of Li's fellow Orientals through overwork and the refusal to implement the smallest safety precautions during the building of his railroad lines. The Californian stood on Leavenworth Street, halfway up one of the city's hills, a vaudeville-house with a seating capacity of perhaps five-hundred and a truly impressive array of backstage mirrors, hoists, electrical lights with colored lenses, pulleys, trap-doors, and duplicate backdrops. Diaz, the day watchman, was still there when we arrived. Antonio Rosales appeared a few minutes later, and repeated to us what he had told the police last night.

"La niña, I take her out of the cabinet at once through the false back, while the Chinaman is still showing the audience there is no false back. Of course, she all excited to be part of the trick. The other cabinet, he has already raise it—"

I mounted the short flight of portable steps to examine the opening in the backdrop which would be opposite the false back of the second cabinet—an opening too small for an adult to pass through.

"I help her through, in the second where Li set off his flash-powder—" Rosales shook his head. "I swear there was no way out of the cabinet."

O'Day said somberly, "They found her shoe in that heathen cabinet, Mr. Holmes. Her *shoe*. Her poor mother fainted when she saw it."

Holmes opened his mouth to speak, then seemed to think better of it, and merely said, "And all else has been left precisely as it was?"

"The police, they come, they look around," provided Diaz. "Me, I stay back. Captain he say, don't touch nothing, and I don't, all day I been here." And as if to prove his innocence in this matter, Diaz retired to a corner of the backstage, withdrew a sack of coarse tobacco from his shirt-pocket, and proceeded to roll and smoke a cigarette.

"Excellent," said Holmes. "Those trunks over there—?" He nodded towards three large steamer-trunks, lichenous with travel-stickers, brass corners winking in the gaslight backstage.

"Those'll be the Count's trunks—Count Paracelsus, the other magician on the bill," said the police-captain. "Believe me, Mr. Holmes, that was the first place we looked. Li had four trunks back there, where that empty space is. They're at the station-house now, what's left of 'em. We had the false bottoms out of 'em, false linings, everything. Not a sign."

"Hmm. Even were Li so inscrutable as to display his kidnapping before three-hundred and eighty-seven people whom he *knew*—being a native of this country—would not hesitate to lynch him, he would naturally hesitate about caching the girl in the false bottom of his own trunk." Holmes looked around him at the vast, dim-lit cavern of the backstage, with its flickering globes of gaslight. "Mr. Rosales, is there any electricity laid on back here? I'm going to need to make a thorough search of the room, and in this light it is virtually impossible to distinguish details—"

The stagehand shook his head. "The only electric is on the stage—"

"Nonsense, man, where's your imagination?" demanded Diggs briskly. "I'm sure Benny Park—excuse me, Count Paracelsus—won't grudge us a little flash-powder in a good cause..." So saying, he dug a couple of lengths of wire and a little tool like a flattened-out salt-spoon from his vest pocket, and proceeded to open the Count's trunk. From a paper twist abstracted therefrom, he shook a few grains of gray powder onto a saucer, spread them out thin with one of his picklocks, and lighted them, resulting in a white glare so brilliant as to be impossible to look at directly.

Diaz and O'Day squinted and covered their eyes. Rosales shook his head, muttered, "You gonna burn the theater down, señor—"

"Nonsense," retorted Diggs. "A few grains at a time should give us all the illumination required."

The two stagehands were relegated to the front of the house, while the police-captain and I retreated to the corner by the door and Holmes, with Diggs following behind as lamp-bearer, made his usual thorough investigation of the whole of the backstage, including both "magical cabinets" and the three dressing-rooms which opened from the backstage area. These last were so crammed with filmy costumes, wigs, and yet more trunks that I feared that between them, Holmes and the Great Oz would indeed set fire to the theater.

This investigation concluded—the cessation of the magnesium-white light made the ensuing gloom almost like blindness—Holmes wrapped his findings, which seemed to me to consist entirely of dust and cigarette-ends, in brightly-colored silk handkerchiefs likewise abstracted from Count Paracelsus' trunk, and called the stagehands back. "Is it certain that nothing was touched here since the girl's disappearance?"

"Nothing," said Rosales. "Have you found anything, señor? If you have, tell us, man! When I think of that poor little girl—" He mopped his brow—I noticed, bemused, that he must be a ladies' man enough to seek the illusion of youth in a dye-bottle—and wrung his hands with anxiety.

"I know nothing," murmured Holmes. "Yet. When is the floor swept here backstage? I observe it's fairly free of accumulated dust—"

"I go over it good, about three in the afternoon," said Diaz, "so it's clean for the evening show."

"And you did not do so this afternoon, on account of the police?"

"That's right, señor."

"Thank you," said Holmes, and handed each of them a half-dollar. "Captain O'Day, might it be possible, without going into any specific names—" He touched his breast-pocket where the letter of introduction from Connington resided, "—to keep the theater closed down for yet another day? I will relay an account of your obligingness to...*whosoever* I feel would be interested to hear it." He smiled a secretive smile. "Now perhaps we could speak with Mr. Li?"

Julian Li was tall for a Chinese, in his late twenties, and wore his hair in the traditional queue. He spoke perfect English with the usual flat American vowels, and though when first we entered his cell—it was now about ten o'clock at night—he started up in wary alarm, but when he saw Diggs with us he relaxed at little. In the dim gaslight I saw that one of his eyes had been blackened, and his face bore other bruises. His friends at the boarding-house had not been far amiss in their fears of a lynching.

"And I'm afraid it won't stop with me," he said, almost whispering, when I exclaimed at his hurts. "My parents have already left town, but if a mob formed, no one would ask if the Chinese whose houses they were burning were related to me or not. A Chink is a Chink." Bitterness wrung his voice like poison. "One's as bad as another."

"I am assuming," said Holmes, "that anyone who wished to kidnap a child wouldn't do so in so public a venue as the Californian theater—"

"Good God, no!" cried the young man, truly distressed. "When I opened the cabinet and saw nothing there but her shoe, it was like someone had knocked the wind out of me with the end of a pole. I was too shocked to speak, and stood there like a fool until her mother screamed. What did they expect I would have done? Shouted, *Ha-ha, I have spirited away your child?*" He clasped his hands, which shook at the memory of the shock.

"Precisely," said Holmes. "Therefore this is an attack upon the child herself—and twenty years in my business has shown me that one cannot discount the possibility of an obsessed madman—upon the child's family, upon yourself, or upon the Chinese community here as a whole. Which do you yourself think it might be?"

Li's eyes shifted. He looked aside, and for a long time sat silent, his hands pressed together. Then he said, "There is always hatred for my people, since the time my grandparents came to this country."

"A rather elaborate way of stirring it up, I should think," said Holmes, watching the young man's face intently. "As far as Captain O'Day could tell me—and so far as any newspaper knows—John Redwalls and his wife are completely unremarkable people without enemies. How did you happen to choose Miss Redwalls to assist you in your act?"

"Well," said Li, and his gaze returned to Holmes' face, "I generally pick a child—you've seen the apparatus of the cabinets, and a small opening in the backdrop can be concealed much more easily with mirrors and lighting than a larger one. And people pay more attention when it's a child. They keep their eyes on the first cabinet while she's being slipped into the second. I watch their faces as the audience comes in, and look for one who's bright and who…who looks outward, who'll go along with it when I whisper—" His voice shifted into the accents of melodramatic stage-pidgin, "—*Honorable Miss will not split on insignificant Li, will she?* It makes them laugh," he added, with a faint smile. "You can tell looking at them, who might think it's funny to come out of the cabinet and shout to the audience, *It's all a trick.* Miss Redwalls wasn't that sort. She was a perfect accomplice."

He pressed his hand suddenly to his mouth, his face working with horror and shock.

Holmes asked, "Was the shoe fastened or unfastened?"

Li raised his head, his eyes haunted. "The laces had been cut with a knife."

"But there was really no way of telling in advance," Holmes went on, "which child in the audience you would choose for your act?"

"No."

"Only that it would be a child."

Li nodded. "Did you find anything at the theater? Was Rosales able to tell you anything?"

"One or two items of interest," said Holmes. "Would Rosales himself have had any reason to take the child?"

"I can think of none. He came to the theater well-recommended. I think he's had experience as an illusionist himself, so he needed very little coaching in his duties."

"Yes, I thought he had," said Holmes. "When the Great Oz lit up some flash-powder to aid in my investigation of the scratches on the floor, I noticed he turned away and shaded his eyes beforehand. And the dyed hair points to the stage as well. Do you think he is a man who could be bribed?"

"By whom?" asked Diggs in surprise, and Holmes turned back to Li, and raised his brows.

The prisoner whispered, "Any man can be bribed."

"Surely in so horrible a crime," I objected, "the man behind a bribe places himself in the hands of his accomplice. And if the man *were* bribed, who then would bribe him? And why?"

"Why, indeed?" Holmes kept his gaze on Li, who continued to look down at his own hands, and did not reply. "Is this all you have to tell us?"

After several more minutes' silence, Li whispered, "It is."

"The man is screening someone!" murmured Diggs, as a police-officer showed us out of the cells and along the corridor to the watchroom. "With his life—and the lives of hundreds of people, perhaps, in Chinatown—hanging in the balance."

"Obviously," returned Holmes, in an undervoice barely louder than breath, "someone of critical importance to him."

It was now close to midnight, the fog outside the station-house a black wall only dimly pierced by far-spaced street-lamps. As there was now no question of me or Diggs being able to cross the Bay back to Berkeley, Holmes inquired of the nearest hotel, which was on Union Square, a few blocks along. I admit I was not sorry about this, for the day had been an extremely tiring one and my own constitution had not recovered from my illness of the spring. We had gone but a half-block, when I touched Holmes' arm, holding him back. The three of us halted, and for an instant, I heard the moist tap of feet behind us in the fog before they, too, stopped.

Holmes' hand touched mine, signaling that he had heard, and we walked on, then stopped again. Again the following footsteps silenced. Holmes said—for the benefit of our unseen friend—"Damn this fog! We shall be lost like Hansel and Gretel in the woods."

"The Great Oz knows all things," chipped in Diggs serenely. "This way…Do you call this fog, man?" He led on, and Holmes slipped away into an alley between two buildings. "Why, when I went into battle against the Wicked Witch of the East and her evil minions, she called darkness a thousand times more dreadful than this, just by pouring ink onto her mirror—"

His voice must have successfully lured our following footpad past Holmes' hiding-place. The next thing we knew, I heard a sharp scuffle behind us, and a voice gasped, "Oh! Let me go!"

Diggs and I doubled back at once, groping our way along the wet brick wall in the darkness—away from the blurry glow of the few street-lamps it was like being at the bottom of a cavern—until we reached Holmes and his captive. "You have trailed us from the police-station, Madame," Holmes said. "Yet had your intentions been honest, I think you would have screamed to find yourself seized—"

"I will scream," threatened the young woman, as Diggs and I came up.

"My dear young lady, there is absolutely no need to do so," said Diggs. "You obviously wanted to follow us, out of all the middle-aged gentlemen in the city, so here we are at your service…Are you a friend of Mr. Li?"

She whispered in a small voice, "I am."

"Then come with us to the parlor of what I hope is to be our hotel for the night," he said, "and tell us all about it."

Her name was Diana Prince, and she worked as a typist for a firm of importers on Grant Avenue, near the wharves. In the better light of the parlor of the Kearney Hotel, I took note of the worn and slightly faded condition of the neat jacket, skirt, and shirtwaist she wore, and of their exquisite neatness. The cameo at her throat was no piece of costume jewelry, but a simple and expensive piece that precisely matched her ladylike, well-educated manners and speech. In her hazel eyes was the calm strength of a woman who, though young, has had to make her own way in the world; in the firmness of her mouth, the determination of a woman who knows her mind…and her heart.

"I didn't dare go to the station myself to ask to see Julian," she told us, with a glance across the parlor at the desk where the night-porter dozed. "I knew it would only make matters the worse for him, if the men there suspected he was engaged to a white woman. Yet he's told me about you, Professor Diggs—" She smiled at the wizard. "—and I've seen you on stage, when you and Julian were on the same bill. I hoped to speak with you alone, not knowing who your friends were."

"Is it only the opinion of the police, and the public, that you fear?" inquired Holmes. "Or is there opposition from another quarter as well?"

Miss Prince raised her chin. "If you mean my family," she said, "I have had no contact with my father for three years now. I was of age when I left his house, and will need no permission of his to wed. Still, Julian and I have been deeply discreet. I doubt my father even knows where I am living. But you see what this country is, Mr. Holmes. I'm sure you can guess at the kind of violence that would be unleashed against a man of Julian's race, should he take unto himself an American bride. Now that you have found my secret, I can only beg of you to keep it—and to tell me, is there any hope of finding the true kidnapper of that poor child? For only in recovering her unhurt—and that, quickly—will there be any salvation for the man I love."

"It's true," I said, for Holmes' interest in sensational crime had given me, over the past twenty years, a great knowledge of the darker paths of human conduct. "God save him if the child is found dead."

"Three hours ago, Miss Prince," said Holmes, "I would have said your fiancé's fate hung in the balance. Yet I begin to see a glimmer of light, and I hope, by tomorrow evening, to have better news to tell you, if, as Watson points out, the child is not found dead in the meantime. Do not wait up for me, Watson." He fetched his own greatcoat and our guest's well-worn cloak from the rack beside the porter's desk. "I shall return to the Palace once I have seen Miss Prince to her lodgings, and shall probably be abroad as soon as it grows light enough for the ferries to run. But please tell Mrs. Carey that I shall come to the boarding-house for dinner tomorrow evening—this evening, I should say, rather, for it is all of three o'clock!

And then, if you aren't knocked entirely into horse-nails by our adventures, perhaps we three can pay a call tonight."

Professor Diggs and I had taken two adjoining rooms with a sitting-room the size of Mrs. Hudson's dining-table between them. As we ascended the stairs, Diggs sighed, and shook his head. "It's a bad business, Watson. A bad business. When I left this country, forty years ago, we were in the midst of a war to make an end of slavery; to make an end, many of us dared hope, to injustice as well. And in the years I spent away—organizing the realm and building a city of emeralds, and trying to convince the real witches that ruled that country that I was not only a real wizard but more powerful than they—I often dreamed of my own land, and of what it had become and was becoming in my absence...Something beautiful, I hoped. Something shining and filled with promise, better even than the magic realm where I ruled. And coming home I have found..."

His brow contracted, with grief and pain.

I reflected on the men I'd seen gathered outside the jail, and on what I knew would happen should the poor child be found dead on the morrow. I had to admit that in recovering his sanity (for so I interpreted his "return" from years in his private world), he had perhaps not had the best of the bargain. But I said, "We go where we are sent, Oz, that we may fight the battles we find there. It is all men can do."

"I suppose," said the wizard. "And all we can do is our best. But on nights like this, I do sorely miss the City of Emeralds. Good-night, Watson. And thank you."

Professor Diggs and I returned to Berkeley mid-morning, and that same afternoon Sherlock Holmes arrived, driving a rented buggy behind a fast-stepping team and clothed—improbably if extremely convincingly—as a Methodist preacher, an outfit which he quickly changed (with the critical assistance of half of Mrs. Carey's boardinghouse) for the calico dress and gray wig of an elderly practical nurse. He gave a few instructions to Diggs as to the contents of the carpet-bag he should bring along, and within forty-five minutes the three of us were on the road again, bound for the small communities of wine-growers and ranchers on the hills above Point Richmond.

"I have found the man, and I have found the girl," he informed us shortly, as he drove. "I can keep him busy for perhaps twenty minutes, but certainly no more than that, as his suspicions may have been aroused by my visit earlier today in the guise of the Reverend Cleaver. There's a small waste-space at the peak of the house, above the second floor. Its only ventilation is a screened and louvered opening at the gable end, half-concealed behind the exposed roof-trusses. The gable end of the house faces the loft of the stable."

"Hence," said Diggs grimly, "your request for a rope and my air-gun." And he opened the carpet-bag to show me an air-rifle which had been modified to fire a spring-activated grappling-hook. "The secret of my version of the Indian rope-trick," he added ruefully. "It's quite amazing what people don't see, if you convince them to look the other way."

"Precisely," responded Holmes, "what the three of us shall be doing this evening."

"But how did you find the man?" I asked. "Was it indeed a madman who had somehow become obsessed with the little girl?"

"It is a madman," said Holmes, and his gray eyes glinted coldly behind the fussy spectacles of his latest disguise. "Yet not in the way that you think, Watson. A coldly calculating and monstrously vain madman—ah!" he added with satisfaction. "Here we are. We shall walk from here. The vine-rows will give us cover, almost to the stable itself."

I was taken aback at the wealth and comfort implied by the property to which we had come, a handsome ranch not far from the village of San Pablo. Like many wealthy Californians, its owner had planted several acres in vines, and, as Holmes had predicted, he, Diggs and I were able to crouch between them and traverse the ground from the back-lane where we left the buggy, almost to the rear wall of the stable which backed the house. Twilight had come by this time, and the staff had gone to their dinners in the bunk-house. "We are just in time," whispered Holmes. "He knows we are on his track. He waits only for darkness himself, to get the girl away from the house. You must be swift, for he has a certain amount of wealth and power, and all depends upon catching him red-handed."

So saying he left us, and I saw him—as he walked toward the lane that led to the house from the main road—shrink his tall form into that of a formidable old lady, as he tottered, leaning on his stick, towards the door. Meanwhile Diggs and I scrambled up the ladder to the loft-room, Diggs assembling his air-gun and grappling-hook as we crossed to the loft-window that overlooked the house.

"Even at a moment like this," I sighed—more in bemusement than exasperation, after all the years of our partnership—"he cannot bear to speak a word of what is going on…"

"My dear Watson," replied Diggs. "He would not be Sherlock Holmes if he were not a showman in his soul. Certainly he would never be able to convince our culprit that he is a garrulous old lady who must be dealt with, were he other than he is. What a prestidigitator he would be!" So saying, the wizard braced his feet, took aim at the sideways K of trusses that lay just under the overhang of the gable-end roof, and fired, the grappling-hook—with some thirty feet of light rope attached—whipping soundlessly across the distance and engaging itself in the woodwork with barely a clank.

"Now, listen," said Oz, as he wrapped our end of the rope twice around a rafter, and put the end in my hands. "Once I cross over, I'm going to free the grapple and re-tie the rope onto the beams. When I give the rope a shake, you're to pull hard. You must keep constant tension on the knot, or it will give way. I should be back—" He slipped a pulley-mount over the rope, "—in five minutes—"

"But have you the slightest idea whose house this is?" I asked. "Or why he would have kidnapped a child – or *how* he would have done so, for that matter?"

"Not the slightest," replied the wizard cheerfully. "Does it matter? I'm sure Holmes will explain it all, after our exclamations of delight. And even did he not—" He slung a loop of strapping beneath the pulley, and slipped his head and shoulders through it, "—so long as the child is recovered, and justice is served, is he not free to serve Justice in whatever fashion he chooses? Alley-oop!"

And with me hanging hard onto the end of the rope, Oz crossed the line like an acrobat, hanging from the pulley, to the truss-beams of the house. The slow settling of the twilight prevented me from seeing clearly, but I assumed he had chisels and a screwdriver in his pockets, for a few moments later I saw the louvered screen beyond the truss-beams change to a gaping black square, perhaps eighteen inches in width. The rope was shaken, and I leaned upon it with all my strength, and within moments I felt again the weight of the man as he re-emerged and hung from the harness, the child clinging to his back.

For all the horrors of her experience, Emily Redwalls must indeed have been, as the Celestial Li had described her, a bright and outward-looking little girl—game and not cowed—for she clung to Oz's back as they crossed on the spider-thread of the line over the stable-yard, thirty feet across and a good twenty-five feet above the dirt. When they reached the loft window in safety and I slacked my hold on the line, Oz knelt so that Emily could reach the ground, then turned back to give a vigorous shake to the line on which his own life and the child's had depended. Hair-raisingly, it promptly released the knot that held it to the beams on the other end. He gathered it in as I knelt before Emily.

"Are you all right?"

She nodded. Even in the near-dark of the loft she was a pretty child, her blond curls disheveled and the light-colored calico of her dress rumpled and dirtied from the attic where she had been kept. She shed not a tear, only clung around my neck as the Great Oz and I hastened down the ladder and through the vine-rows back to the buggy. Holmes was waiting for us, once more in shirt and trousers, and stripping off his wig even as we came up.

"Is this she? Good girl!" he cried, as Emily settled on the buggy-seat between us.

"And not a sound," said Oz approvingly. "You'd think she'd been being rescued from dungeons all her life, eh, Emily?"

"I know how to make a getaway," replied the girl with dignity. "Can I go home now?" And she clung for a moment to the wizard's hand.

"We need to make one stop," he promised, as Holmes lashed the team into a canter. "At the sheriff's office in San Pablo, to arrest the man who kidnapped you—What was his name, Holmes?"

"Prince," said Holmes grimly. "Marshall Prince."

In fact, we made two stops before returning Emily Redwalls to her parents, for the San Pablo sheriff, even before Holmes could suggest it, immediately returned with us to the ranch-house, to find Diana Prince's father shouting at his stable-hands to hurry as they harnessed his buggy and loaded his carpet-bags into it. "Prince," said the sheriff wryly, "I'm pleased to see you on your feet. I hear tell as you've been ill this past month."

"I have," snapped the rancher, a tallish man with the swarthy sunburned skin of an outdoorsman, and a thick shock of white hair. "And I'll thank you—" He looked past the sheriff at Emily, sitting in the buggy between me and Oz, even as Holmes, coming up on his other side, reached over and with a quick tweak pulled the white wig from Prince's head. The transformation was startling. With the black hair underneath – even given the bad lighting of the stableyard, and Prince's white mustache—the face of Antonio Rosales seemed to leap into being.

"No, you don't," added Holmes, catching Prince's wrist as the rancher grabbed for something on the buggy-seat. The sheriff whipped his sidearm (this was America, after all) from its openly-worn holster, and held a revolver on Prince while Holmes removed the pistol from the buggy-seat.

"I'll have your job for this!" Prince yelled at the sheriff, as he was taken away. "I got you elected, and I can have you broken!"

"My attention was first drawn to Antonio Rosales," said Holmes, much later that evening, in the cozy parlor of Mrs. Carey's with perhaps the most appreciative audience of his life gathered around on the worn couches and pouffes, "by the circumstance of his hair having been dyed. This I saw the moment Diggs provided decent lighting for my search with Count Paracelsus' flash-powder. It was white at the roots. The man might simply have been vain of his appearance, but coupled with the fact that he was clearly familiar with the techniques of stage magicians suggested a direction in which to look. My suspicion increased when I found no fewer than four cigarette-ends crushed out on the backstage floor—commercially manufactured cigarettes. Old Judge, in fact, when as you saw, the local Mexican workingman like Mr. Diaz invariably smokes hand-rolled Bull Durham."

"And Diaz swept the backstage floor before going off-work every night!" cried Gino Moretti triumphantly. "So they got to have been Rosales'!"

"Precisely," said Holmes, much pleased.

"Where did he put her?" asked Oz. "I'd have thought in a false-bottomed stage-trunk, but they searched all of Li's—"

"What they didn't search," replied Holmes, "was the trunks in the dressing-rooms. Fresh scratches on the floor showed me that a trunk had been dragged into the backstage from the alley door that evening, dragged from there into one of the dressing-rooms, and dragged out again, probably much later that evening when everyone was gone…"

"My father had several," said Diana Prince quietly. "He was a magician before he went into banking – he never would tell us, my poor mother and I, where his money had come from." Her hand closed around that of Julian Li, sitting beside her on the overstuffed chesterfield, as if she could not believe that he had actually been released in safety. "He used to lock me into one of them, when I was little, as punishment."

"The sheriff found such a trunk in your father's basement," said Holmes. "The lining still reeked of the chloroform he used to render his victim unconscious. He's lucky," he added, with the coldness that was always a danger-sign with Holmes, "that the poor child was still alive when he finally brought her out of it."

"Is she all right?" asked Li, and Holmes nodded.

"I think you underestimated your father's power, Miss Prince," he said. "And his vindictiveness, when it came to his ears that his daughter had become secretly engaged to a Chinese—and a vaudevillian, at that. As a banker and a wealthy rancher, he could have used his influence to hush the matter up, but that was not good enough. He had to end the matter—to make sure nothing came of it, by whatever means came to hand."

"Would he actually have killed the girl?" asked Rozanov the dog-trainer. "It is inconceivable—"

"Unfortunately," said Holmes, "it isn't. And, yes, I believe that after Professor Diggs and police-captain O'Day managed to disperse the first mob that approached the jail the night of Li's arrest, Prince's next step would have been to have the girl's body found—in whatever shocking circumstances he could devise—to make certain that the jail was mobbed, and his unwanted prospective son-in-law lynched."

"It's why he threw her shoe into the second cabinet," said Diana Prince quietly. "That was just like Father—that showmanship, that *melodrama*. Yes," she said, turning to Rozanov, "he would have killed her, with no more thought about her being a human being than he had about Julian being a man like himself. Like me, they were only *things* that got in his way."

Holmes, Diggs, and I all testified at Marshall Prince's trial for kidnapping, and were duly sued by his lawyers, not only for slander but for breaking and entering, charges which were summarily thrown out of the California courts.

Prince was convicted, and sentenced to twenty years' imprisonment. Nevertheless, Julian and Diana Li left San Francisco and re-settled in the Chinese community in New York, from which residence they continue to send myself and Holmes small notes and Christmas greetings each year.

Holmes' eventual discovery that Hollis Connington's entire persecution had been arranged by the railroad magnate himself, as a means of purging his family and corporation of disloyal members, resulted in Holmes leaving his employ a few days after the Prince trial—and in Connington's repudiation of the Palace hotel bill. Fortunately, we had purchased return-tickets.

On our journey back across the country to take ship for Liverpool, I had occasion, in Omaha, Nebraska, to look up Oscar Zoroaster Diggs. And I learned—rather disconcertingly—that the Professor Diggs we had known in San Francisco was something of an imposter himself. The original OZ Diggs, who had indeed vanished in a ballooning accident in 1861, had been at that time some sixty-three years of age, making it impossible for our Professor Diggs to have been one and the same man, unless of course one believes that a man stranded for forty years in Fairyland does not age. Who he really was—and why he had taken on the earlier Great Oz's identity—I never learned.

As for Professor Diggs himself, he vanished the following year, during another ballooning expedition in Central California. I have often wondered whether that remarkable little madman – far saner than the madman Prince, whom he had helped Holmes bring to justice—ever in fact managed to find his way back to his City of Emeralds.

I can only hope that he did.

The FOLLY OF FLIGHT

by
Matthew P. Mayo

As *is my habit, I, John H. Watson, Doctor of Medicine, have set down this tale in part in an effort to amuse readers. If at the end of it you come away half as entertained as I have been in the writing of it, then my efforts will have been well spent.*

This curious event took place some years ago, and involved a pairing of two of the most singular minds of the time working together, something to which they were unaccustomed, being as they were, and remained, on opposing sides of the law. It will become apparent even to the casual reader that certain of these circumstances required decisions not wholly in keeping with the statutes of the day. Though in the end, justice won out, even if certain laws were pushed and pulled a bit.

As with most of these accounts, this tale benefits from the distinct advantages of the passage of much time and the favorable views of hindsight. In order to present as full and true a narrative as is possible, you'll note that I relied on first-hand accounts of the participants, the principle of whom was most frequently my friend, Sherlock Holmes, who begrudgingly related to me the various events for which I was not in attendance.

He was not the most loquacious of fellows in such instances, preferring, as he said, to let the science of deduction take center stage. Though in truth, I fancy that when I was occupied elsewhere, he did not mind reading these accounts of our adventures, or what he called my "wholesale abuse of poetic license."

Though you would never hear it from him...

"Ha! Watson, if you would be so kind." Holmes flung the folded newspaper towards me. I took the action to mean I would be reading aloud something mundane. I was not incorrect.

It was a two-month-old newspaper folded to the third page. The only full article was about a visit to Lord Ruddy's estate in Little Dimpling by famed French aeronaut Professor Henri Plouff. I had read the article when it came out, of course, having a secret fascination with ballooning, especially as a means of human conveyance. I was most familiar with Plouff, a leader in this field in which the French had excelled since 1783, when the Montgolfier brothers first successfully rose skyward in their balloon. I had even entertained the notion of one day clambering aboard a balloon and sailing over the city of London. How exciting that would be, I thought as, for Holmes' benefit, I launched once again into the article:

"Famed French Aeronaut to Visit Lord Ruddy: The residents of Little Dimpling are excited to hear of the impending visit of Professor Henri Plouff, famed French aeronaut and air-travel pioneer to their town. Attempts to learn more about this visit have met with unfortunate resistance by Lord Ruddy's household. It is understood that Professor Plouff is an old acquaintance of Lord Ruddy, who himself is a keen amateur aeronaut. Air-travel aficionados will no doubt look forward to further word—and perhaps a sky-high sighting or two—when Professor Plouff appears in English skies."

"Good God, Watson, who teaches these young men nowadays to be so ham-fisted in their attempts to approximate the subtle craft of journalism? Is it too much to hope for a snatch of news that is actually newsworthy?"

I ignored my friend's rant and continued narrating the article. After I finished, I said, "I had wondered whatever came of the visit. When I heard nothing more of it, I assumed it never materialized."

"That is what the public were supposed to think. In truth, Plouff has been a guest at Lord Ruddy's estate these two months."

Before I could respond, Holmes turned from the fireplace and pointed his pipe stem at the door. "Mrs. Hudson has just received the telegram I am expecting."

Within seconds we heard our landlady's soft footsteps on the landing outside the door. Mrs. Hudson knocked, then entered, proffering the silver breakfast tray, on which sat Holmes' suspected telegram, the corner poking from the tray's edge. He snatched and peeled it open in one quick movement, then scanned it and looked up.

"Oh, Mrs. Hudson. You are still here."

"Well, I never—" The poor lady set down the tray with a clatter and exited the room. The slamming door caused us both to flinch.

"Holmes, is it really necessary to treat her so?"

"Of course, Watson. I shouldn't want her to hear anything that might put her in undue danger."

"Danger? But what does the telegram say?"

He plumed blue smoke at the ceiling, then read:

"The dimpled lord has fouled the air stop Future skies in doubt stop Plans changed hands but where stop With your help truth will out stop AL stop"

"I knew Plouff's visit to Lord Ruddy smacked of artifice, Watson. I had in fact made up my mind to travel to Little Dimpling this very day, since there is nothing else to be had in London by way of excitement." He spread his arms wide to indicate that the whole of London at present perturbed him—or more to the point, that it hadn't perturbed him in some time. And then just as quickly, he smiled. "And now this." He wagged the thin sheet of folded white paper. "Practically an engraved invitation, Watson!"

"I'm afraid you've lost me, Holmes."

Holmes looked at me as though I were an addled street urchin. "The headline, dear fellow. Reread the headline."

I complied: "Famed French Aeronaut to Visit Lord Ruddy." Indeed, I thought, it couldn't be more blunt or less newsworthy. People visited other people all the time. Especially the gentry, forever hobnobbing the world over. And this trip by Plouff to Lord Ruddy's estate seemed to me to be nothing more than two old friends spending a pleasant visit together.

"If I am not mistaken," I said, "Lord Ruddy's mother was at one time close friends with the Queen, was she not?"

"Indeed, she curried royal favor for quite some time before she betrayed the friendship with lurid gossip mongering. In fact, while still in favor, she was given several pieces of jewelry. It is rumored that one in particular, an exquisite ring, a sapphire offset by diamonds, was requested returned by the royal family, but the Ruddy family claimed it had become lost. Can you imagine?"

I failed to see what Plouff's visit to Lord Ruddy's estate had to do with the cryptic telegram. "But who is 'Al'?"

Holmes exhaled in disgust. "No, no, no, Watson. This just won't do! It is A.-L., Arsene Lupin, who sent the telegram!"

"'A.L.'—of course! Lupin!" I paced the room. "That dandified villain!"

Holmes snorted.

"You can't possibly think otherwise, Holmes."

"I do not. But neither can I deny that the man is impressive at what he does. Do you recall the theft of the DuFau Collection of Egyptian artifacts? Vanished from a locked, sealed, guarded chamber in the heart of that supposed impregnable gallery. And where does it turn up next? In shipping crates on the very steps of Egypt's seat of power!"

I held up one finger. "Minus one small, priceless stone carving, let's not forget. He is a thief, Holmes. Hardly garden variety, and I will admit he does sport a strain of philanthropy, to be sure, but still…"

Holmes laughed as he whisked toward his room. "Come, Watson. Every moment we are here is a moment we are not where we should be."

"Just where is that, Holmes? And why the hurry? I for one wouldn't mind a bite of Mrs. Hudson's breakfast." I stared with longing at the silver dome that shrouded a stack of piping hot scones.

Holmes poked his head around the doorframe, his eyes glinting, his nostrils flexing like a thoroughbred on race day. "There is no time, man. We must away. Don your rambling togs, Watson, and pack for a night free from Baker Street. We shan't require evening dress." He disappeared into his room, then poked his head back out. "And Watson, bring your service revolver. Good man."

"Yes, yes, but what's all this about that Lupin character? If he is mixed up in this, I'll wager we're in for a bumpy ride."

"Ha! You have a talent for fixing the fluttering word to the board, Watson. But, really, we have a train to catch."

Within minutes of lurching up to full speed northwestward toward Little Dimpling, Holmes fixed me with a hard gaze, no wry smile underscoring it. We each lit cigarettes, then I said, "Why should Lupin want to contact you? I don't recall reading about any recent thefts that might fit his modus operandi."

"You are correct and incorrect. A theft has occurred, but it was not perpetrated by our dandy."

I thought again about the old headline. "The French aeronaut Plouff? What of his was stolen?"

Holmes drew deeply on his cigarette, then let the smoke leak out of his mouth in a thin, gray stream. He stared out the window. "If I am correct, though I pray I am wrong, the theft is two-fold." He turned his attention to me. "It is a double theft with potential global import that may affect lives the world over for years—perhaps decades—to come."

"But Holmes ... what was stolen?"

Holmes stubbed out the glowing nub of his cigarette. "A man's life." He looked at me. "And a man's life's work."

"Not the aeronaut...."

He nodded. "The very man."

"You don't think Lupin did this?"

Holmes' indulgent smile flitted, then dropped. "You are right, of course, to think so, but no. It is Arsene Lupin who has asked for our help. He has reason to suspect the foulest of play regarding Professor Henri Plouff. And rightfully so. Were I in Lupin's shoes and I had as little time to interrupt this spiraling series of dastardly events, I, too, may have sought help from a mind of such ... similar ability."

"It's as bad as all that, then?"

"Yes. Yes, it is. I curse myself for not trusting my instinct and making this journey all the earlier."

"How could you know? The first we heard of it was via the telegram."

"That was the first you heard of it. I, however, had ample reason to suspect impending foul play for days preceding it. I made inquiries sufficient to satisfy myself that the situation bore nothing more than close scrutiny. Never could I have suspected that the man would be murdered. At least not so soon."

"Why was he murdered?"

"Why, indeed."

And that was all I could get out of him on the matter for some minutes more. I occupied myself with recounting all I knew of Professor Henri Plouff. He was a famed French pioneer in the burgeoning field of aeronautics. Professionally he was well thought of, kept a tight rein on his private life, and rarely spoke with the press, which he regarded as an interference with his work. I also recalled reading that the man had a daughter, but was himself a widower. He had been described as solidly built, which in my experience is a journalistic nicety for saying the man was portly.

"Might I ask why he needs you, Holmes? Arsene Lupin is hardly mindful of the law."

That snapped Holmes from his reverie. "I should think that was obvious, Watson. The seedy and vicious aspects of this instance are, sadly, more in my line, whilst high-level thefts are something that Lupin has vastly more experience with. At least that is how I choose to divide up the basic elements of this case." He glanced sideways at me. "At least for the time being, that is."

"I say, there isn't the off chance that we are about to help Lupin commit a crime, Holmes?"

Sherlock smiled. "It is true, Watson. We may well be heading toward a great duping, but I suspect there is more to it than that. I have had occasion to humiliate the great gentleman thief a time or two in the past. But this time, Watson, there is more potential for evil at stake. This time there is a distinct undercurrent of malevolence that I perceive far exceeds any petty theft or challenge Lupin might care to offer. Something…"

Holmes' voice trailed off as he sank back into the leather banquette and stared out the window at the landscape rushing by.

We stepped down from the train at the bustling town of Little Dimpling, and Holmes headed towards the telegraph office. Inside sat a dapper young man in the midst of a snowbank of white paper scraps.

"My good man…" Holmes snapped his walking stick across the man's desk. Papers fluttered upward. "I wonder if you could tell me the way to Lord Ruddy's estate."

The young man's open face tightened and he leaned forward. "Begging pardon, sir, but you don't want to be going to Ruddy Manor. Oh no, sir. That man …" The youth leaned closer to them. "He's not … well. Yes, that's it. He's unwell. It's the only thing, really, that might account for his dark humors. I daren't say more."

Holmes did his best to stifle a snort. "By the way, do you happen to recall the man who sent a telegram yesterday evening to a Mister Sherlock Holmes at 221B Baker Street, London?"

"Of course I remember that. Who'd forget sending a message to someone so famous? And from a man who was so … different."

"Different? How?"

"Well, he was tall, with blonde hair, blue eyes. Acted as if he was a royal, but he was dressed like a beggar. Oh, and he's a Frenchy." The young man narrowed his eyes. "Here, are you him?"

"Him?" said Holmes.

"Sherlock Holmes, I mean."

"I cannot deny it."

"Good, 'cause he give me another note, just this morning. Said if you made it here, you should have this." He proffered a folded note. "He was in a awful hurry, though."

"Did you notice in what direction he traveled when he left your office?"

"No, not me."

Holmes grunted and plucked the note from the young man's hand.

He handed the note to me, touched a glove to his hat brim, and we left the lad to his toils.

Outside, I read the note:

> "Look to the trampled glade, southeast of the ancestral
> pile. Lovely beech. —A.L."

"Lupin."

Holmes nodded.

"I take it this less cryptic note is a set of directions."

Holmes nodded again and strode toward a public house—The Dimpled Arms.

I smiled, thinking refreshment was forthcoming, but was shortly proved wrong. Instead, Holmes arranged for rooms for the night, then hired a surrey. And all the while, we managed to gather that not only did no one in the town particularly like Lord Ruddy of Ruddy Manor, they were all afraid of him as well.

Not much was said as we clopped out of town toward the very manor so many people had warned us to stay clear of. We paid the driver and he rattled off at a brisk pace without a backward glance.

Holmes moved with the lithe, sure movements I had come to expect when the man was on a case. The tall detective dropped to one knee, then both as he circled an area that had seen recent activity, judging from the crushed grasses and pocked earth.

"Holmes," I said. "Don't you think you'd better be on the lookout for…"

Holmes regarded me from grass height, his brow furrowed.

"The sheep, Holmes. They've been all over this field."

"Watson, this is not a field, as you so quaintly put it. This is a pasture. Of course the sheep have been in it. As for dung, I doubt very much I should have chosen detective consultation as an occupation if I wished to remain free of the aromatic stuff."

He resumed his scouting expedition amidst the grasses. Soon he stood and, flicking off stray particles from his gloves' fingertips, recited what he knew of the dead aeronaut. "He's French, he was a fat man, wore a tweed outing suit. He sported handlebar moustaches, goggles, and one of those tight-fitting leather caps with a chin strap that all aviators insist on wearing."

"Really, Holmes, how do you surmise all that from an oft-trod patch of pasture?"

Holmes stopped halfway to the treeline, pointing at the trunks ahead with his walking stick. "Because I listened to what you said when you read the old article to me but a few hours ago. Really, do you not take in the news as you read it, Watson?"

He pointed overhead. "And there—you see those whitened leaves, dead for days now—that is the location where the balloon drifted and crashed after our aeronaut toppled to his death." He waited for me to catch up with him. "Or," he said, "at least that is what we are led to believe."

"What do you mean, Holmes?"

He strode forward, his black stick twirling, the silver tip glinting in the sun as it arced. "I predict that we will find evidence very soon that is contrary."

"Such as?"

Holmes ignored the query and gazed at the towering beech before him. "If you would be so good as to hold these accoutrements, Watson. I shan't be long."

He lunged upward, his gloved hands finding purchase on a lower branch. His judo-honed form swung upward and he made his way, catlike, from one branch to successively higher branches. Soon, Holmes crouched near the dark nexus of several stout branches. Out came his portable glass, then a match flared. "Ah ha!"

Next, with all but his feet hidden, he ventured into the green cloud of branches in full leaf. I half-expected to see Holmes plummet the thirty feet to the ground, but within minutes and after several more exclamations from within the branches, Holmes climbed down again, then dropped lightly to his feet, smacking his hands together and grinning.

"Such as… " he said, retrieving his hat, stick, and coats. "The fact that someone else was in that balloon with the good Frenchman. And that someone else, I shouldn't doubt, pushed the body out of the basket. I say body because I am convinced—and I hope to prove it if I'm able to conduct an examination of the body—that the poor aeronaut was dead, or nearly so, before he dropped from the sky."

"Do you mean to say—"

"Yes, Watson… " He was already striking back in the direction from which we had come. "I mean to say that Lupin's guess is correct and that this was indeed murder. And I know the why, too. I might even know the who, but proving all these points is the key element. And in order to do so, I'll need the help of yourself, and our mystery man, Arsene Lupin."

"Where is he?"

"That's where we're headed now, Watson. I will admit I half expected him to show up here." Holmes scanned the pasture and into the forest beyond the beech.

"I confess to being a bit confused. For such a dire situation, Holmes, you seem to be enjoying yourself."

"Indeed, I am. When Arsene Lupin is involved, there is always an edge of disruption tickling the periphery. Don't forget there is a world of difference between intention and action. And if my guess is correct, then we may well be the wedge between the two. But we must hurry, Watson."

I hustled after my friend, and in two minutes of hard walking we crested a steep berm. Before us sat a grand manor house, appearing as if by magic on the landscape. Those architects knew what they were after. Surprise is all.

At the edge of the wood, where the manicured greensward began its roll toward the great pile, Holmes put a hand out and stopped me. "I will part from you here, Watson."

"What? But Holmes, I thought we were in this together."

"And so we are, but it is no good. I have met Lord Ruddy on two separate instances. And both times, I am afraid, I had occasion to incite in him some strange sort of animosity, the memories of which I fear will instigate a sneering remembrance in him. He is, how shall I put this? Rather an unpleasant sort of fellow. And frequently his type needs little provocation to become unpredictable in their behavior. " He regarded me a moment, then said, "But have no fear, you have not yet met the man."

"I'm not so sure I want to now," I said in a low voice.

Holmes barked a quick laugh. "You are the end, Watson, it is true. Don't ever change. Now, do you recall all that I spent the past few minutes relating?"

"I do."

"And you have your revolver on your person?"

Again, I nodded.

"Excellent. If all goes according to plan, within a few short hours we will be enjoying a thimble full at the Dilly Dally Arms, or whatever that dreadful little public house is called down in the village."

"And if not?"

Holmes turned back and regarded me a moment. "Then God save Queen and country. For we will have failed."

Neither of us spoke for a moment, then Holmes said, "Oh, and one more thing, Watson. Give Lord Ruddy's hand a good shake, and watch his face. Take the measure of the man." He emphasized this request with a curious piercing look, then he turned and was off.

I broke from the scant cover of the copse in which we had discussed our plans, and strode directly toward the house. I breathed deep and walked with the purpose befitting the bold stranger of Holmes' odd directives, straight across the manicured lawns. A peafowl's harried call threatened to distract my thoughts from turning over and over again what was required of me.

All too soon, I found myself crunching across the circular drive at the front of the house. I lifted and let fall twice the great brass knocker that formed the lower half of a menacing lion's jaw. The echo seemed to spread throughout the great house. For long moments, I stood still and held my breath. Soon enough, I heard the unhurried, echoing footfalls of whom I assumed was a butler. And then the great black door swung slowly inward.

Holmes paused just outside the kitchen, the glossed white door open before him. Three strides inside along a narrow passage he spied the broad back and wide rump of a massive woman, apparently in high dudgeon, remonstrating someone with a tongue thick with German. Holmes stood still and cocked his head to better hear.

"You were a beggar! I give you food, you were to give chores! Then you say no to this by sneaking in Lord Ruddy's house! I vill call the policemen und they vill take you away!"

A muffled voice cut her off. "No, no, my dear Madame Hammelin, I can assure you that will not be necessary. Come, let me out of this closet and I will better be able to explain myself, non?"

Even through the closet door, Holmes recognized the unmistakable aristocratic French lilt of Arsene Lupin's voice. Here is an interesting kettle of fish, thought Holmes. Ah well, in for a penny. He cleared his throat. The effect was as if he had fired a derringer in church. The great hams of the woman's rump quivered as she spun, and a red, jowly countenance exuded anger as she bore down on him.

Holmes stood his ground and even managed a smile. "Good day to you, good Frau Hammelin. I dare say you find this a bit awkward, though no more so than our mutual friend in there." Holmes gestured with his stick beyond the advancing juggernaut.

"You know this … this sneak?" She folded her brawny arms over her apron.

"Indeed I do. And while I cannot disagree with your assessment of him, I must request that you release him at once."

"What? Why…" She lunged forward.

Holmes did not budge. "Frau Hammelin! Really, this will not do. If you attempt to molest me in any way, I shall be forced to call in the police."

She stopped once again, her eyes still narrowed as she regarded this stranger before her.

Holmes stood straighter. "I doubt you really want to see the police just now, do you?"

"I do not know what you mean." But her big face softened.

"Come now, madam. Let us not play games. I need you to do two things for me."

She grunted and made to move forward, but Holmes held up a hand and shook his head.

"No no no. Hear me out, madam. For if you do not comply with my two demands, then you and your husband shall come to regret it—for a long, long time. Do we have agreement?"

Again, her features softened even as they bore the full brunt of her confusion. She stood facing him, her giant form filling the doorway. Finally, she nodded.

"Excellent. First, you will release that miserable wretch you have tucked in that stairwell closet. Come now, proceed."

She turned and padded down the short hallway, her large feet quiet on the worn flags of the floor. Soon, a tall, thin man emerged from out of the closet, his blonde hair mussed and his rumpled and patched clothes hung off his trim frame.

"Monsieur Lupin, it is a singular experience to see you again."

"Monsieur Holmes, so you received my telegram and perhaps my note? I knew I would soon see you here. Where there is murder, there is Holmes, eh?" The French dandy chuckled.

"And wherever something is not, there you will find unmistakable trace of Arsene Lupin." Holmes' wry smile barely cracked the false beggar's chipper façade.

As they spoke, Frau Hammelin watched them, her big arms again folded across her chest.

"Now, step number two, good lady. Would you be so kind as to show us to the remains of Professor Henri Plouff? I know that he is here and I know that you and your husband, Hammelin the butler, have been sworn to secrecy by Lord Ruddy. If you do not comply, you will both be arrested on the charges of accessories to murder."

She clapped her thick, dimpled hands to her mouth.

Lupin nodded. "Yes, madam. I assure you the matter is that serious."

After surveying the faces of both Lupin and Holmes, Frau Hammelin nodded, her shoulders sagging. "Follow me, gentlemen."

They trailed after her, Holmes insisting that the Frenchman precede him. "Your reputation, Monsieur Lupin. I find that my pockets are light enough at present, thank you."

Below the kitchen, in the chill of a stone-walled meat pantry, a pudgy form lay prone, wrapped in canvas, atop the wooden carving table. An oil lamp held by the nervous Frau Hammelin lit the proceedings.

"Lupin, distasteful though you may find it, I'll nonetheless need your help."

"But of course, Holmes. Nothing would give me greater pleasure."

The two men proceeded to unwrap the body, both making sure that the large cook stood well away from the door, should she be tempted to lock them in.

As Holmes poked and prodded the dead man, he said to Lupin, "You were here, then?"

"Alas, yes, but not when it happened. Only too late. Professor Plouff was still warm to the touch."

"There was a struggle…"

"Yes, Holmes. But how did you—? Ah, but of course, you are Sherlock Holmes."

"It is a trifling matter. This wound here," Holmes wagged a gloved finger near the back of the dead man's head, "indicates that the man was struck before he dropped. And since there is a copious amount of blood, you will note that the blow, while ultimately lethal, did not kill him. A dead man does not bleed. But the fall—or rather the sudden stop at the end of the fall—most surely finished the job. So we can conclude that the man suffered a blow to the back of his skull, then was pushed, or fell, from the gondola."

"That is exactly what happened, Monsieur Holmes. Exactly. You see, I arrived at the field, in shadow, in time to see that Lord Ruddy and Professor Plouff were arguing in the basket, not far from the ground. Perhaps thirty, maybe forty feet in the air. I could hear them and see them quite plainly."

"And they were arguing about Plouff's latest invention."

Lupin nodded, amazed. "Yes, I heard the balloon before I saw it, then of course I saw it outlined against the sky, a beautiful sight, to be sure and unexpected, too. It was a small, hot air balloon, merely for pleasurable outings. But I heard Professor Plouff call Lord Ruddy a fool, told him it was obvious he didn't know the first thing about flying a balloon. He accused Lord Ruddy of luring him to Britain under false pretenses. He said Lord Ruddy only wanted the plans, plans for something he called his 'omnidirectional flying balloon.'"

"Now that is interesting, Lupin." Holmes bent to examine the dead man's gloved hands. "What happened next?"

"Predictably, Lord Ruddy overreacted, shouting and threatening. But Professor Plouff merely laughed at him, and told him that the money Lord Ruddy had paid him only assured that the project could be completed, and that he was taking the entire project back to France immediately, since Lord Ruddy could obviously no longer be trusted. I then heard Lord Ruddy shout, 'Never!' I saw his arms come up, then down again, and heard a grunt and groan. It was horrible, Holmes. Professor Plouff pitched backward over the edge of the basket and hit the ground but twenty feet from where I was hiding."

"Yes, I thought I recognized your footprints near the base of the beech tree. Go on."

"Well it was obvious this is not what Lord Ruddy intended, but he was so inept at flying the balloon that he crashed it into that very beech tree under which I was hidden."

Frau Hammelin cleared her throat. "Lord Ruddy told us this had been an accident. Why would he lie about this? Why would he kill the man?"

"Why, indeed, madam. Shrewd of you. But the answer is obvious, is it not, Lupin?" Holmes narrowed his eyes. "What of the Professor's plans? They were on his person, were they not?"

Lupin stared stone-faced for a moment, then said, "It is true, in their argument, Plouff said he possessed plans to his latest invention. I was sure that Lord Ruddy's intentions were to clamber down and ransack poor Plouff's pockets for these mysterious plans."

"So, being the man that you are, you got to them first."

Lupin smiled. "While Lord Ruddy was busy swearing and growling and fighting with the tree branches, I dashed out of hiding and went to Plouff. But he had already died. I did find the leather tube, like a small map case, that he kept on his person at all times. It is this tube that his daughter, the lovely Clarice, told me about. A quick peek in one end told me these were the plans Lord Ruddy was so desperate to have—so desperate that he would murder for them. I dashed away then, just as Lord Ruddy's form became visible in the branches. I saw that his leather gloves were scraped raw and bleeding on the palms, the gloves themselves shredded and in poor repair, and that he was having a difficult time gripping the tree."

"That would explain the blood staining and bits of leather I found in the tree. You are to be commended, Lupin, for your keen powers of observation. But, then again, I expected no less. Do go on."

"I waited in hiding, concealed flat to the ground behind a nearby thatch of tall grass. Most unpleasant. That is a sheep pasture, you know."

Holmes smiled. "I had been made aware of that, yes."

"At any rate, I watched in some satisfaction I don't mind admitting, as Lord Ruddy conducted a fruitless and increasingly angry search of poor Plouff's body."

"It was at this point that you contacted me."

Lupin nodded. "I dared not call attention to Ruddy's foul deed, for fear of revealing myself. I think it fair to agree that I have a certain, ah, reputation, you see. Not only would I not have been believed, but it is quite probable that I might have been arrested for the actions of Lord Ruddy. But I knew that you would be able to assist me in this way, and you have, most ably."

Holmes smiled faintly. "Where are these plans now?"

Lupin said nothing.

Holmes held out his hand, beckoning with his fingers. "Come now, Lupin. I've no interest in retaining the plans, but I must examine them. Need I remind you a murder has taken place? And after all, I am here assisting on your invitation."

Lupin sighed and pulled from the depths of his ratty coat a brown leather tube scarcely a foot long and placed it in Holmes' outstretched hand.

Holmes untied the leather thong the held the tube closed. "Whilst I peruse these, see that Professor Plouff is well covered. I shouldn't want anything further to happen to him."

As he shrouded the dead man with the canvas, Lupin said, "The plans would do you no good anyway, since they are in a code only Plouff and one other person knows the key of."

"Ah, the mysterious daughter." Holmes watched Lupin's face, but learned nothing. "So now we come to it. Your motives are only partly personal. No doubt you came here at her behest."

Lupin nodded. "She was worried, and felt that her father was in danger."

"An intuitive young lady, poor thing. Still, she will be most appreciative of your successful return of the plans. Small solace, considering the grief she will soon experience."

"Yes, poor rabbit. She does not yet know of her father's death. Indeed, the world as yet is ignorant of the fact that it lost a great mind, a great Frenchman."

"Careful, Lupin, your national pride is showing."

"I don't know what you mean, Holmes."

"Come now, Lupin. It is obvious. Plouff was forced to look outside his beloved France for investors when the French government refused to further fund his experiments. Probably because he has that peculiarly French trait of not producing results in a timely fashion. At least not quick enough for a government's liking. Am I correct?"

"Yes, damn them. The fools in power in France confuse money with genius. They are so short-sighted. They only think of the next minute and then the next and the next. Never the next day or year. And Plouff's new airship design, if what I have seen can be believed, is a major advance and could revolutionize travel—and more importantly, warfare. "

"And if it fell into the German Empire's hands?"

Lupin looked at Holmes with eyes wide. "No, no, don't even joke about that, Holmes. Plouff may have gone to an Englishman for money, but he would never go to a German." Lupin glanced at Frau Hammelin. "No offense to you, madame, but your government, ah, it is hardly trustworthy now, is it?"

The woman said nothing, but even in the dim light of the cold chamber, Holmes saw her sneer at Lupin.

"Not to mention the bitter rivalry between the German Empire and France where airship innovation is concerned, eh?" said Holmes. "Sadly, it appears as if Plouff did indeed sell to the Germans, in a manner of speaking."

"What?"

"Lord Ruddy. His allegiance is with Deutschland, is it not, Mrs. Hammelin?"

Instead of the bold denial Holmes expected, the woman merely nodded her head. "Lord Ruddy told us it was an accident." She whispered between her plump fingers, as if half-covering her mouth might protect her from the dire situation.

"Ha," said Holmes. "If it was an accident, why hasn't he contacted the authorities? No, Lord Ruddy is a mean-spirited and wealthy bully who will stop at nothing to get what he wants. And I suspect what he wants most is to buy his way into Count von Zeppelin's good graces. I have no doubt that he has the two of you wriggling under his thumb."

She began to speak, but Holmes held up a hand. "I do not wish to know the particulars. At least not at this juncture. Perhaps later your admission will help shed light on this nefarious affair. For now, however, we must make our move if we are to prevent him from absconding with those plans. In the wrong hands, they will prove disastrous on a widespread scale."

"Indeed," said Lupin, his head bowed. "And France would be blamed."

"A heavy burden that you may yet avoid. Come!" With that, Holmes handed the leather tube back to Lupin, turned on his heel, and bolted down the long passage that led to the interior of the house.

"Good day, sir." With my hands behind my back, I offered the butler a brief nod.

"Yes?"

I cleared my throat. "At the risk of being forward, I should like to speak with Lord Ruddy. I am Doctor John Watson and, among other things, I am an amateur aeronaut. Or rather I am a keen enthusiast." When my smiles and hurried explanation failed to elicit anything more than the same silent stare from the stone-faced butler, I continued. "It is my understanding … that is to say … I was told that the famed French experimental aeronaut Professor Henri Plouff is a guest here at Ruddy Manor. I would like very much to see him."

"You are mistaken, sir. There is no one here by that name."

"I have been traveling for some time to meet the man and as I happen to know he is here, I demand to see him."

"If you persist in this matter, sir, I will be forced to have you removed from the premises, sir. Good day." With that, the butler swung the door to close it.

I can tell you, I felt my opportunity slipping from my grasp, so I blurted out the first thing that occurred to me: "I'll just make my way back to the village, then, and inform the authorities that something is definitely amiss at Ruddy Manor, and that I strongly suspect the esteemed Professor Plouff is in some sort of trouble."

Just before the great wood door clicked shut it paused. Then slowly swung inward again. The butler stared at me. "One moment, please." Then he shut the door in my face.

I stood on the broad top step, unsure what my role in this strange little case was, and what I might do next. That I had set myself up as an amateur aeronaut was one thing, but I couldn't very well hope to occupy much of Lord Ruddy's time on the basis of such a thin premise.

Before my worried thoughts proceeded further, the great door once again swung inward and there before me stood a broad-chested man in a gray woolen suit, impeccably tailored. Atop the suit sat a wide, florid face, sideburns framing great bristling moustaches. And underscoring it all, a broad, mirthless smile mirrored the angry dark eyes that regarded me as a predator might an intended victim. It was an unsettling countenance, I don't mind admitting.

"I am Lord Ruddy."

The man's voice matched his demeanor, low and dark. In an attempt to follow Holmes' advice, I stepped forward and grasped Lord Ruddy's gloved right hand vigorously. I squeezed it hard and gave it several good pumps, clapping my other hand on top, for good measure. The big man's face whitened and a thin breath escaped his mouth.

"It is my distinct pleasure to meet you, Lord Ruddy."

The lord stepped away from me, yanking his hand free. I could see on the man's face a struggle to maintain his composure. So Holmes, as I suspected, was hoping to learn something from the man's reaction. Something about the man's hands. Come to think of it, I thought, why was Lord Ruddy wearing gloves in his home?

"Hammelin here tells me you're a keen amateur aeronaut," said Ruddy, swallowing and attempting another grim smile. "And that you are interested in meeting Professor Henri Plouff."

"Yes, indeed. I was told that he is—" But before I could continue, the man turned away.

"Yes, yes…. Do come in, let me offer you refreshment. Follow me."

I followed Lord Ruddy down a long central hallway, where motes hung in shafts of afternoon sun angling in from high-up windows. We walked to the far end of the hall, which I took to be near the back of the house. The big man turned in at a door on his left and without looking back, beckoned that I should follow.

As I passed into the room, from the shadows to my right I heard a single step, then a hot rush of pain flowered up the side of my head. I caught a glimpse of the interior of the richly appointed room before dropping to a hard, carpeted surface. Rough hands patted me, found my service revolver. My vision wavered, narrowing at times to golden pin pricks bursting against a black velvet backdrop.

I battled with my waxing and waning consciousness and finally managed to retain enough of my wits to realize it was Lord Ruddy who had assaulted me. In my dazed condition, he had also trussed my hands and feet and placed a gag around my mouth. Try as I might, I could not work up anything more than a twitch and a moan.

Then with a grunt, the great brute heaved me up onto his shoulder. Balancing me there, he pushed against what looked to be two volumes of *Plutarch's Lives* in a bookcase. I heard a muffled click, then a pinging sound, and the entire section of shelves popped outward a couple of inches. He tugged on the shelving and it opened to reveal a stone staircase winding upward, enclosed within a tower.

It was a mighty effort for me to maintain some semblance of consciousness as Lord Ruddy clomped up the worn steps, stiff-legged under my nearly dead weight. I heard what sounded like him giving a mighty kick to a wooden door, then I was dumped without ceremony onto a hard stone surface. The last I recall is hearing his footsteps descend the stone stairs. I fancy I heard the secret entry door click shut, and then I recalled no more.

From deep in the house, in a corridor near the kitchens, Holmes, Lupin, and Frau Hammelin heard the summoning bell.

"It's Lord Ruddy's study," said the cook.

"Perfect," said Holmes. "It is time we end this charade. I'm quite sure Watson will be relieved. I'm afraid I left him to fend for himself at the hands of that insufferable lout."

A moment later, they heard Lord Ruddy roar for Hammelin. As they trekked down long, still corridors, they passed numerous antiques and expensive artworks. Lupin's eyes swiveled, taking in each treasure.

"Why do I have the feeling that you are mentally cataloguing everything in this place, Monsieur Lupin?"

"Holmes, you underestimate me. For that which you claim I am doing has already been done, long ago. I must make such a trip worthwhile, after all."

Holmes smiled. "I should think assisting your government—not to mention a grieving daughter of a French genius—would carry its own rewards."

"Oh, this is true, but come now, how selfless do I look?"

This time, Holmes did laugh.

"Hammelin, there you are! Where have you been, you blasted fool!" Ruddy's wide red face glared at the demure butler, who looked down at his shoes. "Did you examine him? Where the devil is it?"

"What would that be, sir?" said Hammelin.

"It, damn you. It, the leather case ... with the plans. Plouff, he entrusted them to me, you see." Lord Ruddy licked his lips and leaned forward. "I must have those plans. I need your help to find them. They simply must be here. We'll go over his things one more time. Did you examine him again as I asked?"

"Yes, sir."

"And nothing?"

"Nothing, sir."

In the shadows outside the Lord's study door, Holmes caught Lupin's grin. They listened a moment longer, awaiting the right moment to rush in and brace the murderous Ruddy. Then, without warning to the others, Holmes stepped into the study, his stick in hand, a smile on his face.

"Who the devil are you?" Lord Ruddy began to rise from the chair behind his massive desk.

"No, no, don't get up, Lord Ruddy. You may remember me—Sherlock Holmes. We have had occasion to meet twice in the past. They are both meetings that I have yet to forget, despite my very best efforts."

Lord Ruddy turned his angry stare at Hammelin. "What is the meaning of this? Two strangers in one day invading my home? Is nothing sacred, man?"

Before he could get out the words, Arsene Lupin stepped into the room beside Holmes. He still wore the clothes of a beggar.

"What is this outrage!" This time Lord Ruddy did rise from his chair. "Who is this … this creature?"

The newest member of the party, apart from Frau Hammelin, who shuffled in quietly behind Lupin, spoke up. "Arsene Lupin." He offered a peremptory nod and half bow.

"Let us cut to the quick, Lord Ruddy," said Holmes. "We know that you killed Professor Henri Plouff, esteemed aeronaut and engineer."

"Whaaat!" Lord Ruddy roared, slamming his pink fists into his desk top.

"Spare us the histrionics, Lord Ruddy. We know you killed him because this man was a witness to the incident and we have examined Plouff's body. We also have the cooperation of your cook, Mrs. Hammelin."

"What? You ungrateful…"

Hammelin the butler looked at his wife, who narrowed her eyes and nodded. That was all the indication he needed that he should follow his large wife's advice in this matter.

"No, Lord Ruddy," said Holmes. "It is you who are ungrateful. You found out that Professor Plouff had run up heavy debts in order to finish his prototype airship. But he needed still more money in order to make the thing operational. You approached him quietly, using the excuse that you are something of a ballooning enthusiast and would like to be his benefactor, provided he relocate his operations to your estate.

"Unbeknownst to you, Plouff had already been approached with similar offers by Count von Zeppelin, of the German Empire. But Plouff had no intention of becoming entangled with the Germans, and especially not von Zeppelin, who had become something of a nemesis to Plouff. But an offer of financial assistance from an English lord, now that was a different story. So Plouff accepted your kind offer, and he had his equipment shipped to your estate.

"In many ways it proved an ideal place for him to work unhindered. But soon, you demanded to be let in on more of the project, and feeling that he couldn't deny you—to a point—Plouff relented. But he grew suspicious of your constant questions. And one recent afternoon, while enjoying a pleasurable balloon ride over your own property, Plouff had had enough and confronted you. There was a struggle, you hit him on the head, then he pitched out of the gondola. Your lies caught up to you at that point, because you had to fly the balloon yourself. Which you couldn't do, and so you crashed it into the beech tree, then ransacked Plouff's body looking for his secret plans."

"You have the plans?" Lord Ruddy rounded his desk and came at the tall, thin detective.

"Stay your ground, man!" said Holmes, steeling himself, walking stick at the ready. "And hear the facts, for only then will you know what we know."

The big man halted, glaring at Holmes, who continued, his own gaze never wavering from Lord Ruddy's face.

"You injured your hands in your struggle with the balloon—rope burns and then the rough, broken branches of the beech." With no warning, Holmes snapped the tip of his cane into first one, then the other of Lord Ruddy's palms. The big man groaned and snatched his hands to his chest.

"Hence the gloves," said Holmes. "Then, you forced the Hammelins to help you retrieve the body and the wrecked balloon. You told them that it was an accident, but because of potential international ramifications, the death must at all costs be kept a secret. Then, to seal the deal, you blackmailed them. Perhaps threatening to expose them as spies, though in truth they are merely a quiet couple in service who happen to be German."

Holmes inclined his head toward the Frau Hammelin and offered a brief smile before continuing. "This is no crime, but your constant overbearing presence in their lives has rendered them helpless to leave your employ. Oddly enough, it is you who are jealous of them. You who yearn for your family's old Germanic heritage. Being a British lord has its benefits, certainly, but for some inexplicable reason you feel an allegiance to the German Empire. I wonder, why is that, Lord Ruddy?"

"Why you—" but the large royal didn't finish his oath. Instead, he spun, snatched a campaign cutlass from the wall, then slid it out of its scabbard with a slicing ring. He waved it before him, menacing the assembled group like a swaying cobra. He backed towards the bookcase, then pushed at it with his boot. With a muffled click, it popped open. Lord Ruddy swung it wide enough to slip inside, then quickly closed it. Even as the four people in his study lunged for it, he barred the door from the inside and dashed up the stone steps.

Holmes turned to Hammelin. "Where is my friend, the other stranger who appeared here earlier?"

Hammelin stared at Holmes, but said nothing. Holmes advanced, snatched at the man's lapels. "Where is he, man? We haven't a moment to waste."

The butler lowered his head and nodded toward the hidden staircase.

"He must have taken him up there. They both came into this room some time ago, but only Lord Ruddy was here afterward."

Holmes shouted, "Watson! Watson! Hang on man! Lupin, quick, help me bash through!"

The two men hurled themselves at the bookcase, clawing volumes from the shelves. "Assistance, if you please, Monsieur et Madame Hammelin," said Lupin, without interrupting his task.

The large woman thrust both men aside and after a few harsh slams, her girth cracked the wood enough that Holmes was able to reach through the broken, splintered boards and slide the cross bar until, with a pop, the bookcase swung into the room. Lupin slipped through first, then Holmes dashed up the stone stairs, three at a time, his walking stick held before him. At the top of the stairs, he flung back a smaller wooden door in time to see Arsene Lupin leap off the parapet.

The Frenchman snagged a rope swinging from a most incredible airship. It had just cast off from its mooring atop the very tower on which they now stood.

Holmes made it to the edge of the tower, seconds too late. "Watson!" Holmes shouted, but it went unheard. In his haste, he nearly toppled from the edge. Mrs. Hammelin snatched him back with a meaty fistful of wool coat.

As Holmes watched, helpless from his perch, he took in the entire scene—he couldn't help but be impressed by the rapidly departing airship, obviously the nearly completed prototype of Professor Plouff's experimental directional flying balloon.

The three watched as the craft wobbled while Lupin scaled the rope. Over the edge of the gondola's rim, Holmes saw the angry, demonic face of Lord Ruddy excoriating the rapidly ascending Arsene Lupin, spittle flying as he shouted oaths at the lithe thief. With one hand on what must have been the tiller, Ruddy hacked with a knife at the Frenchman's lifeline.

"Look out, Lupin!" Holmes shouted.

At the last second, as the rope slithered groundward, Lord Ruddy shrieked and pitched out of sight within the gondola. Even in my trussed state, I had managed to trip up the brute. With haste—and not a little difficulty—I stood, knowing I had scant seconds to deal with Lord Ruddy.

"Watson! Excellent play!" shouted Holmes. I confess his words bolstered my doubting spirit.

As I worked at detaining Lord Ruddy, to my great relief, the poorly knotted rope securing my legs together slipped free, allowing me greater power over my adversary. At that moment, I spied someone's hands grasping the gondola's rim, then a handsome smiling face appeared between them. It was that indefatigable villain, Lupin! The Frenchman dragged himself upward, and managed one leg up and over. I offered him what awkward assistance I could, all the while kicking Ruddy enough to keep him from regaining his footing.

Soon, Lupin had the thrashing lord restrained enough to help me loosen my gag and wrist bonds, then we both set about trussing Lord Ruddy with the same materials he used on me, though we did not gag his mouth, something I'm sure we both regret. All the while, I felt the craft putter away from the tower to which it had been tethered. I stood and confirmed my suspicions as I watched Holmes, the butler Hammelin, and a large woman all recede from view.

"Doctor," Lupin handed me my service revolver. "Can you work this thing? Good, then might I suggest you train it on him." He kicked lightly at Lord Ruddy's bucking legs. "I will turn this craft around."

"You can fly one of these?" I asked him.

"Well, we shall soon see, non?" Lupin laughed, and it felt as though I were in Holmes' presence, so similar did the two men seem to me at that moment. Though I had met Arsene Lupin on previous occasions, I believe I saw then, in the balloon, for the first time what Holmes saw in the man: Here was a *bon vivant* with a penchant for nothing more or less than living life to the full.

I managed a smile as the aircraft, what seemed to be part balloon, part combustion engine, wobbled and putt-putt-putted in a slow, wide arc. I breathed deeply and looked about me at the landscape below. We were barely topping the trees, but the altered perspective jarred my still-reeling senses. And the sensation of floating was both awkward and thrilling, and one that I will not soon forget.

Within the basket, twice as long as the standard man-length gondola commonly seen, I took stock of the contents. At first I was confused—until I recalled that I was traveling with the Gentleman Thief, Arsene Lupin....

Paintings leaned in one corner, braced in place with a large canvas sack brimming with what looked to be an assortment of silver items—candlesticks, chalices, and the like. In the opposite corner sat a wooden crate stuffed with straw and cradling three Chinese vases. Astounding.

Before I could make comment, I saw that we had come to a hovering halt once again directly over the tower. We each tossed a guy rope down to Holmes' companions and the craft soon steadied.

None too gently, Lupin flopped the still growling Lord Ruddy to one side, and lifted a trap door in the floor. With his help, I dropped down to the tower beside Holmes.

"And now, your prisoner, Monsieur Holmes," said Lupin. With our help, he lowered Lord Ruddy, trussed and seething, down to us. The big man flopped to the stone floor with a grunt.

Lupin's face appeared in the trap door opening. "Monsieur Holmes et Monsieur Watson, *mes amis! Merci beaucoup* for your invaluable assistance in this matter. *Et ... au revoir* to you!"

He saluted, then closed the trap door. Seconds later, the two guy ropes held by the Hammelins slithered down on top of their heads, and the aircraft rose skyward, then leveled off, slowly turned, and headed east.

"*Bon chance*, Lupin!" Holmes touched his hat brim.

"Holmes!" I said, looking skyward and rubbing my red wrists. "Surely we're not going to let him get away. You should have seen that gondola, Holmes." I leaned toward my friend. "It was filled with artwork and sundry other items pinched from a certain manor house."

Holmes laughed. "Once a fox, always a fox, eh, Watson?"

Lord Ruddy growled, "He's getting away! Getting away with my possessions! Stop that thief!"

"I shouldn't think you'll be concerned with such things where you are going, Lord Ruddy," said Holmes, looking down his long nose at the florid man.

"What do you mean, sir? Do you know who I am? I demand to be untied, then I shall summon the authorities."

"Oh, rest assured the authorities have been contacted, Lord Ruddy. But I very much doubt that you will ever again be free."

"Ha, you haven't a shred of evidence and no one to support your claims." He nodded toward his servants standing nearby. "They won't say a thing against me. Wouldn't dare!"

"I shouldn't count on it, sir. What say you, Hammelin?"

The small butler stepped forward and cleared his throat. "On behalf of the entire staff, that is to say Mrs. Hammelin and myself, I would like to say that not one of us will visit you in prison, Lord Ruddy."

The big man's face grew the color of a ripe plum—alarming but hardly worthy of my sympathy.

Holmes regarded him for a silent moment. "I am confident in saying that your belittling, bitter, and bullying days are behind you, Lord Ruddy."

"What about my things? Those items he stole are precious to my family." The Lord's bottom lip quivered.

"What family?" said Holmes. "Correct me if I am mistaken, but are you not the last of your line?"

At this, Lord Ruddy said nothing. Then, as if on cue, we all turned our eyes skyward in time to watch that most amazing of inventions puff and steam and corkscrew itself eastward toward France, loaded with a small fortune in stolen items and commandeered by one smiling thief.

"A most singular invention, Holmes."

"A most singular thief, Watson," said Holmes. "And thank God for that."

With that, Hammelin and his wife prodded their former employer in the backside, herding the blubbering man toward the tower stairs.

Holmes and I remained atop the tower, still squinting at the receding speck in the sky.

"Such a diversity of pursuits, Watson. Or perhaps more to the point, obsessions. Thieving, deduction, lineage, flight—what a wonder is man, Watson. What a wonder."

"So you're just going to let Lupin escape?"

"Oh, he'll be back, Watson. Rest assured, he will be back."

"How can you be so certain, Holmes?"

As we turned to descend the cold stone stairwell, I spied the law wagon rumble full tilt up the long drive to the house, the result of a note left with the innkeeper to be given to the constabulary at a given time, had we not returned to the village before then.

I also noticed a glinting in Holmes' gloved hand. I looked closer, and there, pinched between Holmes' thumb and forefinger sat a most distinctive and large sapphire surrounded by equally impressive, though slightly smaller, diamonds.

"He hates to lose, Watson. And I like to win."

"That is a most impressive ring."

"Yes, and it belongs to Britain's monarchy, not to France. The rest of his haul? Piffling trifles compared with this. It was given to Lord Ruddy's mother by none other than Queen Victoria herself. And in Britain it shall stay."

"But how did you, and not the master thief, end up with it?"

Holmes looked skyward. "I happened to find it inside the leather tube containing Professor Plouff's airship plans. Lupin was reluctant enough in allowing me to inspect it, that I surmised the tube contained more than mere plans. No doubt Lupin had secreted the ring there on one of his pilfering trips throughout the manor. It was a mere matter to slip it out again when that opportune moment presented itself."

"Fantastic," I said, still eyeing the ring.

"Even better, Watson," Holmes smiled, one eyebrow arched high. "I replaced it with a beech nut."

Sherlock Holmes
and the Other Eye
by
Richard Dean Starr and E. R. Bower

"WE never sleep," I said, wearily, staring down at the newspaper spread across my lap. The date below the masthead read Tuesday, May the third. Had I been asked what day it was before receiving that morning's edition of the *Times*, which I had yet to read, I might have sworn that it was actually Monday the second.

"Try not to be melodramatic, Watson," said Sherlock Holmes, gazing out through the front window of our sitting room on the second floor of 221B, Baker Street. "While it is true I require less rest than you do, on the whole I would say you sleep quite well, and often."

"It certainly doesn't feel that way," I said. "We have closed not less than three cases over the past two weeks, the last one just this morning, and during that time I have managed to obtain, on average, less than four hours of sleep each night. I think you can agree that is not very much at all, Holmes!"

"And prior to the two weeks in question? How many hours a night did you manage then?"

"About seven. But that is neither here nor there, I must get my rest!"

"Seven hours or four," said Holmes, idly, tamping some tobacco into the bowl of his pipe. "I see no great advantage in one over the other. I would suggest that you consider taking a cold bath, Watson."

"A cold bath? You must be joking!"

"In my experience," said he, lighting the briar-root, "the benefits of submersing oneself in well-chilled water can be substantial."

He drew in a deep breath, held it for a time, and then exhaled. For a moment his head was encircled by a small cloud of ash-gray smoke and the room quickly filled with the scent of bergamot and sandalwood.

"I daresay a cold bath might also help to nullify your persistent desire for marriage," he added, tipping his head to study the various pedestrians making their way along Baker Street.

I frowned. "I can't possibly see how a cold bath would have anything at all to do with my relationship with Mary. Nor do I fathom the connection between chilled water and rest."

My friend looked up for a moment, and I thought a fleeting smile appeared ever so briefly on his long, angular face. Then I wondered if it was anything other than my fatigued, over-active imagination at work.

"It is hardly a unique insight, Watson," Holmes said. "It is a well-known fact that prodigious amounts of cold water *do* have a tendency to 'wake' one up, in every sense of the word."

His tone, which could often be sardonic, was suspiciously lacking in obvious irony. I grimaced. Before I could formulate an appropriate reply, he had already returned his attention to the street below.

"Fascinating," he said, suddenly. I saw him take an uncommonly quick draw on his briar-root and then exhale it equally quickly. "Most interesting."

He turned back to me and frowned. "It appears that sleep, let alone reading the paper, will have to elude you for some time to come, Watson. I suspect we are about to have yet another client."

"This seems a bit soon, Holmes," I said, earnestly. "Would you not consider it prudent to allow some time to recuperate from our recent endeavors?"

"I think not," he replied, seemingly unaffected by my momentary distress. "Even if I did wish to grant you the sleep you desire, this person is of...particular interest to me."

I was momentarily taken aback by this declaration. There are very few men or women for whom Sherlock Holmes would express a unique fascination. Among them were the alluring and dangerous Irene Adler, and the nefarious Professor James Moriarity. For various reasons, I knew that the individual in question could not be either one of them.

"How do you know that this person will become a client, Holmes?"

"Elementary," he said, removing the pipe from his lips and staring thoughtfully into the bowl. "The visitor that Mrs. Hudson is presently receiving is none other than the notorious occultist, Aleister Crowley."

Holmes pointed to the newspaper in my lap. I looked down and saw that morning's headline, which in my fatigued state, I had as yet failed to read:

Sir Fallowgrove Dead; Noted Occultist Sought!

Below it was a drawing of the infamous Mr. Crowley, which in its dark and scowling representation, made him appear more than a bit sinister. To the right of the sketch was a second column topped by an equally sensationalistic headline:

Famed 'Other Eye' Blue Diamond Missing!

"I find it unlikely," said Holmes, "that such a man—especially one in what appears to be his present predicament—would seek us out simply for afternoon tea, Watson."

"'Death,'" said Aleister Crowley, regally, "is the wish of some, the relief of many, and the end of all'. And that, Mr. Holmes, is the essence of why I find myself on your doorstep today, for I fear that death may soon be the end of me!"

Sherlock Holmes sat back in his chair, taking long draughts from his briar-root and studying the man who sat on the settee across from him. I was seated to one side, listening intently and watching both men with equal fascination.

Crowley, whom I had read much about in the press, was more impressive than one might have expected from a man of his dubious reputation, and not particularly sinister at all. I noted with some surprise that he was dressed as well as any Mayfair gentleman, in a conservative and well-tailored suit. His dark brown hair was parted high and severely on the left, which served only to emphasize the pale and generally unhealthy pallor of his skin. Most notably, I could not help but observe that his pudgy, round and vaguely aristocratic face bore an expression of unshakeable confidence and conviction. Even when seated, he exuded a strange magnetism not unlike that of Sherlock Holmes himself.

"And was it not Lucius Seneca who also wrote, 'It is the power of the mind to be unconquerable'?" said Holmes, evenly. "It occurs to me that a man with powers such as those you claim to possess would be immune not only to death, but to the mundane efforts of such entities as Scotland Yard."

I searched my friend's expression for any signs of mockery, but his hawk-like features remained as implacable as ever. Crowley's face darkened for the briefest of moments, and in his keen eyes I saw a quick flash of immense rage. Then it passed so quickly that it might not have been there at all.

"Well, Mr. Holmes," said he, with a sudden smile that was disconcertingly affable, "you appear to be everything I've heard—and undoubtedly more. I hope, then, that you will consider my case. Have you by chance examined this morning's edition of the *Times*?"

"I have."

I was not aware that Holmes had already read the paper, which was now draped face-down over my knee. When I had come through the door that morning it had still been resting on the foyer rug, apparently untouched.

My confusion must have been evident upon my face, for Holmes noticed this and said, "That is why too much sleep leaves a man always a step behind, Watson, and why I counsel so much against it."

"But why," I asked, peevishly, "would you put the newspaper back down as if unread?"

"I have observed," replied Holmes, "that discovering a fresh newspaper each morning is an important part of your daily ritual. In fact, you seem to find it quite energizing. Given your excessive dependency upon sleep, I believe such a small and harmless delusion to be beneficial to your daily vitality."

I opened my mouth to protest, but upon reflection, found that I could not disagree with him. Reading the newspaper after it had already been paged through by other hands was not nearly as satisfying to me as being the first one to open it.

I was loath to admit this fact out loud to my friend, however. I was also abruptly aware that it was uncommon for us to have such an exchange in the presence of a client, so therefore I elected to remain silent.

"As you may have read," interjected Crowley, impatiently, "the police have convinced the editors at the *Times* to help turn the public against me by suggesting that, as the so-called 'Wickedest Man Alive', I was somehow involved in the theft of the blue diamond as well as the death of

Sir Francis Fallowgrove."

"More precisely," said Holmes, "the paper suggests that you performed certain spells which caused the stone to vanish and subsequently led to Fallowgrove's demise." He stared intently at our visitor. "Would you consider this to be a true statement of fact, Mr. Crowley?"

Our visitor blinked once. Then he laughed, sardonically. "Oh, most certainly! In fact, you may not be aware of this, Mr. Holmes, but I actually *am* in the routine habit of casting spells which kill everything from annoying children to the occasional small pet—especially those that bark incessantly."

He grimaced and shook his head in apparent disgust.

"Come now, I'm astonished that a rational man such as yourself could even consider such an idea. Really!"

"I did not suggest that I believe such a thing to be probable, or even possible," replied Holmes. "In point of fact, I have no belief or trust in the supernatural whatsoever. However, whether or not *you* believe that you are capable of such an act, and that certain others might agree, is entirely relevant to the present situation, I think. After all, Mr. Crowley, a man's actions are most often predicated by his beliefs."

He stood up and studied his pipe again for a moment, then stared intensely at Crowley. Our infamous visitor attempted to meet his gaze with equal force. However, following the example of my friend, from whom I have learned much of the art of close observation, I immediately took notice of a faint tremble at the corner of Crowley's mouth. He was, I realized, a man barely in control of some deeper fear.

"Let me be frank, Mr. Crowley," continued Holmes. "Although the *Times* implied that you are being sought for questioning, I am certain that Inspector Lestrade of Scotland Yard has, in fact, ascertained your whereabouts and shall be arriving at my door any moment, fully intending to place you under arrest."

Crowley's already pale countenance whitened even more, an effect I would have previously thought impossible, and in the somewhat muted light of the sitting room, his skin seemed momentarily translucent, each vein as clear against his face as the lines on some ancient parchment.

"But Holmes," I asked, puzzled by his conviction, "how could you possibly be sure of such a thing? And in all of London, why would Inspector Lestrade come *here* looking for Mr. Crowley?"

"When Mr. Crowley made his appearance," said Holmes, "I could not help but notice that he had been followed by one of Inspector Lestrade's sergeants. That very man, wearing a rather plain suit and bowler hat, immediately began skulking about on one of the stoops across the street."

Crowley started to reply, but before he could utter a single word the pounding of several pairs of boots sounded on the stairs, followed by a powerful and sustained knocking upon the door of our apartment.

"And there you have it," said Sherlock Holmes. "It seems that the good Inspector has indeed arrived."

The entrance of Inspector Lestrade was uncharacteristically dramatic, something I knew appealed to my friend, although I also knew that he was not likely to openly betray such an emotion.

When Holmes opened the door, the plainclothed Sergeant that he had noticed earlier entered first, followed by a uniformed officer and another, stouter man whom I did not recognize. Then Inspector G. Lestrade made his entry, his penetrating eyes peering out from a narrow face whose skin was nearly as waxy and plain as that of Aleister Crowley. He took in every detail of the room, his rodent-like gaze pausing only for a moment on Crowley before coming to rest on Sherlock Holmes.

"I must confess, Mr. Holmes," said he, loftily, "I am a bit surprised to find you in the company of such a man. Did you not see this morning's *Times*?"

"I did," said Holmes. "It was, in fact, the events described within it which led Mr. Crowley to this very doorstep."

Before Lestrade could reply, Crowley stood up, indignantly. "I resent your inference, Inspector," he announced, imperiously.

The stout man with Lestrade, whose somewhat pudgy face seemed nearly taken up by enormous dueling eyebrows and a thick, well-pronounced moustache, remained silent but studied Crowley with intense focus, as if he might somehow evaporate at any moment.

"Sit down, Mr. Crowley," said Holmes, firmly. "And unless you wish to make your circumstances direr than they already are, please keep silent until I instruct you otherwise."

Crowley examined my friend's steely expression, then returned to his place on the settee, crossed his arms impetuously, and made the prudent decision not to speak. Holmes, disregarding Lestrade's comment, indicated toward an empty wooden chair beside the window.

"Please have a seat, Inspector," said he, "and introduce us to your companions."

Lestrade scowled slightly then lowered his slight frame into the chair, which was bereft of any padding at all. He shifted about somewhat uncomfortably, and I suppressed an impulse to smile knowingly. On certain occasions Holmes would invite a visitor to sit in that very seat when he wished him to be unsettled by the experience. Having sat there myself, I knew that in short order it could become taxing to the spine, not to mention the rest of one's lower anatomy.

"Of course, of course," said Lestrade. He gestured toward the plainclothed man in the bowler hat. "Holmes, you undoubtedly recognize Sergeant Litster from the Yard, and my other man here is Constable Powers." He nodded at the stout mustached man. "And this gentleman is William Pinkerton, here from America at the behest of Sir Francis Fallowgrove."

"The *late* Sir Francis," corrected Pinkerton. "However, since his death, I am now in the employ of Lloyds, which held the policy on the diamond while it was on display."

He stepped forward and jutted out one large, beefy hand, which my friend seemed to study much the way he would a rare insect or a mysterious crystal which had formed among his experiments during the night. Then, realizing that Pinkerton meant for him to respond in kind, Holmes took hold of the American's hand, his narrow fingers instantly dwarfed by those of the bigger man.

"I've been looking forward to meeting you," continued Pinkerton, pumping Holmes' arm with great enthusiasm. "Lestrade here has told me a great deal about you, and his tales of how you've helped him close various cases have piqued my curiosity."

Holmes studied Lestrade with one quizzically raised eyebrow. The Inspector shifted in the chair and became suddenly fascinated by the cuticles of his slightly ragged, yellow fingernails. Of course, my friend was content to allow Lestrade to take full credit for Holmes' contributions to their occasional collaborations, preferring instead to remain quietly in the background where his deductive abilities could be best put to use. Nevertheless, I suspected my friend had to be surprised that Lestrade had made such claims so boldly in front of him. Upon reflection, I realized that this said a great deal about the inspector's regard for the American, William Pinkerton.

"Inspector Lestrade," said Holmes, gravely, "can be prone to a certain amount of exaggeration when the mood strikes him."

I nearly laughed out loud at his serious tone, but restrained myself. Lestrade coughed into his hand and stood up. "Since you have read the *Times*," said he, quickly, "then you must know why we are here."

"I can easily deduce it, given the disappearance of the blue diamond being followed so closely by the untimely death of Sir Francis," answered Holmes. "I can also see that you have come with more men than you would normally require for the detainment of one unarmed prisoner. One, I might add, who seems perfectly sedate, and for the most part, accommodating. However, the more fundamental thing which I cannot discern is the evidence you have that merits the arrest of Mr. Crowley at all."

"I believe," said William Pinkerton, stepping forward once again, "that I am the best man to answer that question, Mr. Holmes."

He removed a small leather-bound notebook from his vest pocket, opened it, and began to flip through its pages.

"We have a witness that claims Mr. Crowley performed some type of heathen ceremony two nights ago. The witness further stated that the purpose of this observance, which involved, and I quote, 'an aspect of the Hindu Sita', was to rid the suspect of his enemies, whoever they might be."

"When we learned of the death of Sir Fallowgrove," interjected Lestrade, "and examined other facts, which in the interest of justice I am not yet free to reveal, we were able to conclude that Mr. Crowley was a most suitable suspect for both crimes."

"Is that so," murmured Holmes. "Well, then, Inspector, am I to assume then that you subscribe to the supernatural as a means to theft and murder?"

Lestrade's dull face darkened. "Of course not!" he said, peevishly.

"And you, Mr. Pinkerton?" asked Holmes. "Do you believe that a man is capable of summoning the otherworldly in his quest for vengeance, or even greed?"

Pinkerton frowned. "I am sorry to say that I find your question to be... offensive, Mr. Holmes. I am a Christian man, and I give no credence to fairies, ghosts, and the like. It is pagan, and against my faith. More directly, I can honestly say that such things are defied by all that I have seen and heard thus far during my life."

"And yet, here both of you stand," said Holmes, "each prepared to arrest a man on the basis of claims which you both assert to be false."

"As I said," replied Lestrade, testily, "there are things about this case which I cannot speak of, Holmes. For now, we have enough evidence to take Mr. Crowley into custody, and that we are going to do."

"Please, Holmes!" cried Crowley as Sergeant Litster and Constable Powers took him by the arms and lifted him from the settee. "I am innocent!"

"Fear not," said Holmes. "Inspector Lestrade is a fair man and you will not be poorly treated in his custody. I shall take your case, Mr. Crowley, for I believe you are innocent."

"I think you have chosen poorly this time, Holmes," said Lestrade, even as the still protesting Aleister Crowley was led from the apartment and down the stairs. "And I must say that it will not please me to see you proven wrong."

"On the contrary," said Holmes, "should Aleister Crowley be found guilty of the crimes for which you have detained him, I shall be pleased to acknowledge my error, Inspector. It is my hope, too, that in the 'interest of justice' you will allow me to be of assistance in whatever form that may take."

After the police and Pinkerton had gone and the door was once more firmly closed, I turned to Holmes with more questions than answers.

"How can you be so certain that Mr. Crowley is innocent?" I asked.

Holmes picked up the paper and opened it to the second page. There, the front page story continued, stating that the occultist was alleged to have called upon the Hindu goddess, Kali, during the course of his ceremony, with no other details given.

"I believe Mr. Crowley is innocent," said Holmes, "because of two things. First, when Mr. Pinkerton recounted the statements of his witness, he said that the ceremony in question involved an 'aspect of the Sita'. However, Mr. Crowley did not object to this characterization."

"And what is the significance of that, Holmes?"

"As it happens, Watson, in the interest of general knowledge, I have made a study of Hinduism and can say categorically that Kali, the dark goddess known as 'She Who Destroys', has nothing whatsoever to do with Sita, a goddess considered to be the daughter of Bhumi Devi, goddess of the Earth."

"I must confess," said I, puzzled, "I still do not see the connection."

"The *Times* story quotes an anonymous source that associates Mr. Crowley's activities that evening with Kali," said Holmes, patiently.

"Because Mr. Crowley did not object to the Sita reference, we can thereby conclude that Mr. Crowley believes the goddess Kali to be an aspect of Sita. That belief, as you now know, is incorrect."

"And the second thing?"

"That is less a question of fact than of personal belief," replied Holmes. "I am in general agreement with Mr. Pinkerton, in the sense that I have yet to encounter anything which leads me to believe in the supernatural or the spiritual. Furthermore, Watson, I happen to think that if the supernatural *did* exist, then it most certainly could not be manipulated by a man such as Aleister Crowley!"

It was just past six o'clock the following morning when Sherlock Holmes and I found ourselves delivered by Hansom Cab to the intersection of Cornhill and Threadneedle Streets. At that early hour, the city of London was shrouded by a thick and damp fog, and a bitterly cold wind gusted out of the east, whipping our cloaks about our bodies. I pulled mine tighter around my shoulders and glanced at my friend who, as usual, appeared unaffected by either the unfavorable temperature or the miserable dampness.

To our right the enormity of the Royal Exchange building rose into the pervasive dreariness, the columned Romanesque façade partially obscured by tendrils of gray-white fog that curled hazily around the high-peaked roof. Barely visible along the lower frieze of the portico were engraved, in Latin, the letters: *Anno XIII. Elizabethæ R. Conditvm; Anno VIII. Victoria R. Restavratvm.*

Because it was still quite dark, the coachman removed one of the side-lamps from the cab and held it aloft so that we could better make our way across the open paved courtyard, past the regal statue of the Duke of Wellington, and ascend the portico steps. Once there, we discovered that the gates which protected the enormous entranceway had been opened and secured, but beyond it remained two towering wooden doors, both tightly closed. Each was banded with thick metal and punctuated by a large, iron door knocker, and it was one of these that Sherlock Holmes grasped with his gloved hand and rapped hard against the backplate, causing a great booming sound to echo across the broad arcade.

After a moment we heard a deep rumble as the right door began to grind inward across the stone floor. Then a thin ribbon of light fell through the widening rift, and we saw illuminated in it the sour face of a man who looked none too pleased to be greeting us while it was so dark.

"Who are you?" he said, without preamble, staring at us with squinted eyes that glittered with a black and foul combination of impatience and distrust.

"I am Sherlock Holmes," replied my friend, "and with me is John Watson. We are here to see Mr. Peter Curtis of Lloyds."

"So he's expecting you, then?" asked the man, scowling.

"Without question," said Holmes. "Please announce our arrival, if you would be so kind."

"No need," said a voice from behind the door. "Admit them, Pack, and then lock up again."

"Yes, sir," muttered the scowl-faced man, reluctantly.

He stepped back from the opening and held his lamp higher, highlighting the narrow foyer behind him. At the edge of the lamp's glow stood a tall and exceptionally thin gentleman, expensively dressed in a suit of fine gray wool. His narrow, fox-like face was expressionless, and his eyes, while not as poisoned by the darker emotions as those of the watchman, nevertheless studied us with a level of weighted calculation.

During the course of my years of association with Sherlock Holmes, it was a look I had come to know well, one most often possessed by the cynical such as bankers, stockbrokers or policemen—and all too often, criminals.

"Mr. Curtis, I presume?" queried Holmes, stepping into the foyer.

I followed closely behind him. As soon as we were inside, the watchman slid the door closed behind us with some effort, and the sound of the heavy wood scraping along the stone was greatly magnified within the narrow confines of the space. As we followed Curtis out into the inner courtyard of the Exchange, I could hear the man, Pack, muttering darkly beneath his breath, but could not make out specifically what he was saying.

"Indeed," said Curtis, coughing into a white handkerchief that had clearly been soiled by repeated episodes of the same. "Welcome to Lloyds, Mr. Holmes." He glanced at me with quite obvious uninterest, but nevertheless extended his hand with at least a modicum of courtesy. "And again, you sir are...?"

"Watson," I said, taking his hand and briefly shaking it. "John Watson, M.D."

"A physician, then?" replied Curtis, raising one eyebrow. "Impressive, sir, impressive, indeed. You must pardon my impertinence, however, but in regards to Sir Fallgrove, it strikes me that the time for a physician has passed. Wouldn't you agree?"

I felt my face flush with momentary anger. Before I could respond, Holmes said, "Dr. Watson is my friend, but also a valued associate, Mr. Curtis. I think that you will find his input significant as we examine the facts of this case."

Curtis seemed to consider my friend's words, then sighed. "Mr. Pinkerton speaks quite well of you, Holmes," he said. "I can only assume, then, that Dr. Watson is also comprised of much more than he appears. If you would, please follow me."

The gentleman, whom I now began to see as slightly emaciated, led us across the courtyard and into the westerly hall of the Exchange, then up a flight of tiered stairs to a broad landing. On each side were numerous offices, some of which overlooked the courtyard below. After leading us through a series of corridors and rooms as bewildering to me as any ancient maze, we found ourselves in a large windowed meeting room. In one corner sat a modest chimney, and within it a fire burned, casting the room in a warm light. At the center of the chamber stood an enormous polished table, its elaborate surface embedded with a variety of rare and beautiful woods. Around this magnificent table sat the American, William Pinkerton, and another, younger bearded man with whom I was unfamiliar. As we entered the room, the two of them stood up to greet us.

"Good to see you again, Mr. Holmes," said Pinkerton.

"Indeed," added the second man. "It has been quite a while since we last encountered one another."

I glanced at my friend with some surprise. Given the extensive time we had spent together over the past years, I thought I had come to know nearly everyone of Holmes' acquaintances, but this man was a complete stranger to me.

"When we last met, Ian, I believe you were a laboratory assistant," said Holmes. "It was mentioned to me last year that you had been taken on as a surgeon with Scotland Yard. I would say that congratulations are in order."

The man inclined his head, which was largely bereft of hair, and smiled, faintly, from beneath his generous facial hair. "After a great deal of education and altogether too much poverty, I must say that my station in life has, indeed, greatly improved."

"I do not believe I have made your acquaintance," I said, impatiently. "Would you care to introduce us, Holmes?"

"Of course," said Holmes, blithely. "Forgive me. Dr. Watson, allow me to present Dr. Ian Gallagher, formerly of the Royal College of Physicians and the London Hospital, now of Scotland Yard."

"I gathered that much," I replied, a bit irritably. "A pleasure to meet you, sir."

"Likewise," said Gallagher, unsmilingly. "I must say, it would have been better to have met for the first time under more favorable circumstances, Dr. Watson."

"Unfortunately, in our profession it is too often that colleagues meet at similar, melancholy junctures," I replied. "You are involved in the Sir Fallowgrove case, then?"

"Alas, replied Dr. Gallagher, "it was my sad duty to undertake Sir Fallowgrove's post-mortem examination."

Each of us took a seat around the table, and after a moment a servant entered the room carrying a tray bearing a silver tea service and a small plate of biscuits. He placed them at the center of the table and then backed silently from the room, leaving us to discuss the events at hand.

"Tell me," said Holmes, helping himself to a cup of tea, "what did you discover during your examination?"

"Although all indications were of a heart attack, Inspector Lestrade instructed me to search for any signs of foul play," recited Dr. Gallagher, his tone altogether clinical. "This would have included any marks indicative of violence, such as shiv wounds and the like. However, I found nothing of the sort." He shrugged. "In addition, I examined Sir Francis for any manifestations of toxic poisoning, including needle injection marks and so on. However, there was nothing at all detectable, no punctures of any kind, nor any chemical traces apparent in the stomach or in the tissue samples I examined."

"Thank you, doctor," said Holmes, "for your thorough examination and for sharing your findings with me. I must admit, I do find your profession fascinating. However, as I am hardly an expert in your field, perhaps you would be willing to enlighten me as to the procedural limits of such an examination?"

Dr. Gallagher looked perplexed. "I'm not sure what you mean, Holmes."

"For example," said Holmes, "was there anything else which caught your attention? Anything at all, no matter how trivial?"

Gallagher seemed to consider Holmes' question, then frowned. "There were two somewhat unusual things, but I'm sure they were unrelated to his passing."

"Perhaps so," said Holmes. "But please continue, if you would."

"Very well. The first were a number of small rashes evident on the palm of Sir Francis's left hand, as well as the Antebrachial surface of his right arm. However, I attributed them to his hobby of gathering woodland plants for his garden. In this case, the rashes were most likely caused by exposure to *Toxicodendron radicans*."

"Excuse me," said Pinkerton, irritably, raising his great, bushy eyebrows. "If you wouldn't mind speaking English, sir, I'd be quite grateful. Unfortunately, you have exceeded my rather limited grasp of Latin."

"*Toxicondendron radicans*," explained Holmes, patiently, "is more commonly referred to as Poison Ivy, while *Antebrachial* is the anatomical term which refers to the lower portion of the human arm."

"The forearm, as it is commonly called," I added, helpfully.

"Rashes," said Holmes. "Very interesting. Tell me, Doctor Gallagher, was Sir Fallowgrove frequently exposed to toxic plants?"

"Nothing that could be directly confirmed by anyone in his household," replied Gallagher, "but it did seem logical to me, as Sir Francis was a collector of certain wild plants, especially those located in the depths of the forest. On occasion he would even collect specimens nocturnally, which obviously would heighten the chances for accidental exposure."

"I see," said Holmes. "And what was the second unusual characteristic that you noticed?"

"An internal one, actually," replied Gallagher. "During the surgical autopsy I discovered that Sir Fallowgrove's lungs displayed a number of fresh scars."

"And to what cause did you attribute them?"

"When I interviewed his staff, they related to me that Sir Fallowgrove had been visiting friends in the countryside a few weeks past. Apparently, at some time during the journey he found himself assisting a fire brigade in suppressing a burning coach house. As such, I determined that the scarring had most likely been caused by excessive heat or by smoke inhalation."

"Very good. Thank you." Holmes turned to Pinkerton. "Tell me, sir," said he, "what are your thoughts thus far?"

"When I originally arrived in London," said Pinkerton, "I was in pursuit of the master thief, Adam Worth, a rogue you may be familiar with, as his exploits have been reported extensively throughout the press on both sides of the Atlantic."

"I am familiar with the name," said Holmes. "I believe the press calls him America's own 'Napoleon of Crime'."

Pinkerton winced as if the characterization pained him. "Worth has been called that by some yellow journalists, yes. And I'm sorry to say that, to date, he has eluded my agents at every turn. Even now they continue to scour the countryside for any sign of him."

"And how, if I may ask, did your pursuit of Mr. Worth lead to your involvement with Sir Fallowgrove and the blue diamond known as the Other Eye?"

"I believe I am the best one to answer that question," said Curtis, self-importantly. "But first, I should acquaint you with a brief history of the Other Eye and what is perhaps more relevant to this discussion: the alleged 'curse' rumored to accompany it."

For a moment there was a long and awkward silence around the table, and then the American, Pinkerton, leaned back in his chair and waved his hand dismissively.

"Absolute poppycock," he said. "As Holmes and I agreed upon yesterday, there is most certainly a mystery here but I am entirely convinced it is not at all supernatural in nature!"

"And I will reiterate," said Holmes, "that I quite agree with Mr. Pinkerton. However, the accusations against Mr. Crowley are already gaining credence amongst members of the public, as well as the press. I think it is in the best interests of justice to examine every aspect of the case no matter what our personal convictions may be."

"Do as you will," said Pinkerton, with a grunt. "But it seems a waste of time to me."

"Pray continue, Mr. Curtis," said Holmes.

Curtis steepled his fingers beneath his chin, seeming to consider carefully what he was about to say. "When Sir Fallowgrove first made the decision to display the blue diamond at his home," he said, "he approached Lloyds to act as the insuring agent. We were, in a word, skeptical, as the tale he told of how he acquired the jewel in question seemed too fantastic to be believed."

"Did he happen upon it while playing a game of Loo?" I asked, innocently. "I must confess I never excelled at it myself."

"This hardly seems the time for humor, Watson," admonished Holmes, staring at me disapprovingly.

"Actually," said Curtis, gazing balefully from eyes sunken into a face that now appeared to me to be quite emaciated, "that is not too far from being accurate. In point of fact, Sir Fallowgrove claimed to have won the stone in a legal settlement against the owner of a small West Indian shipping company. Not a card game, precisely, Dr. Watson, but I imagine one could assume such an arrangement would provide better odds than most of them."

"Quite so," said Holmes, absently.

I noticed then that he was paying particular attention to Curtis's right hand, which was still positioned beneath his chin. I saw immediately what my friend was looking at: a burn mark on the leading edge of Curtis's palm, small but easily visible if one happened to be looking for it.

"That appears to be a rather painful burn you have there, Mr. Curtis," I said, indicating toward his hand.

"The perils of tea, Dr. Watson," said Curtis, lightly, "or to be more precise, the preparation of the hot water used to steep the leaves. I carelessly placed my hand too near the fire some days ago, you see, and received this for my inattention."

"I'd be inattentive, too," said Pinkerton, dryly, "if I began every day well before the dawn, as you seem to."

"Please continue with your recollection, Mr. Curtis," said Holmes, with some impatience. "I am especially interested in the curse that you mentioned."

"Of course, of course," said Curtis. "According to Sir Fallowgrove, the blue diamond, which he coined the 'Other Eye', was originally discovered more than one-hundred years ago by a grave robber in a temple somewhere along India's Coleroon River, and only recently resurfaced in the possession of the shipping company owner from which he received it."

"That story is familiar to me," said Holmes, rubbing his chin thoughtfully. "Are you suggesting, Mr. Curtis, that the *Times* is correct, and that the diamond in Sir Fallowgrove's possession actually is the lost companion to the famous Tavernier Blue?"

"What's that again, Holmes?" I asked, puzzled. "I'm not familiar with that particular gemstone."

"I am not surprised," my friend replied. "You would know it better by its current and much more familiar name, the Hope Diamond."

"But that's impossible!" I said. "There is only one such stone and at present it is in the possession of Lord Francis Hope."

"Had you found the time to examine yesterday's paper, Watson," said Holmes, "you would have stumbled across a brief history of the Hope Diamond contained therein."

He took one of the biscuits from the silver tray and bit into it with surprising delicacy, then took a moment to flick the fallen crumbs from his waistcoat. I opened my mouth to protest, but before I could speak he continued on, ignoring me.

"And had you kept reading," he said, "you would have discovered that the Tavernier Blue, as it was then known, was originally a much rougher stone and theorized to be one of two 'eyes', both stolen from the inveterate remains of a pagan god. Or the statue of one, at least."

"Quite right! Very good, Mr. Holmes," said Curtis, admiringly. "Of course, this brings us to the curse I mentioned. You see, gentlemen, the Hope Diamond has long borne the reputation of delivering upon its recipients all manner of bad luck—and under certain circumstances, even death."

"Which, if one grants credibility to such stories, would begin with Jean Baptiste Tavernier," said Holmes, reaching for a second biscuit. "He is, of course, the gentleman who allegedly removed the stone from the temple. Apparently, sometime after selling it, Mr. Tavernier journeyed to Russia, and while there on holiday was promptly torn apart by a pack of wild dogs. A thoroughly charming story, yes?"

"Not especially," I muttered, gazing sadly at the plate with its few remaining biscuits. I had been considering sampling one of them, but now my appetite seemed to have abruptly forsaken me.

"Quite the entertaining story, Holmes," said Pinkerton, irritably. "But it can be just as easily explained by coincidence. As I told you yesterday, I'm a Christian man and have no use for such ideas. Besides, I fail to see how these fairy tales bring us any closer to solving the murder of Sir Fallowgrove, or to recovering the stolen diamond!"

"If you would," said Holmes, "I would like to beg your indulgence for just a while longer, Mr. Pinkerton. As a consulting detective yourself, I am certain you will acknowledge that the best way to determine the facts of a case is to observe everything that is available to be seen—or in this case, unseen."

Holmes turned his attention to Curtis. "You mentioned that Lloyds was initially reluctant to insure the Other Eye because of the account Sir Fallowgrove related about how he came to possess the stone. What about its provenance provoked your doubts?"

Curtis shrugged. "We simply felt that his story was too convenient, as it were. Sir Fallowgrove cited privacy reasons and would not say how many pounds were at stake in his settlement with the shipping company owner. This made it impossible for us to determine the plausibility of the diamond being used as a settlement for that debt, especially given its high value. Of course, while that omission alone was not proof of any nefarious dealings on the part of Sir Fallowgrove, it still piqued our curiosity."

"I see," said Holmes. "And yet you ultimately chose to insure the stone anyway?"

"Yes. After examining it thoroughly—a task which I personally undertook along with two expert gemologists—the board agreed that the stone was legitimate and that Lloyds would insure it for the stated value of sixty-thousand pounds. Simply put, Mr. Holmes, we could proffer no reasonable explanation as to why we would not be willing to do so, as the contract promised to be quite profitable for us."

"And that," said Pinkerton, gruffly, "is where I had the bad luck to come into all this. When Mr. Curtis learned I was in London, he approached me at my temporary office with a proposal to provide security for Sir Fallowgrove. With every lead in the Worth case gone cold, it seemed a simple matter to provide the necessary security."

"It must have also been apparent to you as well," said Holmes, casually, "that your involvement with Sir Fallowgrove and the Other Eye would result in a great deal of positive press coverage for the Pinkerton Agency."

The American's face reddened. Before he could speak, Curtis said, "What makes it particularly embarrassing, Mr. Holmes, is that the Pinkerton men were on guard the entire night. It strikes me that this illustrious 'agency' has been made a mockery of by Aleister Crowley, a man who is little more than a degenerate murderer and thief."

"And that is why," said Pinkerton, fiercely, "I am determined to resolve this case as expeditiously as possible, one way or the other. To that end I will accept all the help that I can muster, even if it happens to come from the man working on behalf of the villain in question."

"Actually, you are mistaken," said Holmes, evenly. "While it is true that I have agreed to take up the case of Aleister Crowley, I do so not out of any special concern for his well-being, but as I have said more than once, in the greater interest of justice."

Shrugging, Pinkerton sat back in his chair and stroked his moustache absently. "Whatever your reasons, I'm quite content to allow them to remain just that—yours. What concerns me now is the reputation of my firm in London, not to mention the rest of Europe."

"Your concerns, Mr. Pinkerton, are duly noted," said Holmes. "I must admit, however, that one aspect of this case is particularly puzzling to me. It is my understanding that when the Other Eye was discovered missing, the display was nonetheless still locked and sealed. Is that correct?"

"Indeed," said Pinkerton, glumly. "It was as if the stone simply evaporated into the air." He shook his head sadly. "As much as it pains me to do so, I find that I agree with Curtis here. The Pinkertons are not accustomed to appearing as fools, but this case has become a public relations catastrophe for us!"

"Perhaps," said Holmes, calmly, "dire would be a more apt word. I do not believe that a catastrophe—a word with much more…permanent connotations—is a certainty at this point in time. One thing that *is* certain, however, is that the death of Sir Fallowgrove and the disappearance of the Other Eye cannot be attributed to the supernatural."

"Perhaps not in the usual sense," said I, sensing an opportunity to contribute something of use. "However, I am aware of numerous instances where those who profess a belief in the supernatural have displayed severe psychosomatic symptoms after being 'cursed' by another person."

"Impossible!" exclaimed Pinkerton.

"Not at all," I said. "In point of fact, on certain occasions the subject of a so-called curse has died, ostensibly from his own conviction that death was now a foregone conclusion."

"I have read of such cases myself, actually," said Dr. Gallagher. "It is quite true that the human mind is capable of remarkable—and sometimes horrifying—acts upon the very body which serves to protect it."

"Assuming that you are correct," said Pinkerton, "then there may be an explanation here that makes some degree of sense."

He removed a slender notebook from his coat pocket and flipped through the pages, finally stopping in the middle of the book.

"Ah, yes, here it is. Apparently, Crowley has quite the reputation as a skilled hypnotist; perhaps he was able to employ some kind of power of suggestion to kill Sir Francis. What do you think of that, Holmes?" My friend seemed to consider the proposition for some moments. "I think not," he said, at last. "I, too, have some skill and experience in that arena and have studied the field for many years. I can tell you with absolute certainty that the human mind possesses great power over the body, but that it is, at the same time, ruled by a tremendous prohibition against self-harm. While it is true that some unstable individuals can on occasion cause themselves injury, it is my considered opinion that a man of good mental health could not be hypnotized to cause himself significant harm. Based upon what I have learned thus far, I have no reason to doubt that Sir Fallowgrove was of sound mind."

Pinkerton frowned. "I see your point, Holmes. So what do you suggest, then? This seems to lead us back to where we began."

"Not entirely," said Holmes. "I think that it is time for us to visit the scene of the crime. Most significantly, we must summon the witnesses to Aleister Crowley's pagan ceremony, as well as Inspector Lestrade and Mr. Crowley himself, so that we may put all of the facts of this case in their proper perspective."

He looked into my eyes and I saw his pupils shining with a familiar anticipation that I had come to know well over the many years of our friendship.

"Come, gentlemen," said he, addressing the entire room, his voice betraying none of the excitement that I knew now gripped his imagination. "The game, as they say, is afoot."

Within the hour, Peter Curtis and his man, Pack, had dispatched a messenger to Inspector Lestrade as well as arranged for several hansom cabs, operated by a gaggle of street Arabs who had risen early and were available for the commission, to convey the five of us to the home of the late Sir Francis Fallowgrove. We were barely settled into our respective conveyances, each with its capacity of two passengers, when the crack of multiple whips echoed in the fading darkness, nearly in unison, and we plunged off down Threadneedle Street, the six sets of wheels and the horse's hooves making a terrible clatter in the relative quiet of the early, fog-shrouded morn.

As we rattled along, I noted that Sherlock Holmes was gazing out into the drifting fog, seemingly far away from the moment and deep in some thought, the meaning of which I could not readily discern. Ordinarily I was loathe to disturb my friend during such moments of introspection, but today I found myself bothered by thoughts of the resurgent supernatural aspects which seemed to plaque the case at hand.

"Tell me, Holmes," said I. "Do you truly believe we'll discover some mysterious meaning to all of this at the home of Sir Fallowgrove?"

"Undoubtedly not," said my companion, gravely, turning his gaze upon me. "You know all too well my philosophy on matters such as these." He waved one gloved hand in the general direction of the dark and torturously narrow side streets and alleyways which comprise so much of the city of London. "Mankind strives to find deeper meaning in all things, Watson, but he does so in deliberate avoidance of the prosaic reality which so slowly and inexorably consumes him. To put it more simply, the human soul is a darker and far more convoluted labyrinth than any city, and one need not look to the supernatural to understand that."

"How can you be so certain, Holmes?" I asked. "As complex as the human soul undoubtedly is, the world is also a large and intricate place, and there is much we do not yet understand. Why, just last month I was reading in the *Strand Magazine* an article which stated that the explorer, Sir Randolph Ceasley, recently discovered no less than three varied species of frog in the jungles of South America, all previously unknown to science."

"Unknown," said Holmes, dryly, "but hardly supernatural, Watson. Please alert me the very first time that a frog performs a verifiably magical act, and I will be suitably impressed."

I grimaced, but could think of nothing immediate to say, so I looked instead to the now fading darkness, which remained filled with a multitude of passing buildings and passageways, all of which I was utterly unfamiliar with.

"Is it my imagination, Holmes," I asked, suddenly, "or do the structures here seem...tidier than most?"

"It is not your imagination," said Holmes. "We are entering the district of Belgravia. I am sure you are familiar with it?"

"Of course," I said. "It's among the most fashionable districts in London!"

"Indeed," said Holmes, absently, as our coach began to slow. "Would you expect a man of Sir Fallowgrove's apparent wealth to reside anywhere else, Watson?"

At last, our cab came to a stop before a long row of adjoining four-story homes, all constructed of white alabaster, each with its own columned portico topped by a small, wrought-iron balcony overlooking the street. At this early hour most of the windows remained dark; however, a single gas lamp mounted beneath one of the porticos was lit, and I deduced, without much effort, that this must be the residence of the late Sir Francis Fallowgrove.

As we stood on the pathway in front of the house, two carriages approached from the opposite end of the street and pulled to a stop. A number of individuals stepped from each one, and as they hurried across the road toward us, I immediately recognized the thin, pale form of Inspector Lestrade as well as the broad, yet slightly stooped figure of Aleister Crowley, among the group.

"How do you do, Holmes," said Lestrade, irritably.

My friend merely nodded toward the other people who accompanied the Inspector, the curiosity in their faces clear in the ashen twilight. "Can I assume that these are the witnesses to Mr. Crowley's ceremony, Inspector?"

"Indeed," said Lestrade, "and they're none too happy to have been dragged out here before the sun's come up. Same goes for me, as a matter of fact. I hope you have a bloody good reason for calling us out this early, Holmes."

"Have patience, Inspector," my friend replied. "I believe you will find that all will be made clear in the next hour or so."

"I, for one, would much rather be warm in my bed," said Crowley, his pale, moon-like countenance creased by a sour pout that made him, in the moment, appear more boy than man. "And at home, mind you, not in some hideous cell at Lewes prison!"

"Shut up, you," said Lestrade, blithely. "You'll be lucky not to be hanged from the neck before this year is done, Crowley, so you'd best be silent for now."

The officer beside Crowley placed one hand on his shoulder, and I immediately recognized Sergeant Litster of Scotland Yard, whom Holmes and I had first met in our apartment on Baker Street just the day before. He nodded toward me in the cordial yet guarded manner so common to the members of London's police force, and I nodded politely back to him.

"So what now, Mr. Holmes?" asked Peter Curtis. He pushed his hands deeper into the pockets of the heavy, dark gray overcoat he now wore over his lighter gray suit. "I believe I speak for everyone when I state that frankly, I'm fascinated to see what you've come up with."

"And so you shall," said Holmes as he turned to climb the three short steps to the front door of Sir Fallowgrove's former home and then knocked upon it. After a moment, the door was flung open by a plump, matronly housekeeper dressed in a plain but well-made skirt and jacket, her hair neatly covered by a pretty lace cap. Her face appeared sorrowful, as if she had spent some time collapsed in tears, and I found this indication of loyalty to the late Sir Francis Fallowgrove to be quite touching.

"Oh!" said she, clearly startled to see the group of people standing on her porch so early in the morning. "You've arrived much sooner than I expected."

"My apologies," said Lestrade, gruffly, "but Holmes here felt it was necessary that we visit the scene of the crime at once."

"Quite so," said Holmes. "It is always advisable to pursue the facts of a case as close to the actual commission of the offense as possible so as to ensure that the recollections of all involved are suitably fresh, as it were."

"Old or new memories," said Pinkerton, "it strikes me that people will remember whatever they will, as they desire to."

"Possibly," said Holmes, cryptically, as we followed him into the home. "Or possibly not. I have found that the recollections of witnesses have something critically important in common with the physical location of a crime: it is best to preserve both, in their original state. And that is why I requested that Mr. Pinkerton keep the two original guards on duty, even going so far as to have them sleep here, so that the integrity of the crime scene would remain intact and unbroken until our arrival."

The housekeeper, whose name was Mrs. Georgina Rusnak, had been in the service of Sir Fallowgrove for more than ten years. She led us with assuredness to the large parlor where the Other Eye had been displayed, and where the empty case still remained, flanked by the two Pinkerton men whom Holmes had just mentioned. As we entered the parlor, the witnesses crowded in behind us. The two Pinkerton agents on duty immediately saluted their American supervisor in a fashion which seemed decidedly military, and which I greatly approved of.

"Nothing has been disturbed over the past forty-eight hours?" asked Pinkerton, without preamble.

The two men replied that nothing had, and that the room and the empty case remained undisturbed.

"Very well, then," said Pinkerton, "good work, men. Holmes, it's now in your hands. Take it away, then, as they say."

My friend studied the room, and then the empty case, pausing to rub his chin in that most considered of ways of which I knew so well. As for myself, I could see nothing special about the solid pedestal and the small pillow upon which the stone had rested before its disappearance; likewise the four panes of thick glass which surrounded it. Only the locked, copper lid was particularly unique, shaped as it was to resemble a diminutive Hindu temple.

Holmes turned back to the guards. "Tell me what you saw the night that the Other Eye disappeared, and leave out no detail, no matter how trivial you may believe it to be."

The two men glanced at each other, and I saw not guilt in their expressions, but embarrassment. They seemed to fidget for a moment, and then the taller of the two stared defiantly at my friend. "Truth be told, we hain't seen nor heard a thing," he said, "not two days ago, and not last night, either."

"'Tis true what he says!" exclaimed the shorter guard, whom I could see was greatly vexed. "Mr. Pinkerton pays us well to do our duty, and do it we did. Hain't nothing moved nor made a sound here since we come on duty!"

Holmes nodded but did not immediately speak. Leaning closer to the case, he took a short, deep breath through his nose, but did not reach out to touch the glass or the copper lid.

"Tell me," he said at last, "you men have—if you will pardon the unavoidable pun—touched upon two of the five human senses: sight and sound. In this instance I do not believe that the third sense, taste, is pertinent to the facts of the case. However, the fourth sense, touch, could very well be a different matter. During the night the diamond disappeared, did either of you men touch anything in this room?"

Both men declared that they had not, upon the specific orders of Sir Francis Fallowgrove. "He told us 'taint no one to touch the case," said the taller guard. "On his command we weren't to allow anyone within three feet of it, and weren't no reason for us to put our hands on anything else in here."

"Very good," said Holmes. "Continue guarding the case and do not allow anyone but myself, Mr. Curtis, or Mr. Pinkerton to touch it."

"There is one other sense," said I, "which you did not mention."

"Ah, yes," said he, "the sense of smell. Very good, Watson, I was just about to address that."

"How," said I, "will an examination of the olfactory provide you with any insight into this case, Holmes?"

"Patience, Watson," he replied. "As it happens, the sense of smell may very well provide the final clue necessary to bring clarity to this case." He turned to the guards once again. "Tell me, did either one of you notice any odd scents in this room during the night?"

"Not me," said the taller guard. "We stood separate watches, so there was only one of us on duty at a time, but I can tell you I hain't smelled nothing strange."

The other guard grimaced. "There was something," said he, "two nights past. For an hour or two I smelled something powerful strange, but it seemed to come and go. I di'nt think no more of it once it was gone for good. Figured it was from the sewers or somethin' like that."

"Strange smells, no one in sight, and a diamond missing from a locked case," said I, annoyed. "Once again, I find myself no closer to unraveling all of this than I was a day ago. Tell me, Holmes, what do you make of it all?"

"As I said, patience, Watson," repeated he, a bit sharply. "I assure you that all will be made clear." He turned to the witnesses, all of whom stood together along the parlor's back wall. "I understand that each of you attended Mr. Crowley's ritual where he claimed to have summoned Kali, the Hindu goddess? Is that correct?"

One of the witnesses, a young man perhaps twenty years of age, stepped forward, his jaw thrust out in defiance. "We all saw the Master perform the consecrated ritual, and we beheld the goddess, Kali, as she was sent forth to exact her revenge for the theft of the sacred stone!" When he spoke, his voice quavered slightly, yet I could see in his eyes that he was clearly a true and passionate believer in the teachings of Aleister Crowley.

"It's true!" cried a plump, older woman standing just behind the younger man. "Sir Fallowgrove brought the vengeance of Kali upon himself! He was given the choice to return the stone to the place from which it was stolen, but he refused and has now paid the price for his arrogance!"

Holmes raised one eyebrow and studied the woman thoughtfully.

"Refused?" he said. "If you would be so kind, please explain what you mean."

"On the first night that the stone was displayed," replied she, much excited, "we accompanied the Master here, each to bear witness to his warning. The Master foretold that the stone must be returned to India, and to its rightful place in the lost Temple of Sita."

"I do recall them, Mr. Holmes," said the smaller guard, peevishly. "They came the first day the diamond was on display, but Sir Fallowgrove would have none of it. He ordered us to throw Crowley right out the door." He nodded at the woman and the other witnesses. "And meaning no disrespect, but we threw these ones out right along with him."

Holmes glanced at Aleister Crowley, who appeared to have become rather puffed up from witnessing the devotion so evident in his followers. "I would not be so pleased with yourself, Mr. Crowley," said he, sharply. "Such theatrics may play well before an ignorant crowd, desperate to believe in nonsense, but it will be of no help to you in a trial. In fact, your success may become the end of you, as you so capably predicted yesterday."

Crowley's face flushed with anger. Then, just as it had in our apartment on Baker Street, it resolved back to the contented and vaguely arrogant expression which I had come to believe was his de facto condition, as it were.

"I will risk my fate with any jury," declared Crowley, imperiously, "for I command powers much more potent than the law, and considerably greater than the judgment of any man!"

"Quite," said Holmes, dryly. "But while you may win the battle of credibility with your followers, Mr. Crowley, your statements may, at the same time, cost you the war for your very survival. My counsel is as it was a day ago, sir: remain quiet so that I may, if possible, move to save your life!"

"So what shall we do now?" I said. "This all seems rather a condemnation of Mr. Crowley, Holmes, as circumstantial as the case against him may be."

"That would appear to be true," said Holmes. "However, I believe that we must seek further information before allowing the Inspector here to send Mr. Crowley to the gallows, Watson."

Mr. Lestrade opened his mouth to respond, but Pinkerton waved him off. "If he was, indeed, responsible for the theft of the diamond," commented Pinkerton, "not to mention the murder of Sir Fallowgrove, it strikes me that it would serve him right, Mr. Holmes."

"Once again, you assume guilt on his part," replied Holmes, calmly. "As I stated to Inspector Lestrade, I do not believe Mr. Crowley to be guilty of the crimes for which he is charged."

Lestrade laughed, sarcastically. "How can you be so sure, Holmes?" he asked. "There is no information pertinent to clearing Mr. Crowley of suspicion which you do not already possess."

"That is not entirely true," said Holmes. "When you arrived at 221B, Baker Street to arrest Mr. Crowley, you stated that there were additional facts of the case which you were not free to disclose at that time. I would suggest that now is the time to reveal them, or you risk sending an innocent man to his death."

Lestrade glanced at Pinkerton, who shrugged indifferently.

"Very well," said Lestrade, "but I am convinced that this information would be of no assistance to you, Holmes. In point of fact, it actually helps to condemn your client, rather than help him."

"Your indulgence, please," said Holmes, pleasantly. "If you would, tell me what you know, Inspector."

"On Monday, the day after the diamond disappeared," said Lestrade, "Sir Fallowgrove sought out Mr. Crowley and openly accused him of stealing it. The altercation took place in a public restaurant, with many witnesses, several of whom recounted that the two men nearly came to blows. Mr. Crowley was ordered to leave the premises, and as he did so, was heard to utter several threats against Sir Fallowgrove."

"Pretty damning, eh, Holmes?" asked Pinkerton, rhetorically. "When you take that confrontation into consideration, it seems that we have quite the case against Mr. Crowley here."

"I would not be so sure," said Holmes, cryptically.

He stared intently at Peter Curtis, who had remained silent since entering Fallowgrove's parlor.

"Mr. Curtis, please confirm for me," said Holmes, "that the case has not been opened since the Other Eye was first placed within it."

"We've recounted to you all of the facts, Mr. Holmes," said Curtis, angrily. "Once again, the case has not been opened, and the Pinkertons have attested to that."

"Indeed," said Pinkerton. "If you'd like, Holmes, we're more than happy to open it for you now."

He took two steps toward the case, reaching his arms out toward the elaborate Hindu lid, when Sherlock Holmes took two great steps across the room and placed his hand upon Pinkerton's arm, interrupting the act.

"I would advise against that, Mr. Pinkerton," said he, gravely. "However, one of us must, and therefore I think that perhaps Mr. Curtis is the best one to assist us with this task."

I glanced at Curtis, and to my great surprise, noted that his skin had paled to such a degree that it resembled the unhealthy shade of spoilt milk.

"I...I would be honored," said Curtis, haltingly.

He removed a pair of gloves from his overcoat pocket and slipped them on. Holmes studied them curiously, and sensing the question unasked, Curtis proceeded to explain.

"At Sir Fallowgrove's request, no one is to touch the case without gloves," said he. "More specifically the lid, which is quite ancient and valuable."

For a moment, I thought Holmes might smile, and then his eyes appeared to darken in that ineffable manner which had so characterized the many cases we had worked on together. I now knew that my friend was near to revealing all, and I found myself thrilling in anticipation of this last, final bit of the game.

"By all means, then," said Holmes, "wear your gloves. But please be brief, Mr. Curtis, as the day is now wearing upon us."

Curtis stepped up to the case. I saw him lick his lips, nervously, and then reach for the lid and lift it, with some effort, from its resting place atop the glass. Almost immediately a pungent odor flooded the room, and Curtis hurriedly turned his head away and moved back from the open case, setting the lid down upon the floor.

"What is that wretched odor?" said Pinkerton, grimacing. "I've never smelled anything quite like it."

To my great astonishment, I realized that I recognized the scent, which had quickly dissipated, almost immediately. I opened my mouth to speak, but Sherlock Holmes held up his hand in warning, and so I remained silent.

"Now that the case has been opened," said Holmes, "I would request that you remove your gloves, Mr. Curtis, and examine the inside; more specifically, the area around the pillow which held the diamond."

"Whatever for?" cried Curtis, his forehead shining with sudden perspiration. "This is a complete waste of time, gentlemen! Look for yourselves; it is clear that the diamond is no longer there!"

"Ah, but it *is* still inside the case," said Holmes, "I can assure you of that. Please remove your gloves, Mr. Curtis, and do as I ask. Simply touching the cushion will reveal the diamond's location, I promise you."

Curtis pulled off his leather gloves, and all who were in the room could clearly see that his hands were trembling. He reached for the case, hesitated, and then burst into tears, shaking his head violently. After a moment he retreated to the nearest wall where he stood alone, shuddering and sobbing uncontrollably, as the occupants of the room looked on in shocked surprise.

"I don't understand any of this," said Pinkerton. "Why will he not reach into the case? The diamond is gone, so what harm could it do?"

"As I said," replied Holmes, "the Other Eye is still there to be seen, if one only knows how to look for it."

"I'm not following your explanation, Holmes," said Lestrade, with a frustrated grimace, "for even I can see that the case is empty."

"All of these events," said Holmes, "have at their source the most prosaic of explanations. During our ride here, I actually spoke with Dr. Watson about the manner in which most human beings are absorbed by what they believe to be profound or important ideas, which nonetheless mask the more mundane aspects of their lives. For some, greed is as complex an idea, and a purpose as important, as any others one might imagine. This particular case is a clear example of what can happen when the basest of desires becomes the central focus of one's existence."

"Which means what?" I asked.

"Nothing more than that this case is about greed," said Holmes, "and little more. I will endeavor to provide all of you with the order of events as clearly as I can. Watson, please do not hesitate to add anything which I may have overlooked and which you feel is relevant."

"Very well," said I.

"First," continued Holmes, "please tell us what the strange odor was that briefly filled the room, Watson, if you would be so kind."

"Of course. It is hydrofluoric acid, an unusual and quite deadly chemical commonly used by etchers. I became familiar with it while purchasing a gift for my dear Mary, which I wished to have engraved with her name."

"Most excellent, Watson," said Holmes. "When the case was opened, I saw upon your face the realization of what was happening, but the time was not yet right to reveal that information."

"It would explain why Curtis would not reach inside the case," I said. "To do so would without a doubt have meant certain death. Even the fumes can be poisonous enough to kill a man."

Several of the occupants in the room shifted nervously, but Holmes set them immediately at ease. "There is nothing to be concerned about," said he, confidently. "Most of the chemical in question has already evaporated, and the stench of what remains is relatively mild and will not be harmful to us. The cushion inside, however, is a different matter altogether."

"Very much so," I said, peering at the cushion through one of the glass panes. "This stuff is quite difficult to work with, and in fluid form, is rapidly absorbed by the skin—or a cushion. For so much of it to be detectable after several days, it is reasonable to conclude that liquid hydrofluoric acid was utilized in this instance."

"Precisely," said Holmes. "If you would, Mr. Pinkerton, please have your men remove Mr. Curtis's coat and suit jacket, and then roll up his sleeves so that we may examine his hands and arms."

The two guards moved toward Curtis, who offered little resistance, and they were able to quickly strip away his coats and pull up his shirtsleeves.

"There, you see," said Holmes, "there are burn marks visible on his arms, in addition to the one on his hand which we took note of at the Lloyd's offices. As Dr. Gallagher indicated, similar marks were discovered upon the body of Sir Fallowgrove, and in addition, there were recent signs of scarring to his lungs. One can deduce that both men came into contact not with poisonous plants, as Dr. Gallagher had surmised, but the liquid form of hydrofluoric acid."

"Which, as I already mentioned, when absorbed into the skin can have deadly consequences," said I. "As it happens, when this type of acid interacts with blood calcium it is known to cause heart failure."

"And that," said Holmes, "is what I believe occurred here. Clearly, Sir Fallowgrove inhaled more of the fumes than did Mr. Curtis, which resulted in his rapid demise."

"But to what point, Holmes?" asked Lestrade. "Why would the two of them take such risks? I fail to see how this acid plays a significant role in the disappearance of the Other Eye."

"That is perhaps the most ingenious aspect of their plot," replied Holmes. "Please have your men turn over the lid of the case. Carefully, now, Inspector, and please ensure that their skin does not come into direct contact with the metal at any time."

Two of Lestrade's policemen moved over to the lid and bent down beside it. Both men were wearing gloves, but they still moved carefully as they turned it over, revealing the bottom.

"If you examine the inside of the lid," said Holmes, "you will see that there are the remnants of a small, glass capsule attached there."

"Well I'll be damned," said Pinkerton, "he's right!"

"Ah, but this time, Holmes," said Lestrade, smugly, "you've hurried out the facts of the case without considering all of the ramifications. Even this rare acid cannot dissolve a diamond. Everyone knows that."

"You are correct, Inspector," said Holmes, and Lestrade's eyes widened in surprise. "The strength of a diamond could not be compromised in any significant way by this acid, most especially one of this size."

"You see," said Lestrade, "even the finest of investigators can overlook a critical fact, Holmes. I would not feel too bad about it."

"Again, you are correct, Inspector," said Holmes. By this time Lestrade fairly beamed with anticipated victory over the great Sherlock Holmes, but alas, my friend had not yet finished with him. "There is one thing you did not consider, however, and that is that the diamond never existed at all."

Lestrade's mouth fell open, but thankfully, he stayed silent this time.

"It is my belief," said Holmes, "that Sir Fallowgrove and Mr. Curtis conspired together to create a fake diamond. Based upon the faint stains which I detected upon my examination of the cushion inside the case, I believe it was most likely constructed from jeweler's paste." He pointed to the lid. "The glass fragments there are all that is left of a vial which contained a substantial amount of hydrofluoric acid, which, among its many properties, is capable of eating through glass. Once that occurred, the acid dropped slowly down upon the false diamond, eventually dissolving it and leaving nothing behind but a slight odor and the most minimal of stains. I detected both when I first examined the case, and as you can see, the evidence which has now been revealed confirms my theory."

"And how did Curtis play into this?" asked Crowley, suddenly, from across the room. "I'd like to know, as he very nearly cost me my life!"

"Elementary, Mr. Crowley," said Holmes. "Sir Fallowgrove required the cooperation of Mr. Curtis in order to authenticate his fake diamond, as well as to facilitate the insuring of it by Lloyds of London. Undoubtedly, Mr. Curtis bribed his 'experts' to confirm his findings about the Other Eye, and this final act set in motion the events which followed."

"Unfortunately, he's not directly responsible for the death of Sir Fallowgrove," declared Pinkerton, "or we'd hang him, sure as the day is young."

"I believe you would have no need to do so," said Holmes, dispassionately. "Curtis has been exposed to the acid as well, and while it may take him some time longer for his life to end, I have no doubt that a premature death will ultimately be his fate."

"And so it goes," said I, "for those who seek to unlawfully acquire the possessions of others."

"As Sir Walter Scott so aptly wrote in his memorable poem, *Marmion*," said Holmes, "'Oh! what a tangled web we weave, When first we practice to deceive!' Sir Fallowgrove and Mr. Curtis have no one to blame but themselves, Watson, and in the end they will have both paid dearly for their actions."

"I must say, Mr. Holmes," said Pinkerton, "that I am greatly impressed. Very much so!" He reached into his vest pocket and removed a flat metal object and thrust it toward my friend. "Please take this as a token of our appreciation and respect, sir, and by all means, feel free to call upon us should the need arise."

Holmes took the item, which I now recognized as a Pinkerton National Detective Agency badge, and slipped it into his coat pocket.

"Thank you, Mr. Pinkerton," said Holmes. "I shall bear that in mind."

"Please do," replied Pinkerton. "As it turns out, bringing you on board was the best decision I could have made." He turned toward Inspector Lestrade, who had suddenly become quite busy herding the witnesses from the parlor. "Had I left it up to the police, the Pinkertons might very well have been left with a highly visible *black* eye!"

"I am pleased to have been of service," said Holmes, "but now the sun is well up and I believe it is time we considered breakfast. Would you not agree, Watson?"

"At the risk of being rude, I would very much like to join you, Mr. Holmes," said Pinkerton. "Given your success with this case, I'm quite curious to hear your thoughts on our pursuit of Adam Worth."

"Perhaps another day, Holmes?" I asked, pleadingly. "I am ready for a nap, and a full breakfast will only compound my desire for rest."

"Remember, Doctor," said Pinkerton, with a thin smile, "there is no rest for the wicked. And because of that, a Pinkerton never sleeps!"

"You make an excellent point," said Holmes, thoughtfully. "I must confess, I find Mr. Worth's activities to be of substantial interest. Please, do join us for breakfast."

"A Pinkerton never sleeps," said I, wearily, "and so it appears, neither do we."

* To paraphrase Sir Arthur Conan Doyle's own editorial note from the end of "The Hound of the Baskervilles", "This story owes its inception to our friends, Matthew Baugh, who helped us in the general plot, and Tim Powers, who assisted us with some of the local details." – RDS & ERB

THE ADVENTURE OF THE
MAGICIAN'S MEETINGS

by

Larry Engle and
Kevin VanHook

THE *magician stands in darkness. He turns in a circle, seeking an exit from the nothing, and* sees *nothing. He is used to dark places, has been locked in steamer trunks, milk cans, a coffin six feet below the earth, but this is a new experience for him, this total absence of all. He cries out, listening for his voice to bounce back to him and give a clue to the size of...of wherever this is. The magician is not a religious man, has even been accused of heresy in his day, but a word occurs to him that frightens him:* Purgatory. *He is a logical man, and even though he does not remember dying, this does not mean this has not happened. As he contemplates a blank eternity, he becomes aware of a subtle shift in the void. Some of the darkness has gotten darker. He concentrates. Narrowing his mind to the space immediately ahead, gradually he can make out shapes. Writ in black, limned in black, the magician's fate materializes before him in the form of great yawning grotesqueries the likes of which exist on no earthly plane. Horns. Teeth. Talons. Eyes. All in horrible proportion to each other and in terrible numbers. The sound of a chasm ripping into existence below his feet, and he is falling; falling and screaming one thought. This is not* Purgatory. *This is surely* Hell.

It was early March in the year 1898, and the London spring was slow in coming. I was drawn up before the fire in the study on Baker Street, idly reading *The Times*, trying to forget the snow that even then was threatening to drift us in and thinking that there were worse places to be. An article caught my eye, and I must have "hmphed," because Holmes, who had been staring intently at the fire from his perch in the easy chair opposite mine asked me what it was.

"They've dragged out that dreadful Whitechapel business again. Seems today is an anniversary of one of the murders."

Holmes turned to look more fully at me. "I see. Nothing new, I suppose."

"The same old business. A full recounting of the murders, a police theory or two. Seems they think the killer must have died or been caught for another crime, thus explaining the abrupt stop to the spree."

I felt Holmes' gaze even more intently, and turned to him.

"Nonsense," he said, and reached for his pipe on the table and started to pack it. "I don't believe the 'Ripper', as they call him, died, or was caught for something else, or even stopped his crimes."

I didn't ask, but he continued.

"First, a man possessed of an urge to destroy in such a spectacularly grisly manner is not going to spend his waking hours committing petty crimes for which the law may grab him. As to his death, he would have been a man in the relative prime of his life, with the ability and strength to overpower women used to handling their fair share of abuse. Such strength would not be in an old man, so death of old age is unlikely. Granted, a fatal incident, such as an accident, or even death at the hands of another could easily have occurred, but I highly doubt it."

I was growing slightly uncomfortable with the conversation, but I knew it was best to let him have his head, and he would soon finish with the subject.

"Consider..." Here he lit his pipe, and settled back into the chair, "that unsolved killings occur every day, everywhere. Likely one a day, at least, right here in London. Any man with the ability to elude detection through five confirmed murders and ten years would be able to commit his crimes anywhere he wished. He would simply play an area out, then move on, or possibly wait a considerable time before starting up again. I would have to say that absent any definite proof that he is dead, and with no confession of a living prisoner, I would be comfortable in the assumption that our man is alive and well, doing just as he pleases, where he pleases."

I had to ask. "Why did you never attempt the case?"

"I was never asked." Before I could digest this, he sprang from his chair and went to the window, drawing the curtain aside.

"Ah, the sound of a cab on such a harsh evening, and stopping just out front. We have a visitor!"

Indeed, within a few short moments, we could hear Mrs. Hudson's tread upon the stair, and her knock upon the door.

The visitor she brought with her was a man, rather on the short side; I estimated his height at no more than five and a half feet, and muscular. He had a round face with a prominent chin, and after he removed his hat, I saw that he wore his hair in a curious fashion, parted in the middle and combed across either side, giving his head a rather flat look.

Holmes crossed toward him a few steps and spoke.

"Welcome. It must be an urgent business indeed that would bring you out in such dreadful weather."

Our guest looked keenly at Holmes, gave me a glance, and nodded. Holmes asked Mrs. Hudson for coffee, and as she withdrew, offered the man brandy.

"No, thank you. I am not a drinker."

"Ah. But I see you *are* American, recently arrived, engaged in an occupation that requires athleticism and manual dexterity, and you have been to a tailor in the last two days."

The man laughed. "Yes. In fact, I have only arrived in your city this week, I am indeed in a physically demanding profession, and I visited a tailor just this morning!" The man flipped his hat with a particular flourish, and it landed neatly upon the sideboard.

"Let me see. My accent told you my nationality, of course. You surmised that I have recently arrived as I have yet to pick up the regional lilt." Holmes nodded, and the newcomer went on:

"My build surely gave away the physical requirements of my career, and the length and musculature of my hands led you to my need for nimble fingers?"

Holmes nodded again, frowning slightly.

The man cocked his head a little to the right, and brought one of those slender fingers to his chin. "As for my trip to the tailor, I have no idea how you could have known."

Holmes' frown disappeared, and with a slight animation in his voice, which I knew to be his closest approximation to glee, he pointed to the man's leg, near his shoe. "Just there, on the outer edge of your cuff, I can see the chalk-line where a near-sighted man has made your adjustments, then failed to erase all the line. You could not have had them long, or the mark would have faded."

The man smiled and extended his hand. "Excellent, sir! You must be Sherlock Holmes." He turned to me, and I swear he winked. "And that would make you Dr. John Watson?" At my nod, he rubbed his hands together." Gentlemen, my name is Harry Houdini, and it is a great pleasure to make your acquaintance."

Mrs. Hudson arrived with the coffee, and after our visitor had been seated near the fire and handed a cup, he proceeded, without any drawing out by Holmes, to tell us his singular problem.

"You surmised correctly the requirements of my profession, Mr. Holmes, but you did not deduce my exact career. It is an unusual one, to say the least, and it bears directly on my reasons for coming to visit you."

Holmes said nothing, merely inclined his head, indicating Mr. Houdini should continue.

"I am a stage magician, sir, an illusionist, with an emphasis on the art of escape. I have come to your city on a series of engagements. These are meant to raise my reputation, as I have gotten pretty far in my own country, and now wish to perform abroad."

"I see," said Holmes. By the upturn of his chin, I could tell that he was interested in what this man had to say. "Please, go on."

"In addition to my regular vocation, I have a sort of hobby. It is an unusual one, to be sure, but I am quite passionate about it." Houdini paused to sip from his cup, then looked earnestly from one to the other of us, settling back on Holmes.

"I investigate paranormal phenomena."

Holmes put away his pouch, and lighting his bowl, puffed softly. Tendrils of smoke escaped his nostrils. "Do you mean the spirits, hauntings, and things of that nature?"

I began to roll my own tobacco, feeling that the brief meeting had reached its end. Mr. Houdini had come to the wrong man.

"Perhaps I should have stated that differently. I investigate circumstances in which people use claims of supernatural ability to perpetrate fraud. It dovetails nicely with my professional life, as I sometimes call upon the spirits in my act, and often use a device I call the 'Ghost House' in my escapes from manacles and chains. All humbug, of course."

I laid my smoking materials down without lighting them.

"I see. And you are on such a trail now?" asked Holmes.

Houdini set his cup down and leaned back in his chair. "I am, sir, and that is why I have come to you." He pursed his lips, and Holmes leaned forward.

"I am afraid that I may not be able to prove fraud, as fraud may not exist."

Holmes leaned back, steepled his fingers, bade Mr. Houdini continue, and I knew the hook had been set deep.

"The man who promotes my stage show is an Englishman, James Farnley. I have only known him several weeks, but I believe he is honest, which is harder to come by in the show business than you may think, and intelligent. James Farnley is aware of my little hobby and this last week he came to me with a proposal.

"He told me of a man here in London that he, James, believed to be a true spiritual medium, a channeler of the spirit world, a go-between of sorts..."

Holmes held up a hand. "I am aware of the terminology. Please go on."

Houdini sat a little forward in his chair.

"Very well. As I said, I trust James, and he doesn't seem to me to be the type to fall prey to a charlatan. I asked him to introduce me to his man, and he readily agreed, then in short order informed me that he had arranged a meeting for me with a Mr. Harker Bellamy, spiritualist." Mr. Houdini paused, and Holmes shook his head.

"The name means nothing to me, Mr. Houdini. Continue."

"Please, you may call me Houdini. That is what I go by." We nodded, and Houdini went on.

"James called for me at my hotel at seven last night, to make the meeting at seven-thirty. Upon arrival, I saw that it was a large house, on its own grounds, which encompassed a garden and a small greenhouse. As we waited for someone to come to the door and admit us, I remarked upon the greenhouse, as I thought it was curious to have a lock on such a structure, and James told me that some people grow rare and exotic plants, some quite valuable.

"James rang the bell, and we were admitted by a man introduced to me as Mr. Bellamy, our host for the evening."

"There was no servant, in such a large home?"

"None that I saw. Mr. Bellamy appeared to be a man accustomed to taking care of himself; he was certainly stout enough to take care of any chore that may arise. The place was neat as a pin, and after seating us in the parlor, he asked us to wait to serve refreshments until the others arrived, as we had come some few minutes early.

"We chatted idly of nothing, and when the bell rang, Bellamy, who had not yet taken a seat, excused himself to the front door. When he returned, he had in tow two women, older, obviously sisters or other close kin. These ladies were introduced to us as the Misses Mae and Mary Jacobs, and they were introduced as sisters. No sooner had they been seated than the bell came again, and Bellamy showed in and introduced the Dr. Wesley Williams and his wife, Emma, who was a younger sister to the other women, and our group was complete. I was made to know that aside from myself, this was a repeat visit for all. Bellamy brought the coffee and a decanter of brandy, then, and excused himself, to 'make preparations.' He went through a door to another part of the house."

Holmes finally lit his pipe, and waved the stem idly as wisps of smoke from the rank tobacco he preferred made small eddies.

"I have an idea of Harker Bellamy as a hale fellow, strong and capable," Holmes said. "The sisters Jacobs would be matronly types. Mrs. Williams I see as a younger version. Would you please describe the Doctor for me?"

"A man in his middle forties, I would guess, tallish, with a full head of blond hair, a small moustache. Thin through the shoulders, with a bit of weight in the middle."

"Did he rasp when he spoke?"

Houdini's right eyebrow rose a fraction, but he betrayed no real surprise. "You know the man?"

Holmes merely waved his pipe and gave a gesture for Houdini to continue.

"Bellamy left the room and was gone for some few minutes, during which I tried unsuccessfully to prize some information from my companions about our host. I had given up the questions when the man himself reappeared.

"'Is everyone ready?' he had asked. I had thought he asked the question of the group, but I saw he was looking only at the Doctor, who gave a small nod."

"'All right, then,' Bellamy said. 'Let us repair to the other room. I feel that the spirits are ready, as well.'

"At this, we all rose, and Mr. Bellamy led the way to the door he had used earlier, and stood by as we filed in, ladies first, the Doctor last.

"On the other side of the door was a large room, furnished as a dining room. A table and eight chairs took up the majority of the area, with a sideboard, a dish cabinet, and the like, with a large chandelier above. All of these I examined as surreptitiously as I could while approaching the table, mindful of confederates in hiding with strings, trumpets, noisemakers and other tools of the huckster's trade. I saw no one, and waited to be seated. I know from experience that the medium controlled exactly where each person sat, placing the victim, or pigeon, closest to him. That way, the seer fills the person's whole view and attention, and that person more than any other is likely to be ignorant of other things going on in the room.

"Even though I saw nothing immediately, I was on alert, for frauds have a thousand tricks. I could write a book. All of this I took in quickly, and Bellamy was just shutting the door when I turned to look at him and wait for my assignment. To my surprise, he took the chair immediately in front of him, and gestured for us all to be seated."

"And how did you end up arranged?" asked Holmes.

"At the foot of the table, with his back to the door we had entered by, was Bellamy, then James Farnley at his right. I was to James' right, then it was Emma Williams; her sister Mae sat at the head, facing Bellamy, then her sister Mary, a blank chair, and Dr. Williams sat immediately to Bellamy's left."

Holmes rested an elbow upon the arm of his chair, and his chin upon his hand.

"The meeting was nothing like any I have ever attended," Houdini said, "and that is more than a few. At first, we simply sat quietly. I took the chance to examine my surroundings again, and I had just about decided that the phony spirit, or ectoplasm, would descend from the chandelier once the lights were out. I was ready to get on with it, and I was opening my mouth to say so when I heard a small gasp from my right, which came from Mae Jacobs. I turned to look at her, and her eyes were lifted up to the chandelier. 'So quickly this time,' she said with a soft, almost dreamy smile upon her lips. My suspicions confirmed, I looked upward myself, and I saw…"

Here, I leaned forward. At last, the meat of the tale!

"…Nothing. The lights were still on, and the fixture gave such a glow that it distorted one's eyes. I was trying to decide if I should get up and try to it see from her angle, but just then Mr. Bellamy spoke up:

"'What is it, Mae?'

"Mae Jacobs turned her head, not toward the man who had asked the question, but as though she were following the path of something around the room. I tracked with her, and still saw nothing.

"'Mae?' Bellamy asked again.

"The woman said nothing, as first Bellamy, then her younger sister and then myself tried to communicate with her. I believed she was insensate. I have seen such things before. A person is so desperate to believe in the medium's message they become capable of a sort of self-hypnosis. I had never seen it occur so soon into a meeting, but her actions up to this point had marked her in my mind as the likely target in this fraud. I believed she had been conditioned to a particular belief, to the point that she very likely would have swooned if Bellamy had not even been there, and she were told that he was present in 'spirit'.

"I rose to my feet, intending to examine her for her own safety, when I began to feel a slight pressure behind my eyes. It quickly grew in intensity, and I sat back down without ever reaching the woman. I leaned forward, placing my elbows on the table, my face in my hands. I felt an arm slide across my shoulders, and was relieved, because I knew that James was coming to my assistance. I knew my eyes were open, but my world had gone dark, and…"

Here Houdini related his experience in a world of darkness, and he was able to communicate the utter desolation he had first felt, the curious apathy he had experienced on contemplating his possible death, and finally the sheer terror in the belief that he had been sentenced to Hell.

"I came to myself right where I had been, sitting in my chair around the table, surrounded by the others. I was still quite upset, and James muttered some excuses and escorted me out, then home in a cab. On the way, he tried to reassure me, saying that each one of them had had an 'experience' that evening, and that it was different for each of them. I had told no one of what I had seen and felt, and upon waking this afternoon, after what was for me an unusually deep and long sleep, and suffering a headache, I determined there was only one man in all of London that could help me." Houdini's voice had grown quiet in the telling, until finally he sat back in his chair, drained from reliving his vision. No one spoke for several moments.

Without reference to the chilling story we had just heard, Holmes began asking for details.

"When you first arrived at this estate and saw the greenhouse, did you notice if it connected to the house, or stood apart?"

"I cannot tell you. Only part of the greenhouse was visible, it extended beyond the end of the house and back out of my view."

"Very well. Tell me, when Harker Bellamy returned after leaving you for a few minutes, did he show any indication of having been outside? Snow on his clothes, a red face, perhaps?"

"I didn't notice anything like that."

"Before you entered the room where these strange events occurred, coffee and brandy were served. Did you drink the coffee?"

"Yes. I needed to take off some of the chill of the evening."

"Good. Now, I need you to remember. Did Mae Jacobs drink anything?"

"I poured coffee for her and her two sisters."

"Excellent." Holmes leaned forward, and asked, "Did your friend, James, drink anything?"

"He mentioned an aversion to coffee, and had a shot of the brandy."

"I see. Now to Dr. Williams; Did he have coffee or brandy?"

"I believe he had brandy. Mr. Holmes, is all this important? The spirits I am concerned with do not come in decanters."

Holmes' features took on a severe cast, then softened. "I assure you that I do not ask irrelevant questions. Now I have but a few more things, then we shall be ready to put your medium to the test."

Holmes asked our new friend a few more questions, gave him some instructions, one of which was to ask for another meeting with Mr. Bellamy, with Holmes along as a wealthy friend and *devotee* of the spiritual. He then sent him on his way with assurances that answers would be had.

On his way back through the room from showing Houdini out, Holmes stopped by the shelf containing his indices to noteworthy Londoners. He selected the volume *W*, passed it to me, and sat back in his chair. Without his telling me, I turned to what he wanted me to see.

> *Williams, Wesley R. Dr.*
> Son of Dr. W. Williams & Lady P. Williams
> Born Stratford-1840 Graduate Medicine Oxley
> Married E. Jacobs 1865. Pioneer Abnormal
> psychology studies, loss of license 1870,
> reinstated 1897.

"Well, Watson. It seems this particular volume needs an update. I must find the time."

I closed the book and laid it on the side table, knowing that Holmes would never feel his records were quite up to the minute. "What are you thinking?"

"Dr. Wesley Williams was an employee of the Crown from his graduation up until his marriage, a low level doctor in a public sanitarium. When he married Emma Jacobs, he wed a considerable amount of money. Her father did well in South American gold futures, or some such, and he made a wedding present of a healthy account of her own. Immediately upon completion of the nuptials, Dr. Williams retired from the public life to open a private hospital, which he could administer to his own whims."

"Sounds reasonable enough. How did he come to lose his license to practice? It must have been something serious, indeed."

"I would say so. He was…experimenting on his patients. He put forth that it was research, but Williams Sanitarium was a beastly, tortuous place, overseen by a Sadist of the highest order. Forced deprivation of the senses. A diet of foods not fit for human consumption. Pharmaceutical experiments."

"Dear God. I see how he lost his practice. How did he get away with it for so long?"

"Evidence was hard to gather. People placed under his care were legitimately in need of treatment, and thus any mention of the barbarous practices was written off as the ravings of a lunatic. It was a very difficult situation for all involved. His sins came to light when a patient managed to slip his restraints, grab the doctor by the throat and twist him into unconsciousness, and make off with the skeleton key. The patient was able to make himself believed, and Williams received a damaged voice as a souvenir."

Pharmaceutical experiments. I thought of Holmes' addiction, and shuddered.

"How could he possibly have gotten his license back?"

"His father-in-law was a very influential man. He set Williams up as camp doctor at some of his mines in South America, then got him licensed there, and you and I both know a piece of paper is as good on one continent as another."

I was disgusted, but Holmes would speak no more on the matter, and for two days, nothing of much import happened at our address. It was time I spent catching up on correspondence with old army comrades, and in which Holmes sat rapt, poring over one volume after another of I-don't-know-what.

Late in the evening of the second day after our meeting with Houdini, a telegram arrived for Holmes, and he read it in great earnest.

"All is well, Watson. By tonight, we shall have the answer to Houdini's little problem. He has made some preparations, and now I make my own."

Holmes walked over to the sideboard, and after a moment's searching came up with a close-fitting pair of kid gloves. These he shoved in a pants pocket. He put on his waistcoat, and asked for and received permission to take my revolver from its place in my desk.

As he donned his hat, he said, "Sorry, Watson. I must go to this alone. Two new people at one of these meetings may put Williams on my scent. I have had Houdini play me as wealthy venture capitalist just in from Canada, interested in the hospital game. My name for the evening is Mycroft. Everyone in the city knows Sherlock Holmes, but very few have heard of Mycroft Holmes. Oh, and I seem to be out of copper. Could you spot me? I need to stop by Bradley's for some shag."

I dug in my pocket, flipped him a coin, and he was off.

The rest of the tale, I did not learn until it was all over, and Holmes and Houdini were safely back in Baker St.

Holmes had arrived at the Bellamy house half an hour before the appointed meeting, and bypassing the front door, had gone straight to the greenhouse. There, he removed the padlock, which was open, but had been hung in such a way to give the impression that it was shut. He spent a few minutes inside, and upon leaving, locked himself out. He went straight to the road, turned back up the walk, and approached the house. He was now just a few minutes late for his meeting, and went to the door, where he was admitted by Bellamy. Introductions were made, after which the group, minus Williams, who had gone with Bellamy to see about something in a back room, was amused by Houdini in the parlor for a few moments with sleight-of-hand. He went around to each cup of coffee, and making a funnel of his hand and a newspaper, made the liquid disappear. A shot of brandy was had by all except Houdini. Holmes played the part of a hospital investor for the benefit of Mrs. Williams, and when Bellamy and Williams returned, the group moved into the dining room with the large table. They were seated in the same random matter as before, with Holmes contriving to be at the head of the table, opposite the door, Houdini on his right, and Bellamy and Williams sitting in their previous positions, closest to the door.

The three sisters sat quietly, waiting to see who would be struck first with a spiritual vision. Houdini never took his eyes off Holmes, who in turn never took his eyes off Williams.

After several minutes of throat clearing on the part of Bellamy, and increased fidgeting from the older sisters, Holmes pulled out his pocket watch, marked the time, and stood.

"Enough, gentleman. I have some things for you, and then we'll be leaving."

Bellamy leaned forward over the table. "Mycroft, if you will wait but a few more minutes, I can assure you that…"

"Don't bother." Here Holmes pulled a small tin from his pocket. It was red, and stamped with the mark of Bradley's Tobacco. Next, he produced the gloves and laid them next to the tin. Finally, he brought out my old service pistol, and laid it in a row with the other objects. Houdini had started at the production of the gun, and Holmes spoke without looking at him. "It's insurance against a man who would be reckless with the lives of others, but wouldn't dare face his own death.

"Dr. Williams. I gather from the expression on your face that you have deduced what is in my little box. Care for a look?" He made to open the tin.

Williams jerked back from the table as if he had received an electric shock. "Mycroft, you just leave that thing right where it is. What I want to know is how you got it."

"My friend, Houdini, is a magician. Magicians pick locks. I merely told him what to look for, and after opening the greenhouse, he found it. It was, however, a bit of an effort on my part to secure one of your little friends without doing myself great harm. And, now, Williams—let's just drop the

Doctor bit, shall we? — I give you your fate." Holmes opened the tin, and with a flick of his wrist, tossed it across the table. Williams was gone like a shot, shoving his way past Bellamy and his own wife—straight into the arms of Inspector Lestrade of the London police force, whom, having been alerted earlier by Holmes, had entered the front room with a group of officers at just about the time Holmes stood from his chair. During all this, the women sat motionless with shocked expressions, dumbstruck.

Later that evening, Holmes and Houdini were filling me in on what I had missed.

"Good Lord! What on earth could have been in such a little box that would send a man screaming for his life?" I asked.

Holmes laughed. "It's not what was in the box, it's what Williams *thought* was in the box."

"Well, come on, man. What did he think was in there?"

From a pocket, Holmes pulled a stoppered glass vial with a small wad of cotton and a brightly colored marble inside, and passed it over.

"A live one of these. Do not open that vial."

I looked closely. "A frog? Williams was afraid of a baby frog?"

"Hand it back, Watson. Gently, now. This is a Patagonian Thistledart. A most interesting little creature, it is found only in a certain type of rainforest on the South American Continent. When provoked, it secretes a waxy substance, odorless, tasteless, and highly prized by the natives for its hallucinogenic properties. I understand that it is used in religious rituals, rites of passage, that sort of thing. However, direct skin contact with the secretion in its undiluted state effects a rapid onset of psychosis, progressing to catatonia, and finally to death with a one-hundred percent rate of mortality within four hours. There is no cure. It is far too dangerous to handle even in optimal conditions; the tin was empty. I brought out the gloves to give the impression that I had collected one the frogs."

"Williams was using that to poison his wife and her sisters? To what end?"

"Greed, Watson. Simple greed. After his father-in-law's death, Emma Williams held the purse strings. A vast sum of money was left in trust to the three sisters, which produced a nice income of its own accord, but it was not enough. Williams hoped the visions created by this little fellow, coupled with his wife's and her sisters' susceptibility to belief in spiritualism, would lead her to 'donate' large sums of money to psychic research, which would actually fund a new hospital for himself, into which he would then commit his unfortunate wife and her sisters, gaining control of the Jacobs' fortune."

Houdini spoke up then, from his position by the hearth. "I don't see how you put it together. I was there when you sprung the trap, and I'm still lost."

Holmes passed the vial slowly from hand to hand. "I felt from the beginning that the greenhouse was the key. I knew that Williams had spent some time in South America, interacting with natives. There are plants there that grow nowhere else, and I knew that many were capable of producing the visions and symptoms you described, the deep sleep, the headache. I spent the time between your leaving here and the telegram you sent telling me all was set, reading everything I had on deadly plants. It wasn't until I actually got into the greenhouse, however, and saw no dangerous plants, that I realized I was on the right scent, but the wrong trail. I then narrowed my search to plants only found in South America, and found only one. A dwarf conifer I recognized as only occurring naturally in the sub-tropic region of Patagonia. The greenhouse led me to the tree, the tree led me to the poison frog."

"I understood having me unlock the greenhouse, but what was the business of having me vanish the coffee?"

"As I said, the undiluted secretion is death. However, a preparation approximating one part to one-hundred, in something as innocuous as water, or coffee, will produce the desired effect with no lasting harm. I knew that whatever the drug, it must be in the coffee, because you told me that Williams only drank the brandy, and I knew he would never poison himself.

"Unfortunately, that is also how I knew that your promoter, James, was in on the scheme. I wondered how he could have possibly known of these meetings, having no vested interest in anyone present, but you told me that James also drank only brandy, and was in shape to take you home after your experience."

Houdini shrugged. "I told you that I thought he was unusual. What was his connection to Williams, anyway?"

"James Farnley, prior to his life as an entertainment promoter, was, along with Harker Bellamy, an orderly at the former Williams sanitarium."

"But then why bring me into it at all? James knew that I would attempt to debunk them, which is exactly what we've done."

Holmes took his pipe off the mantle, fiddled with it, couldn't find his tobacco, and absently stuck his pipe in his vest pocket, stem upwards.

"I believe it was ego, mostly. They thought that if they could fool you, they could fool anybody."

"I have to thank you again, Mr. Holmes. Although I am disappointed that like so many others this instance turned out to be a fraud, it was an adventure I'll never forget, and we stopped some very bad people from harming someone else." He approached me, and I stood to shake his hand. "Mr. Watson, I hope you find this episode interesting enough to someday chronicle it."

"I believe there is the potential," I said. "It was a pleasure meeting you."

He turned and shook Holmes' hand. "Goodbye, gentlemen. If I can ever be of service to either of you, you have an eternal friend."

As he crossed the threshold to the stairs, he called back. "Oh, could one of you gentleman tell me the time?"

I reached into my vest pocket, and pulled out Holmes' ratty old pipe by the stem. I stood looking dumbly at it as Holmes pulled my watch from his pocket, calmly opened it, and obliged the man.

THE ADVENTURE OF THE
ETHICAL ASSASSIN

by
Matthew Baugh

"I must agree, Watson," Sherlock Holmes said. "Even the keenest mind can be prone to making rash statements, on occasion."

I turned from the window of our lodgings at 221B Baker Street where I had been gazing at the fog. My friend sat in his favorite chair, smoking a pipe of the shag tobacco he preferred. "I don't think I shall ever get used to that, Holmes," I said. "If I didn't know better, I'd suspect you had learned how to read my mind."

Holmes rewarded me with a thin smile. "Not your mind, my dear fellow, but your thoughts are an open book to one who observes carefully."

"Then, please, enlighten me, for I have no clue."

He waved his hand dismissively. "It is no great thing. I see my friend, Watson, gazing out into the fog, his mind filled with thoughts of assassins. He is thinking how easy it would be for a killer to strike his target and then vanish on a night like this. I see a silent look of amusement on his face. He is remembering how I stood before that same window, not three weeks ago and declared how fortunate it was that there are no such fogs in the lands where assassination is common."

I raised the *Times*, which I had been holding. "And you knew I was thinking of assassinations because I was holding this. You circled three articles about prominent men, all killed in the last month. Carruthers and Blankenship killed by a bomb-wielding anarchist, and Lord Saltire, shot dead while hunting foxes."

"Watson, you excel yourself," he said with a note of triumph. "Yes, it seems that we are beset with a wave of assassinations."

I placed the paper on a table and moved to my seat, opposite him. "But surely these crimes are unrelated."

"They may be," he said, steepling his fingers in front of his face. "I confess, I have no compelling reason to think otherwise, and yet..."

He rose and crossed to his desk, which was cluttered with a thousand pieces of paper of every size and description. It has often amazed me that the man with such an efficient mind should be so careless when it came to his personal papers. After a moment he produced a folded note and passed it to me with a flourish.

"Take a look at that, Watson, and tell me what you think."

I opened the paper, a pink tinted bit of foolscap of the finest quality.

My Dear Holmes, it read, *You were of great service to me in a most delicate situation three years ago. I find I am in need of your assistance again on a matter of even greater urgency. Please call on me today at my rooms in the Langham.*

It was signed *Wilhelm Gottsreich Sigismond von Ormstein, Grand Duke of Cassel-Felstein and hereditary King of Bohemia.*

I looked up at Holmes, surprised. The name was familiar to me, for I had also been involved in the case. "What does it mean?" I asked. "Can the King be involved in some new scandal?"

"I think not," Holmes replied. "It must be something serious for him to seek me out once again, but if it were a simple scandal he would have come here. Instead, he summons us to his hotel."

"That may simply be to avoid being seen," I said. "If the press knew that he was consulting Sherlock Holmes they would assume the reason."

That prompted a sharp laugh from my friend, who rose and crossed to the hearth, where he paused next to a picture the King had given him, a framed photo of the American actress, Irene Adler. "Very good, Watson, I would cede you the point if this were anyone else. But his majesty was not shy about visiting me when he was entangled with *The Woman*, why should he be now?"

"Now he is married," I said. When the King had come to Holmes before, he had feared that his past entanglement with Miss Adler would interfere with his engagement to the daughter of the King of Scandinavia.

"Ah," Holmes replied. "But if you followed the continental newspapers, as I do, you would know that King Wilhelm has often embarrassed his queen. No, Watson, marriage has done nothing to tame his wanderings.

If anything, he is far bolder now that he is safely wed; he feels no such constraint."

I felt myself flush with anger at this. "It is bad enough that any man should treat his wife in such a shameful manner, but he is a king!"

Holmes continued to look at the photo of the woman both he and the king had admired and, when he spoke, his voice had softened.

"It is foolish to expect any man—or king—to rise above his nature." He turned toward me, a playful smile lighting his face. "This is a fearless man, Watson. He does not worry much over his reputation, property, or physical safety, for his rank and wealth are his protection. Despite this, he seems unwilling to venture out into the London fogs, even when his errand is of great urgency. Can you not see what this means?"

"I confess, I cannot."

"Unless I am very much mistaken," Holmes said, "His Majesty wants us to prevent his assassination."

Holmes was lost in thought as the hansom carried us to the hotel on Regent Street and I found myself stating into the fog. This was a true London Peculiar, smothering the city in its oily embrace and transforming the picturesque West End into a scene of Limbo. The world seemed to fade away after a dozen or so feet in any direction.

Holmes was right: this would be a playground for murderers and other blackguards. One need only take half a dozen strides in any direction to vanish, completely.

We arrived at the Langham at a quarter past nine. The building, oldest of the "grand hotels," served as a massive anchor, bringing my thoughts back to the material world, and the matter at hand.

We were ushered to the King's suites, where a Germanic manservant took our cloaks and presented us to His Majesty. The King was much as I had remembered him, a handsome fellow, some six and a half feet tall with an athletic physique, and a look of firm character bordering on obstinacy on his handsome features. He was dressed in a tasteful English suit, which was somewhat at odds with his flamboyant jeweled rings and stick-pin.

We bowed. I thought Holmes' gesture somewhat perfunctory, but the King seemed to take no notice.

"Mr. Holmes," he said, "I am gratified that you have come."

"I am at Your Majesty's service," Holmes replied.

King Wilhelm nodded, gravely, and gestured to a young man who stood slightly behind him. "My assistant, Herr Haas. He has been invaluable to me and, I trust, will be to you, also."

Haas clicked his heels together and offered a stiff, military bow.

"I presume that he is a part of Your Majesty's Secret Police," Holmes said.

"He is," the King replied, a look of delighted puzzlement on his face. "How did you...? No, that is not important now. Please, I have much to tell you."

He gestured us to chairs and we sat, all except Haas, who prowled the room as the rest of us talked. He was of average size and lean, but the way he moved gave the impression of great strength, and tigerish agility. Though he was youthful, his cheeks were sunken, badly scarred by acne, and his dark eyes seemed to blaze with fanatical intensity. It was as if an intense flame burned within him, fueling his energy but also consuming his body.

"I perceive that Your Majesty is in fear of his life," Holmes said. "Why else employ such a fearsome watchdog."

"Mr. Holmes, there have been threats," the King replied. "There has also been an attempt on my life only three days ago, in Prague."

"What manner of attempt?"

"A bomb." The king took a deep breath. "Forgive me, gentlemen, this matter is most upsetting. To murder is a terrible crime, but to threaten a king's life? It is unthinkable, unnatural. It breaks the laws of man and God!"

"How was this bomb detected?"

"Haas found and disarmed it. It was hidden underneath my bed."

"It is my custom to inspect His Majesty's quarters regularly," the man said.

"And what manner of device was it?" Holmes asked.

"A dynamite bomb with a clockwork timer," Haas replied. "It was set to explode at two in the morning."

"When I was certain to be sleeping." The King shuddered at the memory.

"The staff was questioned?"

"Yes, the Czech police were very thorough. Sadly, they were able to turn up nothing."

"I take it the room was unoccupied, aside from Your Majesty."

The King stared at Holmes closely. "Is there some innuendo in your question?"

"I neither imply nor seek to judge," Holmes replied. "However, I must insist on having all the facts. I am paralyzed without them."

"I can hardly see how this pertains."

Holmes stood. "Forgive me, Your Majesty, for having taken so much of your time. I regret that I cannot be of service to you."

King Wilhelm stared at my friend in shock as I also rose. "You cannot be serious," he said.

"I assure you that I am," Holmes replied. "If I am to be of service, I must be given all necessary cooperation. I will not work half in the dark."

The King locked gazes with Holmes for a moment, then forced a chuckle. "I see that you are a man of the world, Mr. Holmes, and I am sure that I can trust in your discretion. There was a young woman with me, an actress named Milena Jebavýová."

"I shall need to interview her."

"She is still in Prague."

"And the bomb?"

"Also in Prague," Haas said. "The police had disassembled it for examination."

"Your wife was not with you on that trip?" Holmes asked.

"Certainly not!"

"But she is with you, now?"

"I did not feel safe leaving Clotilde in Bohemia," the King replied. "My enemies might attempt to strike at me through her."

"Have any of the threats been directed at her?"

"They are not so specific, Mr. Holmes," Haas said. Reaching into his coat he produced three folded notes. They were all on a plain foolscap with words painstakingly cut from newspapers and pasted to the pages. The first said, "*Tod zu allen Tyrannen*," the second, "*Smert všem tyranům*," and the last, "Death to all tyrants."

"The note in German came to me in Cassel-Felstein a week ago," the King said. "The second arrived at my hotel in Prague the day of the bomb, and the last came here, today."

Holmes took the notes and began studying them with a magnifying lens.

"Do you suspect anyone, Your Majesty?" I asked.

"It is the work of Anarchists," Haas said.

"Though why they should target me is a mystery," the King added. "Still, who can understand the ways of madmen?" He moved to the window and pulled back the curtain to gaze into the fog.

"Your Majesty, I would advise you not to do that," Holmes said. "Even on a night like this you do not want to expose yourself to—"

He was interrupted as the window imploded. In a flash, Haas had tackled the King to the floor. Holmes crossed to the window and, taking care not to expose himself, drew back the curtain to look out. I rushed to the King's side.

"Your Majesty," I said. "Are you injured?"

King Wilhelm did not answer, for it was clear he did not know himself if he had been hurt. He lay on his back, clutching his forehead as it gushed blood. It took a moment for me to ascertain that the wound was merely a gash where a fragment of glass had embedded itself.

"I think I see him," Haas cried, peering over the sash. He sprang to his feet and ran out of the room, Holmes following a step behind.

"Stay here, Watson," my friend cried from the doorway. "Look to the King's safety."

I closed the drape while my patient held a handkerchief to his forehead. I chanced a glance at the street below but the fog was so heavy that I could perceive nothing. Haas' feline qualities must have extended to his eyesight for him to have spotted anyone.

"Wilhelm, what is happening?"

I turned to the new voice and saw a young woman, tall, with a strong jaw and pale-blue eyes. She was not conventionally pretty, though she had lovely chestnut hair, and carried herself with such a dignified air that I found her striking.

"Clotilde," the King cried. "Back to your room, woman! There has been another attempt."

"Are you shot?" She had a strong contralto voice and a noticeable Scandinavian accent. A pair of servants, a man and a woman, appeared in the door behind her. The woman appeared to be a lady in waiting, and the man had a military bearing. I guessed that he was another is His Majesty's bodyguards.

"See to the Queen's safety," Wilhelm said, overriding her attempts to protest. "Take her to her room and keep her away from the windows."

The man took the Queen's arm and she flinched away from him, as if his grip had caused her pain. Fixing her husband with a look of cold anger, she exited the way she had come.

I retrieved my medical bag and took out a suture kit. The King, in the meantime, had poured himself a glass of brandy and seated himself in an armchair. He sat there, in sullen silence as I fished the shard of glass from his forehead and stitched the wound shut.

"You cannot be serious," I protested, but Holmes ignored me as he continued to pack his bag. We had returned to our lodgings in Baker Street, where I had retrieved my service revolver and he had announced that he was leaving for the continent, immediately.

"You know my methods, Watson," he said. "I am an investigator, not a bodyguard. I will be of much greater use to the King if I am free to ascertain the identity of his assailants.

"But surely they are anarchists, as Haas said."

He paused in his packing, an intense light burning in his eyes. "Surely? My dear Watson, *nothing* is certain in this case. We have only been involved a few hours and already we have seen a bewildering mass of contradictions."

"Contradictions?" I said, struggling to think of what he could mean.

"Ah, Watson, you yourself commented on the peculiarity of a sniper choosing such an unlikely night. And then there is a matter of the bullet."

"But you never found the bullet."

"A most significant fact."

"Suggestive of what?"

"It would be premature of me to say," he replied. "Ah, Watson, we are in deep waters here, as we have seldom seen before. I implore you to take nothing at face value. Nothing and no one."

He closed his satchel and rose.

"Holmes, perhaps I should accompany you. If you are not a bodyguard, I am even less so. Surely Haas can manage."

"Haas is another unknown," Holmes said. "You observed his eyes, did you not?"

"Indeed," I replied. "He seems fanatical in his devotion to the king."

"A fanatic, yes. I have seen his type before, Watson. He is a driven man who will let no word of argument or pang of conscience deter him in his duty."

The thought made me shudder. "But is that not a useful thing? Who better than a fanatic to act as bodyguard?"

"I do not trust such men," Holmes said. "Such devotion, unchecked by conscience makes a man inhuman, and unpredictable. That is why I need my trusted Watson on the scene; not only for your dedication, but for your decency and common sense."

He laid his hand on my arm and spoke with such sincerity that I found myself deeply moved. "I shall do everything in my power to keep him safe," I said.

Holmes smiled triumphantly. "Then I can do what I must, knowing that he is in the best possible hands."

The next two days were pure tedium as I sat with the King in his suite. Anxious about a repeat of the sniper incident, Haas ordered the drapes drawn at all times. Between this and the lingering fog, we had to keep the gaslights on at all hours, which I found dispiriting.

King Wilhelm obviously found it so, also, for he grew increasingly sullen, his silences broken only by the occasional fit of pique against the servants. Queen Clotilde remained in her room with the door locked and took her meals in solitude. This also seemed to wear on the King, and he drank heavily through the second day.

I retired early, weary of his sullenness and temper. Around midnight I woke and ventured into the suite's common room. There was no sign of the King, but Queen Clotilde sat near the fire, reading a book. One of her maids, a pretty blonde girl of about fifteen, sat nearby, knitting. The Queen glanced up as I entered.

"Good evening, Dr. Watson," she said.

"Your Majesty," I replied with the best bow I could manage. "I hope I have not disturbed you. I could not sleep."

She smiled, a sad expression, but one that softened her countenance and brought out its warmth. "I could not sleep, either. On nights like this I find relief in reading my Bible."

"I am sure there is great comfort in the scriptures," I replied.

She smiled again, but this time the expression was hard. "What I am reading is not of much comfort, I'm afraid. Do you remember the story of

Jael, from the book of Judges?"

I shook my head.

"It is the story of a woman in an...unhappy situation."

It seemed to me that the Queen had more than a little sympathy for this woman, but I could think of no tactful way to ask why.

"My husband is not here," she said.

"What?"

"He went out while you were sleeping."

"Went out?" I was stunned that the King would do such a foolish thing, and without waking me. "Do you know where I can find him?"

"I do not," she said, "though I know the kind of place where he must be. He said that he felt stifled here and that he would rather take the risk of going out than remain in the hotel one more moment."

"Forgive me, Your Majesty, but that seems most..." I let the sentence die on my lips. There are things one does not say of a king, especially to his wife.

"My husband is a fool," she said, quietly. "I do not object when he goes out, however, for it gives me some relief."

"Your Majesty—" I said, shocked at her frankness.

She rose, stiffly, and moved to the young woman. "I hope I can trust in your discretion, Doctor. I would very much like for you to understand."

She said something in Norwegian to the girl, then raised her arm. The maid helped her pull back her sleeve to reveal a bruise of violet, brown and sickly green hues. I moved closer to examine the mark and saw that it had been made by the grip of a large and very powerful hand.

"The King?" I asked.

She nodded. "Three days ago, though he has often given me similar in the past. He is careful not to mark me where others may see."

"But why?"

"You could as well ask a mad dog why it bites," she said. "He would tell you it is because he wants a son and I refuse to let him into my chambers. Perhaps it is the duty of a queen to ignore her husband's wanderings and to produce an heir, but I cannot bear his touch knowing of all of his actresses and others."

I nodded, not knowing what to say.

"Sometimes, he forces his desires on me...or on another if I am unavailable to him." She exchanged a glance with the little maid, who turned her eyes down in shame. "I do not blame Sylvie," she continued.

"My husband did not ask her consent. He took her, as he takes me, by brute force."

I felt a rush of rage at this. In that moment I thought that Holmes and I were engaged in a fool's errand in trying to save such a man, king or not.

"Your Majesty, I...I do not know what to say."

She graced me with another of her sad smiles. "That is not necessary, Doctor. I am grateful for your confidence and your kindness in listening."

It was nearly two in the morning when the King's carriage arrived. Queen Clotilde took little Sylvie into her quarters with her. I heard the key turn in the lock behind them.

Moments later the King entered with Haas and two of his men. He had a young woman on his arm, a lovely thing with dark hair and blue eyes. Except for Haas they all seemed to be deep in their cups.

"Your Majesty, I must protest," I said. "It was dangerous to go out and moreso to return with a stranger."

King Wilhelm glared at me for a moment, then let out a bellowing laugh. "Come, Doctor, Haas was always with me. Besides, the idea that this lovely creature is an assassin is absurd."

"Majesty," I replied, "if your enemies know of this weakness for the fair sex, they will seek to exploit it."

"Weakness?" His voice rose in anger. "I will forgive your impudence for the sake of Sherlock Holmes, but you should mind your tongue when speaking to your betters."

I looked to Haas for support, but he only stared at me with his blazing eyes.

"Your Majesty," I said, "I am only speaking out of concern for your safety."

"You think I am in danger from this slip of a girl?" He passed a hand over his face and spoke in a calmer tone. "Perhaps you have a point, Doctor. What do I need her for when I have a loving wife waiting for me?"

He strode to the Queen's door and, finding it locked, began to pound on it with his fists. "Clotilde!" he shouted. "Open up, damn you, woman! I am your husband, do you hear?"

After a moment he turned back to me, a dark expression on his face. "You see how she treats me? What man should have to endure this?"

When I did not respond, he took his companion by the hand and entered his own room.

The next morning I was awakened by the news that a messenger from Holmes was waiting to see me in the lobby. I dressed and went down to find an elderly man with great mutton-chop whiskers and a fierce moustache waiting for me. He wore civilian clothes, but with enough accoutrements that I did not need Holmes' acumen to know he had served as an officer of Her Majesty's Army in Afghanistan and India. He introduced himself as Major Kildaire and took me to a waiting carriage.

"Are you taking me to meet Holmes?" I asked. "I had assumed that he was still on the continent."

"My dear Watson," the man said in my friend's voice. "I have been in England all along."

"Holmes?" I said, peering at him closely.

He grinned. "Forgive me, but I find this a useful method to test myself. If I can fool you, surely no stranger can pierce my disguise."

"But I thought you had gone to Prague."

"Forgive my deceit," he replied, "but I had a line of inquiry to pursue here. The illusion that I had left the country made it easier for me. I left the fact-gathering on the continent to an associate. Do you recall me speaking of Francois le Villard?"

"The French detective," I said.

"Indeed. He has excellent insight and a keen mind, though he is somewhat lacking in his breadth of knowledge."

"What did he find?"

"He said that Miss Milena Jebavýová, in addition to being a dainty creature, is someone of intellect and quick wit. That sounds rather familiar, does it not?"

"Like Irene Adler."

"Yes," Holmes replied. "Sadly, it seems that His Majesty's taste is for women who are unlike his bride."

I felt myself flush angrily as I remembered the King's shameful behavior. "And did she have any light to shed on this matter?"

Holmes's laugh was derisive. "M. le Villard seemed quite taken with her charms, but his interview with her yielded nothing of interest. The

Gallic temperament is not well suited to this sort of work. The French are too easily distracted by a pretty face."

"Then there was nothing to be learned?"

"From the girl, no," he said, "but from the bomb? Ah, there we make significant progress. Villard described it to me in the most exacting detail and it was a marvelous piece of machinery, something to make a Swiss jeweler blush with envy."

"Rather an expensive way to blow someone up," I said.

"It is most suggestive, is it not?" Holmes replied. "It fits with what I have discovered in my own inquiries. I knew from the first that this was not the work of anarchists. They are zealous, but consistently amateurish in their attempts at murder. No, this is the work of a specialist."

"A bomb specialist?"

"An assassination specialist, Watson. A skilled professional belonging to an organization ready to hire their services to any person or group that cannot undertake murder on their own."

"But that is monstrous!"

"Indeed," he said, "and yet they have been operating secretly in London for months. I believe they were responsible for the deaths of Carruthers, Blankenship, and Lord Saltire, among several others.

I was stunned by the news and could only shake my head in disbelief. Holmes smiled, bitterly, and spoke with barely controlled anger. "Secretly! They carry out their depredations in *my* city and I had no knowledge of it."

"But who are they?" I asked.

Holmes' laugh was pained. He handed me a business card, blank but for the words:

THE ASSASSINATIONS BUREAU, LTD.

"This organization is set up on the lines of a legitimate business," he said. "It is run by a Russian expatriate who calls himself Ivan Dragomilov, though I suspect that is an alias. It is he with whom we have our appointment."

My shock must have showed on my face, for Holmes laughed again, this time with real humor. "That is the reason for my disguise, Watson," he said. "We are going to meet with the chairman of this Assassinations Bureau to commission a murder."

"And who is to be the victim?" I asked.

"I am," Holmes replied.

Ivan Dragomilov's offices were comfortably appointed. As we waited, Holmes scanned the shelves where the works of Stirner, Marx, and Rakhmetov sat side by side with Russian editions of the novels of Tolstoy, Chekov, and Dostoyevski. On a table by the entrance sat a stack of magazines and popular novels. One of these, a slender volume titled *The Noise that Shook the Mountains* caught my eye. It had a garish red cover on which a young woman in scanty costume was depicted. It seemed out of keeping with the rest of the surroundings and, curious, I picked it up and opened it.

There was a flash, accompanied by a lout retort and the smell of cordite. I dropped the book and backed away while Holmes turned toward me, an expression of concern on his face.

"Good afternoon, gentlemen." The speaker was a tall, slender man who had entered the room while the explosion had distracted us.

Holmes had moved to examine the book, which contained a clever mechanism designed to set off a paper cap when it was opened.

"An interesting toy," he said, using Major Kildaire's voice. "Though I don't see why you would play such a crude joke on your clients."

The man smiled an icy smile. Indeed, I'm not sure he could have offered a warmer expression. His hair was so blonde as to seem prematurely white, and his complexion was nearly that of an albino. Even his blue eyes were so light in color as to suggest an Arctic wilderness.

"I find that many of my clients have a fetish for explosives," he said. "That is certainly true of anarchists, who like their vengeance as dramatic as possible. Ironically, I have discovered that they also often seem to feel a positive terror about actually being in the proximity of an explosion."

"You mock them?" I said. "I should think that you lose a number of customers that way."

"My services are not to be sought lightly," he replied. "If something so slight chases them away, then they should not have come to me in the first place."

"You have some contempt for anarchists," Holmes said.

"I agree with many of their aims, but find their methods deplorable.

But come, we are here to discuss your business, not my philosophy. How may I be of service?"

"I am Major Bernard Kildaire," Holmes said. "This is my friend, Dr. Sigerson."

"I am Ivan Dragomilov," the man said, shaking our hands. I noticed that his grip was astonishingly powerful, and believed that he could have broken my hand with the strength of those slender fingers. He gestured us to chairs and sat behind his desk.

"We would like to employ your bureau to eliminate Mr. Sherlock Holmes," Holmes said.

"Why is that?" Dragomilov asked.

"Does it matter?"

"My Bureau does not accept any commissions it does not deem morally justified," the assassin replied. "We have nothing to do with personal vendettas or business disputes. Before I give the order to remove a man from life, I must be convinced that his passing will leave the world a better place."

"I can assure you that many of my associates will be eternally grateful for his death."

Dragomilov smiled, indulgently. "That sounds rather self-serving, Major. I can assure you that I have no interest in making the world a safer place for criminals."

"But you are a criminal, yourself," I said.

"Technically, that is true," he replied. "I have placed myself and my organization outside the confines of the law, but only in order to serve the greater good. I would think that you would appreciate that, Major."

"And why is that?"

"Because I know that you are actually Mr. Sherlock Holmes."

I have rarely seen Holmes taken so off guard. He stared at Dragomilov, clearly weighing his options. After a moment he relaxed and began to peel off his wig, whiskers and makeup.

"Don't be upset, Mr. Holmes," Dragomilov said with a smirk. "I make a habit of thoroughly investigating anyone who seeks an appointment with me. Had I not known who you were, I should have never seen through your disguise."

"It will do you no good," I said, reaching for my pistol. Dragomilov did not move, and the superior smile never left his face. Holmes reached across from his seat and caught my arm.

"We are in his hands, Watson. This man is a master of assassins and he knew we were coming. It is only at his sufferance that we will leave this room alive."

"There is no need to fear, Dr. Watson," Dragomilov said. "I have no intention of harming either you or Mr. Holmes. We are surgeons, not butchers, in my Bureau. We only strike down the guilty."

"So you say," I replied.

"Would it surprise you to know that I have already turned down half a dozen offers to have you killed, Mr. Holmes?"

"Indeed?" Holmes said. "Only half a dozen?"

"You are one of the most popular requests, but I have always turned the offers down on ethical grounds. I admire you greatly, both for your gifts and for your interest in justice. Indeed it has long been my hope that we might collaborate."

"Outrageous!" I said. "Sherlock Holmes cooperate with a professional killer?"

"Do not be so hasty to dismiss the idea," Dragomilov replied. "I imagine there have been quite a few times when you knew that someone was guilty of terrible crimes, but have been unable to do anything about it. How many murderers have slipped through your fingers? How many blackmailers? How many who have shattered people's lives but not left behind enough evidence to convict them?"

"Not so many," Holmes snapped.

"From what I have read of you, even one left unpunished would be too many."

"Don't be deceived," Holmes replied. "My biographer has a tendency to oversimplify and exaggerate."

Dragomilov shrugged. "As you will, but remember the offer is always open. And for a man of your integrity, my prices would be reduced."

"My only interest in coming to you is to discuss one of your current commissions," Holmes said. "Is it true that you have agreed to kill the King of Bohemia?"

"It is."

"I am engaged by the King to prevent this."

"Yes," Dragomilov said, a ghost of his former smile returning to his pale lips. "It does seem that we are at cross purposes. I suggest you stand aside, for my Bureau has never failed."

"You have failed twice already," I said, "and you will continue to fail as long as Holmes opposes you."

"It would be an interesting contest," Dragomilov replied.

"Perhaps it need not come to that," Holmes said. "Who is your employer in this matter? Is it an anarchist group, as he believes?"

"That is a confidential matter."

"But you have been convinced that the assassination is justified?"

"Would you try to convince me otherwise?"

"*Thou shalt not kill*," I said.

"I cannot accept that as a predicate," he replied. "Come, Dr. Watson, you are a man of medicine. You know that diseased tissue must sometimes be excised for the good of the patient. So it is in the world at large. Imagine the tens of thousands who could have been saved if my organization had existed in the time of Bonaparte. Think of the terror that could have been averted if we had been there in Robespierre's day."

I was outraged, but could think of nothing to say to counter his arguments. This man was as clever as the Devil.

"I cannot see any point in continuing this conversation," Holmes said. "You are right to assume that I am often frustrated by the law and all its inefficiencies, but I am hardly willing to abandon it."

Dragomilov nodded. "Then we are at odds in this matter. Believe me when I say I wish it could be otherwise."

"What do you make of him?" Holmes and I had returned to our lodgings at 221B Baker Street, where he was changing from his disguise.

"Dragomilov? Aside from the fact that that is not his real name, that he is ambidextrous, is the son of a nobleman, has a blonde daughter about two years old whom he dotes on, and had some knowledge of the Japanese system of wrestling, I can say very little."

"Holmes!" I said. "I don't doubt you, but how could you know?"

"You know my methods, Watson."

"Ambidextrous…" I said, thinking. "Did he have calluses from holding a pen on both hands?"

"Capital!" Holmes said with a short laugh.

"But the daughter?"

My friend waved his hand impatiently. "You must have noticed how immaculately Dragomilov was dressed."

"Certainly."

"A man who cares so much for his appearance and yet his left trouser leg was wrinkled, as if a small child had hugged his leg. Add to that several long strands of blonde hair clinging to his knee, and a matching strand on his shoulder when he, no doubt, picked up the girl to cuddle. Who but a daughter would a man like him allow such liberties?

"As for his martial skills, if you had studied Baritsu, as I have, you would recognize the unique tread of the master whose motions all originate in his center of mass."

"Remarkable," I said. "But his ideas, do you think he sincerely believes them?"

Holmes looked up from the towel he was using to wipe the last of the makeup from his face. "Yes, I do. In his own way he is as much a fanatic as our friend, Herr Haas."

"Well, we know that his assertion that he only kills the guilty cannot be true."

"How is that, Watson?"

I grinned, pleased at having beaten Holmes to a deduction for once. "Because, my dear Holmes, there was no way the sniper could have known that he had the right target. On such a foggy night the best he would have seen was a vague silhouette at the window, yet he fired anyway."

Holmes froze in mid-motion, his face rigid.

"Watson, I have been a fool!"

"What do you mean?" I asked.

"I shall explain on the way, I only hope that my blunder has not doomed the King."

"I don't understand," I said. Holmes had tipped the driver and our four-wheeler was moving with frightening speed through the foggy mid-day streets.

"Do you remember the missing bullet, Watson?"

"Of course."

"Your comment made me realize that we could not find the bullet because there was none. A man like Dragomilov is too exacting to take the kind of chance you mentioned. He will strike when the King, and only the King, is a possible target."

"But we all heard the shot," I said. "And the window shattered inward."

"I have seen a device, an invention of the Russian hunter, Zaroff, for hunting dangerous game fish or alligators. A blank shotgun cartridge is attached to the end of a spear. When the tip of the spear is thrust against the body of the fish the shell detonates, killing it.

"I believe that our 'sniper' used just such a device. He stood on the ground outside the hotel and thrust his weapon up to strike the window. The explosion shattered the glass and created the illusion of a sniper. Then the man flattened himself against the side of the building; the last place anyone would think to look."

"That is ingenious," I said, "but what is the purpose?

"The same as the purpose of a sophisticated bomb that is too easily disarmed. The attacks were distractions, intended to make us believe in the mythical anarchists, when all the time the assassin was in our midst. When the time came they could kill the King and we would be too busy chasing phantoms to suspect the real culprit."

"But who is it?"

"Think, Watson. Who disarmed the bomb?"

"Haas!"

We were informed at the front desk of the Langham that the King had dismissed his staff for the afternoon. He, the Queen, and Haas were in the suites with strict instructions not to be disturbed.

"We're too late," Holmes said, and raced up the stairs as I struggled to keep up. He reached the door before I did and tried the knob.

"Locked," he cried. "Watson, use your revolver."

I had already drawn the Webley and now fired three shots into the lock before it shattered. We pushed through to find King Wilhelm seated in one of the chairs, his wrists securely bound to the arms and his ankles to the legs.

"Holmes!" he cried. Beware, Haas is—"

I didn't hear the end of the sentence, for at that moment a body slammed into me from behind with enough force to bring me down. Haas had heard us and had hidden behind the door. He was as strong as I had feared and twisted my arm, creating such pain that I lost the gun and very nearly all consciousness. A moment later the pain stopped but it was a moment before I could clear my head and look up.

Holmes had caught Haas from behind and was trying to apply a choke hold to him, but the smaller man was struggling so fiercely that it seemed he must throw my friend off in a moment. Holding my injured right arm to my body, I cast around with my left for the pistol. After a moment I found it and pointed it at the pair of them.

When Haas saw the weapon, he stopped his struggling and stared murder at me with those wild eyes. Holmes twisted his arms behind him in a Bartitsu hold that I did not think even this human tiger could escape.

Then I heard the gunshots. I spun to see Queen Clotilde emerging from her room. She carried a small revolver in her hand and fired shot after shot into the King's body. He cried out at first, but after the third wound, his eyes rolled up in his head and he made no more sound. This did not stop the Queen, who continued to advance on him. Even when the hammer fell on empty chambers she continued to pull the trigger.

I approached her, and gently took the weapon from her hand. As she turned to me, tears streamed down her face but, otherwise, she seemed unnaturally calm.

"I have misread the situation again," Holmes said. "Haas was never the assassin, he was merely the arranger, hired to prepare the murder."

"Holmes, we must protect her," I said, guiding the Queen to a chair. "Trust me when I tell you that she has as much reason to kill her husband as any woman ever has. It would be unthinkable for her to suffer more than she has, already."

"Are you saying that Dragomilov was right, Watson? Was this killing ethically justified?"

I found I could not speak but, as much as it galled me, I nodded my head.

"Take the Queen," Haas said. "Get her away from this place and I shall see that none of this ever comes to her door. It is what I was hired for."

The newspapers said that King Wilhelm was tragically killed in a freak gas explosion in his room. Fortunately the staff was away and the blast was limited to His Majesty's suites. At first it was feared that Queen Clotilde had also been killed, but it turned out that she also had left the hotel for the afternoon.

Haas vanished so thoroughly that it seemed he had never been born, and by the week's end, Ivan Dragomilov's offices were abandoned and he was not to be found in London. After some investigation, Holmes concluded that he had sailed to America under the alias of Sergius Constantine.

"Will you pursue him?" I asked as we sat in our lodgings on a January afternoon mercifully free of even a hint of fog.

"To what end, Watson?" Holmes asked. "I cannot convict him of any crime of which the Queen is not also complicit. Indeed, it would be hard to prove that Ivan Dragomilov has broken any serious laws.

"No, let him make what he will of his life in his new home, but if our paths cross again, I shall not rest until I bring him down."

"Holmes," I said. "As much as I despise his methods, we did end out working towards the same end. Are we really so different from him?"

He stood and began to fill his pipe with the tobacco he kept in the toe of a Persian slipper. "I believe so," he said. "Men like you and I are sometimes forced into these situations where there is no good way, only a choice of evils, but men like Dragomilov seek them out."

"I wish he could see that in using such methods he is actually causing more harm than good."

"What a thought," Holmes said with a sharp laugh. "If he does ever come to that conclusion, our ethical assassin will be honor bound to do away with himself."

THE ADVENTURE OF THE
IMAGINARY NIHILIST

by
Will Murray

O NE of the most remarkable experiences in all of my dealings with the illustrious Mr. Sherlock Holmes began with the simple act of opening a door.

It was half-past three in the afternoon, when the brass knocker gave up a resounding clamor.

Holmes was deep in the study of a pamphlet on something or other and looked up to request, "Be good enough to answer that, would you, Watson?"

"Are you expecting a client?" I inquired.

"I daresay I am always *half*-expecting a client. But this afternoon, no."

I threw open the door and took a sharp inward breath of surprise.

The man standing at the stoop was of military bearing. He stood no less than six feet in height, and his black eyes snapped under a shock of dark hair shot with glints of gray. But these details were not what flummoxed me at first sight, rather it was the vague yet alarming resemblance to Holmes himself. It was in his gaunt face, in the steely look in the man's eyes. The predatory nose, the sharp features. All of it.

I found myself searching this man for other familiarities, when he said in a brusque American voice, "I should like to see Mr. Sherlock Holmes. If I may."

He presented me with his card. It read:

COLONEL RICHARD HENRY SAVAGE
U. S. Army
Retired

"One moment," I requested.

Taking the card to Holmes, I waited expectantly for some sign of mutual recognition. There was none.

Instead, Holmes laid his pamphlet to one side and arose.

"Bring him in," Holmes said.

I did as instructed and when the two men came face to face, they did so as evident strangers.

"Mr. Holmes, I understand that you accept private consultations," said the American colonel. His manner was direct, and admirably to the point. There was an air of brisk, nervous energy about the colonel that reminded me again of Holmes, but in a rather different way.

"If the matter is of sufficient moment to interest me," Holmes allowed. "Pray be seated."

The two men sat down without the preliminary of a handshake.

Holmes appraised the man with his inquisitive eyes. "You are a man of the world, I take it, Colonel?"

"I consider myself an old campaigner," Savage replied.

Holmes nodded. "They are much the same thing."

Holmes lit his pipe thoughtfully. I often saw him doing this as a cover for sizing up visitors. He resumed his inquiry.

"You are an author, I take it?"

"Yes. You have heard of me?"

"Your novel, *My Official Wife*, received an enthusiastic review from the *Times*. I recall the reviewer wrote that 'It is a wonderful clever *tour de force*, in which improbabilities and impossibilities disappear, under an air of plausibility that is irresistible.'"

"You have a remarkable memory, Mr. Holmes. I believe that those are very nearly the exact words employed."

"They are *precisely* the exact words," said Holmes. "They impelled me to lay hands on your extravagant novel, which I have read."

The colonel's dark eyes seemed to light up, only to dim as Holmes went on with his characteristic frankness. "I found it to be, in the *Times*' words, 'wildly extravagant.' But I congratulate you upon its success, Colonel. Now, what service may I render you?"

"That you have read my little novel greatly reduces the need for explanation, as you will see," said Savage. "I am a world traveler, and have seen many lands."

"Among them, Russia," Holmes suggested.

"Yes. I was present in that vast land when Tsar Alexander II was assassinated a decade ago. You see, the events as described in my story have a basis in actuality."

"Say no more. Watson, have you read the colonel's novel?"

"I confess that I have not," I admitted.

"Simply told," said Holmes, "it is a fanciful account of the colonel gallantly passing off a Russian Nihilist as his wife, as she fled the Russian Secret Police in the wake of the assassination."

"Exactly," said Colonel Savage. "The woman in the matter was no figment of an author's imagination, but a creature of flesh and blood like ourselves. Although I took liberties with the greater portion of the tale, up until our arrival in St. Petersburg, the story is, with only minor embellishments, the truth."

"I see," said Holmes. "And now you seek my aid in determining her fate?"

The colonel gave a short gasp. "How the devil did you deduce that?" he fairly exploded.

"It is quite elementary, my dear Colonel. If the woman in question is taken from life and the factual account ceased at St. Petersburg, therefore her fate must be unknown to you."

The colonel composed himself. "Yes. Of course. Allow me to finish. I am in London in response to a secure wire that was signed by a *nom de guerre* known only to me. It is the selfsame *nom de guerre* used by my Nihilistic friend during our brief time together. Naturally, I was astounded to receive such a communication, since I had assumed that the woman in question had been captured by the Royalists and no doubt shot, or quietly strangled for her political activities."

"Go on, Colonel," Holmes urged.

"Arriving in London I went straightaway to her hotel. But the clerk swore up and down that no one of that name, or any name by which I knew her, had taken rooms there. Nor did anyone on staff recognize her description, which I gave most minutely."

"Therefore you suspect a hoax, perhaps some enemy luring you to London for dire and murky motives?"

"I admit that such has crossed my mind. But my chief concern is the woman. Did she survive? Is she now in London? Have agents of the Tsar tracked her down? Has she been—"

"Murdered?" Holmes supplied.

"Yes! You can understand that although I am a married man, and happily married to boot, having assumed this woman long dead, I could not resist the siren call to find out for myself."

"And you have had some luck in your quest, I take it?"

Savage started. "However did you guess that?"

"I did not. I am a student of human nature. If man crossed the Atlantic in order to track down a long lost traveling companion and compatriot, one who was presumed dead, only to find an empty hotel room, I daresay he would be depressed. On the contrary, you are enervated. You have found more than a blind alley filled with questions."

"It is true," said Savage, "I was reconnoitering the streets of London when I chanced to spy her in the crowd. I called out her name. I ran after her. But she fled. And I lost her in the teeming throng, damn the luck."

"A glimpse of a woman in a crowd is hardly sufficient to ascertain identity," Holmes offered.

"This was no ghost. I would swear that it was she!"

"A trifle older, I imagine."

"Not so that I could have been fooled," Savage countered. "She is in London. And I must locate her, Holmes. Will you help?"

"Having read your book," Holmes essayed after a pause, "I confess the mystery intrigues me."

At this point I interjected, "But, Holmes. Why would the woman in question wire Colonel Savage to come to a certain address, then disappear into thin air?"

"Ah, Watson. She did not vanish. She was never at the address to begin with. Don't you see? Fearing for her life, she dared not relay her actual lodgings. But they cannot be far. For how else could she monitor the colonel's arrival?"

Colonel Savage leapt to his feet. "Then you will consent to come with me, my dear Holmes?"

"Colonel Savage, I deem it your second chance to entertain my fancy," said Holmes, rising, taking his revolver from a drawer and pocketing it.

As the four-wheeler drew us along London's substantial cobbles, Holmes pressed Colonel Savage for additional details.

"I never knew the woman's true name," the colonel related. "She called herself Helene Marie Vanderbilt-Astor Gaines—a concoction no doubt derived from a close reading of the news of the world mixed, perhaps, with gleanings from tawdry shop girl romances.

"Describe her, please," Holmes prompted.

Colonel Savage painted a portrait in words that any artist might transfer to canvas without difficulty. He was a keen observer, of that there could be no doubt.

"This is a delicate matter for you, is it not, Savage?" Holmes said after absorbing the careful description.

"Indeed. I left my wife at New York, lest there be any misunderstanding."

"No doubt," replied Holmes. "But I was referring to your connection to the Russian Royal family."

"You know of that!" Savage sputtered.

"Tut-tut. You give me overmuch credit. Widespread publicity attended the publication of your popular novel. It was reported that your daughter is married to the Chamberlain to the throne."

"True. And the survival of the unfortunate Nihilist might lead to political complications with the Russ. For I have done considerable diplomatic work in my time, much of it of a confidential nature."

"Complications that it would be best to avoid," said Holmes.

Savage bowed his head gravely. "Your discretion would be greatly appreciated, Holmes."

"My discretion is at your disposal, Colonel."

At length, we arrived at our destination.

Alighting, Holmes invited, "Now, Colonel, if you would be so good as to show us the precise spot where you spied the beautiful Nihilist."

"This way, gentlemen."

The colonel went to a street corner where a tobacconist had his little shop. Taking a position, he faced slightly northwest, and lined up his penetrating dark eyes with a far alley.

"There!"

We followed him to the area in question.

"It was much busier than it is now," Colonel Savage explained. "But I am certain that I ran to this very spot, by which time she was no longer present."

Holmes took a position on the designated spot. He turned about in a slow circle, eyeing the view from every possible angle.

"Any number of avenues by which she might have fled," he mused. Then he selected one, by what means of calculation I confess that I do not know. But Holmes strode with the purposefulness of a fox on a scent until he arrived at a certain door.

"The woman you spied," he announced suddenly, "vanished through this door."

"What leads you to that conclusion, Mr. Holmes?" Savage asked, without a trace of surprise in his voice. Evidently, he was fast becoming accustomed to Sherlock Holmes' rapid deductions.

"Look about you, Colonel. Do you see any other means by which an adult woman might disappear from sight of a throng of passersby?"

"I do not," Savage admitted. And I could not gainsay him. It was the only door close enough to the spot where the woman was last seen which could be reached in the time it would have taken the colonel to cross the street from the far corner.

That settled, Holmes gave the handle of the door a firm tug.

The door surrendered easily. It proved to open into kind of cul de sac where ash barrels and rude tools were stored. Its confines were small, to be sure.

"I daresay a woman might have loitered here undetected if one did not possess the wit to try the door," Holmes said.

"I am not in the habit of opening strange doors," Colonel Savage said stiffly.

"I meant no offense, Colonel," Holmes said hastily. "I was merely thinking out loud. For two things are now obvious."

"Not to me," said the colonel.

"The first is that the lady in question did not wish to be found by you at the time you came across her. That much is evident by her seeking refuge in such squalor."

"And the second?"

"The second is that she greatly desires a meeting with you, but under circumstances far more to her liking. I would judge that she deliberately showed herself to further that end. "

"What makes you say that?"

Holmes pointed to a fragment of lace handkerchief he had removed from under the rim of an ash barrel's dented lid. He was looking at it in the dim light. With a flourish worthy of a stage conjuror, he turned it about, presenting one face. On the faintly soiled surface a solitary word had been written in ink, apparently in a woman's delicate hand:

Blackness

"Good Lord!" Colonel Savage said hoarsely. "What can that possibly mean?"

"Not possibly," returned Holmes. "Definitely."

Not a quarter hour later, Holmes had guided us to Charing Cross station and as nightfall smothered the surrounding towns, we were whisking south to some unknown place.

"If I may inquire, Holmes," asked I. "What is our final destination?"

"Blackness," said Holmes gravely. "Nothing more and scarcely less."

Puzzlement was evidently written on my face, for Holmes swiftly dispelled it with a singular sentence.

"Have you never heard of the village of Blackness, near Crowborough, Watson? I know that Colonel Savage is unlikely to be familiar with it, man of the world that he is entirely notwithstanding."

I confessed placid ignorance.

"What type of place would be cursed with such a foul name?" asked Colonel Savage. "Is it the lair of thieves?"

"Actually, it is quite unremarkable," Holmes related. "I daresay we may not find it so prosaic if my suspicions are proved to be true."

"And precisely what are your suspicions?" Savage asked.

"Only that your woman of mystery fears to meet with you in the city, where she might be observed. Beyond that, I am still working on the problem."

"But, Holmes," asked I. "How can you be certain that the village of Blackness was meant by the scrawl on the handkerchief?"

"While I deduced that the message was written by a woman, based upon the unavoidable fact that man would scarcely employ a woman's handkerchief to leave a message, the handwriting itself was sufficiently bold to proclaim the author a person of some mental fortitude. The choice of message might have been improvised, or preplanned. But the manner in which it was conveyed suggests one accustomed to the writing of secret messages calculated to mean little or nothing at casual inspection, but which are fraught with hidden meaning to the initiated. In short, the colonel's charming conspirator of old."

"Bully good logic, Holmes!" cried the colonel. "But by what arcane skill did you ascertain that the village of Blackness was meant?"

"By a skill no more remarkable that the ability to read the King's English." From a pocket Holmes produced the handkerchief in question and invited us to examine it anew.

We studied it a moment. The truth became distressingly clear. Colonel Savage spoke it one jump ahead of my unuttered thought.

"The B is capitalized," said he.

Holmes nodded sagely. "In the heat of the discovery, this simple fact was overlooked. It is often thus."

Savage settled back into his cushions. "Now how do you propose to flush our fugitive quail out of the underbrush?"

"I confess that I have no idea," Holmes admitted, closing his eyes as if desirous of sleep. "But inasmuch as we will not arrive at our destination for some time, we have ample time to ruminate on the prospects ahead."

With that, to the colonel's visible disappointment, Sherlock Homes dropped off into a deep sleep from which our unbroken conversation failed to rouse him.

At Crowborough Station, we commandeered a four-wheeler, which took us straightaway to Blackness, which, given the late hour, seemed well named.

"Is there an inn?" asked Holmes of our driver as we approached.

"But the one. The Ruddy Fox."

"Take us to the Ruddy Fox, then."

"We would like to engage rooms," Holmes told the innkeeper upon our arrival.

"For the night, sir?"'

"At least."

"Very good. This way, please." As our genial host led us to our rooms, Holmes asked, "Have you given lodging to a woman traveling alone in the last day or so?"

"Why do you ask, sir?" the keeper asked with the studied caution of his breed.

Colonel Savage interjected. "She would be aged about 30, and possessed of marvelous caramel hair."

"A relative of yours?"

"My wife, as it were," Colonel Savage asserted boldly.

"Odd. She did not say to expect you."

"We are…estranged. I believe her to be traveling incognito, as the saying goes. Mrs. Savage has been under much strain these last months."

"Shall I announce you, Mr.—"

"Colonel Richard Henry Savage. United States Army, retired."

The innkeeper's eyes grew wide. "The author, sir?"

"The very same. And since it is so late, and Madame Savage has doubtless retired for the evening, I think any announcement can await the rosy dawn."

"Very good, sir. I will leave that to your discretion."

After the innkeeper left us to our rooms, Sherlock Holmes paid our companion a rare compliment.

"Well played, Savage."

"Thank you. Now what is our itinerary?"

"A stealthy reconnoiter, I should think."

"Why not knock on 'Madame Savage's' door?"

"We do not know for certain the identity of your mystery woman, so I should judge that imprudent, if not rash."

"I bow to your superior instincts in these matters," Savage said.

We went out into the gathering evening. There was but a sliver of a moon, yet Holmes refrained from use of his pocket torch. He seemed preoccupied, and spoke little. I noted the unimportant fact that the fleet-winged swifts of summer had arrived early. Their startled cries as we passed were unmistakable.

After we had thoroughly circumnavigated the vicinity, Colonel Savage asked, "For what are we searching, Holmes?"

"That most illusive and imponderable of earthly stuff."

"Yes?"

'Time," said Holmes.

"We are seeking time?"

"No, we are killing it."

Savage frowned darkly. I confess that my countenance must have resembled his in that wise. For I was as perplexed as the American colonel.

Beyond that cryptic pronouncement, Holmes could be induced to say no more.

Once midnight had come and gone, Holmes abruptly changed course, leading us back to the Ruddy Fox.

"And now?" asked Savage as we reached the door.

"Now," said Holmes. "To bed! And a good night to you both."

He left us standing in our boots, exchanging glances of studied consternation.

The day was still assembling itself when Holmes and I and Colonel Savage foregathered in the inn's quaint breakfast room to take tea.

"I fear you must prepare yourself for dire tidings," said Holmes.

Colonel Savage glowered over his morning cup.

"Your faithless 'wife' has fled the inn," explained Holmes.

For a moment, I thought the American would storm out of the room. His predatory features colored angrily. But he soon mastered himself.

"It is as I anticipated," Holmes went on without evident concern. "In fact, I rather hoped that she would do so."

"Hoped!" Savage flared. "Why, I sought your assistance precisely so that she would not escape me a second time!"

"Her escape," said Holmes, "was entirely unavoidable. In truth, you could no more have arrested her flight than you could have apprehended a spirit of the dead."

"I do not entirely take your meaning, Holmes," said Savage, his ire subsiding somewhat.

"All will be explained," Holmes promised. "Come, finish up. We must be off."

We went out into the milky morning, where the horrid screech of the newly-arrived migratory swifts resounded. Holmes led the way, as he had before. He seemed to select a direct course into the Ashdown Forest and followed it unerringly like the proverbial sleuth hound.

"How are your tracking skills, Colonel?" Holmes asked after a time.

"I can read sign. We are following boot tracks."

"Male or female?"

Savage studied the ground as we walked.

"Both, I should say."

"What leads you to that conclusion?" asked Holmes.

"Two heavy sets. One rather light. Suggesting a dainty foot."

"Very good. You will be our guide whilst I scan the higher reaches."

"For what?"

"For whatever may be discovered," said Holmes.

Savage favored me with another doubtful glance, and we could think of nothing better to do than to follow the enigmatic detective.

We pushed far into the forest when Holmes suddenly cried, "Halloa! What have we here?"

Stopping at the foot of a sturdy copper beech tree, Holmes set aside his walking stick and began a climb that would have intrigued a monkey. Reaching a high bough, he sat astride it and seemed preoccupied with what he discovered there.

At length, he called down, "Watson, do you recall the disappearance of one Mary Morgan?"

"How could I not? Her slain body lay in woods very much like these, utterly unfindable owing to decomposition and the actions of animals."

"Indeed. She might never have been found expect for the natural habits of an enterprising woodpecker, who in constructing her maternal nest, plucked ginger hairs from the dead scalp, employing them to feather her nest, as it were. By that reckoning alone, was the unhappy girl's body unearthed."

Holmes lowered himself out of the tree in careful stages.

"May I present," said he, "proof of the mortal remains of your Helene Marie Vanderbilt-Astor Gaines."

Accepting the clump of caramel hair, Colonel Savage gave a profound gasp. "She is deceased!"

"So it would seem."

I glanced at the hair, and offered, "The color is yet vibrant. No sign of weathering."

"Suggesting that the body is fresh and not far off," Holmes snapped. "Let us continue. The game is afoot."

Still clutching the caramel hair, Colonel Savage followed woodenly. For his part, Holmes picked up his pace. His dilating nostrils resembled those of the hound after the fox.

"If I am not mistaken," said he, "the malefactors are not far ahead of us."

Rousing from his new-found grief, Savage swore, "This outrage will be avenged." He brandished a substantial revolver. "We'll give them Billy Hell!"

"Caution foremost, Colonel," said Holmes. "Vengeance later, perhaps. If you still possess the appetite for it."

Holmes' suggestive words were still ringing in our ears when we happened upon the discarded kidskin glove.

Retrieving it, Holmes unexpectedly took its mate from a coat pocket.

"Wherever did you get that?" I cried.

"From the empty room of the former Miss Gaines," explained Holmes. "I thought it odd that there was only the one."

"The fiends!" Savage exploded. "They are disposing of her personal effects piecemeal."

Holmes seemed unperturbed. We pressed on through the purple heather and yellow gorse that feather the High Weald so charmingly.

We caught up with them in a dell. At sight of us, they startled like so many flushed quail before the advancing sportsman.

One called out, "We told you to come alone!"

A pistol shot rang out. Then another. The whistle of bullets through foliage sent us ducking in turn.

Savage coolly returned fire, causing the trio to scatter wildly.

Holmes swung his walking stick, knocking the revolver from Savage's grip.

"Enough!" he cried.

"The murderers fired upon us!" Savage retorted.

"They are deliberately aiming high—and you are the last person on earth they wish to harm."

Savage looked thunderstruck. Holmes snatched the revolver from the ground and ran forward, his own pistol still pocketed, I noticed.

Colonel Savage drew abreast of us. "You are a brave man, Holmes."

"Tut-tut. The only danger is that of misadventure."

"They have killed once already! Return my pistol, please. I am not so foolhardy as to blunder into a gun fray unarmed!"

Without delay, Holmes did. Savage took the firearm, neglecting to notice that the cylinder was now empty of shells. I take pride that I spotted the brass cartridges tumbling to the ground after Holmes broke the action open, then knocked the weapon sharply against his hip to dislodge them.

We soon surrounded one of the fleeing men. He was of small stature, and utter terror marked his eyes. Unarmed, he wore a cap pulled low over his wan and rather delicate features.

"What have you done with Miss Gaines!" Savage demanded, thrusting the pistol barrel into the man's heaving chest with intimidating force.

When the culprit spoke, his accents betrayed his national origins. "I have done nothing with her. For she is my sister."

"A Russ!" Savage cried. "Tell me, man. Where is she?"

The man gulped air greedily, and it was possible that he was playing for time, hoping for succor from his fellows.

Holmes interjected, "Come now. The game is up. There is nothing to be gained by denying the facts of the matter."

At length, he spoke, his words and accent thick. "You ask where my sister is. I will tell you now: Dead in her grave."

"Scoundrel!" Savage snapped. "You murdered her!"

"Nyet, nyet! For the woman you knew as Helen Marie Gaines Vanderbilt-Astor Gaines is long in her grave—although where she lies buried not even I, her only brother, know for certain."

"Holmes, what does this mean?" I cried out.

"This man is lying," Colonel Savage insisted. "I saw Miss Gaines in London, only days ago." He grabbed the small man by the collar and shook him vigorously, as if to shake the living truth from him.

"Lies. All lies!" the culprit sobbed.

"My eyes do not lie, sir!" Savage returned with steel in his voice. He placed his formidable revolver to the man's forehead, cocking it.

"It was all a plot, sir. I swear it."

"Allow me to explain," Holmes interjected. "Colonel, look to this man's boots and pray tell me what you see."

Colonel Savage stepped back and regarded the boots with which the captive was shod.

"My God!" he cried. "He is wearing her boots."

"Yes, just as he once wore the kidskin gloves I retrieved. In his haste to flee, he had time only to don such articles as were at hand. For the innkeeper had apprised all concerned of our arrival."

"He promised confidence," Savage said.

"Promises, alas, are often sealed with gold. He was paid to alert his mysterious guests of your coming. The fact that you did not come alone made the conspirators uneasy. They slipped a note under your door, then made their escape during our midnight ramble, as I imagined they would. While you slept, I took the liberty of fetching the note from under your door with my pocket knife. Here it is."

Savage took the envelope and saw that it had been unsealed. Removing the paper within, he read the contents.

"It is a request that I meet Miss Gaines at a clearing two miles northwest of the Ruddy Fox. And to come alone."

"This very dell," said Holmes, "where they waited for you."

"For what fell purpose, Holmes?" I asked, failing to follow the skeins of the scheme.

"An old story, I am afraid," said Holmes. "Blackmail. Extortion."

Consternation enwrapped Colonel's Savage's haggard features. "Nonsense! I am above reproach!"

"Pray let me tell the tale," said Holmes. "In Miss Gaines' room, I discovered certain articles which led me to suspect if not conclude the truth of the imposture. With full knowledge that they awaited you at this spot, I set out, giving the impression that I was following an obscure trail."

I asked, "But why conceal the truth, Holmes?"

"Out of an abundance of caution, I must confess. And owing to a dawning belief that I had erred in an earlier deduction, when I prematurely concluded that the note inscribed on the lady's handkerchief had been written by a woman."

"It *was!*" Savage insisted. "It *must* have been!"

"Logically, yes. But among the articles I unearthed in the abandoned room were a man's straight razor and a woman's wig-stand. Yet the room was occupied by a single party. These items led me to doubt my original assumption."

"I fail to understand the significance of that curious combination," Savage said.

Holmes raised an admonishing finger. "Knowing that this is the height of swift nest-building season," he continued, "and understanding the habits of the redoubtable feathered migrants, I merely kept a weather eye cocked for new birds' nests. Such, I reasoned, would prove more fruitful than a tedious canvas of the forest floor."

"For what?"

"A discarded caramel wig," replied Holmes.

"Wig!" The words left Colonel Savage's lips with the force of an explosion.

"If you will trouble yourself to examine the clump of hair I retrieved from the swift's nest," invited Holmes, "you will discover for yourself an absence of natural roots. In short, you hold strands of Miss Gaines' hairpiece."

"But you implied that she had been killed—"

"No, you inferred such," responded Holmes. "Miss Gaines was in truth dead, as I indicated. But she has suffered from that unfortunate condition for several years now."

"But, Holmes," I interjected. "What of the woman who tantalized Colonel Savage like an apparition?"

"She was entirely imaginary," said Holmes. "Yes, she wanted to be seen. But only that. She wished to lure the colonel to Blackness, there to consummate the bold plan."

Colonel Savage spoke up stiffly. "As I have indicated, Holmes, I am not subject to blackmail."

"No? You penned a novel of your exploits in Russia with a woman not your wife and let the world know that the tale was half-true. On that alone, you might be extorted. But the scheme was more clever than that. You were to be presented with a facsimile of your long-lost Nihilist, and appeals were to be made to your generosity. Gallant soldier that you are, no doubt you would have succumbed to an opportunity to aide a woman you thought long dead. For here was a golden opportunity to rescue your charming co-conspirator. If not, blackmail was still a possibility."

Colonel Savage's military bearing took on a crestfallen posture. His revolver wilted in his hand.

"Then who wore the caramel wig?" he asked at last. "Who could possibly have succeeded in passing herself off as Miss Gaines?"

"Who else but the one person on earth who most resembled her?" returned Holmes. "Who but her own brother?"

With that, Sherlock Holmes snatched the rough cap off the head of the man who wore woman's boots. The features thus exposed were fair, the close-shorn hair a hue akin to caramel.

"When the three confederates fled," Holmes explained, "they dared not leave behind the wig, for its distinctive color would doubtless expose the imposture. Nor could they risk being caught with it, if apprehended. I reasoned therefore that they must dispose of it in the forest. No doubt other bits of Miss Gaines' costume will be discovered there."

"*Da*," said the miserable blackmailer. "We did not foresee the hiring of English detectives."

Colonel Savage exhibited all the symptoms of a man struggling with great emotion. Hoarsely, he asked the conspirator, "She is in truth dead?"

The man nodded gravely. "The fame of your novel reached even imperial Russia. I saw in your fame an opportunity to profit. But now I am lost." He hung his head.

"Let us escort this man back to the Ruddy Fox," Holmes suggested. "There we will alert the local authorities. No doubt it will be a good morning's work to capture the other two. But capture them, I am certain they will."

"Capital!" said Colonel Savage. "Simply capital."

I regarded the American colonel with wonder. "You are in good spirits for a man who has suffered a grievous wrong and an even greater disappointment."

"The contrary. To this very day, I have never been certain of the fate of that improbable but unforgettable woman who was temporarily my wife. Now I know the truth. For that I have you to thank, Mr. Holmes. How can I repay you?"

"You may begin," said Holmes, "by accepting as a present these bullets to replace those which somehow fell from your revolver while it was in my possession."

The HOUSE ON MOREAU STREET

by
Don Roff

The Manchester Guardian: Monday, February 21, 1910
Ghastly Murder in the West-End

A SECOND murder, more atrocious than the one at King's Row last Saturday, was discovered early this morning. Gerald Manley Thompson, a tobacconist, discovered the disfigured body in an alley next to his shop.

Police later identified the mutilated corpse of Wilford P. Tomkins, Jr. of Chelsea. The son of Iron Works founder Wilford P. Tomkins, Sr., the victim inherited the wealth of his late father after the founder's demise in 1907. The body of Tomkins was found stripped. The throat of the victim had been torn out as if by some wild animal. The right arm of Tomkins was also torn off and located approximately 50 yards from the site of the murder. The victim, who was usually known to carry large sums of cash and who wore an expensive watch and rings, was apparently robbed, as those possessions were not found on or near the corpse.

Police speculate that the assailant was a large man, as Tompkins was over 17 stone in weight and was a champion bare-knuckle boxer during his college days at Oxford. It is believed that a group of men could have overpowered Tompkins, and then had a large dog, owned by the gang, kill him. It is unknown why the victim's right arm was carried away from the site. The investigation continues.

The Daily Telegraph: Tuesday, February 22, 1910
Gone! Rare Burmese Ruby Ring Vanishes

While staying at the prestigious Ulmen Hotel, Russian Chancellor, Prince Karl Alexander, who had in his possession a rare Burmese ruby ring, has notified London Police of its disappearance.

After returning from dinner Monday evening, Prince Alexander placed the necklace on the hotel dresser, then went into the closet to select his evening wear. When the prince returned to the dresser, not more than ten minutes later, the Burmese ring was gone.

The staff is being questioned, but the Chancellor saw no one entering the hotel room. The window to the room was unlatched. However, the room is seven floors up and investigators consider it unlikely—if not humanly impossible—anyone could have climbed the side of the building.

Authorities see no apparent connection between the missing ruby ring and diamond bracelet that vanished from the hotel room of Parisian Madame L'Espanaye last week.

The police, at this time, have no leads.

From the files of Sherlock Holmes by Dr. Watson:
Wednesday, February 23, 1910

It has been over 24 hours since the disappearance of Holmes. The last thing that he told me was he was "stepping out" but failed to specify or purposely withheld information on where he was going. Previous to his departure, he spent much of his time in his study. He wouldn't divulge what he was working on. Several meals brought to him were left untouched and he worked well into the early morning hours. What he was working on, I do not have a clue. There is one thing, however: a scrap of paper with one word in his handwriting scrawled upon it. It's curious, as I don't know the reference. Holmes has never spoken of a man with such a name. There is no street with that name in London, or a shop that bears it. It is a French name: *Moreau.*

From the case studies of Dr. John Evelyn Thorndyke,
compiled by Christopher Jervis: Thursday, February 24, 1910

The police called Dr. Thorndyke in for another crime scene analysis. Inspector Dickinson was also on the case. His nose, which is long and very distracting, looked like a misshapen potato. "A fairly cut and dry case," the Inspector said to Dr. Thorndyke and myself. "Looks like a robbery gone bad—the assailant, obviously insane, killed this woman when she wouldn't surrender her earrings, and then fled into the night." The Inspector's statement was not only invalid, it was ridiculous. The victim, who was recognized as Missy Allan Watkins by the identification in her handbag, wasn't just killed—she was beheaded. The head, found a few yards from the victim, had been thrown aside like a child's ball. The earlobes were both torn, indicating that the earrings that she wore, apparently valuable, had been ripped away with great haste and force. Missy Allan Watkins had been a rising stage actress, her expensive earrings, we are told by her friend and flatmate, Marla Grimes, a gift from a wealthy, anonymous admirer.

Dr. Thorndyke noted that little blood had been emitted from the earlobe wounds, indicating that Miss Watkins' head was ripped from her shoulders, carried off, and then relieved of its jewelry.

Inspector Dickinson failed to mention that it would take a man of incredible strength the tear a human being's head off. It would have to be a man of superhuman strength. "Obviously a sword must have been used," the Inspector sums up, as if on cue. "A particularly jagged one as you'll note from the torn edges of the skin."

Dr. Thorndyke, however, was far from convinced by the police detective's faulty hypothesis. "The fact that you are able to practice any form of law enforcement at all is the crime here, inspector," Dr. Thorndyke said. There are deep marks, like claws, near Miss Watkins' clavicle. Dr. Thorndyke finds some strands of reddish-brown hair. "These hardly look human. We'll have Nathaniel analyze them back at the lab to confirm." The doctor then made a quick but highly accurate and detailed sketch of a bloody print next to the woman's corpse.

"I will venture, Jervis, that we have connected cases to the murder in King's Row on Monday." The doctor shook his head in disgust. "The crime scene was undoubtedly contaminated by these bumbling fools, but perhaps a sojourn there will enlighten us on any missed details."

The Manchester Guardian: Wednesday, February 23, 1910
Mysterious Disappearances from the East-End

In the streets of Whitechapel, it is not uncommon to find homeless men and women begging for food, money, and other charitable handouts. However, in recent days, it has been noted that there are noticeably fewer homeless people occupying the back alleys and street corners of the city's east end.

"One-Eyed Pete used to come around and I would give him scraps of bread," Emma Drysdale, an employee of Whitechapel Bakery on Montague Street, said. "We all loved Pete. He was a gentle soul. Many of London's homeless are wicked and cruel, but not Pete. He would sometimes sweep up the back room for something to eat. But now he's gone and no one has seen hide nor hair of him."

Managers of flop houses and day labor facilities have made note of several disappearances of their transient employees, too. "They don't clock in for work," Mason Sinclair, a manager at a day labor site, said. "Sometimes we send someone out to look in the alleys and building alcoves to see if they're sleeping off a bender. That sometimes happens. But lately, those places where the homeless usually bed down are empty, too. Where is everybody going?" Police, at this time, have no leads to the disappearances.

From the private papers of Sherlock Holmes: March 17, 1910

I estimated that I was unconscious for the better part of a day, and then drugged. Judging by the intoxicant, it was a plant-based derivative. There was also the smell of jasmine. This indicated that my captor was either a person of wealth or well-traveled.

I awoke, my clothing removed, bound by my hands from a basement rafter. The knots that secured me were tied with occupational skill, which led me to believe that the person who had done the tying had spent some time at sea, particularly on a commercial vessel, as the knot, though unique, was a common one among modern employed seamen.

My head swam and shadows along the stone wall took on monstrous shapes. There was the smell, too, under the odor of rotting wood and stale vegetables, another smell. An animal smell. Like that of a stable. Upon first olfactory observation, this led me to believe that I had been consigned to the country. However, I heard the low rumbling of a motorcar minutes later; several, in fact. I was in the city.

I flexed my wrists to loosen the binds; however, this proved difficult, as my captors saw fit to hang me several inches from the floor, suspended by my arms. It was laborious to gain purchase without the advantage of stability, the weight of my bare feet on the floor.

Obviously, I was important to my captor, as I was still alive. I could see marks in the rafter where the rope had been. I was not the only individual who had been held prisoner in this dim, subterranean cell.

I began drifting off, weak from the drug and lack of nourishment, when an animal roar, like that of some jungle-bound creature, echoed through the chamber. It came from behind a wooden door at the far end of the room. A heavily bolted wooden door, either to keep something out or something *in*. I made an attempt to distinguish which part of London that I occupied by the color of the soil in the basement. However, the dim light, and the fact that the soil was moist, made the assessment all the more problematic and speculative. But my esteemed estimate was that this building occupied the South Eastern portion of London, the dockyards. This would explain the exotic smell of jasmine, and perhaps, the animal braying. These items were imported.

Then I heard the gruff voice of a man: "You know the Law. The Law is not to kill. You have violated the Law. And now there is only pain."

There was then the most, agonized, pained "screaming" that I have ever heard. It sounded both human *and* animal, which seemed impossible. Later, of course, I would learn different. I would learn how much misery a human being could inflict on another; it would be notable if not so diabolical.

I fought my mind's probability to black out. I was not successful.

From the files of Sherlock Holmes by Dr. Watson:
Friday, February 24, 1910

Looking through the extensive library in Holmes' study, and among the disarray of newspapers, the only name I was able to find was a Dr. Moreau. He was a noted physiologist in the city before he was exposed for some gruesome experiments in vivisection, which involved the cutting of living organisms for scientific study. It seems that the trail went cold there. Moreau disappeared shortly after that and has never been heard from again.

In another newspaper dated 1896, there was some ranting from a gentleman named Edward Prendick about finding Moreau on some remote tropical island and him experimenting on both humans and animals, but this was all written off as ballyhoo. Prendick survived a year on his own after a shipwreck and his sanity was in question.

Could there be some connection between the lost doctor and the lost Holmes? In the clipping, there is mention that Moreau had a sister, Molly M. Basehart, who still resides here in London's West End.

I must clear up this matter if I am to find any trail to Holmes.

The Times: Friday, February 25, 1910
"Beastman" Spotted by Constable in Harrow Alley

"He was the most 'orrible thing I've ever seen," was the first thing Constable Roland Thomas said when he described what he saw last night. "I was making the usual rounds in the Harrow Alley neighborhood when I heard a scream. It was foggy out that night. I ran toward the direction of the scream, which was a bit confusing within all of the mist. The scream seemed to erupt from all directions, echoing off the brick walls and blind alleys. Then I saw the slumped form of what looked like a woman lying on the sidewalk. And standing above her was a man, or what looked like a man. He wore clothing, at least trousers and a work shirt. But his feet were bare. And what feet they were—long with curled nails like that of a lion, from the illustrations I've seen of those African beasts. But the face was the most repugnant. The 'man' had a tuft of dark hair around his neck like that of a lion, and moon-yellow eyes that just stared at me. They looked like they hung there in the mist, lit up with a light all of their own. He 'grinned' at me, baring rows upon rows of jagged teeth. He stood there, frozen for a moment, and then he charged. I had my billy club at the ready. The next thing I know, however, I was waking up on the street. The 'beastman' must have knocked me down and out."

The victim, Myra H. Brown, 23, was only marginally harmed, a slight gash on her forehead. She has no recollection of being attacked or the events of the previous night. "All I can remember," she said, "Is that I was walking home from my seamstress shop and then next thing, I was waking up in the street with a wide-eyed peace officer standing over me. It's all a bit confusing."

Constable Thomas' story is being checked out. However, it remains doubtful at this time that there is a "beastman" roaming the streets of London. There is little doubt that someone attacked the policeman. However, with the fog and the knock on the head as factors in his bizarre testimonial, there are clouds of doubt as to what actually transpired the previous evening.

In any case, however, residents of the Harrow Alley neighborhood are asked to walk home in pairs, particularly at night. If there is a man who is unafraid to attack police officers, this could be a dangerous culprit indeed.

From the files of Sherlock Holmes by Dr. Watson:
Saturday, February 25, 1910

The meeting with Molly M. Basehart in London's West End proved to be an educational one, and also one that provided me with some possible clues as to Holmes' recent disappearance.

Mrs. Basehart, quite understandably, was hesitant to share any information with me or to allow me to gain entrance into her expensive, well-tended townhouse. However, when I informed her that it was a police matter and provided her with some proper identification, she was more willing.

Over afternoon tea, Mrs. Basehart answered some questions regarding her brother, Dr. Moreau. Naturally, she was hesitant to speak of her sibling, trying to bury the past and not bring it out into the open once again. I could see her neck muscles tighten. Mrs. Basehart was rather thin, not frail, with long limbs and neck. She wore a black dress buttoned all the way up her neck that seemed to shroud her form in as much secrecy as her hesitant nature. She was as odd as I suspect that her brother had been.

During the brief, and forced, conversation, I learned a few vital details. One, that Mrs. Basehart had a son, Augustus Phineas Moreau, who lived in London. He lived in the Southeastern part of London and owned and operated Exotic Imports Limited. They specialized, she told me, primarily in bringing in animals for zoos and to universities and hospitals for scientific study, also in delivering many herbs and spices, coffees and teas to expensive restaurants and hotels. She told me that she had a falling out with her son some years ago regarding an argument about his uncle, Dr. Moreau. Mrs. Basehart and her son had a disagreement about Dr. Moreau's experiments. Mrs. Basehart said that her brother was "interfering in God's domain." Her son had stated that perhaps "God interfered with learning the natural ways of the world." Mrs. Basehart had told her son that he was being blasphemous and asked him to leave. The two have not spoken since. She informed me that she still does, however, receive a monthly stipend from her son for living expenses. Mrs. Basehart is a widow. Jacob Basehart, her husband, died of yellow fever in Panama a few years ago during an industrial trip.

After tea, I excused myself and left Mrs. Basehart's townhouse. I heard the distinct clack of the door bolt behind me. I pretended not to notice the pensive resident sneaking a glance at me from behind a lacy curtain.

Was it Augustus P. Moreau who Holmes was tracking? Was there a connection? It was time to pay a visit to Exotic Imports, Limited on the south side.

From the private papers of Sherlock Holmes: March 18, 1910

I had one of the most bizarre dreams I've ever encountered. Three men stood around me. Only they were not men. They were humanoid in form, with two arms and two legs, standing upright. However, they were not men, but animals, at least in appearance. One man had the distinct markings of a tiger. Another, shorter man, had the tusks of a wart hog. A third man had the dark mane and eyes of a lion. It was only then that I realized that I wasn't dreaming. This, in fact, was a grim reality. I was still naked and bound to the ceiling beam in the foul-smelling basement in some southern part of London.

These three "awakeners" seemed to have some kind of animalistic agenda on their "hands." Whatever their cruel intent could be was a mystery. The "hog man" snorted. "When you are free, you come with us." The "tiger man" brandished the most impressive claws I've seen from his right "hand." They glinted in the dim light. "You try to run after I free you," the tiger man grunted in barely discernable speak, "and I will gut you like a gazelle."

I only had the strength to nod. If I were indeed meant for death, I would be already. There was some other intent for me. My only chance for escape was to play along, perhaps even feigning more weakness from hunger than was the reality. Often times, the opossum's greatest defense is in remaining inert, playing dead, allowing for escape when the attacker grows uninterested or distracted. An inactive defense was my best hope in the moment. With the ease of a sharpened machete cutting through elephant grass, the tiger man sliced through my bonds. My bound hands fell limp at my side and my nude form crumpled, part voluntary, and part, I assure you, involuntary, upon the filthy floor of the basement.

I felt the hairy paws of the lion man and the tiger man lift me under the crooks of my arms. Their strength was incredible and they lifted me with ease. The hog man led the way to the waiting, closed door. He opened it and my feline counterparts escorted me through.

The adjustment to the light was quite blinding. I was in a well-lit, white-tiled room that had the antiseptic smell of rubbing alcohol and the pungent smell of animal hair. Two tables sat in the middle of the room. On one table was the macabre corpse of a man. He, however, wasn't all man. He had the markings of a leopard. I was laid on the table parallel to the corpse. The hog man then bound my arms and legs with leather straps. I made sure, however, to flex all of the muscles of my body. This would allow some slack in my bonds that would allow me to wriggle free when the opportunity arose.

My mind began to piece together the sinister purpose of my remaining alive.

Of course, the name Moreau drove itself home. It was apparent that this Augustus Moreau, whom I was investigating, nephew to the illustrious Dr. Moreau, was carrying on his uncle's bizarre and cruel experiments of fusing man with beast. Edward Prendick had reported all these events some years ago. But they were dismissed as flights of fancy from a man marooned on a tropical island alone for almost a year.

"Good afternoon, Mr. Holmes," a voice said from behind me. It was a voice of refined English and proper education, obviously not belonging to one of the beasties that had brought me to this laboratory. Then the voice had a face. I recognized him as Augustus Moreau, the proprietor of Exotic Imports, Limited. He was not dressed as a simple businessman who plied his trade in the export business, however; he was dressed as doctor about to perform a scientific experiment—wearing a lab coat and a soiled apron. The blood of many previous experiments stained it. "Welcome to my home. I trust that you have had a pleasant stay."

"What is your purpose?" I asked, stalling for time while I worked at the bonds at my hands, flexing my wrists, relaxing, and then flexing again. I could feel significant slack in them both.

"Since, my good man," Moreau said, "I seem to have you at a disadvantage, I will tell you. I am merely carrying on my uncle's experiments." He pointed to a thick notebook on the nearby counter. "Luckily, my uncle's notebook was spared from the fire that consumed his compound. He was making great progress and it would have been a shame for all of that to have been lost."

"I have my doubts that petty robbery was part of your uncle's scientific study," I said.

Moreau waved his hand with a vapid indication. "Scientific study requires financial backing. And since there are many who do not understand the very forward nature of these experiments, I must collect my own, how should I say, 'charitables?'" He smiled. "In time, I hope that I can abolish such petty operations and that these grand experiments can be shared with the rest of the scientific community."

Moreau looked at his tiger man and lion man. "Back into your rooms— go." The two "men" obeyed, shuffling their padded feet against the cold tile floor. The hog man remained. His tusks looked more yellow and soiled against the sharp contrast of the snow-white transpose walls. His dim, dark eyes betrayed little intelligence behind them.

"You will make a fine addition," Moreau said, turning his attention back to me. "You're a specimen of both remarkable physical and mental form. You have the cunning of a jungle panther." He turned and prepared his surgical tools. "And so you shall become one, of sorts. I wouldn't be frightened, though, Mr. Holmes. You will most likely find this form liberating, a return to nature, so to speak. You will have indomitable strength and agility to match that superior mind. You will be my greatest creation yet."

"Charming," I said. And the bonds at my wrists grew more and more slack.

From the case studies of Dr. John Evelyn Thorndyke,
compiled by Christopher Jervis: Friday, February 25, 1910

The reddish-brown hair found next to the decapitated Missy Allan Watkins proved conclusively to be that of a tiger in origin. Nathaniel, in Dr. Thorndyke's crime lab, tested the sample against all possibilities of indigenous animals in the London area, particularly stray dogs and cats. When those proved inconclusive, then further specimens had to be checked. The color suggested that of a feline. There was a match when checked against the tiger. However, the London Zoo reported no missing tigers. It seems that it would be noticeable if a private citizen were to have one prowling around illegally as a pet in the streets of London. Then there was the report of Constable Roland Thomas in this morning's *Times*. Though the account was mostly laughed off by investigating officers, Dr. Thorndyke had other notions. "There is, I suspect," he said, "something sinister happening in these London streets that few can comprehend. When the probable has been analyzed and become inconclusive, it's time to investigate the improbable."

I asked the doctor what he intended to do. "Tigers are obviously not indigenous to England, which means they need to be imported. There are several importers who make their living with such trade; that will be our next step."

From the files of Sherlock Holmes by Dr. Watson:
Saturday, February 25, 1910

Saturday evening proved to be another foggy one as I ventured to the docks on London's south side. As I suspected, Exotic Imports, Limited was closed; the office hours posted on the window enforced this. I knocked on the door but there was no answer. Then, by strange coincidence, a peculiar figure appeared from behind me in the shadows—two figures. One was officious looking in a top hat and cloak, the features of his athletic face tight. The other, a shorter man, reminded me of a bit of Sancho Panza, Don Quixote's faithful companion in the yarn. "Dr. Watson, is it?" the man said. I nodded. "Dr. Thorndyke and my assistant, Christopher Jervis."

"Is it strange coincidence that brings us both here or something else?" I said.

"It appears we might have to gain some other entrance to this facility," Thorndyke said, noting the office hours and ignoring my question entirely.

And that was when the rumble of an explosion rocked the brick building, breaking windows. Acrid smoke began to billow out of the basement windows, rising up, and then mingled with the nightly fog.

From the private papers of Sherlock Holmes: March 18, 1910

"We first start with a powerful anesthesia," Moreau said. "Then the surgery can begin." He prepared a syringe. If I were to make my move, it would have to be now. With the amount of anesthesia he was preparing—morphine, most likely—I would be slipping into a delirium within moments of administration. The binds were loosening but I was still not able to pull myself free. I noticed that Moreau seemed to favor his right hand, which made sense because he was right-handed. However, he was careful not to move his left arm, keeping it close to his side. The shoulder on his left side was slightly lower and slumped than his right. The way Moreau gingerly moved suggested a recent injury.

"Hold the patent's right arm still," Moreau commanded the hog man. "Make sure he doesn't wriggle as I insert the needle into his vein."

The hog man moved towards me. I was able to pull my right arm free. I would only have less than a second to incapacitate the hog man before he would arrest my free arm. A second was all it took. A well-placed hammer fist into the groin of the pig man sent him howling and doubled over with pain. My left hand was now free.

Moreau rushed at me with the needle poised, apparently obsessed with putting me into a morphine haze. I grabbed his left arm—his injured one—and jerked down like I was pulling the chain of a Swiss clock. He howled—much like his beastly creation—in pain. He dropped the syringe and moved back. I rose up—fueled by pure adrenaline. I was able to pull my ankles free. I leapt up off the table, perhaps in the jungle panther way that Moreau had attributed to me. The hog man came at me. A sharp blow to the stomach and he slumped to the floor a moment later. I snatched the syringe of morphine off the floor and injected it into his jugular.

An axe handle whistled past my face. Moreau, who apparently had the weapon stashed somewhere in the lab, wielded it with one hand. His left hung limply at his side. I closed the gap between us, rendered the swinging arc of the potential weapon useless and dispatched a combination of punches to his face and sternum. The axe handle fell back against the table, breaking beakers of chemicals—and an explosion erupted in the tiny room. My ears immediately rang with a perpetual bell. The drone immediately drowned the volume of my surroundings out. The leather-bound journal of Dr. Moreau was consumed with fire. The cantankerous nephew went after the book, trying desperately to extinguish the flames—until they, too, consumed him. The ringing in my ears drowned out any possible screams of anguish from my opponent. Noxious fumes from the chemicals and heat drove me out of the white-tiled room, now filling up with smoke.

From the case studies of Dr. John Evelyn Thorndyke,
compiled by Christopher Jervis: Saturday, February 26, 1910

It proved to be one of the most compelling Saturdays in recent memory. While investigating the origin of animal hair from a well-known importer, we were joined by Dr. Watson, collaborator with the infamous Sherlock Holmes. Our rendezvous was short-lived, however, after an explosion in the townhouse office we were investigating.

That wasn't the most unusual portion, however. A lion man, like the one the police constable described, rushed out of the front door of the building. He knocked poor Dr. Watson out of the way as though he was made of straw. The beastman, his eyes filled with both rage and terror, then came at me. I was frozen with fear until a large crack—the report of a pistol—erupted in my left ear. The lion man, a tiny bloody hole now in his forehead, dropped to the ground. Dr. Thorndyke held a small derringer in his hand. "Pity about that," he said. "I would have loved to interrogate him."

Moments later, the weakened form of Sherlock Holmes appeared in the doorway, smoke now roaring out of the front door. Holmes had a dark overcoat draped over his nude form. Holmes said only two words before he collapsed into unconsciousness. The two words Holmes had uttered confirmed all of our suspicions about this case. The name that was notorious in the scientific community: "Dr. Moreau."

From the private papers of Sherlock Holmes: August 20, 1910

It has been nearly six months since my encounter with Augustus Moreau. Yet there is not a week that goes by where my mind does not wander back to that place in south London. How easy it had been for me to be overcome by those sinister perpetrators and how nearly was I transformed into one of those beastly abominations myself.

Exotic Imports, Limited is now nothing but a condemned hollow shell, completely burned out by the chemical fire. All traces of Augustus Moreau, and his manically prodigious uncle, have literally gone up in smoke. But their memories have not. It is in my most quiet of times in my study when I reflect upon those mental images. The images of hog men and tiger men; the images of sterile labs and anatomical experiments too terrible to mention.

Indeed, this case will remain in my collective conscious for quite some time.

THE ADVENTURE OF THE
LOST SPECIALIST

by
Christopher Sequeira

THE year 1903 saw my friend Sherlock Holmes involved in several cases of capital importance, all worthy of presentation to attest the man was at the height of his skills, and in demand for his expertise internationally. Indeed, Holmes' decisive actions that year in the affair of the depraved Herbert West and the grave-robbings in Essex County, Massachusetts, prevented a mass panic, and his investigations into the Panama Hat Murders circumvented a serious diplomatic disaster that might have blocked that nation's bid for independence. But the issue I set down now—and set down only at Holmes' insistence—actually afforded *very little* opportunity for him to demonstrate his peculiar genius for deduction and instead allowed him to show the bravery and quick reflexes that saved lives during many a dangerous case, and also marked the end of the official part of his career. It was the final case he was to take as a referral from Scotland Yard, and it was the last matter he was to deal with before he moved to semi-retirement on the Sussex Downs. As will become apparent, although in many respects the case serves as a capstone to my friend's career, the episode is, in many ways such a total perversion of Holmes' dedicated adherence to provable facts in the face of wild conjecture that I have made sure the executors of my estate understand the published account must have no currency in Holmes' lifetime.

It began on a cold October morning. Holmes was seated at the breakfast table, smoking a cherrywood pipe and cutting pieces from *The Times* for his scrapbook. I was nearer the fire, scribbling notes for a paper I wanted to submit to *The Lancet* on some of the most interesting medical aspects of the Victor Savage murder that Holmes had solved with my help—the matter that saw print as *The Dying Detective*. Victor Savage's uncle, the famous American doctor and adventurer, had corresponded with both Holmes and I and his additional researches on the deadly disease used to murder his poor nephew were very worthy of adding to the published lore on the illness. With his consent I was readying an article.

Into this scene of quiet concentration quick footsteps were suddenly heard bounding up the stairwell leading to our rooms, and Holmes looked at me with a smile. I squared my papers away as I, too, recognized the signature of Inspector Tobias Gregson.

"Gentlemen. Good to find you at home," said the inspector, as his large frame entered our sitting room doorway.

"Ah, Gregson, equally a pleasure to see you—the last time was the Red Circle episode?" Holmes said with a laugh.

"Very true, sir," said Gregson, doffing his hat and smoothing back his flaxen hair, and then helping himself to a cup of Mrs. Hudson's coffee. "And I'm afraid it's more of the same, Mr. Holmes. Murder and mayhem. But there is a mystery solved at the same time as a mystery begun in the business I'm here about today."

Holmes had moved his chair and a third one over to the grate and gestured to Gregson to occupy one. "Excellent," he said. "Please explain, and we shall make a decision about whether to take the train to Endover this morning or this afternoon."

Gregson stared, then looked himself over, inspecting his coat, waistcoat and pockets, and the hat he'd laid down, then turned a steely eye at Holmes. "Not fair, Mr. Holmes, I've no train tickets or letters sticking out of my pockets or hatband. How did you know my intentions?"

"The newspaper, Inspector. It contains a report of a body discovered in the West country, at Endover, last night—not described as murder, but as 'cause of death—unknown, the matter having been referred to Scotland Yard'. You are here at eight in the morning, well before you normally arrive at your desk, ergo the matter relates to an issue from yesterday, or one you were urgently contacted about overnight. You mention murder, not mysterious death, so you do have information the paper is not privy to. Finally, Endover is normally outside your jurisdiction, unless of course it relates to some other matter, already in progress. I submit in the case of a newly discovered body that would then have to be a previously notified missing persons matter. If you are here, you have not been to Endover, and I must assume you seek our company for the trip on either the morning or afternoon train that makes that run."

Gregson's blue eyes twinkled as he interrupted with a chuckle. "Very good, sir! Since May I have been trying to clear up the matter of a missing man, an engineer, a specialist in locomotive and engine design named David Twykham. Only thirty years of age he was a lecturer in engineering at Camford, too. Quite brilliant, or so I'm told."

"Earlier this year Twykham left his house in Endover, in the West, to visit the barber, a regular occurrence, his family say. But he never arrived at the scheduled appointment and he never came back. A man of extremely regular habits, so the matter was exceedingly odd. However, there was some talk of a woman at the university he was overly friendly with, so a scandal was whispered of. But when this woman—an assistant in the library—was questioned she went into shock. She knew nothing about Twykham's disappearance, and in fact had been planning to introduce him to her family, as he wanted to broach the topic of marriage. Inquiries were made, his entire family and known friends were canvassed, but nothing was determined. A complete mystery."

"Was he engaged on any project of significance at the university?" said Holmes. "Perhaps in the military line—anything our friends in rival nations might either want to prevent this emerald isle completing, or which they would rather acquire first themselves?"

"Not as far as I can tell, sir. Twykham was working with the rail company on new engines, and even some track specifications, but nothing that would be confidential, as far as I can tell, just refinements of existing designs, as far as anyone can tell me."

"I see," said Holmes. "Now, Mr. Twykham's body has been found, and by the circumstances murder is your straightforward conclusion, yet you have not seen the body, thus I assume a witness is involved? And as you are here in my consulting rooms, I assume some unusual aspect to this case awaits us?"

The big man grinned. "Indeed, there are features that suggest your 'unorthodox' lines of inquiry might be valuable, sir. Because the witness you have correctly deduced exists has made quite a claim."

"Claim?" I ventured, "That suggests doubt, Inspector. What is this claim?"

Gregson placed his hat back on his head. "That David Twykham was shot in the back by a man who looked exactly like *himself*."

Holmes tapped his almost empty pipe into the grate. "I believe we should catch that morning train, Watson."

Holmes always enjoyed traveling via the railway, as a first class carriage provided him both a comfortable situation and a place to smoke, as well as the sense of activity that his restless nature craved. He reviewed the facts with Gregson and I once more as the carriages rattled along, but for the most part he was silent—his gray eyes surveying the countryside outside the windows dispassionately.

I could only recall Gregson traveling with us once before—during the Adventure of the Cardiff Giantess—and it was clear he was still unaccustomed to Holmes' lack of effort to entertain or respond to idle social remarks. Eventually the Inspector gave up and directed his dialogue solely at me, and I must confess his interest in football matches tested me—as rugby was the only game that had remained important to me since my university days.

We eventually alighted at Endover and were met by a reedy constable named Kenners. I was anticipating a four-wheeler ride, but such was not to be as we simply walked a few minutes beyond the main train station platforms to a group of several buildings adjacent—the Endover Roundhouse and Repair Yards being the chief structures. Kenners began to explain, whilst Gregson headed off to see the Controller of the Yards, to make sure we could have access to all the grounds for our search, if need be.

"Endover Railyards ha' been built this past tenyear, big job war that, we are the top of the line, in more ways 'un one." He giggled, somewhat childishly, I thought. "Over thar—" He pointed to the massive green roundhouse. "—we set 'em oop and turn 'um through, and t'pride o t'coompany we be. This business, this murder business be a blight."

Holmes exercised that special capacity he had for putting a person he'd just met at ease. "Mr. Kenners, you have my sincere sympathies. An enterprise this size tells me much faith has been placed in the local community to support this operation. To suffer the grim occurrence of murder—well, sir, that must be a shock."

Kenners nodded and as he led us to what was the key location he launched into an almost incomprehensible listing of the functions of the different buildings on the allotment, which Holmes seemed keen to absorb. He then told us the strange tale of Twykham.

He had been patrolling the Yard the previous afternoon when he saw a man leaning against a shed, arguing with someone who was on the other side, out of view. He got closer, and the argument seemed to have altered in tone, receded to calmer words. He had decided it was not worth looking into further, and walked away, when he heard a shot.

He turned and saw Twykham had fallen and the man who shot him came out from behind the shed. He looked *exactly* like the dead man.

"It were his twin, no doubt—even dressed the same." I were a little bamboozled, I 'esitated-like, then rounded t'shed a minute later—and this be the hard part, sir—he war gone. Nowheres tar be seen."

"Well, Holmes, a twin certainly narrows the field," I commented, a trifle obviously.

"Yes, Watson, except when he has no siblings. But why dressed identically? I—"

Gregson suddenly appeared and interrupted our discourse, looking strangely wild-eyed.

"Gentlemen, this is extraordinary!" he said. "Back at Endover Station, a train has pulled up—a Special, commissioned yesterday. It was apparently called for by David Twykham!"

"What?" I exclaimed. "The man found dead?"

"Indeed. It seems he organized it here and it was to run up from London. It must have been not far behind us! What's more, a number of parcels were placed on board at London."

Holmes was staring at Gregson's face; there was puzzlement in his eyes, an odd look.

"Well, Holmes, shall we go?" I ventured.

My friend suddenly regained his alertness. "Of course," he said, but again, I noticed him staring at the Inspector. Then he rubbed his hands together, briskly. "I daresay we have a look at such items as are on this train."

We arrived at the station shortly thereafter and saw the Special. It was a gleaming new engine, emblazoned with the word "Pascal" on its cabin. Gregson spoke to the engineer whilst Holmes and I boarded. We began an immediate search for the parcel.

We had covered the entire carriage when a violent lurch threw us to our feet. The train was leaving the station! With a suddenness that I was not anticipating, Holmes sprang from his seat and darted to the compartment door. I followed as quickly as I could.

Out of the window the station was being left behind and I saw a disturbing sight—Gregson stood there looking at us, laughing with an expression of complete contempt. I was shocked.

"Watson," Holmes said before I could articulate my rage at what seemed to be a stupid prank, "what color are Gregson's eyes?"

"Why, blue," I spluttered.

"Indeed," said Holmes, "they were blue at Baker Street. But when he returned from the Yard Controller's office they were dark brown."

"My, my word, you're right. I thought he seemed different. But eyes cannot change color, though the pupils may dilate and give that impression, perhaps. Dilation of the pupils can indicate a drug has been administered. Holmes, Gregson must have taken a drug of some sort or had one administered whilst he saw the Controller! What does it mean?"

"I suppose so. But yet I have a certainty that his actual eyes were brown, though I could make no sense of observing that change in his appearance." Holmes then fell silent, as we turned our focus to our current plight.

The train began to move faster, and faster, and it began to rock on the railings, the speed we were traveling seemingly dangerously accelerated. Holmes and I ran to the external doors, but we discovered a weird sight; the doors were closed, and it was clear they would not open—they had been nailed shut!

We then ran throughout the carriage to the front-most part of the car, to where a door between carriage and engine was, and it was the same: the doors there were nailed shut. We went back to the doors whence we had originally entered the special, and though these were not nailed shut we found we were still, in fact, sealed in by an iron trellis that had somehow been deployed from doorway to floor, carefully hidden when we'd entered. This grate was a single piece of steel fabrication.

"We were brought here as part of a well-prepared plan," said Holmes. I could only nod in agreement.

The windows were all now barred from the outside; some similar ploy had been used that had allowed them to appear as ordinary windows when we boarded but allowed our captor—for that is what we were, captives—

to surreptitiously lower the metal grilles that prevented escape whilst we traveled unaware. Had we been able to smash the windows we would not have been able to use them for egress; the bars left insufficient space. Whatever locking mechanisms were used were exterior to the carriage and my revolver would be no help on the iron.

Holmes began systematically battering the wooden paneling of the carriage's interior, quite methodically, even as I felt a sense of despair alternating with my anger.

"For the sake of Heaven!" I said. "Will we die in a railway carriage? The prosaic nature of such a sinister campaign!"

Holmes ignored this and began smashing the iron ferrule of his walking stick across the ceiling. When the stick did not puncture the wood he pointed to it.

"Quite amazing craftsmanship—metal painted as wood—what efforts have been made to keep us here! I am suitably impressed!"

I failed to share my companion's admiration, and I directed my attention out the windows, trying to discern our destination. The train was getting faster and the scenery was blurring by. We seemed to be moving along spiraling tracks, splitting off from one junction point to another, then another, nothing but rock and trees visible to either side.

The view became hypnotic, frightening and compelling. The walls of the carriage were violently vibrating, and the engine roared as we sped on, and on. I had a sensation we might be on some vast circle of track, perhaps some odd siding, as the view was monotonously unchanging, but we veered right as often as left—leaving me doubting we were simply traversing a loop.

Finally, a huge plume of steam painted the windows, throwing us in semi-darkness, and stirring me from what was almost a trance. The vapor cloud lifted and I cried out to Holmes, but he saw what I saw also: we were pulling into the Endover Roundhouse! As we rolled within its huge confines I peered from window after window, but I could not see a soul at work in the yards, although it was still day, though fading day.

The train moved in and came to a halt. The iron trellis that had appeared over the door we'd used to come aboard rattled and by some hidden automation of gears it rose and disappeared into the door jamb. Holmes pushed in front of me, gently. "Steady, old fellow." There was a tone to his voice I'd never heard before, one I did not care for; it sounded too much like fear. He exited the door and I was directly behind him.

We left our carriage with the steam-clouds within it, like fog, making it hard to see, and giving the place an eerie atmosphere, save for the very center of the Roundhouse, which was brilliantly illuminated by gas-lamps on poles, arranged in a circle. I could see that all the berths of the Roundhouse contained carriages, just like ours, and I tugged at Holmes' arm, for I felt I was losing my mind, my sense of time and place. Our carriage and all the others—none had engines in front of them! I could not see how we'd been shunted in here, our carriage prison uncoupled and wheeled away, without our being aware of it, but that was precisely what seemed to have happened.

"He will have the answers, though I am not sure I wish to hear them," said Holmes, as if to an unspoken question of mine, and he pointed to a doorway that faced us in a far wall on the opposite side of the circle of light. The door was open and a man was coming through it and towards us, walking at an almost jaunty pace, his feet ringing out in the stillness. His features slipped in and out of clear view as the steam, which emanated from nowhere in particular, roiled around. He reached the edge of the circle and waved at us, and seeing no reason not to, Holmes and I kept walking towards him.

The man who stood waiting was tall, and wiry, dressed in a dark suit of clothes. He looked anything between forty and sixty, for his face was smooth and unlined but he had completely white hair, receding. The features were sharp, and the eyes were clear and compelling. There was an energy about him, as with an athlete; he seemed coiled as if to move at any time.

I had never met him before, but I felt a dryness in my throat once I accepted that I knew him by his photograph all too well, except for one fact: The man before me, I had believed, had been dead for more than a decade.

He spoke, clearly, with a well-projected voice. "Yes, doctor, I am the man you think me to be. I am James Moriarty."

"Holmes!" I exclaimed. "This man did not die at Reichenbach Falls? How could you conceal this from me? Why? I accepted all you had to say about your own falsified death, but this?" I looked at Holmes not angrily, but with pleading.

Holmes' expression was different to what I would have expected. He looked at Moriarty with contempt. Then he looked at me.

"Watson, I give you my word. I saw this man's body—*that is, some man's body like it,* in a mortuary in Switzerland, a week after he died. I was in disguise and wanted to be sure his menace had ended before I commenced my three-year hiatus. Believe me, the ruined corpse…

"Was not me, Mr. Holmes," said Moriarty.

Holmes peered at the man, was angry when he spoke. "I do not know what the nature of this farce is, but I shall let you know I have no time for this charade. James Moriarty died in front of my own eyes, when he fell after trying to kill me at Reichenbach. I have no remorse over acting in self-defense, none whatsoever. I know not whether you be his twin or a look-alike effected through very impressive make-up, but you are not he. In any case, his criminal empire ended long ago. If this is about familial revenge, you may do your worst, although I would prefer you leave my friend out of such matters."

Moriarty spoke again, as relaxed as if we were recounting the weather. "Dear me, dear me, Mr. Holmes. No, no. My pursuits, since Reichenbach have been directed away from crime. They have been in other fields entirely. Science. Transportation. And a unique nexus between the two, one might say."

"You remember my vast financial resources, and no doubt lamented the fact the authorities failed to get to my accounts in time to find all but pennies. Those funds were turned to good purpose. Through a series of proxies and agents all paid to carry out my strictest instructions. I have supervised the construction of this building we are now in, and more importantly the miles of track you rode upon to get here, and the 'Pascal Engine' that pulled your carriage. It cost much, but it has been a profitable investment, too. Young Mr. Twykham was my Chief of Construction, and he performed a marvelous job. His contract did have to end when he fathomed some of my purpose, but I blame his rather limited religious beliefs. He could not reconcile them with my employment, and alas, he had to be replaced. With someone like him."

The man laughed and the echoes of that outburst reverberated through the structure. I wanted to leave that building, I wanted to run from it, but Holmes was firmly planted, not taking his eyes off the man, who continued.

"You see, I redirected my entire criminal enterprise into transport and logistics; a wildly flourishing sector of business, let me assure you. The entire metropolitan railway network has been clandestinely suborned to my methods. I extract ten percent of all revenues of all goods that traverse it, a tidy sum. The simplest of accounting artifices ensure the funds are commuted to me without ever appearing on the ledgers of the railway institutions."

He continued, gesturing at our environment. "We stand, in many ways, at the center of a vast web of commerce that brings me what I desire and allows me to move forward and seize what objectives I need, as I need. I believe, incidentally, I have made British rail more efficient by twelve percent since I took hidden control."

Holmes shook his head. "A colorful story. However, I fail to see the point of it at all, despite its grandiosity. You claim to be Professor James Moriarty, and you claim to have a new empire of elicit activity. Yet no shred of proof applies."

"No proof is needed," Moriarty said. "For the proof was in the journey you just took. The track-work you just traversed was designed to drive your train-carriage through what I refer to as a Moebius Point, an aperture in reality that allows one to journey to points that are normally inaccessible, but by dint of harnessing higher mathematics as a propulsive force are at last attainable. You are now in the Roundhouse, and the Roundhouse is a nexus, where realities converge."

"Holmes, this fellow is speaking gibberish." I was annoyed that this self-confessed railways embezzler—if he was nothing else—was largely ignoring me in the conversation, as provocative as it was. "What does he mean, 'realities?'"

"I mean the answer to riddles, Holmes," said Moriarty, "and if nothing else, riddles will command your attention, your oh-so-weak attention span. Answers to questions about how David Twykham could be seen to have killed himself. Why Gregson betrayed you. Why you saw my corpse in Switzerland, yet here I be. Why Professor James Moriarty had a brother, Colonel James Moriarty, who defended his academic sibling's name in the press vehemently, yet James Moriarty's birth records show him as an only child."

Holmes looked at Moriarty. His voice was flat. "The binomial theorem."

"Yes," said the other. "You do comprehend."

Holmes nodded. "Your masterwork, the treatise on it. I'll admit I could not understand the applications you made reference to. As with your other books, few actually understood the work you did with imaginary numbers—but now, now. It was this, wasn't it?"

Moriarty was shaking his head, side to side, a sadness in his eyes. "You, you are truly a marvelous, prodigious *natural* talent, Mr. Holmes. My aptitudes were slow in developing, and required massive effort in childhood on my part, but you are like quicksilver. Such a shame, such a distinct shame I shall be terminating your existence. But I cannot allow my personal feelings to assail my plans."

Moriarty straightened his shoulders and looked at us both again. "I had divined that the multiplicity of realities are as real, as tangible as iron and steel, but were separated by the most gossamer of divides, and that divide was a philosophical construct we call *choice*. Only we—only the one, thinking animal on this plane can exercise this capability. We generate the matrix for this in our brains and we even catalogue all its potential shades in memory and fantasy, and then we bring it into being. Thus, if we can create an infinitude of outcomes—"

"We might travel between those outcomes," said Holmes.

And the way Holmes made this last utterance made me feel very cold. He believed what Moriarty was saying, and because he did, I began to consider it possible, too.

"Yes, it is my belief that every thinking man, woman and child actually does travel from one world to the next whenever they exercise a choice. They can only travel, of course, to a place occupied by themselves after making such a choice. The Pascal was my engine for making use of these principles to travel from one point to the other by another means, and to travel to universes where we had made other choices, lived other lives. Or even visit those worlds created by another's choices."

"Thus the three of you," Holmes snapped. "Moriarty, the professor, who died at Reichenbach. The Colonel. And you, the Station Master of this little show."

"All James Moriarty, and all the same man, but from differing universes. Once I had fathomed the mechanism, I had no more to fear in this world of consequence. I could simply plot in my mind the action I wanted to take, such as chasing you to Switzerland where I might destroy you. I conceived that my plan *might* fail, thus the Special I engaged to follow you from London all those years ago was in fact the maiden journey of the Pascal, traveling to *here* before I left England, *and I brought one of my counterparts from the divide*. He was eager to risk death to face you. Since poor choices he had made in prior years had left him with advanced syphilis, his time was short and he was prepared to risk much. He openly wept for joy when he laid eyes on me; our plan was agreed upon in minutes.

"He was reckless," said Holmes, "prepared to kill me in hand-to-hand combat. I appreciate why now. And the third incarnation, the Colonel?"

"When you defeated my counterpart at the falls, I decided to avoid the temptation you would present me of revenge. I know my own mind, you see. The desire to settle the score would be a huge burden on me. I would be driven to act rashly, and think superficially, it would be difficult to concentrate on the development of my new sphere of influence—logistics—while you were in this world. So I vacated it for the place of my self-sacrificing doppelganger, and enjoyed the fruits of his labor for some time. His illness had prevented him advancing his criminal empire to the degree I had and as a result he was a Napoleon of Crime in theory only. You will be intrigued to hear your own counterpart had no interest in him, had not even been attracted to his few, profitable isolated criminal ventures. But I could not leave you completely unwatched, so I traveled on the Pascal to a universe where I had made not a career decision to be an Army coach, but to be an actual military leader itself. That was from whence faux brother Colonel James Moriarty issued, and he was most supportive of the enterprise. In return I provided him some designs for army rifles that will likely deliver him a more obvious form of power, one whose progression I will be keen to see should I visit him in five or six years. He may have annexed all of his Europe by then; such promise."

I decided to make another attempt at pushing away the absurdity of this subject matter that Holmes and his old enemy were discussing so calmly; I hoped I might be able to squash flat this outrageous raving, even though my friend was acknowledging it.

I barked: "This is a ridiculous, elaborate hoax! Like that American Buffalo Bill, this is nothing but a cleverly arranged dramatic contrivance! I'm sure H.G. Wells and his ilk might write wonderful romances on the topic, but one *cannot* live in a world of one's imaginings."

Holmes was silent. I hoped he was preparing to challenge our adversary's madness after having lulled Moriarty into false confidence. I clasped Holmes' shoulder in a gesture of solidarity, with the intent we move against Moriarty. Then Moriarty held up his right hand in warning and using his other hand made a languid gesture at the carriages that surrounded us.

"Ah, Doctor, not only can one do just that, but this building we stand in and the methodology that brought you here were designed to do better. Not only can one journey to an adjacent reality, one can bring its inhabitants here. And if one gives the matter sufficient thought, one can invite inhabitants to visit that have the greatest desire to *replace the original inhabitants—permanently.* Haven't you ever wondered what would happen if you made the 'other' moral choice? And what if you did so in a world where the choices had been different for many, many people? With enough intriguing variances the nature of *being human* might even be different."

"The answer, my friend," he continued, "is in understanding universes, or what the American philosopher William James has termed *the multiverse.* But, again, for proof, don't ask me. I'd prefer you ask *them.*"

Moriarty pointed at the dark, steam-clouded expanse behind us. As if by some pre-ordained signal the doors of the other eleven carriages in the roundhouse opened and from each one emerged people, in every case just two people. Soundlessly, in a way that was redolent of a dream—and, indeed, in many ways whatever one thinks happened that day, dream may be the right term—the couples came and stood surrounding us, on the exterior of the circle of light, all of them shrouded in darkness and steam.

I peered and I at last understood—even as I refused to accept. Holmes and I were surrounded by eleven pairs of men, and each one was a dark mirror of Holmes and myself; *they were Shadows of us.* Their aspect may have differed from pair to pair, but there was a common thread—a malevolent, hateful gaze at Holmes and myself that was disturbing. But as I studied these figures, as the dark and the vapor that swirled around that chamber allowed me periodically to see more details of them, the more I began to feel not just loathing, but horror.

"'There are more things in Heaven and Earth, Horatio, than are dreamt of in your philosophies,'" said Moriarty. He laughed.

I had my revolver out, but the shadows remained outside the arena of gaslight Moriarty had arranged. I began to think there was some force that ensured that. If so, it was a blessed mercy, the only thing that stopped me from dashing in retreat from the Roundhouse. Instead I surveyed what I could of the Shadows.

Here was a Holmes and Watson who looked exactly as Holmes and I, save they seemed more "brutish", a nose flattened, teeth missing, small facial scar, and when I observed an obviously prison-made tattoo on my reflection's wrist the pattern was complete.

Another pair of shadows seemed less threatening at first glimpse; they even seemed somewhat frail and undernourished, until a curtain of steam in the room parted briefly and I noticed their eye sockets were black and oozing, the hands were rotting, and what looked like worms writhed in their hair.

Another pair were dressed in bizarre, torn clothing, their faces mutilated like some sort of primitive savage's, with silver and gold rings and chains piercing their faces in the nostrils, cheeks and ears. Bizarre slogans and symbols were daubed in paint across their very clothing; the overall effect was of mad, self-vandalism.

Another two were covered in shiny black and silver scales that glinted in the darkness, their eyes distended and round, as a fish's.

Two others at first glance seemed just like myself and my friend, yet when a ray of light pierced the atmosphere outside the gas-lit circle I saw their skin was etiolated, bleached white. The Holmes-shadow grinning in his dark purple frock had hair that seemed acid-green, whilst his Watson, who glared at me evilly through a monocle, possessed a nose like a broken beak. His hands, which clutched an umbrella, had suffered some deformity that had fused the fingers together.

I began to yell, before I even knew I was going to. "Impossible! A childish stunt. Do not think that we will cower, man, do not think we will! I faced worse odds in Afghanistan!" My head was pounding.

The Station Master raised his own voice to the Shadows. "You heard the man—he does not believe. You have received your invitations and accepted. The offer is valid. If any want the place of these two, now is the time to take it! I leave the outcome to you, all of you to determine!" A murmuring ripped through the shadows. Some voices muttered, so much like the sounds of my own and Holmes'; so, so terrifying because of that.

I turned to my friend. "A trick—a league of actors trained and prepared to frighten us, to get our guards down, before a genuine attack."

Holmes looked at me; he was silent.

The figures waited, I could feel they wanted—that they hungered for some event, as a crowd before a sports contest may be hushed but you can still feel their animal desire to witness a conflict, to see a party vanquished.

The Station Master withdrew, the steam parting for him, and disappeared into the doorway in the wall from whence he had come originally. Strange light seemed to play from that open door as he slipped in, but my eyes could not penetrate, and my attention was on the threat around me.

Two figures emerged from the steam-shroud, and into the arena, only two. The first to become distinct was so like Holmes at initial inspection that I turned to where my friend stood beside me, expecting to see him gone, but no, he was still next me, his face, grim, angered. I looked back and saw why. The creature was like Holmes in build, height, even similar in clothing, sporting an Inverness cape - although this cloak was jet-black. But the face became quickly distorted; cruel lines stretched the eyes and mouth in a grimace, the eyebrows swept up wildly, and the jaw was open and grimacing, sporting enormous, snakelike canine fangs. The eyes were not the cold gray of Holmes', but red, an almost phosphorescently glowing red. A stench issued from the thing; the vampire version of my friend.

Worse still was the mockery of me that accompanied the creature. Our wardrobes might have come from similar sources but for the fact this shadow's suit adorned a figure much, much larger than mine. For it was near seven feet tall, and massively proportioned, and it looked like some sort of walking corpse, with a hideous disfigured face, a face, I realized from the hideous scars that adorned it, that was a patchwork of many faces, many swatches of human tissue. The head was lank-haired and the eyes watery, like a drowned man, the brow somehow exaggerated and distended, as if bone and skin had been reinforced with more bone and skin. Two odd metal plugs or posts adorned each temple, embedded in the flesh. The thing looked as if it had been strung together from disparate human anatomical parts like a mortuary jigsaw, the gray skin at the wrists and hands stretched over huge bundles of muscle and tendon. Hands the size of hams clenched and unclenched. This, the hideous Monster companion of the Vampire Holmes, looked at me with heavy-lidded, pure hatred and I knew it would rend me if given the chance.

As the two nightmare distortions moved towards us in the light-circle, the others outside receded into the steam, as if they had never been there. I knew that silent communion had been made somehow. If Holmes and I fell here that would be an end to things. If we could survive, the others would make no attempt on us, but the reason for this chilled my mind; these two invaders were thought to be unlikely to be stopped. Our deaths were viewed as assured, not just possible.

The Monster lumbered towards me, quite slow, and I retreated as quickly as I could, trying to find my revolver. The thing made some strange gurgling noises as I managed to get away from it and I thought to head to the doorway the Station Master had made his exit from. But as I darted that way I heard a creak and looked behind me, and that gesture saved my life. The Monster had hefted enormous broken-off sleepers from a pile of rubble at one side of the Roundhouse, one in each massive paw, and held them above its head!

It threw them at me and I narrowly escaped as they smashed against the wall and rebounded off in dozens of fragments—and I quickly noted the door remained unbreached. I turned and the monster was coming for me, another piece of sleeper held in its paw like a club. Again it was slow, yet implacable. I knew if it got hold of me my life would be forfeit.

I turned and braced myself and carefully took aim with my service revolver. I fired. Three times, aiming right for its head. The creature fell back into the steam clouds.

I glanced at Holmes, and his battle. The Vampire stood before him, the red-eyed face was animalistic; actual drool spilled over the open lips and out. But Holmes was surprisingly calm in the face of this nightmare; he actually lunged at the dark creature and grabbed its arm, and slammed his hip at the beast, a baritsu move I had seen him use once before in a street brawl when he was attacked by the John Clay gang. The Vampire was flipped up and over Holmes' body and I expected to see it fly crashing into the ground, but in mid air the thing tucked its feet under itself gracefully and performed an acrobatic roll that saw it land unhurt. As it rose to its feet it smiled; it was clearly also a master of the fighting art.

Holmes, however, had not waited for it to land. He had run for the wooden railing at the back of the carriage we had entered by and once there he kicked it with his foot, smashing it. I wondered why he might favor a piece of such kindling as a weapon, but I soon understood. Holmes extracted a broken railing and its broken cross-bar, then snapped off the ends and suddenly was holding forth a make-shift cross. He thrust it at the dark version of himself and muttered some word of blessing. His adversary whirled away in a rage, shielding its face from the sight of the Holy Object.

Holmes had his shadow at a disadvantage, kept thrusting the cruciform at it, causing the thing to snarl and turn away, as if it were being lashed. But it would swiftly turn and try to attack him from another angle. Its speed was amazing and Holmes only narrowly was managing to keep turning and being able to brandish that cross between himself and the Vampire. I could see that the creature was not without a strategy; Holmes was being backed ever so gradually into a corner where he would have nowhere to turn or flee if the vampire got the advantage. I could have fired my pistol but the risk with the two of them darting around was that I might hit my friend.

Then Holmes threw the cross *at* his foe! The Vampire flinched back and raised its cape to protect its face. Astonishingly, when the cross hit the Vampire the cape burst into flame and smoke, and the creature howled in fear. But the moment was brief, for the cross then fell to the ground and when the fanged one raised its head now it showed a look of red-eyed triumph. Holmes had run across the chamber. The Vampire literally hissed with glee and when it leapt a distance no man could make, straight at my friend—who was stooped over—it was clear the vampire would be upon him.

But Holmes had a fragment of sleeper the monster had smashed apart, and he simply turned, reminding me of nothing less than a Spanish bull-fighter, and the Vampire was suddenly skewered right through the shoulder on the end of the broken shaft by its own leap at Holmes! The creature uttered a string of curses, and almost fell to its knees; my friend had the beast at his advantage.

But before I could see how this would play out I heard a roar from the darkness and I looked up. The Monster that was my shadow was back, apparently unharmed. A few welts on its forehead were the only sign I had fired at it; clearly all I had done was temporarily daze it.

I did not have my revolver ready. I had returned it to my pocket and the thing was almost upon me, so I swung at the Monster with my walking stick, which had the advantage of being a solid oak staff with a lead-filled head. The blow struck the thing soundly in the face and there was an audible thud, but the gray face was unmarked. It was like hitting stone, and if a bullet hadn't killed it a blow like mine was a desperate move. I hit the thing again and again, and it moved somewhat slowly but I soon realized with horror it was amused. It watched me with evil mirth, not caring what I was doing. Then suddenly a black-nailed hand flicked out and knocked me to the ground, and before I could rise, the thing picked up my stick and squeezed and snapped it into two like a pencil, ostentatiously letting it drop in pieces to the ground. I saw then that I was a rat being played with by a cat.

So I withdrew my revolver, and fired at the thing's heart—perhaps the bony ridged face was too well armored. The shirt the Monster wore exploded, but a gaping hole revealed more of the gray skin and the skin was undamaged. I fired again, and nothing happened; this corpselike giant had a hide like some prehistoric beast.

It lunged and grabbed me. Agony fired through my ribcage as the thing crushed me in a sick embrace. I could barely breathe and I smashed my pistol at the thing's face—to no effect. It locked eyes with me and began to laugh, a horrible, nightmare sound that issued between huge, uneven, broken teeth.

I do not know to this day what made me act the way I did then; perhaps wild desperation, perhaps divine insight. Where the idea came from I really cannot fathom. I raised my pistol and stuck it hard up against the side of the monster's head—right against one of the small metal posts that extruded from the thing's temple—then weakly squeezed the trigger, discharging the final round in the revolver.

The sound of the bullet discharging was like a cannon in my ears. I was completely disoriented and it took me a moment or two to appreciate I was no longer in the grip of the thing, but standing in front of it. The beast was standing, bellowing like a wounded bear. My shot had blasted the metal cap off, and taken a small chunk of the dead, leathery gray flesh, but no blood flowed. A gaping wound left a strand of wire exposed—which began to issue furious, hot sparks. The Monster raised its hand to it and then screamed. Its hand seemed stuck to the side of its own head, but did nothing to diminish the furious sparks which soon had its coat-sleeve burning.

The Monster jerked around like a macabre, gargantuan puppet being idly tugged about by invisible strings. The air smelt of a lightning storm, and the sparks flew intermittently from the hole in one side of the head and the still intact post on the other side. The horrible face writhed in grotesque transformation, or agony, or ecstasy, for I could not tell; the contortions and twistings were hard to interpret in a face so misshapen.

The huge creature flailed about, then fell to its knees, then flopped sideways onto the ground. An arm spasmed out a few times, clutching at empty air. I looked at the features; the pitted and scarred face, and most of all the dead eyes. I saw no reflection of myself—and wondered if one hid behind those eyes—and I said a silent prayer of thanks.

My prayer was premature. Something hit me and knocked me to one side—almost off my feet, and then the fanged Holmes-shadow had its hands about my throat. The immediate pressure was frightening, and I used all the strength I had to try and stop its fingers from tightening. I had slipped my fingers under its own to try and save myself but I the pressure was increasing. I felt the bones of one of my fingers crack, but terror of death stopped me screaming and kept me struggling—futilely—I knew.

Then Holmes slammed the broken-off shaft of my stick into the fanged demon's back. It released its hands from my throat slowly and stepped back. It stared at the front of its body and the shaft protruding from its shirtfront. Black blood was oozing out of its chest around the stake. It fumbled with one taloned hand at the stick and I had a presentiment it would pull it loose and the black fluid would become a fountain, but it dropped its hands to its sides. It stared at Holmes and its features softened. For one terrible second they looked exactly like those of my friend, then a paroxysm of pain distorted the Vampire's face. It resumed its inhuman cast and fell to the ground, on top of the remains of its Monster companion.

"You once told me my taste in sensational criminal literature and natural history was unparalleled, Watson. I'm thankful it is. I would refer you to the case of vampires in the writings of Augustin Calmet—hysterical village criminal matters where the remedy is always the destruction by stake through the heart…"

"Really, Holmes," I gasped. "I thought you'd been reading Bram Stoker!"

"Who?" said Holmes.

The Vampire and the Monster were one unmoving mass, and a change began to take place in that pile of remains. Both corpses—if that be the correct term—as one, began to quickly liquefy into a huge, repulsive mass of whitish slime, which began to dissipate. It stunk in a way that reminded me of the corpses on a battlefield, and I moved away from it, even as the fluid sank into the ground and became reduced to a stain, wisps of white gas coming from it.

The remaining Shadows could be heard conferring amongst themselves, each shade of me communicating in hushed, obscured tones with its counterpart of Holmes. Almost as one they could be seen faintly in the miasma again, but stepping back into their own carriages and closing the doorways.

Holmes laughed, a touch of hysteria in his chortle, but he brought himself under control. "Just what I would have advised. Time to return home."

I had been leaning on Holmes for support. My leg was aching, my blood was pounding in my ears, but I found I could ignore the feelings. The situation still seemed so unreal as to prevent me feeling panicked and even though my heart was racing, my mind was calmer than it would normally be in this situation. I'd found my footing and Holmes, satisfied I was all right, had just let my arms and shoulder loose when the Station Master appeared before us, holding a pistol. He shouted at the Shadows in the carriages.

"Very well! I shall deal with this myself!"

Holmes spoke sharply: "They know, don't they? This is not the natural order of things? There is a risk, a danger of sorts in bringing...us together, isn't there? They don't want to end up affected by that danger, do they? But you don't care, because your obsession rules your mind, overrides even your sense of self-preservation—just as you said you feared it would. In that sense, you are a madman."

"Irrelevant," the Station Master said, and he extended his arm and pointed the pistol at Holmes' face.

There was a noise and the Station Master turned away from us. There was someone standing behind him, presumably whomever it was had entered from the doorway behind him. It was clear from Moriarty's face as he turned that this visitor was a surprise to him, as much as to us.

I say this visitor was "someone" but even as I do, I need to qualify the description. The new arrival to our scene was *not* a man; that much was clear. It was some sort of device, a construct, in the rough form of a man! It had arms and legs and a torso and a head, but they were fashioned from a copper-colored metal of some kind. It stood at about five and half feet in height and was very slender in shape, and it was terrifying. I thought at once of the possibility that a man was concealed in some sort of burnished armor, but the legs were almost like thin brass pipes; they did not conceal a man's, or even a child's lower limbs. The aspect of it that transfixed me the most was the thing's head. It was larger than an average person's, and had odd little metal flags and cones that were moving on it, like portions of a clock, or some small rotating weather vane. And the eyes were round and green, and a faint glow radiated from them, giving the thing a ghostly aspect. If I were not a man of the modern age I am sure I would have assumed the thing was some demon of the pit, some specter, but there was something mechanical about the thing.

It spoke, the voice emanating from the head, but from no mouth I could discern. Its voice was male, clear and fluid, quite beautiful, in fact.

"No," it said, and raised one arm and hand. A puff of gas flew forwards and into Moriarty's face, then his eyes bulged and his skin whitened, and he screamed a horrible noise. Then a rattle-like sound escaped his lips. The Station Master died, but ere his body even fell to the ground, the thing caught it by the collar of the shirt, with swiftness and economy of movement so precise it seemed like a flywheel on a motor whirring into action, and held it, so that the dead man did not hit the floor, only his legs folded under him.

The thing held the Station Master's body like a doll, effortlessly. It turned its awful face at us, and shook the body as if gesturing with a toy.

"I can use bits of this," it said. It looked at Holmes.

"We're not *all* like him," it said, "but too many of us are. I certainly *was*. Until someone like you made me see the error of my ways, made me see the misery I caused and how profoundly...*irrational* that behavior was."

Holmes mouth was open, but not a word came out.

The creature held up its free 'hand' and a small aperture opened, from which a greenish light emanated—dim at first, then brighter.

"A pity I had to get thrown off a cliff over a waterfall to achieve that, but that's how these things go."

The light brightened, fiercely, and I had to shut my eyes.

I did not fain, I did not collapse. All I did, or at least all I remember doing, was close my eyes for a few seconds, to shield them from the bright light. But when I opened them again it was clear that my recollection was false, or, failing that, some sort of transference of time and distance had taken place.

I was standing, dressed in exactly the same clothes as when I had shut my eyes, but I was outdoors and it was daylight! Holmes stood next me, in the same relative spot to me as before, and he looked confused—a rare sight, I must emphasize. Where we were was more incredible. We stood in the blackened ruins of some sort of wooden structure, some place that had

had been demolished or destroyed by fire. It was Holmes that spoke the impossible. He leaned down and for some reason ran his fingers through the blackened earth we stood on.

"We're in the roundhouse, Watson, but it's been burnt to the ground—and these ashes are *cold!*" I imitated my friend's actions, and the pure insanity of what he was saying made sense to me! I looked around and could see, strewn here and there not far from us on the ground, the gutted fragments of the walls, the blackened rails, the charred and crumpled sleepers.

"Halloa!" It was Gregson, strolling along, notebook in hand.

Holmes looked him dead in the eye. I started to speak, but my friend silenced me.

"Dreadful mess here, Holmes," he said.

Then he turned to a passing worker, a scrawny old fellow with a wisp of beard pushing a trolley of grass cuttings. "This body you found, it was in this building, burnt, was it?"

"Yessir," the fellow said. "Sad it were. He were well-liked."

Holmes and I looked at one another.

"The engineer, Twykham?" Holmes said quietly.

The old man looked puzzled. "Engineer? No, sir, it were the local Station Master from Endover. Mister Moriarty."

Holmes and I returned to Baker Street and attempted to continue the ways of our friendship of so many years, but it soon became obvious things could never be the same. Instead of watching with interest the commerce and society of London traipse past our Baker Street vantage the view had taken a strange cast. Now, sitting before the fire reading a yellow-backed novel whilst Holmes scratched an inspiring tune on his violin was unappealing. Again and again I would surreptitiously look at Holmes' knitted brow over the chemistry table, and fear—just for a second—that an evil hunger might lurk behind it. Lord knows what Holmes thought when he looked at me. In the end, such fears began to swamp one, so, with little discussion, we decided to dissolve the old association. Holmes packed his mass of belongings, including his prodigious library and papers, and decided to retire early, to Sussex, and keep bees. Little creatures who know their roles well and never vary them. I returned back to the small home I had shared with my last wife, which I had been renting to a professional man and his wife and family. In time I even married again.

The reader will now understand why this case must be consigned to my tin dispatch box with the strict proviso that it not be circulated until at least a century has passed – by which time I hope the scientific principles the matter involved have come into better focus and have helped to yield a better society—a society where one understands on a fundamental level that one's choices, however small, for good or evil, have astonishing potential. Alternatively, one-hundred years from the day I write this perhaps progress shall have been scant, the bustle of the modern world having reached its apogee with the wonders of the gas-lit streets and telegraph wires of 1903 that make our cities the glowing hives of industry they are. In that scenario few will take seriously my claims as to what Holmes and I witnessed, and will consider me instead a former military man whose mind finally slipped free of its moorings.

If that be the case, then so shall it be. Better a mad fool, than being any *number* of other strange things.

And how important, how fitting, that my under-signature be also a declaration, the emphatic recording of my identity, standing against a barrage of unpleasant possibilities about that identity.

Thus, do I sincerely hope to remain,

John H. Watson (M.D.)

INFORMATION PERTAINING *to* *the* CONTRIBUTING AUTHORS

MATTHEW BAUGH is a writer and pastor who lives in the greater Chicago area. He has more than 20 published stories and is at work on his first novel. His previous stories for Moonstone have appeared in *The Avenger Chronicles*, *Tales of Zorro*, *The Phantom Chronicles Vol. 3*, and *The Green Hornet Chronicles*. His Blog: http://www.journalscape.com/Matthew/ and his Writer's Blog: http://mysteriousdavemather.blogspot.com/

WIN SCOTT ECKERT is the editor of and contributor to *Myths for the Modern Age: Philip José Farmer's Wold Newton Universe* (MonkeyBrain Books), a 2007 Locus Awards finalist. He has written many stories about adventurous characters, including The Green Hornet, The Avenger, the Phantom, Captain Midnight, the Green Ghost, Doc Ardan, and the Scarlet Pimpernel. His latest books are *The Evil in Pemberley House* (Subterranean Press), co-authored with Philip José Farmer, featuring Patricia Wildman, the daughter of a certain bronze-skinned pulp hero, and the encyclopedic *Crossovers: A Secret Chronology of the World* (Black Coat Press). As Sherlock Holmes is the most crossed-over character in literature, Win is most pleased to contribute to the Great Detective's *Crossovers Casebook*. Web: www.winscotteckert.com.

LARRY ENGLE, a life-long admirer of Sherlock Holmes, exists in Indianapolis. Between trips to the local library and nicotine-caffeine fueled horror movie marathons, he is working on a short story collection purely for his own amusement. Lovers of murder, mystery, and mayhem can find him at larryengle@facebook.com.

MARTIN GATELY was born in Nottingham, England in 1966. His first writing was for D C Thomson's legendary *Starblazer* digest in the 1980's. He worked briefly for the gaming magazine, *White Dwarf*, as an editorial assistant before joining the Civil Service (the pay was so much better...) where he toiled to bring wrongdoers to justice on behalf of the Serious Fraud Office before being seconded to the office of the Attorney General. He has written many articles and episode guides on cult TV series and contributed to *Fortean Times* (where he is the creator of "The Cryptid Kid Investigates" comic strip.) He has been captivated by Sherlock Holmes since seeing Billy Wilder's movie *The Private Life of Sherlock Holmes* on TV at a very young age. Coincidentally, he lived just a short distance away from Baker Street during his final months in London. He now lives back in Nottingham in a dilapidated mansion, that has a view of a former insane asylum, with his beautiful wife and two children.

JOE GENTILE keeps pretty busy running a publishing company, but in his spare moments he has managed to write graphic novels and short fiction stories: *Buckaroo Banzai, Kolchak the Night Stalker, Sherlock Holmes, Werewolf the Apocalypse, The Phantom, The Spider, The Avenger*, and many more! His latest was the critically acclaimed graphic novel *"Sherlock Holmes/ Kolchak: Cry for Thunder"*, which will soon be expanded into a novel. When he's not writing, editing, publishing, or trying to find time to sleep, Joe plays the bass guitar and enjoys a good life with his wife Kathy and their pack of personality-ridden dogs.

BARBARA HAMBLY has been a fixture in the science fiction and mystery scenes for many years. Her newest vampire novel *Blood Maidens* (Severn House) has just appeared in the U.K., and her most recent historical whodunnit, *Dead & Buried*, continues the well-reviewed Benjamin January series. She writes historical mysteries as Barbara Hamilton (*The Ninth Daughter*, and *A Marked Man*). She also writes short fiction about the further adventures of characters from her fantasy novels of the '80s and '90s, which can be purchased via download from her website, www.barbarahambly.com.

HOWARD HOPKINS (www.howardhopkins.com) is the author of 34 westerns under the penname Lance Howard, six horror novels, three children's horror novels and numerous short stories under his own name. His most recent western, *The Killing Kind*, was a Dec. 2010 release and his most recent horror series novel, *The Chloe Files #2: Silver of Darkness*, is available now. He's written widescreen and panel comic books and graphic novels for Moonstone, along with co-editing and writing for *The Avenger Chronicles*, *The Avenger: The Justice, Inc. Files*, and will soon bring *The Golden Amazon* back for a new generation of readers. He's also created a new pulp heroine called The Veil, is the editor of *Sherlock Holmes: The Crossovers Casebook* and *Honey West* anthologies, and has had stories in *The Spider Chronicles*, *The Green Hornet Chronicles* and *The Captain Midnight Chronicles*.

MATTHEW P. MAYO has had short stories appear in a variety of publications, including *Beat to a Pulp*, *Out of the Gutter*, and the DAW Books anthologies *Timeshares* and *Steampunk'd*. His story, "Half a Pig," from the anthology, *A Fistful of Legends*, was selected as a 2010 Spur Award Finalist by the Western Writers of America. Matthew's novels include the Westerns *Winters' War, Wrong Town*, and *Hot Lead, Cold Heart*. His critically acclaimed non-fiction books include *Cowboys, Mountain Men & Grizzly Bears*, and *Bootleggers, Lobstermen & Lumberjacks*. Matthew lives on the coast of Maine with his wife, documentary photographer Jennifer Smith-Mayo, where he protects his family from kill-crazy sea creatures. Visit him on the Web at www.matthewmayo.com. And bring a speargun.

WILL MURRAY has written numerous novels and short stories starring a wide variety of classic heroes. The list grows every year: Doc Savage, the Destroyer, Spider-Man, the Incredible Hulk, The Avenger, the Executioner, the Green Hornet, the Phantom, the Spider, the Secret 6, Sky Captain, Honey West, Superman, Batman, Wonder Woman, and many others. When asked to pen a Sherlock Holmes team-up tale, he selected Colonel Richard Henry Savage, the real-life inspiration for Doc Savage and Richard Henry Benson, The Avenger. While the "The Adventure of the Imaginary Nihilist" is fictional, the background is based upon true events in Savage's life.

MARTIN POWELL is the author of eight Sherlock Holmes adventures, beginning with the Eisner Award nominated *Scarlet in Gaslight*, first published in 1987, which has remained in print more than twenty years. In addition to his acclaimed original tales of the Great Detective, Powell was also chosen to adapt the classic *Hound of the Baskervilles* as a graphic novel for young readers. His *The Tall Tale of Paul Bunyan* won the coveted Moonbeam Children's Book Gold Award for Best Graphic Novel of 2010.

DON ROFF is the author of 10 books, including the bestselling *Zombies: A Record of the Year of Infection* published by Chronicle Books/Simon & Schuster UK. He is also an award-winning screenwriter and filmmaker. A former airborne ranger with combat experience, Roff peppers his fantastical fiction with seasoned verisimilitude. A lifelong reader of crime, mystery, and horror, this is his debut Sherlock Holmes yarn. He currently resides in Washington State. He can be found at www.donroff.com

CHRISTOPHER SEQUEIRA is an Australian writer who works predominantly in the horror, science fiction and mystery genres. His published work includes poetry, short fiction and comic-book scripts (including some *Justice League Adventures* stories for DC Comics, and *Iron Man* and *X-Men* stories for Marvel Entertainment). Sequeira is a longtime member of the Sherlockian society *The Sydney Passengers*, and he has played characters for that group in various dramatic re-enactments (including a filmed-for-Australian-national-TV segment wherein he portrayed Professor Moriarty plunging to his death in battle with Holmes at Reichenbach Falls). Sequeira's Sherlockian credits include a paper on Holmes and Jack the Ripper described as 'brilliant' by authority Leslie Klinger, short stories published in various anthologies, including the award-nominated "His Last Arrow" in *Gaslight Grimoire*, and the current bi-monthly comic-book series *Dark Detective: Sherlock Holmes* for Black House Comics. Sequeira, his wife and two children reside in Sydney.

KEVIN VANHOOK is an author, illustrator and film-maker from Indianapolis, Indiana. He has written and drawn comic books for virtually every comic book company over his career and is possibly best known for co-creating *Bloodshot* for Valiant Comics and writing *Superman* and *Batman* for DC Comics. In the 1990s, he wrote the *Flash Gordon* Sunday Comic Strip for King Features Syndicate. As a film-maker, his movies have been translated into languages throughout the world.

C. J. HENDERSON

KOLCHAK: THE NIGHT STALKER

THE LOST CITY

TWO
original
pocket-thrille
novels!

HOWARD
HOPKINS

THE LONE RANGER

TWO
iconic characters
TWO
master authors!

VENDETTA